A FORBIDDEN LOVE: BOOK THREE
The Author's Story
by
John Williams

Coat of Arms of the Earls of Grafton

Other books in the "A Forbidden Love" series:

Book One

Two young friends are drawn together when their mothers die, embark on a personal journey of discovery about the nature of their friendship. One the son of an earl, the other of a German prince.
They reunite in the early summer of 1914 in London, but are soon sent to the family's country estate in Norfolk where they enjoy an idyllic summer together - largely oblivious to the gathering storm clouds of war in Europe.
With the imminent declaration of war they are summoned back to London by their fathers - and one has to return home to Germany.
Now on opposite sides, each serves their country with distinction.
Will fate allow them to be reunited in peace?

Book Two: Thomas' Tale

In the shadow of Langley Hall, young Thomas Cooper navigates the complexities of friendship, duty and love in Edwardian England. As the son of a tenant farmer, Thomas forms an unlikely bond with Lord John Langley and Prince Christian, two boys from vastly different worlds. Their shared adventures and deepening connections are tested by the rigid boundaries of class and the looming threat of war in the summer of 1914. When tragedy strikes, Thomas is thrust into a role that demands unwavering loyalty and discretion. As he rises through the ranks of service, he must confront his own desires and the painful secrets that haunt him. "Thomas' Tale", is a poignant exploration of love, loss and the enduring power of friendship in the face of society's constraints. Spanning seven decades of British history, Thomas' story chronicles his life from the fields of Norfolk, to a post-war life that includes a liberating road trip across the United States, and also reflects the many changes in social attitudes towards the LBGTQ+ communities.

Book Three: The Author's Story

Book Three intricately explores the life of John Williams, focusing on his journey through trauma, identity struggles, and the pursuit of belonging and reconciliation. Set against varied and evocative settings, from the historic Langley Hall estate and its surrounding village to the urban landscapes of Manchester and London, and the vibrant Greek islands. The narrative weaves themes of personal growth, love, and acceptance into a deeply reflective and emotional story.

Dedications:

In loving memory of my mum and my big sister.

CONTENTS:

CHAPTER 1: SUMMER AT LANGLEY HALL

Summer 1984

The first impression is heat: not the dry, throat-tightening sort I had known during excursions south with my parents, but a broad, reedy suffocation peculiar to this eastern edge of England. The coach groaned to a halt on the limestone sweep in front of Langley Hall, its white facade shimmering in the slow-bleeding sunlight of late July. Dust hung motionless above the drive, even after the engine cut out; it seemed that the air itself was reluctant to move. For several moments I remained seated, one palm pressed flat to my thigh, the other curled round the handle of my battered cricket bag, as if unsure that the world outside would yield to my presence.

The rest of the coach party, other bewildered looking university students picked up with me at Norwich railway station, was slow to stir, the heat tamping down the usual cacophony of arrivals and departures. The driver, a man of considerable girth and considerable humour, opened the luggage compartment and began flinging bags onto the gravel with a studied nonchalance, as if he did not care whether they landed up or down, intact or ruptured.

"Langley Hall," he pronounced, as though the name alone should inspire us to unbuckle, rise, and collect our belongings. He wiped his face with a handkerchief, a gesture as deliberate as any I had seen in the preceding journey, and waited, arms akimbo, for us to file past.

I let the others go first, unhurried, trying to look as if I belonged among them, though I wore the badge of outsider in every stitch. My rucksack, grey, scuffed, the product of five years' use and two hasty repairs, slid awkwardly off the luggage pile, almost tripping me. The cricket bag, an old Slazenger with cracked leather handles, followed. I caught both before they could touch the dirt, and for a moment felt the brittle comfort of competence.

No one greeted me at the threshold. The double doors of the Hall stood ajar, exposing the shadowed gulf of the entrance hall. I could see, through the columned portico, the broad sweep of marble floor and the distant glimmer of chandelier light. Above and beyond, the upper windows; tall, recessed, and absolutely blank, looked down with the self-assurance of ancient wealth.

I paused at the base of the steps. Sweat pooled between my shoulder blades, caught beneath the cheap polycotton of my shirt. Somewhere in the upper air a pair of swifts carved their frantic gyres, their calls thin and sharp as glass. The air near the ground smelled of scorched grass, but as I stepped inside, the temperature dropped and the scent changed: beeswax and leather, a trace of pipe smoke, and something else; old paper, or perhaps the slow decay of wood sealed up for centuries.

The entrance hall was an exercise in overstatement. The floor, polished to a treacherous shine, reflected the columns and mouldings in inverted perfection. There were paintings that were oily, anachronistic, all jowls and powdered wigs, gazing down from impossible heights. A marble bust, chin raised in permanent dismissal, presided over the main stair. I trailed my way across the expanse; the sound of my footsteps drowned in the hush. No sign of the summer's children so I just followed the crowd; I might have been trespassing in an empty museum.

We were herded right down a shadowed corridor into what must once have been a grand ballroom, now hollow and echoing with our footsteps. Suddenly a tall, white-haired man materialised behind us, he was Ted, the caretaker, flanked by a woman I pegged as a mid-thirties' hippie in tie-dyed blouse and jeans. He gestured us into neat rows of chairs, then took his place at the front beside her. I felt both drawn to and alienated by their calm authority.

Once we'd settled, she spoke with breezy certainty: "I'm Sue, manager of the summer camp, and this is Ted." She handed out print-outs, a map of the school, a staff list with duties and room assignments. Then she rattled through health-and-safety bullet points. We were dismissed to explore and find our rooms, told to return to the ballroom in an hour for questions. I left feeling oddly boxed in grateful for structure, yet yearning for more freedom.

I studied the map, heart thumping with indecision, then retraced my steps to the entrance; "The Great Hall", up the "Dowager's Stairs," and up a narrow servants'-stair flight. At the corridor's far end, through a heavy oak door, I found my room.

At first glance it felt like a cell: a spartan single bed shoved into a corner, a tiny desk with a classroom chair, a threadbare armchair, and a built-in cupboard. I bristled at its austerity, then caught sight of the window. Outside, the gravel courtyard gave way to an immaculate cricket pitch, its geometric lines faint reminders of last summer's glories. Beyond, parkland slipped into woods veiled by bluish haze, and overhead the sky stretched vast and chalky, the sun angling low. For a fleeting moment I loved it, then resented how that beauty made the room feel even more claustrophobic.

I stood silent in the centre, torn between resisting and embracing the stillness. At university I'd learned to acclimatise before claiming a space; now I questioned whether I was soothing myself or simply postponing the inevitable unpacking. After less than a minute, I set about it with deliberate slowness. My rucksack spilled out two pairs of jeans, several pairs of shorts and tee shirts, four nearly identical blue shirts, half a dozen pairs of boxers and white sports socks, a plastic case of toiletries, a comb, and two rolls of athletic tape. I aligned the coaching manuals on the desk, placed my black Filofax alongside them, my lone indulgence, and wondered if rituals like these were grounding me or trapping me.

Unpacking the cricket bag was more fraught. Each piece, bat, pads, gloves, boots and trainers, club cricket shirts and whites, and tracksuit bottoms, assorted guards all came out methodically, inspected for damage with a precision that felt both comforting and obsessive. At the bottom, wrapped in a towel, lay the red Duke ball I'd bowled my last over with in Lancashire. Scuffed and nearly split at the seam, it was useless for play. Yet I set it on the windowsill anyway. Ritual, I reminded myself, is not quite the same as sentimentality, but sometimes the line felt perilously thin.

Voices from the corridor: the rustling of someone moving into the room opposite, a distant radio's swelling tune, shouts from the stables, the judder of another window being forced open. Oddly, the ambient clamour soothed me. Their everyday normalcy countered the Hall's ancient grandeur, and my own uneasy mixture of anticipation and dread.

I opened the window, and a rush of cool, damp air spilled in, simultaneously welcome and alarming. The late afternoon heat ebbed away, but my pulse quickened at the shift. I leaned out, elbows on the sill, torn between relief and the inexplicable dread that this new place imposed. Below, a handful of staff kicked a football, their shouts thin and dissolving on the breeze. A man in a green groundskeeper's jumper paced the rope boundary as if every blade of grass might betray him. I felt almost as wary.

Back at the desk, I flipped open my Filofax and scribbled the date in the corner of page one. My pen hovered over the blank expanse, but I couldn't bring myself to write the obvious: I'd arrived. I had nothing to fear. The weeks ahead would blur into matches and drills and decorous small talk. Instead, I recorded the weight of my bags, the angle of the desk lamp, the corridor doors labelled *Oak*, *Beech*, *Elm* in a shaky, old-fashioned script. With each note I made, I wrestled with the impulse to confess how unsettled I felt, and how this place felt too large, too silent under its polite veneer.

After ten minutes I shook my head, unscrewed my water bottle, and took a long swallow of lukewarm, metallic-tasting liquid. I grimaced, shoved it aside, and returned to the window. My watch told me it was time. I'd promised myself I'd present a composed front. I checked my reflection in the narrow mirror by the door. The shirt was hopelessly creased, my hair a tangle, but I forced a half-smile. Good enough. I closed the door, tried to brace myself, and descended the stairs, wondering who or what would greet me.

The briefing meeting passed with mechanical ease: Sue outlined housekeeping rules, answered questions about laundry and mealtimes. My chest tightened at every *'Any questions?'*. No one asked about my real concerns, and the ache of leaving home, the fear I'd never belong. We were led through the Hall to the dining room in the old servants' wing, where a buffet of sandwiches, cakes, and soft drinks waited. Around me, colleagues traded brittle pleasantries: weather woes, travel delays, debating which town had the best university. Their smiles felt provisional, like we all knew how fragile our newfound camaraderie really was.

Afterward, we gathered in the staff lounge overlooking the courtyard. I sipped tonic water while I catalogued names and faces in my mind: Pete Evans, science coordinator, cheerful but distant; Ash Patel, my fellow cricket coach, quiet and obviously ill at ease; Sarah Beecham, dance-and-drama whirlwind, all bold laughter and laser focus; intimidating. Everyone else blended into an indistinct haze, their individual anxieties as masked as my own.

As soon as manners allowed, I excused myself and veered off toward the Great Hall. I told myself it was curiosity as I had to inspect the old estate maps behind the glass panels. In reality, I needed to escape the chitchat, the low hum of forced friendliness that made my skin crawl. My pulse fluttered as I studied the faded lines and place-names, losing myself until a noise behind me jolted my attention.

I turned and saw him: tall, dark-haired, solid in tight jeans and an open hi-vis vest that revealed a lean torso straining with the weight of a trolley stacked with classroom chairs. My heart lurched, relief, recognition, worry all tangled together. I stood stiffly, uncertain whether to speak or retreat, strangely eager and yet dreading the words that might follow.

"Could you?" he asked, his soft Norfolk drawl somehow both gentle and insistent. He nodded toward the closed double doors leading to the ballroom, balancing an awkward stack of chairs.

"Erm… yes," I murmured, heart thudding as I reached for the handles. My fingers brushed his arm which were warm and damp with sweat, and a jolt of something sharp shot through me. I opened the doors, stepping aside. He manoeuvred his load past me, then paused inside and turned, flashing that grin. A grin I shouldn't have wanted to see again.

"Thanks for that," he said, his eyes, those pale, steady eyes, lingering on me.

"Anytime," I whispered, feeling my face catch fire. I fought the urge to tell myself to stop imagining what that smile meant, whether it was promise or mockery. Damn that thought, *'phoar'*, I heard myself think, then immediately scolded my own filthy mind.

I slipped away before he returned, my steps hurried and clumsy down the corridor. In the solitude of my room, I closed the door and leaned against it, trying to steady the whirl of embarrassment and… something else. Longing? Regret? Fear? All of it.

I fetched my wallet from the little table where I'd laid it out so meticulously earlier and withdrew a slightly worn photograph. Small and curling at the corners, its surface puckered from repeated handling, it showed Mark O'Toole, lean, blond, two days' stubble, and that mercurial smile that might be invitation or warning. We'd taken it in that pub off *Hope Street* in *Liverpool*, the last night before exams a year ago sent us scattering like so many summer moths. He'd been wearing a rugby shirt that he probably never wore on the pitch, a sidestep of style, like so many of his feints.

I traced his jawline with my thumb, as if I could bridge the two hundred miles and the weeks of silence just by lingering there. The ache inside me was familiar, a tight vice in my chest, a bitter tang on my tongue. I'd felt it ever since he pressed his mouth to my neck that night two years ago, drank Smirnoff from the bottle and let the lights go down. His fingers had unbuttoned my shirt so naturally it felt like breathing. And I, stupidly, had no shield against the hunger in his look.

From the start, I knew we were playing at secrecy. I told myself the summer would purge me: a purgative of cricket matches, loud children, endless daylight and duty. I would emerge cured, a picture of normalcy with good reports, trusty references, the bland rituals of heterosexual adulthood. This job was supposed to be step one: prove I could hide, could pretend, could endure.

But here I was, in a small room clutching his photo, my plan already unravelling around me. I should hate the memory, I should want to burn it out, but every memory stings with a sweet ache I can't extinguish. And so I stay tangled in conflict: wanting him gone, yet craving the ghost of his smile. My summer of salvation is failing, because I'm already failing myself.

I propped my elbows on the desk and pressed my thumbs into the sockets of my eyes until I saw stars. My body, ever the traitor, responded with a tightening of the chest and a pulse in my throat so strong it felt visible. I tried, as I often did, to imagine an alternative: a parallel life in which desire did not threaten annihilation, in which I might bring someone like Mark to dinner, to Christmas, to the dull regularity of weekends. The thought always brought a kind of vertigo, equal parts hope and terror. And even now, with no one watching, I found I could not sustain it.

The voices in the corridor snapped me back. Someone, Sarah, probably, by the volume and cadence, laughed, then called a muffled rallying call to join the rest in the pub in the village. Instinctively, I snapped the photo back into my wallet, closed the book, and placed both in the bottom drawer of the desk. My pulse refused to slow. I stood and crossed to the window, forced myself to breathe in the evening air and then braved the throng in the corridor.

The Langley Arms was just as I had pictured it: a squat, thatched lump of a building, its flint walls whitewashed so often that the corners had begun to lose definition. The windows were small and reluctant to let in light; the interior was lit chiefly by the efforts of a fireplace large enough to roast a deer. The air was thick with wood smoke and the sour perfume of spilled bitter, overlaid with the faint sweetness of pipe tobacco and old wood.

There were about ten of us in all as Sarah had insisted on the outing, and the others, reluctant at first, had been unable to resist her charm or volume too. The caretaker had accompanied us as far as the gates, then vanished with a thin smile and a parting benediction: "Don't walk home alone. There are stories."

We found two tables and commandeered them. The locals, stooped men in flat caps, a pair of pensioners with gin and tonic, a farmer's wife and her teenage daughter, gave us the usual glance reserved for city folk in rural outposts, then returned to their own conversation. I ordered a pint of lager, which arrived sloshing over the rim, and tried to make myself as inconspicuous as possible.

It was a wasted effort. Sarah was a force of nature. Petite, wiry, dressed in a battered denim jacket with sleeves cut off, she possessed a voice that could cut through stone. She told stories with her whole body, hands slicing the air, chin jutting, eyes always searching for a new listener. Within five minutes, she had the entire table in thrall.

"So, first year at Bristol, I get cast as *Viola*," she was saying. "You know—cross-dressing, gender confusion, the usual Shakespearean horseshit. Halfway through rehearsal, the director decides we're staging it as a rock musical, which means we spend six weeks in Lycra and platform boots. By the end, I could tie a corset in my sleep. Or someone else's."

The table roared. Evans, nearly choked on his scotch egg. Even Patel, whom I had mentally consigned to the camp of the permanently reserved, was grinning openly.

"You'd make a good *Sebastian*," she said, suddenly turning to me.

I blinked, uncertain.

"In '*Twelfth Night*'. You know, the lost twin. Slightly tragic, particularly good at looking confused. Trust me, you'd nail it."

I laughed, more from surprise than agreement. "I always thought I was more of a *Malvolio*."

That got a bigger laugh. Sarah raised her glass in salute. "To *Malvolios* everywhere. God knows the world needs them."

I drank. The beer was flat but cold, and I felt the immediate warmth of it blooming in my chest. For the first time that day, the tension in my shoulders began to ease.

The rest of the group was less vivid, but each played their part. Evans, ruddy and loud, had a running feud with the management of the Hall over resources, which he relayed in increasingly elaborate anecdotes. Patel, soft-spoken but unexpectedly sharp, countered with gentle mockery. The others, general PE, language specialists from Leeds, York, Durham chimed in when they could, but Sarah was the clear centre of gravity.

I watched the dynamics unfold with the dispassionate interest of an anthropologist. There was the usual posturing among the men, a kind of coded bravado, each staking out a position in the pecking order. The two from Leeds, identical in both haircut and opinion, had already begun the process of bonding over mutual acquaintances and shared loathing for '*southerners*'. I recognised, in their banter, the same defensiveness I carried myself; a need to perform, to blend in, to camouflage.

I was careful to direct my own conversation away from anything that might betray me. When the talk turned to girls referred to always, in these circles, '*birds*' or '*totty*', I nodded, smiled, offered the expected platitudes. I named a girlfriend from back home, gave her a plausible degree and hair colour, made her up from the bones outward. I listened for cues in the others, searching for any hint of deviation, but found none. If there were other frauds among us, they concealed it better than I did.

Sarah, for her part, seemed immune to this posturing. She moved between the table and the bar with total self-assurance, laughing off the farmer's son who propositioned her by the fruit machine, then returning with crisps and an armful of refills. She asked questions, real questions, and when she looked at you, you felt for a moment that you were the only person in the room.

Around ten, she nudged me, "fancy walking back?"

I nodded, finished my drink and we stepped outside. The night was thick, the heat lingering but tempered by a slow breeze. The lane back to the Hall was pitch-black; we walked in silence for a minute, both of us content to let the village noise recede. The road was rough, and I stumbled once, catching myself before I went down. Sarah grinned.

"Not much of a country boy, are you?"

"Lancashire has streetlights. And fewer ditches."

She laughed, "true. Even Brighton has its limits. There's a kind of, what's the word, gravitational pull here? Like the dark wants to keep you."

I glanced at her, unsure whether this was a joke.

She shrugged, "I like it, though. It's honest. You can't pretend out here. Not really."

We kept walking. I could feel her watching me, weighing some unspoken question. I looked up: the stars were out in force, the sky brilliant and overwhelming. I realized how long it had been since I'd seen stars.

Sarah said, "you're quieter than the others."

I hesitated, not sure how to respond, "probably just shy."

She shook her head, "no. It's something else. Like you're holding your breath, waiting for permission to exhale."

I was startled by the accuracy of it.

"I suppose I am," I said.

She grinned, satisfied, "you'll get used to it. The Hall, the kids, the routine. It's all theatre. We're just playing parts."

Her words settled in my mind, finding purchase in places I'd tried to keep vacant.

"You're good at it," I said.

"Been rehearsing all my life. You?"

I considered, "I'm still learning the lines."

She nodded, as if this confirmed a theory, "if you ever need a script, you know where to find me."

We reached the gates, passing through before the road turned to the right when The Hall loomed ahead, pale and improbable against the dark. I felt the urge to say something, thanks, or a return invitation, or even a simple goodnight, but words failed me.

Sarah seemed to sense this. She touched my arm, briefly, and said: "see you at breakfast, *Malvolio*."

I watched her go, her silhouette swallowed up by the corridor. I lingered at the threshold, breathing in the silence, letting the last of the night air soak through me. For the first time since arriving, I felt a flicker of something like hope.

Inside, the Hall was quiet. The others had gone to their rooms. I climbed the stairs, moving softly, and let myself into *Oak*. The photograph of Mark was still in the drawer, undisturbed. I did not look at it.

Instead, I sat on the bed and, for a long time, listened to the night sounds; the tick of the pipes, the settling of the beams, the faint, almost imperceptible hum of voices from the pub drifting up through the open window. I lay down, closed my eyes, and rehearsed my lines for tomorrow.

Standing up suddenly, I peeled off my shirt and dropped it onto the bed. My skin was slick, the collar damp. I ran a towel over my face and chest, then stood in front of the mirror and examined myself as though searching for evidence: a mark, a telltale sign, anything that would betray the truth. There was nothing. No scarlet letter, no secret code. Just a young man, thin and slightly pale, except for the *'cricketer's tan'* of a brown V-neck and forearms, with a constellation of freckles across his shoulders and an expression I didn't recognise. Not unhappy. Not content. Something in between.

I returned to the desk and, with a deliberate slowness, began to write in the Filofax. I described the day's events, the faces and voices of my colleagues, the layout of the Hall. When I reached the part about the photograph, I hesitated. My hand hovered above the page. Eventually, I wrote: "I am haunted by things I am supposed to forget."

Below, in smaller letters: "distance is not the same as escape." Over the last two years I had learnt to write in my own code as Mark had once found my then explicit journal and forced me to destroy all mentions of him.

I closed the journal, replaced the pen, and drew the chair up to the bed. The lamp's light cast long bars across the duvet, and I let myself drift, one hand behind my head, the other resting on my chest. I listened to the sound of the night bleeding in through the open window.

I told myself, as I had countless times before, that I could endure it. That with enough routine, enough discipline, I could reset the circuitry, make myself new. I would be a teacher, a coach, a dependable member of society. No one would guess. No one would have to know.

Still, as I drifted toward sleep, I found my mind returning to Liverpool, to Mark's mouth at my neck, his fingers pressed into the small of my back, the murmur of his voice in the afterglow: "it's alright, John. No one will know." A lie, obviously. But sometimes, I believed it anyway. And then the memory of the grateful smile the young worker had flashed to me in the Great Hall, and an honest thin smile hit my face.

The last thing I saw before the dark was the shadow of the photo, still visible against the wood, and the memory of Mark's smile, an invitation, a warning, and something else. I resolved, once again, to forget. But even as I promised myself oblivion, I knew I would look at the picture again tomorrow, and the day after that, and all the days until the end of summer.

Sleep, when it came, was thin and unfinished. I woke at intervals throughout the night, sometimes to the hoot of an owl, sometimes to the rush of blood in my ears. Each time I opened my eyes, the room seemed subtly altered: a shifting of light, a change in the cast of the shadows on the ceiling.

At three a.m., I surrendered. I got out of bed, padded barefoot across the wooden floor, and stood at the window. The view was spectral: moonlight silvered the grass of the cricket pitch, and the park beyond glowed with an almost aqueous clarity. The oaks, vast and antediluvian, loomed like sentinels, their canopies rendered in fine, trembling lines by the wind. There were no cars, no distant hum of traffic; the only sound was the slow breathing of the Hall itself, and the occasional call of an owl somewhere far off.

I stayed there for a long time.

CHAPTER 2: THE CRICKET PITCH

I stayed there for a long time, propped against the sill and staring at the spectral pitch, until the indigo bled into a watery blue and the trees threw their first hesitant shadows across the dew-bright grass. By then, sleep was both impossible and unnecessary. I yanked on the least-wrinkled pair of shorts, a white t-shirt, and my battered trainers. I tried, without much conviction, to comb my hair, then gave up and left it to the mercy of the breeze.

The morning was indecently clear. Already, the drone of a mower haunted the edge of the woods, and the air shivered with the sound of pigeons ransacking the eaves for loose mortar. I made my way down the backstairs, following the scent of burned coffee and warm toast to the kitchen, where Ash was already waiting.

He stood at the counter, methodically buttering bread and not looking at me. His posture was precise, his clothes impossibly neat for so early an hour. I was always faintly jealous of how little Ash seemed to need sleep. Or food, or companionship, for that matter. In three days I'd yet to see him eat more than a single biscuit at a sitting.

"Mornin'," I said, my voice small in the cathedral hush of the kitchen.

He grunted, not unkindly, then gestured at the French press, "if you want, there's some left."

I poured a mug and took the stool across from him. The silence stretched, not unpleasant, but with a steady current of awareness, as if the two of us were stationed at opposite ends of a canal and any words would have to be rowed laboriously across.

"You sleep?" he said at last, when my mug was half-empty.

I shrugged, "a bit. Mostly just…" I made a vague gesture at the window, as though the answer was out there, among the pigeons and the thinning mist.

"Still getting used to it?"

"I don't think you ever get used to it." I regretted the candour as soon as it was out of my mouth. "I mean… places like this. They're designed to keep you off balance. All the marble and the long corridors. It's like being in a museum, only you're part of the exhibit."

Ash considered this, lips pursed, "you think too much," he said, without being unkind. "Come on. Let's get it set up before the kids arrive."

We gathered our equipment in silence, netting, poles, guy ropes, pegs, mallet and the sacred wheelie bag of first-aid supplies. Ash hefted the nets with one hand, then led the way out the back and around the path to the front of the Hall where the practice pitches were.

Langley's main cricket square, immaculately bordered and flat as a snooker table, sat about a hundred and fifty yards from the front of the house, as if the Hall was presiding over it like a headmaster at prize-giving. The grass was still slick with dew, and the chalked lines glowed with a ghostly intensity against the green. I took it in with a mixture of pride and apprehension. There was something sacramental about a cricket pitch at dawn: unmarked, unspoiled, waiting for play.

We worked quickly, each absorbed in the task. I hammered stakes for the net, then double-checked the tension along the top tape. Ash, true to form, triple-checked it, then adjusted the guy ropes. At some point I realised we had entered a kind of wordless ballet, each anticipating the other's moves before they were made. The ritual was oddly soothing, and for a time I forgot about everything beyond the boundaries: my own heart, my own failures, even the looming threat of a day spent corralling forty shrieking eleven-year-olds.

At 9:30, Ash straightened and surveyed our handiwork, then nodded approval, "looks good."

I shielded my eyes from the rising sun, a white-hot coin above the trees, "thanks."

He hesitated, then said, "we should go over the schedule. I'll get the clipboard from the staff room. Be back in five?"

I nodded, grateful for the moment alone.

I did a slow lap of the pitch, checking the surface for stones or divots. The silence was dense, almost sacred, punctuated only by the distant keening of a kestrel. I knelt to remove a clump of moss near the bowler's mark and, as I did, a low rumble rolled in from the park's far edge.

I turned to see a tractor making its way across the morning, a green *John Deere* with a battered cab and a gang mower rig trailing behind like a mechanical serpent. It moved with deliberate slowness, flattening the hillocks and taming the overgrowth. The man at the wheel wore a hi-vis vest and, somehow, scruffy khaki shorts, even in the early chill. His legs, long and fox-brown, were streaked with old scars and newer grass stains.

He drew up at the edge of the nets, killed the engine, and hopped down in a single, effortless motion. I recognised him instantly: the same groundsman I'd seen in the Great Hall the other day, the one with the easy smile and the ridiculous capacity for moving furniture. Up close, he seemed even taller, with a shock of dark hair and arms that looked designed for climbing trees or scaling castle walls.

He strode toward me, wiping his hands on his shorts, and said, "hi, I'm William. The groundsman." His voice carried the same soft Norfolk lilt I remembered, stretched at the edges by something warmer, almost teasing, "are you the John I'm looking for?"

I felt my face heat, the old mortification pooling in my ears, "depends what you're after," I said, then immediately regretted how it sounded, flippant, and maybe even flirtatious. I shot a glance back at the Hall, half-expecting Ash to appear and catch the exchange.

William grinned, undeterred, "cricket. I'm told there's a new wicket to be marked out, but wanted to check the specs before I put the square under the blade."

He was looking at me, really looking, as if nothing else in the world required his attention. I struggled to find a normal, adult answer. "Right. Yes. We're using the far side for the first weeks. Then move inside the square each week."

William nodded, then squinted toward the east boundary, "you're the coach, then?"

"Assistant," I clarified, "Ash is head. I'm just… helping out."

"I saw you bowl yesterday," he said, with the smallest tilt of his chin. "Looked like you knew what you were doing."

"Thanks," I said, the compliment unexpectedly sharp. "It's … well, it's what I do. Did."

He smiled again, then reached down to pick up a ball that had rolled toward his boots. He cradled it in his palm, thumb tracing the seam. "Ever play pro?"

"Not really." I shrugged, unwilling to elaborate. "Lancashire U16s. That's about it."

"Still counts." He returned the ball to me, underarm, and I caught it with the automatic grace that came from a decade of repetition. For a moment, neither of us spoke.

Then he said, "well, if you need anything. Rolling, marking, whatever, you just yell. I'm usually about or hanging around the old stables at the back of the Hall."

"Thanks," I said, willing my voice not to shake, "I will."

He turned to leave, then paused, "oh, and thanks again for helping me with the doors, back in the Hall. Those old hinges hate the summer."

I managed a weak smile, "anytime. I'm good at getting stuck too."

He laughed, a deep and generous sound, then walked back to his tractor. I watched him go, unable to look away from the way his muscles moved under the high-vis vest, or the line of sweat down his spine. I realised, with the slow, dawning horror of self-awareness, that my hands were shaking.

Ash returned with the clipboard just as the engine revved to life. He didn't mention William, or my visible agitation, but I caught the sideways glance he threw me as we knelt to mark the first set of cones. For the next hour we worked in silence, punctuated only by the rumble of the mower as it orbited the field.

After Ash left to go for lunch, I sat alone, with excuse of wanting a quiet cigarette, on the edge of the square, breathing in the smell of diesel and cut grass. I replayed the encounter in my mind, dissecting each line, each gesture, searching for the moment I'd given myself away. Had it been the wink? The stammer? Or just the way I looked at him, hungry, desperate for approval, for even a second of shared understanding?

I pressed the cricket ball to my forehead, feeling the roughness of the seam. I told myself it was just a conversation. Just a man doing his job. But underneath, I knew it was something else, a charge, a current, the old, dangerous spark.

I stood and brushed the grass from my shorts. The sun was high now, and the pitch gleamed in the light. I tried to focus on the day ahead, the admin, the dividing into age groups of Sunday's arrivals and the new long, exhausting routine of summer, but already my mind was running ahead to the next encounter, the next accidental touch, the next opportunity to be seen.

I left the pitch, promising myself I'd be more careful next time. But even as I walked away, I knew I wouldn't be. Saturday dusk came in on a tide of gold, so viscous and luminous that every stone of the Hall seemed lacquered in honey. The children would arrive tomorrow. Tonight was the last exhale before the summer's long inhale, and already the place felt different: a fraction more private, a hair less formal, as if the house itself relaxed the rules at sunset.

Ash had gone to the pub with some of the other staff. Sarah had commandeered the main lounge for a dress rehearsal of something she called *artistic enrichment*, which seemed to involve choreographing a dozen teachers through the steps of *YMCA*. The noise was incredible, and as much as I liked her, I couldn't stand the forced jollity. I found myself wandering through the empty corridors, content to be alone.

I drifted, my footsteps slow and echoing, past the music room (where a baby grand piano glowered under a quilted dust sheet), through the silent refectory (long tables, the aftermath of a staff supper: dried mustard, ghostly crumbs), and out into the Great Hall. The ceiling here was forty feet high and domed with painted gods and monsters: *Neptune* and *Diana* and a host of grimacing cherubs that seemed to leer no matter where I stood.

It was, by any metric, a ridiculous room. The floor alone could have accommodated a basketball court; the chandelier hung so low that I could reach the crystal drops if I leaped from the third stair. Someone had left the wall sconces on, casting a low, flickering light that made the old portraits seem animate.

I paused by the main entrance, where the shadows converged around a glass-panelled door. The staff handbook (which I'd read, twice, *in lieu* of sleep) said that the library could be reached through here, but I hadn't dared try the handle before. Now I did. It opened, noiseless and cold, into a grand room.

The library was a thing apart. Three sets of French doors gave out onto the terrace, which looked westward over the ornamental ponds and the rose gardens. The walls were floor-to-ceiling shelves, crammed with books in every possible configuration: upright, slanting, double-stacked, the volumes sagging and swollen from a century of inattention. The air was close, a mixture of paper, beeswax, and that dry, granular smell of ancient stone.

Behind me, above the largest of three marble fireplaces, hung a painting that dominated the space. Even from a distance I could see it was something special: six feet wide, bright and sharply rendered, not the usual murky parade of nobodies in livery. I found myself walking toward it, unable to resist.

The painting showed Langley Hall as seen from the top of the avenue, with the drive perfectly centred on the portico and elegantly lined through stands of oak and beech. The Hall itself was as it was today, essentially unchanged, except for the absence of cars, the odd geometry of horse-drawn carriages and servants in livery. In the foreground, just left of the drive, three boys' cricket clothing, were captured mid-game: one poised to bowl, the others waiting, frozen in expectation.

It took me a moment to register why this unsettled me. The boys, though rendered in miniature, with the kind of detail only a loving hand could manage, looked like… well, like boys I knew. The one with the bat was thin and sharp-faced, hair parted with military precision. The wicketkeeper had a sullen hunch to his shoulders and wore a cap at a rakish angle. The bowler, blond, was lean and long-limbed, his arm coiled in the act of delivery.

I stared at the scene, trying to guess the date. Judging by the boys' dress and the cut of the trees, I pegged it at *Edwardian* and 1910, maybe. But there was something in the expression of the blond boy, a mixture of pride and terror, that seemed both older and younger than that.

I was so absorbed that I didn't hear anyone approach until a voice, quiet, but with the same drawl I'd heard that morning, spoke behind me.

"It's not a bad likeness, is it?"

I jumped, then turned. William stood just inside the door, still in his shorts, though now paired with a faded rugby shirt and the same battered trainers from earlier. The effect was, well, disarming.

He walked in with the unhurried assurance of someone who knew every inch of the place. He glanced up at the painting, then back at me, "the wicket-keeper is my great-uncle," he said, as if this explained everything.

I tried not to sound incredulous, "seriously?"

"Thomas Cooper. My dad's side." He squinted at the canvas. "He's about thirteen there. Loved cricket. Loved it so much he used to sleep with a bat under his pillow."

I grinned.

He stepped closer, hands shoved in his pockets. I could smell him, the day's sweat, the aftermath of cut grass and gasoline, "you've got a good eye," he said. "Most people walk right past. They want the oil portraits of the lords and ladies, but that one…" he nodded at the painting, "that one's the real Langley. Painted by *Countess Isabella*, around 1910. She was obsessed with cricket. Well, obsessed with her son, really. The painting is supposed to be about him, but she put the servants' kids in, too. Family, but not family, you know?"

I nodded, though I didn't, not really. My own family's lineage was as convoluted as the spines on the shelves behind us.

"Did you grow up here then?" I asked, eager to deflect.

He shrugged, "in Home Farm behind the Hall and stables. Dad's family have had the farm for generation. Mum's people were all in service. My great uncle moved from the farm into the big house to be a hall boy and then was a footman. And then valet, and then butler and finally estate manager for the last earl."

"Do you ever get sick of it?" I asked, "being part of the history, I mean."

He looked at me, head tilted, "depends which history you mean. The Hall's? Or my own?"

"Either."

He laughed, and the sound was softer than before. "The Hall, never as there's always something to fix, or grow, or dig out. The people, though…" He made a face. "They change every year, but they're always the same. City lot, here for the summer, think the place is a great adventure. Or they're scared of me, because I talk like a farmer and know where the boiler room is."

I smiled, embarrassed, "I don't think you're scary."

"Not yet," he said, eyes twinkling, "give it time."

A silence fell, but not an uncomfortable one. He leaned back against the long table, arms crossed, and looked at me in a way that was both challenging and inviting. I felt the impulse to ask something risky, to step closer to the line.

"Do you ever want to leave?" I said, "go somewhere else? Do something else?"

He considered this, biting his lip, "sometimes. I went to horticultural college in Norwich, but hated the city. Hated the noise, the air, the way the sky was always the wrong colour. I came back as soon as I could." He looked away, then back at me. "What about you? Where's home?"

I hesitated, "Lancashire, I suppose. But I moved around. School, university. I'm not… I don't really fit anywhere."

He seemed to understand this, or at least respected the honesty, "that's why you walk the grounds at night," he said.

I blinked, "you've seen me?"

"'Course," he said, grinning, "I'm the only one who does, I live onsite in a flat above the stables. Well, except for the foxes. But they don't judge."

I felt the heat rise to my cheeks, "sorry. I'm not a creep. I just… I like the quiet."

"So do I," he said. His voice had lowered, almost a whisper now, "it's the best time. You see things you'd miss in the day. Badgers, deer, sometimes the old barn owl if you're lucky. You should come out some night. I could show you the river. It's better than the painting."

I met his gaze, startled by the invitation. There was nothing sly in his look, just a kind of open expectation. I wondered what he saw when he looked at me: a sad, itinerant cricket coach, or something more.

"I'd like that," I said. My voice sounded strange in my own ears.

He nodded, satisfied, and pushed himself upright. For a moment I thought he might reach out, might shake my hand or clap me on the shoulder, but instead he just offered a small, conspiratorial smile.

"We'll arrange it once you got the kids settled after Sunday."

He left without waiting for an answer, his footsteps muffled by the library's thick rug. I watched him go, then sat down in the leather chair nearest the fireplace, my heart beating against my ribs like a caged thing.

I looked up at the painting again. The three boys, forever on the verge of play. I wondered if they knew, even then, how their lives would shrink to stories told by someone else, a hundred years later. I wondered if the painter saw more than just the uniforms and the posture—if she captured the nervous energy, the unspeakable things that made the boys themselves.

I sat there until the light failed and the world outside was black as pitch. Then I closed my eyes, listened to the silence, and tried to imagine what tomorrow would bring.

CHAPTER 3: THE FIRST COACHING SESSION

The Sunday dawn came with a gentler hand than I expected, grey, a little sullen, as if the Hall and its acres were themselves hungover from the previous evening's heat. The kitchen air was dense with the scent of milky tea and burnt toast; Ash was already at the counter, eyes red-rimmed but defiant, eating cold *Shreddies* by the fistful. I nodded to him, poured my own mug, and hovered at the backdoor, watching as the world beyond Langley's portico twitched gradually to life.

The first coach arrived at 9.00, precise to the minute, trailing a pale cloud of diesel and hope. It disgorged a battalion of children in matching navy sweatshirts and new trainers, their parents close behind, bearing battered *Samsonites* and *Sainsbury's* carrier bags. The children spread, shrieking, into the forecourt, some toward the lawns, others toward the great marble steps, as if the Hall were a fortress waiting to be stormed. The parents, middle-aged, anxious, followed at a statelier pace. One mother, in a yellow tracksuit and a frosted perm, took a photograph of her twins, then immediately burst into tears.

I pressed my forehead to the glass, willing myself to remain invisible. Through the haze, I could just make out Sue, the camp manager, already on the move, clipboard in hand, her stride both urgent and unhurried. She wore the same faded dungarees as at staff induction, her hair up in a ragged bun, and she radiated a calm that was almost martial. Her voice, when it came, was not loud but sliced through the confusion like a well-aimed cricket ball.

"Under tens this way, please, if you're over ten, find your group leader in the blue bibs. Parents, we'll ask you to stay on the terrace for refreshments and briefing at 9.30 sharp."

Within seconds, she'd imposed a logic on the melee. The smaller children clustered at her feet, the older ones orbited in lumpy constellations, and the parents, reluctant at first, gravitated toward the terrace, where tables had been laid with urns of tea, baskets of dry croissants, and a dozen glass jugs of orange squash. I was reminded, suddenly and sharply, of the opening minutes of a test match: the fielders jostling into place, everyone watching for the first unpredictable bounce.

I'd been told to *'float'*, that is to circulate, to be available for emergencies and questions, but not to seem as if I was waiting to intercept trouble. I took this remit literally, trailing the edge of the crowd and trying to look both purposeful and accidental. In the first ten minutes, I was stopped three times: once by a father who wanted to know whether the children would be allowed to call home ("There's public phones on the ground floor just before the entrance to the ballroom, but their use is restricted to break times or evenings"); and once by a pair of identical twins who simply wanted to be pointed in the direction of the toilets, then promptly forgot the instructions and followed me instead. Most questions were answered with "Sue will explain all of that to you in the meeting shortly" because I didn't know the answer.

By then, the final three coaches had arrived. The Hall's entrance filled, then overflowed, until the ground floor seemed to heave and buckle with the sheer density of children. Some milled in the anterooms, others clumped on the stairs, calling down to their friends or up to the higher balustrades. Everywhere, the noise was raw, predatory, and as shrill as a battery farm, ricocheted off the marble and the high, domed ceiling.

And yet: at the centre, Sue stood, unyielding. She made small adjustments with the skill of a naval officer: redirecting a misrouted child here, soothing a fretful parent there, barking a gentle warning at a boy scaling the banister. I watched her, half in awe, and realised that in her wake the chaos receded, as if the very architecture responded to her presence. By eleven, all but a handful of stragglers had been matched to their dorms, and the terrace, littered with torn muffin wrappers and the clots of parental anxiety, emptied out.

I made my way to the top floor, where the boys' dorms had been hastily renamed in marker-pen for the week: *Oak, Beech, Cedar, Elm.* Asif was already there, standing sentry at the far end of the corridor, his arms folded and his mouth set in a line that managed to look both grave and bemused. He caught my eye and jerked his head toward the first open door.

"Room drama," he said, sotto voce, "two sets of siblings, one bunk-bed, and a moral crisis."

I stepped in, bracing for the worst. The air was thick with the smell of new polyester, *Lynx Africa*, and the heartbreak of forced partings. Six boys, maybe ten or eleven, arrayed themselves in tactical positions: two on the lower bunk, one perched above, two more on opposite corners of the room, and the last, tall, pale, already sporting a faint moustache, standing arms akimbo in the doorway.

A tiny, red-faced child on the bottom bunk wailed, "I have to sleep near the window! Otherwise I'll die!" His brother, less impressed, kicked him gently in the shins, "you're being a baby. I get the top."

"Doesn't matter," said the boy at the door, voice heavy with the indifference of one who has already witnessed a lifetime of disappointment, "we're all gonna get murdered by the ghosts anyway."

The wailing increased, now accompanied by actual tears. I crouched down beside the bunk.

"It's only for a week," I said, summoning my best imitation of a soothing voice. "How about you take the window for three nights, then swap? Or we do a coin toss?"

"Not fair!" both sets of siblings chorused, as if rehearsed.

"Or," said Asif, who had appeared behind me like a silent commando, "we do a first-night trial, then revisit in the morning. If you can't sleep, we'll sort it. If you can, you're braver than the ghosts."

This, miraculously, seemed to satisfy all parties. The wailing subsided to sniffling, and the older boys exchanged a look of sullen respect. Asif shot me a tiny, triumphant smile. I was reminded that he had a little brother back in Birmingham and had once told me, over chips at the induction, that he'd spent half his life arbitrating toy disputes and bed swaps.

We moved down the corridor, poking our heads into each dorm. Everywhere, the same: suitcase carnage, half-unpacked sleeping bags, children simultaneously desperate for attention and mortally embarrassed to be seen needing it. I discovered, to my horror, that the mere act of being tall and wearing a staff name badge made me an instant authority on everything from sun cream to lost retainers. By midday, I'd resolved three bunk disputes, located a missing inhaler, and reunited a crying boy with his invisible friend, who was named (with chilling directness) *'Death Machine'*.

At intervals, I'd catch sight of William outside, tending to the lawns or ferrying boxes to the kitchens. He worked with a kind of economy that was almost theatrical: every movement precise, nothing wasted. He wore cargo shorts and a football shirt, *Norwich City*, for his sins and seemed unbothered by the shrieks and projectiles hurtling past him as he walked the grounds. I found myself watching for him in odd moments, as if drawn to the steadiness he offered amid the madness.

After lunch, a massed feeding at trestle tables, the food as beige and as functional as possible Sue called a staff huddle in the refectory. We gathered, exhausted, around the central table. Her clipboard, now covered in annotations and stickies, looked like an ancient, battle-worn palimpsest.

"Well done," she said, voice light but eyes serious, "nobody lost, nobody sick, and only one minor nosebleed. That's a record for us. Tea at four, activities at five. Get some air if you can. Parents' cars are cleared by now, please check the car park for stragglers before next session."

She dismissed us with a wave, then called me over as I tried to slip away.

"John," she said, "could you take corridor duty this evening? The boys' floor needs a calm head. If you can brief them to respect lights-out later on, I'll owe you a pint."

"Sure," I said, instantly regretting it. I had visions of spending the afternoon running a permanent, low-level hostage negotiation.

But the task, it turned out, was not so terrible. Most of the boys, worn down by travel, anxiety, and the relentless churn of the morning, wanted only to collapse on their bunks and pretend not to be homesick. Some played cards, some read comics, a few even wrote letters home, though I doubted any would actually be sent. I patrolled, making small talk where invited, enforcing the no-shouting rule with gentle reminders, and, when necessary, offering impromptu tutorials in the fine art of pillow-fort construction.

After an hour, Asif joined me. We sat at the far end of the corridor, sharing a packet of crisps and trading stories about the day so far. He seemed more relaxed now, the sharp edges worn down by fatigue or camaraderie.

"How long you reckon till they riot?" he asked, nodding toward the rooms.

"They're already plotting," I said, "it's just a question of when the powder keg goes."

He grinned; teeth white against his dark skin, "you ever work with kids before?"

"Cricket coaching and my teaching practices, mostly," I said.

"Same," he replied.

We sat in companionable silence, listening to the murmured voices from the rooms, the occasional peal of laughter, the slap of bare feet on the old boards. It was almost peaceful. I closed my eyes, just for a second, and let the noise settle over me like a blanket.

I must have drifted, because the next thing I registered was Asif poking my arm.

"Wake up, mate," he said, grinning, "tea's in ten. If we're late, Sarah will set the drama kids on us."

I stood, wincing at the pins-and-needles in my legs. We walked together down the stairs, the air gradually thickening with the smell of jam tarts and instant coffee. As we reached the first landing, a group of girls in matching pink cardigans hurtled past, squealing, "we're gonna be late! Move!" They disappeared around the corner, leaving only a fading echo of perfume and mischief.

In the refectory, the noise was already nuclear. I scanned the room, found my cricket group clustered at a table near the window, and made my way over, bracing for impact. The boys greeted me with shouts and a volley of questions: *'Could we use the nets tonight?', 'Was it true the Hall had a swimming pool?', 'Would I referee a game of 'Extreme Dodgeball' after tea?'.*

I told them we'd see, that if they survived the scones and the sugar rush, anything was possible. I caught sight of William outside, on the gravel path near the service entrance, talking to another groundsman. The sun, dropping fast now, cut across his shoulders and caught in his hair. For a moment, the world seemed to slow, and I felt a curious ache, regret, maybe, or longing, or the uneasy suspicion that the boundaries I'd set for myself were already dissolving.

The boys pulled me back to the present, arguing over who would bat first. I smiled, tried to answer them, tried not to let my gaze wander to the window again.

It was only the first day. Already, I was losing track of which self I was supposed to be.

Tea was a ritual, messy, repetitive, conducted at deafening volume, but a ritual all the same. The Hall's old refectory, once reserved for the servants, now echoed with a hundred children's worth of hunger. Spoons rattled, jam tarts vanished by the dozen, orange squash spilled in sticky rivers down the tabletop's groove. Staff hovered on the periphery, shooing the worst offenders toward the *'clean up'* station and, for a brief window, patrolling for the kind of allergy that could send a week's planning to hell in a heartbeat.

I perched at the end of my table, trying to make eye contact with Asif through the tempest of sugar and sound. He caught my look and raised his mug in mock salute, then mouthed: "ready?" I nodded, even as a small hand closed on my sleeve.

"Sir, " the voice was thin, but urgent, "when is cricket?"

I checked the clock, *16:17*. "Thirteen minutes," I said, then calculated the walk to the field, "actually, ten. Meet at the front steps. Bring a water bottle."

The boy grinned, then turned to shout this intelligence to his mates, who all immediately began a countdown chant: "Ten! Nine! Eight!" The entire table joined in, and within moments a quarter of the room was on its feet, chanting and bashing plastic cutlery against their trays. Sue, up at the serving hatch, gave me the raised eyebrow of an officer surveying a mutiny.

I tried to quiet my group, with limited success, then stood and called out, "cricket group, on the steps! Everyone else, listen for your name!" The exodus was instant and total. In under a minute, twenty-two boys, ranging from eager and twitching to barely-awake, clustered at the Hall's main portico, flanked by myself and Asif. The sun was still high, the sky a relentless blue, the gravel radiating up heat like a kiln.

Asif and I did a quick headcount, then I led the procession out of the front doors to the pitch. The grass was blindingly green; the strip chalked with fresh lines and the portable stumps already in place. I had never seen a wicket prepared so well. I wondered if William had done it himself, and if he had, whether he knew how much it would matter to these children, for whom a *'real'* cricket square was as rare as a miracle.

We divided the group: one team to field, the other to bat, with the plan to swap halfway through. Asif took the fielders, positioning them with quick, efficient gestures, while I gave the batsmen a pep talk about *'rotation'* and *'fair play'* and *'nobody is out for a duck today'*. They nodded, some biting their lips in focus, others already jostling for who would go first.

The game itself was chaos. The first delivery, a gentle delivery, was dispatched square to deep cover, where it was promptly missed, then chased all the way to the rope. The batsman did not run so much as cavort, arms windmilling, his partner trailing behind in helpless laughter. I set up cones for boundaries, kept an eye on the least confident kids, and did my best to manufacture a contest that would, at the end, be close but not traumatic.

Within fifteen minutes, shirts were stuck to backs, shoes kicked off, and faces daubed with warpaint lines of white sunblock. Asif umpired with the fairness of a man who has seen every possible act of gamesmanship; he called wides with a gentle but unyielding tone, and ruled on runouts only after conferring with both teams. I stationed myself near the wicket, offering tips on grip and stance, occasionally patting a shoulder or ruffling hair when a ball was well struck.

But my mind was, increasingly, elsewhere. Midway through the second innings, as the younger boys took their turn in the field, I saw William again, standing at the edge of the drive. He leaned against the battered tailgate of his maintenance truck, arms crossed, watching the game with the faintest smile. He wore the same shorts as the morning, but had changed into a work shirt, sleeves rolled, collar open. Even from a distance, the shape of his arms, the easy athleticism, the set of his jaw, set off something inside me that was not entirely professional.

I tried to ignore him, to focus on the children, but found myself checking the boundary at each over, scanning for movement. At one point, he caught my gaze and raised a single eyebrow, as if to say: *'not bad'*. My face flushed so hot I thought my ears would bleed.

Distracted, I failed to notice that the next batsman, a tiny boy in a hat three sizes too large, was about to loft a skied ball directly toward me. I tracked it late, scrambled forward, and watched, in slow-motion horror, as it slipped straight through my hands and thudded against my sternum. The impact knocked the breath from my chest, and for a split second, all I could see was the bright afterimage of William's smile, superimposed over the infinite blue.

The children howled, a mixture of delight and disbelief. "He dropped it! Sir dropped a sitter!"

I tried to laugh, rubbing my ribs, "fielding lesson one: always watch the ball."

The batsman, emboldened, sprinted for two. The others cheered, "give him a medal!" and, "you can't sack the coach, can you?" Even Asif doubled over, hands on knees, his laughter as clear as glass.

After that, every fumble was an occasion. The boys on my team made a pantomime of my next fielding attempt, crowding round to *'help'* and then shouting, "don't let *Sir* near it!" When I did manage a clean pickup and return, the applause was deafening, more tribute than mockery.

William never moved from his place by the truck, but at the end of the session, as the boys gathered their bottles and trudged back toward the Hall, he walked over to the pitch. I was alone, kneeling to gather the scattered cones, when he stopped just beyond the rope.

"Good show," he said. His voice was softer than I remembered, the accent less rural now and edged with something almost conspiratorial.

I straightened, dusted my hands on my shorts, "you saw the catch, then."

He smiled, kindly, "I've dropped worse. Once lost a cup final that way."

I shrugged, trying to look unfazed, but I could feel the sweat cold on my back, my arms tingling with the aftershock of embarrassment, "the kids will dine out on that for weeks."

"Means they like you," he said. He reached down, picked up a stray ball, and tossed it underarm. I caught it, held it, let the rough seam bite into my palm.

He nodded, thoughtful, "you look settled, though. Like you belong. Not many do."

I wondered if this was a compliment, or something else, "do you?"

He looked at the Hall, then back at me, "most days. Some days, you remember it's just a job, like any other." He paused, gaze flicking to my hands, then said: "you play proper cricket?"

"Yeah, for the Uni team and my local club at home."

"I'd bet you will miss it this summer," he said, and there was a knowingness there that rattled me, "if you ever want any practice, after hours…" He left the sentence hanging, the implication obvious.

The air between us was charged, awkward, charged again. I wanted to say something, anything, but all the old reflexes crowded in: don't be obvious; don't be naïve; don't reach where you're not wanted.

Instead, I said, "sure. I'd like that."

He nodded, once, then turned and walked back toward the car park. I watched him go, my breath shallow, a thousand unsayable things clotted at the back of my throat.

I finished clearing the pitch, then jogged to catch up with my group. The corridor outside the dorms was pandemonium, shoes off, arms swinging, laughter ricocheting off the stone. Asif stood in the midst, arms folded, issuing instructions with the patience of a *Zen* master.

I ducked into the staff room, splashed water on my face, and leaned against the sink. My reflection was a mess: hair damp, shirt clinging, eyes wild with something I did not want to name. I looked at myself, willing the pulse to slow, willing the feelings down to a manageable simmer.

But the flush would not leave. It wasn't just embarrassment or arousal. It was the sense of being seen, properly seen, for the first time in a long while. And though I was ashamed to admit it, even to myself, it felt good.

After the showers, after the shouting, after the long, slow crawl to lights out, I sat at my desk and tried to write the day into my Filofax. I described the game, the dropped catch, the noise and the chaos. But when I reached the moment on the pitch, the line where William looked at me and said, *'you look settled, though'*, I froze.

For a long time, I stared at the blankness. Then I wrote, in tiny, cryptic script: *'sometimes the world conspires to show you what you want'*.

Below that, smaller: *'sometimes you even let yourself want it back'*.

I closed the book, sat in silence, and let the air cool around me. In the corridor, the boys had already begun to whisper ghost stories to each other, their voices a low, conspiratorial hum. Down on the lawn, the grass still held the print of our game, a faint, tangled memory that would fade by morning.

I went to bed, not knowing if I would sleep, but certain that the world would look different when I woke.

CHAPTER 4: AN EVENING AT THE LANGLEY ARMS

Evenings at the Hall possessed a peculiar viscosity: time slowed, thickened, coalesced into a syrupy dusk that pooled in the corridors and under the doors. I finished my circuit of the dorms just as the boys, miraculously, yielded to exhaustion, the last stragglers succumbing to a fugue of homesick tears and bravado stories. For the first time all day, a hush descended, sticky and unfamiliar. I stood a moment at the top of the staircase, listening for uprisings. Nothing but the distant susurrus of pipes and the soft, collective exhale of a hundred children bedding down in foreign rooms.

The corridor itself, *Elm* tonight, I leaned against the cool wall, forearm braced above my head, and let myself sag, letting the day's adrenaline bleed away. I tried to map out my next move, complete assessments, prep tomorrow's sessions, find food, but inertia had other plans.

It was Sarah who rescued me. She materialised from the stairwell, hair dishevelled, a denim jacket slung with calculated carelessness over one shoulder, and a take-no-prisoners smile plastered across her face.

"Survived?" she said. "I've got four still awake, plotting a mass breakout. If they succeed, I'm blaming you."

I snorted, but with more fondness than I intended, "we could leave the doors open, see what happens. Might improve the gene pool."

She cocked her head, approving, "there's a plan. Come on, you look like you need a pint. A bunch of us are heading to *The Langley Arms* before last orders." She paused, examining my posture with a dance-captain's eye. "You in, or are you married to the paperwork tonight?"

I glanced at my watch, *21:35*, the time glowing dim and ineffectual, and considered the prospect of solitary admin versus communal intoxication. "Depends. Is it socially acceptable to show up in trackies?"

"In this village, if you don't, they'll know you're a spy," she said, "grab your wallet, *Malvolio*."

It was an order, not a suggestion. I made a detour to my room, splashed water on my face, and debated a wardrobe change. The tracksuit bottoms were indeed the path of least resistance; I paired them with a clean tee shirt and tracksuit top. My reflection, hair flattened, eyes raw, looked less like a professional and more like the survivor of a minor disaster, which, I reasoned, was about right.

The walk down the drive to the village was brisk and silent, Sarah setting a pace just shy of a jog. She had the enviable knack of inhabiting stillness and motion simultaneously, her stride long and unhurried yet never lagging. I struggled to keep up, feigning indifference to the way my legs threatened to seize with each step.

We reached *The Langley Arms* just as the last orange of dusk bled into the hedgerows. The building itself was a study in anachronism: low, flint walls sunk deep in the earth, windows emitting slits of jaundiced light, the thatched roof almost apologetic in its shabbiness. Inside, the air was a warm blend of hops, slow-cooked meat, and the subtle undercurrent of dog. The clientele was precisely as it had been before, farmers, retirees, the odd couple in from the next parish.

Sarah navigated the room with confidence, weaving through the regulars and snagging a free booth in the far corner. She flopped onto the bench, stretching her arms above her head in theatrical relief. "I could sleep for a decade," she announced, "or at least until these kids go home."

I banished my nerves, ordered at the bar (two pints, plus whatever packet of crisps was nearest the till), and joined her. For a while we let the noise of the room fill the space between us, the clack of darts, the punctuated roar from some event at the LA Olympics on the small TV above the bar, the steady drone of rural gossip. Sarah tore open the crisps, dumped them on a napkin, and attacked them with surgical precision.

I rolled the condensation on my glass into a neat ellipse, the movement soothing in its repetition. Sarah caught me at it, smirked, and said, "you're worse than my mum. When she's nervous, she alphabetises the biscuits."

I laughed, though I was instantly aware of how right she was, "is it that obvious?"

She shrugged, "I teach drama. I can spot a tic at fifty paces. You're not nervous around me, are you?"

"No. Well, yes. But only because you're so…" I waved my hand, encompassing her general aura…"intense."

She barked a laugh, then softened it with a grin, "I've been called worse. You get used to it."

We talked. At first, the standard-issue patter of university, who was in what cohort, where we'd been posted for teaching practice, how much we loathed the bureaucracy. I learned that Sarah was in her second year of a *Dance and Theatre Ed PGCE,* that she'd only come to Langley because the Brighton placement had fallen through, and that she had a secret, burning hatred of interpretive movement but did it anyway because, "it's what the world expects."

She asked about my own studies, and I found myself admitting, before I could recalibrate, that I'd always wanted to teach history, but wasn't sure I had the stamina for actual schools.

She leaned in, elbows on the table, "why history?"

I hesitated, then told her about the day I visited my town's museum with school when I was about ten years old: how I'd stood for two hours in front of the Roman coins, transfixed by the idea that something so tiny could outlive a civilisation. How it felt like proof that time was both immense and heartbreakingly fragile. The memory sounded grandiose in my own ears, but Sarah just nodded, her eyes level with mine.

"That's beautiful," she said, and I felt the weight of it.

I took a long pull of my drink to steady myself. The lager was warm, a little metallic, but it did the trick. "It's just, I don't know if I'm cut out for it. Teaching, I mean. I'm not… I don't have the presence. Or the voice. Or the…" I gestured, helpless, as if the correct noun might emerge from the swirl of bodies in the pub.

Sarah's answer was immediate, "none of us do. That's why we fake it. You think half those geezers in there…" she jerked her head at the other staff table that had been recently populated, where a PE instructor was halfway through a raucous impression of Sue's walk, "actually know what they're doing? Please. The only difference between a real teacher and an impostor is time spent pretending."

I smiled, because it was the kind of lie I desperately needed to believe.

She watched me, then shifted in her seat, her posture softening. "You're good with the kids. I saw you with the twins earlier, how you got them to stop fighting for five seconds. That's half the job right there."

I felt myself colour, embarrassed by the praise, "I bribed them with sweets."

"Exactly. Genius."

We went quiet for a minute, not awkward, just companionable. I caught myself winding the edge of the beer mat around my finger, as if tying and untying a secret knot. Outside, a tractor trundled past the window, its headlights casting slow-moving shadows against the opposite wall. The hour, the beer, the company, all conspired to make me feel, for a moment, that I could settle here, or anywhere.

Eventually, Sarah broke the silence, "what about after this? You going back up north?"

"Yeah, got my last year to finish, but…" I trailed off. I didn't want to admit how uncertain the future felt, how every option seemed to lead back to the same hollow place.

She read it on my face, "you'll be fine. And if not, just run away to the coast and teach sailing to rich idiots. That's my backup plan."

I laughed, genuine now, "if you end up on a yacht, let me know. I'll join as first mate."

She raised her glass, "deal."

We toasted to hypothetical futures, the glasses meeting with a dull, satisfying clink. Around us, the staff tables merged into one large group, the noise of the pub seemed to recede, the world shrinking to just the amber lamplight, the smell of hops, and the easy warmth of shared admission. For the first time in months, I let myself relax. I let myself believe, even briefly, that I could be anyone, become anything, provided I had someone like Sarah at my back to say it was possible.

There's a peculiar hush that falls in rural pubs when the hour grows late and the regulars have made their peace with each other. The staff table, now ballooned to twice its original size, rippled with the energy of people forcibly decompressing after a day spent performing competence. Sarah and I had become part of the current; I was mid-story, a tale about my grandfather's cricket obsession and how he'd once forced me to wear pads to Christmas dinner, when the door clapped open behind me.

A gust of air, thick and sodden with the memory of the day's heat, curled into the bar. With it came William, trailing the scent of rain-on-stone and mown grass. He paused, blinking in the transition from dark to amber, his shirt dark with sweat at the collar and under-arms, the fabric clinging to him in a way that was almost indecent.

My words died. A pulse like a snapped violin string ran up my chest and stopped just behind my teeth. I watched, stupidly, openly, as he raked a hand through his hair until it stood in wet, canted peaks. He wore the same battered rugby shirt as earlier, but in the pub's light it looked softer, the stripes faded to memory.

He saw me, saw Sarah, and offered a small, slow nod before sliding into the next booth over. Two other groundsmen, burly, sun-burnt, nearly indistinguishable, joined him. Their arrival shifted the centre of gravity in the room; laughter grew louder, chairs scraped back to make space.

Sarah followed my gaze with a small, knowing smile, "you al-right there?"

I snapped back to the table, heart still in the process of reas-sembling itself, "yeah. Just lost the thread."

"Wasn't much of a thread to begin with," she said, grinning. "Go on. Pads at the table. Did you eat in them, or just the pudding?"

I forced the story to its conclusion, but my mind orbited the next table. Every laugh that rolled out from William's booth seemed to echo through my ribs. I drank faster, in tiny, nervous sips, until the glass left a sweat ring on the wood. I traced it with a finger, circled the outline, pressed until the moisture beaded on my skin. My knee, unbid-den, bounced a rhythm under the table. I could feel Sarah's eyes on me, assessing.

The table filled up; conversation turned chaotic, everyone talk-ing over each other. Someone started a story about the food fight in the refectory that morning, and the rest tried to outdo it with their own anecdotes: a boy who ate seventeen *KitKats* in an hour, the girl who convinced a whole dormitory that the library was haunted by a Victo-rian maid.

William watched me as I spoke, not staring but always attentive, the corners of his mouth quirked in a way that suggested approval. I caught myself lingering on his forearms, the way the light drew gold out of the hairs, the veins standing proud when he gestured. At one point, his knee knocked mine under the table, a jolt, a static charge, then gone. I wanted to believe it was accidental. I wanted to believe it wasn't.

When the conversation turned to the Hall itself, William became more animated. He spoke about the grounds, how the river flooded every third spring, how the trees along the avenue were older than most of the nearby villages. He admitted, with a sheepishness that bordered on pride, that he'd been born in the Home Farm behind the Hall, and that he never wanted to leave.

Last orders arrived in the form of a brass bell and the barman's measured decree: "ten minutes, folks." The room responded with a collective groan and then a final, spirited rally. Pint glasses were drained, new rounds summoned and dispatched, toasts made with the extravagance of people who knew they'd be regretting this in the morning.

Sarah raised her cider and called, "to surviving week one, mostly intact!" The staff chorus responded with "here, here," the phrase shattering into laughter as half the table spilled their drinks or knocked heads in the attempt to clink glasses. William, across from me, caught my eye and lifted his glass in a subtle, private salute. I matched it, letting the cold, bitter lager anchor me to the moment.

The pub emptied slowly, the regulars melting into the gloom, voices fading into the insect-noise of the lane. Our own contingent spilled out last: a shuffling, mostly coherent parade of teachers, groundsmen, and kitchen staff. The walk up the lane to the Hall was less a march and more an amble, bodies drifting apart and together in a choreography dictated by habit and the narrowness of the road.

Sarah led the charge, arms swinging, already halfway to the front gates by the time the rest of us had gotten up to speed. William and I fell behind, not deliberately but inevitably, our strides matching pace even as the others faded ahead. The sky had cleared during the evening, and the moon cast everything into that peculiar, two-dimensional clarity reserved for summer nights: the hedges black as ink, the gravel path a silver ribbon, every tree skeletal and sharp.

For a while, we said nothing. Just the crunch of our trainers and the ghostly echoes of laughter from up ahead. I tried to walk in a way that looked uncalculated, but with each step, I was more aware of the proximity of William's body, the way his elbow occasionally nudged mine, the way his hand drifted perilously close to my own when we rounded a corner together.

Eventually, he broke the silence, "do you miss home?" His voice was low, as if the night required it.

I considered, "sometimes. Mostly I just miss knowing what comes next. Here, it's all guesswork."

He smiled, soft at the edges, "I know what you mean. It's why I never left, really. Everything out there feels too big. Here, I know every stone in the wall."

"Do you ever get bored?" I asked, not expecting an answer.

He shrugged, "only when there's no one to talk to."

I let the implication hang, then said, "it must get lonely."

He looked at me sidelong, then kicked at a pebble, "it does. But I like the quiet. You ever notice how loud cities are, even at night?"

I nodded, "sometimes the noise helps, though. Drowns out the other stuff."

He thought about that, "I reckon I'm the opposite. I like to hear myself think. Most days, anyway."

We walked on, the Hall now visible ahead, its windows dark, the columns of the portico catching the moonlight like bones. I felt a sudden urge to fill the quiet, to spill out all the things I'd kept shuttered up: the ache for home, the doubts about teaching, the messiness of wanting something I could barely name.

Instead, I said, "my mum wants me to be a headteacher by thirty. She thinks it's the only safe job left."

William snorted, "my dad wanted me to get my own farm. Said it'd knock some sense into me."

I laughed, "did you ever think about it?"

He shook his head, "not once. I'm useless with all the accounts stuff."

We shared a smile, a fragile little thing, but it lingered.

The path narrowed as we neared the Hall, forcing us closer. William's shoulder brushed mine, once, then again, this time with intention. The touch was electric, a brief, grounding shock. I shivered, though the air was warm.

He glanced at me, then looked away, but didn't increase the distance. We walked like that, skin-to-skin, until the path widened again, and I mourned the loss of contact. Ahead, the rest of the group was dispersing: Sarah peeling off toward the staff annex, a few others wandering in the direction of the kitchen or the back gardens.

At the bottom of the steps to the main entrance, we stopped. The Hall loomed above us, solemn and silent, its face picked out in silver. The air smelled of stone and honeysuckle, the faint, chemical tang of chlorine from the old fountain.

William turned to me, hands in his pockets, and said, "who would've thought I'd have a northerner and a Liverpool supporter for a friend?"

I smiled, trying to play it off, "who'd have thought you'd survive the experience."

He grinned, and there was a moment, just long enough for me to measure the space between us, where I thought he might say something else. But he just winked, said, "see you to-morrow, John," and walked off into the darkness toward the stables.

I watched him go, the shape of him shrinking with every step, until he was gone. The silence was absolute. I lingered on the steps, letting the night seep in. I thought about the brush of his shoulder, the warmth of his hand, the way my own skin still tingled with memory. I thought about Mark, where he might be tonight, whether he ever felt this strange, helpless ache for someone. And I thought about tomorrow, and the day after that, and all the unguessable ways the world might change.

Eventually, I climbed the steps, let myself into the Hall, and found my way to bed. The moonlight slanted across my pillow, painting everything in a soft, improbable blue. I closed my eyes, replayed every word and gesture, and tried, futilely, sweetly, to sleep.

CHAPTER 5: THE MYSTERIOUS LETTER

The next afternoon, I barricaded myself in the library. Not for effect, I didn't slam doors or leave a trail of slammed books in my wake, but because the world outside had become intolerable, a sunlit pageant of children's voices, staff-room laughter, and the persistent hum of possibility that I could neither welcome nor escape. The morning had been all motion: bracing wind on the sports field, the gleeful carnage of a paintball session, William's figure in hi-vis moving like a ghost at the edge of the trees. Even when I closed my eyes, his silhouette floated behind the lids, etched in a halo of ozone and yellow.

The library, Langley Hall's great room of memory, stood cool and drowsy behind heavy French doors. I paused a moment inside the threshold, letting my eyes adjust to the wet-green dimness. Outside, the sun's heat pressed at the glass, distorting the rose gardens into a series of trembling watercolours. Within, the light fell in thin, trembling shafts, stripping the air of all its urgency. It was silent except for the sigh of the old house settling and the low, continuous tick of the regulator clock above the fireplace.

I let myself drift along the spines, grazing the shelves with a hand. Here were the bound quarterlies, the fat compendia of agricultural progress, the brittle lives of parliamentarians. The titles, Langley's own, sometimes, recurring with the regularity of a bloodline. But even among the books there was a sense of abandonment: volumes slouched, dust filmed their jackets, one shelf near the window had partially collapsed and never been righted.

I found myself, after a while, at the bottom of the east wall, among the forgotten and the merely useful. Old *Ordnance Survey* maps, estate ledgers, receipts for milk deliveries, and a row of wine-stained *County Records* journals. They were packed tight, but my hand found a gap, and I felt, not a book, but a box: wooden, pale, no bigger than a shoe, its lid secured with a tarnished brass clasp.

Something about it compelled me, perhaps the audacity of a plain wooden box in a room that had once been sacred to parchment and calfskin. I knelt, feeling the bite of the flagstone through my jeans, and pulled it free.

It was heavier than I expected. I set it on the desk and hesitated before opening, as if I might set off an alarm or trip some last line of the Hall's ancient security. My fingers hovered, then snapped the clasp. The lid lifted on a mild resistance, inside, paper. Not the thin, suffering paper of library stacks, but thick sheets, their edges deckled and inked with a variety of hands.

I worked through the first few layers: inventories of livestock, planting schedules from the twenties, a pamphlet on the management of bee colonies, annotated with faint, looping marginalia. I liked the heft of each page, the sense that every item represented a moment of significance, even if it was only the counting of sheep. There was something soothing in it, a counter to the volatility of my own thoughts.

I lost track of time. The voices outside the window blurred to a low drone, the world becoming increasingly distant as I let myself be absorbed by the tactile monotony of record-keeping. For an hour, maybe more, I moved documents from left to right, arranging them in neat piles by date, by topic, by the accidental narrative of their arrival in the box. My mind wandered, always, inevitably, back to William's hands, the way they had handled the cricket ball, the easy competence of him. Each time I caught myself drifting, I pressed harder into the work, as if the weight of these papers could ballast me against longing.

Near the bottom of the box, between two nearly identical inventories of milk yield for 1916 and 1917, I found it: a single envelope with a sheet, folded once, then again, and sealed with a red wax circle, now broken. The seal was stamped with a coat of arms, the one he recognised from outside the pub in the village. The paper was creamy, heavy, and as I unfolded it, the musk of old wax stung my nose, a scent more intimate than perfume.

I hesitated. I did not want to read someone's private letter as the envelope was addressed to a *Lord John Langley c/o Trinity College, Cambridge* and this had a single line through it and the words *'forward to Langley Hall'* written underneath. On the back of the envelope it was written *'recvd 2nd August 1917'*. And yet, even as my fingers protested, my eyes obeyed the old, forbidden instinct to know. The folded letter inside was addressed to the same person, but the address was given as *'c/o The Imperial German Embassy, Lisbon, Portugal'*.

The letter itself was dated *'10 January 1916'*, which meant it had taken eighteen months to be delivered. The handwriting sloped right, urgent and unvarnished, the penmanship of someone who wrote more often with a pencil and a moving train than in the calm of a desk.

My dearest Jonny,

I am now on active duty and on shore leave. I have passed this letter to my comrade in the hope that he can find a chance to post it from his hometown as it would be too suspicious if I did.

I cannot get your voice out of my head. The days here are endless, the nights worse, and when the stars come I lie awake and count everyone I would name after you, if only it were permitted.

For now I sleep only with the memories and dreams of our last summer together, and a firm resolve that after this bloody war we will get to live our dream together in that villa in the south of France

Do not write again as it is too dangerous, instead at least think of me—on the cold mornings, or the long blue twilights, or whenever you stand at the window and see the moon caught on the river.

Yours, always and only,

Kip

For a long time, I did not breathe.

The lines doubled, then trebled, as I re-read them, unwilling to let go of the voice that pressed so close to the bone. My hands trembled; the letter shuddered in my grip as if electrified. The world contracted to the space between the lines, the air in the library dense with the scent of wax and longing. In the deepest part of me, something folded and refolded, recognition, envy, a helpless complicity.

Stolen afternoons. Moments I treasure. The ache of not hearing from you. It was all here, the narrative of hiding, of rehearsed distance, of the unspeakable. The clarity of it cut through me: a story as old as the walls, as private as a touch behind a closed door.

I looked up, panic needling my chest, certain that I was being watched, that someone would see me holding the evidence of a secret as powerful as my own. The library was empty, the clock above the hearth now chiming the hour. Still, I found myself checking the door, the window, the corridor beyond, before letting the letter drop to the desk.

For a while I just sat, my breathing ragged, the room a blur at the edges. It was not just that I had found a kindred spirit in the old house; it was that the words, careful, coded, desperate, were the ones I'd never dared to speak, even to myself. It was all here, in Kip's hand: the wanting, the carefulness, the hope.

I read the letter again. And again.

I put it down, then picked it up, tracing the grooves left by the pen, the broken arc of the seal. My thumb, unconsciously, hovered over the signature. I tried to imagine the hand that wrote it: the angle of the wrist, the set of the jaw, the hours spent drafting, discarding, perfecting these lines before sending them into the blue.

At some point, the sun moved behind a cloud, and the library cooled by several degrees. I felt a cold sweat form at the nape of my neck, an aftershock of the exposure. I wanted, almost desperately, to know what happened to Jonny and Kip. Did they write again? Did the letters go unposted? Did the war erase them, or did they simply subside into the silence required of men who loved wrongly?

I could not say. I could only sit, surrounded by the books, the ledgers, the failed archives of ordinary life, and feel the echo in my own blood.

I closed the letter, folded it once, then again, and replaced it between the inventories. For a minute, my hand lingered on the edge of the box, as if the wood could transmit some last current of memory.

I thought of William, his arms, the sweat at his neck, the way his voice dropped in the blue hour between night and morning. I thought of Mark, his smile in the pub, the press of his mouth to my shoulder, the long, bitter aftermath of losing him.

Above all, I thought of the phrase: *'if you cannot write, at least think of me'*. I wondered how many times that wish had crossed the gulf between two people, how often it had gone unanswered.

At last, I stood, smoothed the rumpled front of my shirt, and closed the box with a click. The library was unchanged, but I felt as if every molecule in the room had shifted, as if the air itself was now charged with something dangerous, vital, and possibly redemptive.

I left the library as quietly as I had entered, the memory of the letter burning in my palm. I told myself it was nothing, a relic, the residue of a life that had nothing to do with me.

But when I got to my room, I sat on the edge of the bed and, with trembling hands, copied out the letter from memory, word for word, line for line, into the back pages of my Filofax. I wanted it, needed it, to survive.

When I finished, I pressed my thumb to the page, as if a fingerprint might make it more real. Then I shut the book, turned out the light, and lay awake until the world went dark.

The morning after the letter's discovery, I walked through my own life in a trance. Children's games rang out through the open windows and bounced, pointless, off the flint walls. The taste of burnt coffee lingered on my tongue. I lost three consecutive cricket balls to the long grasses of the meadow next to the ground, and my attempts at classroom discipline came out in the voice of a man who'd spent the night conversing with ghosts. Every so often I'd catch myself glancing toward the Hall, as though at any moment someone might appear at the top window and beckon me to some necessary reckoning.

I endured it as long as I could. When the lunch bell sounded, a cowbell, struck with theatrical zeal by the kitchen manager, I slipped away from the sports field, followed the shade of the yew walk, and let myself back into the library. I was grateful for Sue's organisational skills as this allowed us all to have a couple of hours a day for admin work.

The box was still there, stashed at the edge of the desk where I'd left it. My hands hovered above it, then, without preamble, I snapped it open. I needed to see the letter again. Not for what it said, but to prove it hadn't evaporated overnight, that I hadn't conjured the whole thing as a self-pitying hallucination.

It was real. The red seal still cracked, the paper still thick and ochre-tinged. But now, as I unfolded it, I saw something I'd missed in the rapture of the first reading: a faint pencilled notation, at the very bottom of the back page. Just a string of numbers and letters, underlined once, so lightly pressed that it could have been the ghost of a previous reader's hand.

I wrote it down on my own notepaper, then checked the inside lid of the box, where a faded index card was pinned. There, column three, halfway down, a matching reference: *'CPT. LANGLEY / COOPER – Corr. – 1918'*. I felt the same jolt as when, as a child, I'd solved a puzzle before my older cousin. Some grownup had known what this was, had made a note, but hadn't cared to read the details.

I set to work, methodically. The rest of the box was mostly account ledgers and estate business, mundane, but meticulous. Every transaction was logged, every receipt initialled, every debt or surplus annotated in the hand of the then butler, a *Mr. Reeves*. There were, however, two other letters, both less intimate, both addressed to *'Capt. J.E. Langley'*. One came from a captain in the *Norfolk Regiment*, dated October 1918; the other, from a solicitor, regarding the signing of a will.

But that name, Langley, set the rhythm of my heart to a new, faster tempo. I spread the documents across the desk, ignoring the dust, and tried to reconstruct the cast. *Lord John Langley*. The surname alone told me he was of the house, not just a namesake. I checked the cover page of the first ledger: *'Langley Hall: Domestic Staff & Expenses, 1914–1920'*.

I leafed through. There, four lines down, was an entry for *'Cooper, T. (Valet)'*, appointed March 1914, twenty-two, *'son of Mr. J. Cooper of Home Farm'*. I recognised, dimly, a thread that ran from this boy to the present, through the groundsman's bloodline.

Everywhere I looked, the names repeated: *'Langley'*, *'Cooper'*, *'Reeves'*. The Hall, for all its apparent grandeur, was a closed system, feeding on itself, its people forever orbiting in tight, invisible circles.

With a trembling hand, I wrote the sequence out in my Filofax:

- 1914: Thomas Cooper valet aged twenty-two

- 1916: J.L. Langley enlists, age (uncertain—guess eighteen?)

- 1918: The letter from Kip to "Jonny" (Langley)

- 1923: Langley Hall reverts to new earl (unexplained)

There was no mention of Kip's surname in the letter itself, but the reference index, my next target, listed *'Lord Christian Langley'* possibly as being *'Kit'*. It didn't help.

I leaned back, the chair creaking beneath me, and let the facts swirl. The young lord of the house, gone to war. The correspondence with *'Kip'*, their relationship, whatever its boundaries, preserved here in the negative, in the silence between lines, in the absence of any open mention. The rest of the world continued: the milk was delivered, the hay was cut, the boys were hired and sacked, the wages paid. But somewhere, in the eye of the great war, these two had found an hour to love, or something like it. And someone, possibly even the butler, had saved the evidence. Not destroyed it. Saved it.

I sat, for a long while, immobilised by the significance. I was not the first to try and fit desire into a place that was not built to contain it. I was not the only one to lose sleep over the memory of a mouth, or the scent of someone's skin on a wet night. Men had been doing this for centuries, and here, of all places, I had found proof.

A movement at the window caught my attention. I startled, heart in my throat, but it was only a sparrow flitting through the rose canes. The library was otherwise deserted, the hush as profound as ever. Still, my hands shook as I closed the ledger and replaced the box. Even an empty room seemed, suddenly, to pulse with surveillance.

I took out my Filofax and began to draft the story as best I could. Each line became a hypothesis, a guess, a wish. In one version, *Jonny* and *Kip* survived the war and met again at the Hall, passing in the corridor, maybe exchanging a glance of recognition, or nothing at all. In another, one or both were buried under a field in France, the letter unread, the desire unspent. In all versions, I felt the same ache: a hunger for proof that happiness was possible, even if only for a moment, even if only in secret.

I tried to imagine *Thomas Cooper*, the young valet, moving through these rooms sixty years ago. Would he have known? Would he have seen the longing between his masters, or understood the signs? Would he have cared, or would the business of survival have obliterated every other instinct? I wondered if William, today, ever felt the weight of that history in his own bones, if he knew he was living on the sediment of buried desire.

The rest of the afternoon passed in a fever. I alternated between scanning the ledgers, cross-referencing the guest lists, and returning, again and again, to the letter. Each time I read it, something new emerged: the sharpness of *Kip's* wit, the way he laced longing with self-mockery, the fragility of the hope. I began to see him as a real man, not a character, not a cipher, but a person who had lived and died with the same doubts, the same cravings, the same need to record the unbearable in ink.

As the light waned, I set myself a task: to find every scrap of their story, to build a record where none had been meant to exist. If nothing else, I owed it to them to *Jonny*, to *Kip*, to everyone who'd ever tried and failed to be happy here.

I gathered the papers into careful stacks, re-shelved the box, and wiped the dust from the desk with my sleeve. The library was deep in shadow now, the sun a memory beyond the trees. The world outside was still, for once, and I could almost imagine that the war had never ended, that the whole house was suspended in that hour before darkness, waiting for a letter, a knock, a sign.

I stood for a while at the window, watching the bats wheel and the slow, patient drift of clouds over the park. I thought of William, working somewhere in the twilight, unknowing. I thought of Mark, probably asleep in a shared room in some city, dreaming of escape. I thought, finally, of myself, not the self I had curated for the world, but the one who, in this moment, was so helplessly, so stupidly alive.

When at last I turned away from the glass, I found myself smiling, though there was no one to see it. There would be time, tomorrow and all the days after, to find out what became of Jonny and Kip. There would be time, maybe, to tell someone else their story.

For now, it was enough to know that it had existed at all.

CHAPTER 6: CONFIDING IN SARAH

The air inside the staff lounge was dense, charged with the particulate tension of a day's spent energy. Someone had set a radio to low, tinny jazz, and the lilt of a saxophone tangled with the miasma of sports drink, chlorine, and overcooked pasta. I was meant to be celebrating. The children, having survived their inaugural match and a plague of bruised fingers, were at last corralled into their dormitories; the other instructors, their shirts two shades darker than at breakfast, lolled against the vinyl banquette with the abandon of soldiers at the armistice. Sarah, queen of improvisation, held court by the kitchenette, using a plastic coffee stirrer as baton to conduct the day's autopsy.

I let them. I clapped and nodded then said, "God, yes," when the story required it. But after the third round of "guess what the twins did next," my circuitry shorted, and I slipped out the fire door before anyone could require my participation in the next exhumation. The sudden quiet was bracing. I stood in the shadow of the annex, blinking at the low sun as it flayed the cricket pitch gold, and felt the ache of my neck where the day's ultraviolet had found unprotected flesh. My limbs throbbed, alive with the day's exertions, and a stripe of salt had dried above my lip.

I had, by some miracle, retained my half-pint of lager. I nursed it as I walked, relishing the cold glass against my palm, the beads of condensation mapping the lazy descent of gravity. With each step, the air changed: from the overripe sweetness of the refectory bins to the burnt mineral of the drive, and finally, after a hundred yards, to the bruised, mossy breath that collected under the ancient oaks by the Hall's northern boundary. I made for the largest of these, an edifice that predated the Hall itself by at least two centuries, its trunk bifurcated and thick as an altar. The ground beneath was spongy, cool. I set my back to the bark and let myself sink.

The Hall was visible from here, half-obscured by the sweep of lawn and a foreground of wildflowers. Its windows, in the final hour of daylight, glimmered back every permutation of sky: cobalt, then flame, then the weird, bruised blue that signalled the coming of night. I tried to imagine the generations that had looked out from those windows, the lineage of boys, girls, and men who had walked these fields before the age of fluorescent sports bibs. My mind made a game of it: which of them had ever felt so desperately alone, and so perilously exposed, as I did now?

A drone of insects rose, then faded. The wind, which had been absent all day, materialized in a sudden gust, shivering the leaves overhead. The movement sent loose a handful of brown, unfinished acorns; one bounced off my knee and rolled to rest by my heel. I picked it up, rolled it between thumb and forefinger, and let the texture, green velvet, rough at the cap, anchor me.

My body was a catalogue of minor failures: shoulder stiff from an ill-advised dive, calf cramping from too many overs, skin everywhere tight and itching from the sun's unkind attention. Even my tongue felt burnt, the taste of cheap lager mingled with the chemical memory of sunblock and whatever institutional detergent the Hall used for its glassware. I shut my eyes, tried to order my thoughts, and found them rebelling, leaping the tracks I'd laid for them.

William.

His name alone was enough to reconfigure the circuits, to send the blood running a fraction hotter. All day I'd watched for him at the periphery of the matches, an unhurried figure with the ballast of a local, never out of place, always at ease. He'd made the pitch perfect for us, swept the creases, set the stumps. Each time I passed him on the way to the pavilion, our eyes met, never for long, always with that sly, checked energy that said: we see each other.

But seeing was not the same as knowing. I told myself this, again and again, in the same way I'd learned to tell myself that I was normal, that my affection for Mark, still burning, still unresolved and was merely a chemical fluke, a misfire that I could ignore if I willed it so. I was supposed to be fixing myself this summer. Not pining, not inventing new obsessions. I thought of Mark back at university, so far away it almost hurt: the cruel clarity of his eyes, the sureness with which he took and withheld affection, the way he could, by the smallest gesture call up all the hunger and terror that made me myself.

He would hate this place, I thought. He would hate its rituals, its sameness, its willingness to accept whatever small joys the world permitted. But he'd find William fascinating. He would tease me about my taste, about my apparent inability to resist "boys with mud on their knees and hands built for breaking." I smiled, bitter, and pressed my thumbnail into the flesh of the acorn until it nearly split.

I told myself to think of something else. To focus on the symmetry of the Hall's façade, the way the sunlight had turned its limestone to amber, the strange floating serenity of the clouds. But the mind is a greedy thing, and the body greedier still. My fingers, restless, tapped the rim of my glass in a staccato that matched the agitation of my chest. I tried to still them, then gave up. I took another sip, felt the shock of cold against my teeth, and let it linger.

From somewhere beyond the lawn, the sound of laughter, a cohort of children, escaped from their caretakers and running amok in the walled garden. Their shrieks carried, thinned by distance, but they reminded me that the world existed beyond my skin. I tried to recapture the sense of purpose that had seemed so attainable in the mornings, when the pitch was new and the boundaries marked with such precision. I tried, and failed.

My skin prickled again, but this time not from the sun. I sensed, rather than heard, the approach of another body, footsteps through the leaf litter, the scrape of trainers against the stone border. For a moment, I thought it might be William. I tensed, heart tripping in anticipation and dread, then immediately resented myself for the hope.

But it was Sarah. She emerged from the copse, arms folded tight around her chest, her denim jacket draped loose and her face schooled into a mask of faux surprise.

"Thought I'd find you here," she said, her voice low but carrying, "you have a habit of vanishing when the party gets good."

I shrugged, unwilling to offer more than a smile.

She dropped to the ground beside me, crossed her legs, and stared at the Hall. For a minute or two, she let the silence do the talking. Then she nudged my shin with her boot and said, "is it the kids, or the grownups, or just the world in general that does you in?"

"Little bit of all three," I said, surprised by the honesty, "mostly the world, though."

She grinned; teeth white in the dusk, "you should've done drama. You'd have fit right in."

I made a face, "I don't have the courage."

"Courage is overrated. We're all just faking it. Some of us get paid to fake it louder."

I glanced at her, and for a second I saw something in her expression, curiosity, maybe, or the quiet pride of someone who recognizes a fellow exile. I looked away, embarrassed.

She said, "I like it out here. The quiet. You can actually hear yourself think."

I nodded, "sometimes I wish I couldn't."

She laughed, but there was no malice in it. She leaned her head against the trunk, just a hand's width from my shoulder, and for a while we let the coming night settle around us. I felt her breath, slow and steady, and tried to match it. Tried to let it carry me away from the churn inside.

But even in company, I could not quiet the war inside my chest. William's name, Mark's face, the endless appetite of memory. The need to be seen, and the terror of being known.

Above us, a single bat veered through the amber air, its wings cutting the dusk with astonishing precision. I tracked its flight until it vanished into the shadowed eaves of the Hall. Then I set my glass on the grass, closed my eyes, and wondered how much longer I could hold myself together.

The answer was: *not long at all.*

Sarah was not a large person, but her presence filled the space between us as if she'd hung lanterns on every branch. Even in silence, she radiated intent: the sharpness in her jaw, the way she tucked a strand of hair behind her ear with deliberate slowness, the creased lines at the corners of her eyes, which deepened whenever she suspected a secret. For five minutes, we watched the Hall together, tracking the long shadows as they crept up the fluted columns. I tried to count the window-panes; I lost the thread at twenty-six.

Sarah drew her knees up and wrapped her arms around them, then looked sideways at me. "Alright," she said, with the careful precision of someone defusing a bomb, "tell your aunty Sarah what's troubling you."

The effect was instantaneous. My composure, so rigorously constructed over years of familial obligation and academic posturing, cracked like the thinnest shell. The ache in my neck sharpened. My hands, already tight around the base of the glass, began to tremble. For a few seconds I did nothing but stare at the grass, blinking rapidly as the pressure in my throat built to an unmanageable surge. When I finally spoke, the words came out thin and uneven.

"It's nothing, really," I said, the automatic phrase of cowards everywhere.

She let that hang. Then: "try again."

I wanted, desperately, to produce the expected answer: anxiety about teaching, imposter syndrome, the loneliness of displacement. All true, all defensible. But none of them would explain the way my body refused to obey, the way my skin prickled and my chest felt cinched tight as a drum. I searched for a safe place to start, and found none.

"Is it home?" she said, voice low.

I shook my head, "not exactly. I mean, yes. But also… it's complicated." The phrase, so bland, so inane, nearly made me laugh. Instead, I choked on it, and the next sound out of my mouth was something between a gasp and a sob.

Sarah's hand, cool and firm, found my shoulder. She squeezed once, not a gesture of comfort so much as a contract: I am here, I am not leaving, you may proceed at your own pace. The simplicity of it shattered me. All the tightness, all the careful architecture of holding in—gone.

I started to cry. Not the cinematic, single-tear variety, but the ugly, stuttering kind that seizes your entire body and leaves you raw. In my mind the familiar feelings of guilt and shame came to the fore — was I about to do to William what Mark was doing to me, or even worse, was I the catalyst of all of this for everyone.

I tried to hide my pain and tears, turned my face away, but Sarah just waited. When I finally managed to breathe, she handed me her napkin, surreptitiously purloined from the staffroom, blue and printed with the Hall's crest and watched as I wiped my nose and tried to reassemble myself.

"I'm sorry," I said, hating how pathetic I sounded.

"Don't be daft," she replied, "if you could see the lot of us, you'd know you're in excellent company."

We sat that way for a long time: me, alternating between sniffling and silence, and Sarah, patient as an old tree, her hand never leaving my shoulder. I was vaguely aware of the sound of distant voices, the squeal of a bicycle from the lane, the dry rattle of acorns against the trunk. Mostly, though, I was aware of the relief, the deep, exhausting relief, of being permitted to fall apart.

The last of the sunlight faded. The Hall's windows went from gold to black, and a single bat resumed its patrol overhead, indifferent to our small drama.

Eventually, Sarah said, "you don't have to tell me now. Or ever, if you don't want. But you're not alone, yeah?"

I nodded, still unable to find a voice that wouldn't betray me. She squeezed my shoulder again, then let go.

"Come back in when you're ready," she said, standing. "If anyone asks, I'll tell them you got locked in the toilet."

That actually made me laugh, wet and hoarse, but genuine. She left me there, under the oak, as the blue hour gathered its strength and the night insects took up their song. Alone now, I let myself lean fully into the bark, and for the first time in weeks, I let the tears fall until I was too tired to resist them.

When I opened my eyes, the Hall was just a shadow, the cricket pitch a palimpsest of footprints and forgotten hopes. I flexed my hands, felt the damp on my skin, and wondered if tomorrow would bring courage, or simply more of the same.

It rained the next morning, a tight, unyielding rain that pooled in the guttering and ran in cataracts down the Hall's limestone cheeks. The pitch became a sketch of itself, every line blurred, each marker cone tumbled by the wind into a new configuration. The children sulked indoors, inventing rivalries over the last of the *Rich Tea* biscuits, and the staff gathered in the lounge, forced to invent themselves anew in the absence of their prescribed duties.

I spent most of the day in a fugue, alternating between overzealous bin duty and half-hearted lesson planning. At noon, Ash cornered me near the service stairs and said, "you good, mate?," in a way that implied he knew I wasn't, but would not press unless paid overtime.

I said, "fine," and walked on.

By evening the rain relented, and the grounds exhaled a fog so dense it erased everything beyond the first rank of trees. At supper, Sarah caught my eye over the pocked expanse of shepherd's pie and mouthed, *'after?',* I nodded, grateful and terrified.

I waited for her beneath the same oak, the ground slick but welcoming, the bench now a dark ribbon of water. I wiped it with my sleeve, then sat. My hands, even in my pockets, would not stop moving. The entire sky was the colour of a healing bruise.

She arrived with her usual purposeful stride, hands deep in the kangaroo pouch of her hoody, hair curling wild from the humidity. She sat, not close this time but at an angle, as if to make the words easier to aim somewhere other than at her.

"Didn't think you'd show," she said, kindly.

"Neither did I," I replied, and was startled by how much my voice sounded like someone else's.

We waited out the first silence together. I watched a bead of water collect on the tip of my shoe, then slide off and vanish into the moss.

"Mark," I said, like lobbing a stone into a pond and waiting for the ripple. "That's his name. I met him at university. Well, technically before, I'd seen him at the open day. He was the kind of person who just… takes up space. Makes you want to be wherever he is, even if it's only to get a reaction."

Sarah nodded, and said nothing.

"He's from the Wirral," I continued. "Plays rugby, but not seriously, more for the look, I think. He's clever, but he acts like he's not. And he's…" I almost said *beautiful,* but stopped myself, "he's got this way of looking at you that makes you feel like you're the only one in the world. Until he stops, and then you're no one."

I tried to laugh, but the sound was small and bitter. "We're not together, not really. Not officially. He has a girlfriend. Or he had, last time we spoke. He's always with someone, you know?"

Sarah's eyes crinkled with understanding. "And you're…?"

"On the side," I said. "Like a spare set of keys. Only useful when he locks himself out."

The confession, once started, became easier, as if the rain had loosened the roots. I told her about the first night in the city, the way Mark had followed me back to my room and shut the door behind him, as if he'd done it a hundred times before. How he'd been gentle, but also matter-of-fact, as if there was nothing about it that needed comment. How the next morning he'd made coffee and then left, whistling, without a backward glance.

I told her about the months that followed, the clandestine meetings, the messages sent in code, the rituals of avoidance. The way my entire world began to pivot around the possibility of seeing him, of being wanted, even briefly. The way he'd sometimes vanish for weeks, and then reappear with a joke or an insult, and how I always, always forgave it.

I told her how I had never said it out loud to anyone, not even to myself most days, and how coming to Langley was meant to be an antidote, my way to forget, to reset, to see if I could live as someone else for a while. But the forgetting hadn't worked. If anything, the isolation had made the memory sharper, the hunger worse.

I paused, then wiped my face with the sleeve of my jacket, "and the worst part is," I said, "I don't even know if I love him. I just know I don't want to be without. Which is pathetic. I mean, I'm twenty-one, not a child."

Sarah exhaled through her nose. The sound was almost a laugh, but not quite, "you're the second person in two weeks to confess something like this to me," she said. "I must have one of those faces."

I smiled, not believing her, but grateful for the lie.

There was a long, gentle silence. I could feel her waiting, not for more detail, but for the shape of the feeling behind it.

I said, "I'm scared. Not of being gay, not really. I mean, I am, but it's not that. I'm scared of being nothing to someone who means everything to me. I'm scared that this is all I'll ever get, and I am terrified that Mark's life would be perfectly normal had he not met me."

I looked at her then, really looked, and saw in her face none of the pity or revulsion I had rehearsed for in my nightmares. Only the steadiness, the simple acceptance.

"I'm not good at advice," she said, "but I do know this: you can't punish yourself for wanting to be loved. Anyone who says otherwise is selling something." She stretched her legs out in front of her, studied the way her boots caught the last of the daylight. "If this Mark can't give you what you need, find someone who can. Or, failing that, learn to want less. But don't make yourself small for someone else's comfort and don't blame yourself because he obviously finds you irresistible. That's just…" She made a face, "it's just a waste, is what it is."

I snorted a laugh at the thought of me being *irresistible* to anyone. I let the words settle, and then nodded, "you're the first person I've ever told."

She grinned, feral and proud, "I'll get a medal struck. I can put it next to my world record for marshalling year six girls through the netball changing rooms."

We sat for a while longer. The light fell and the bats came out again, zigzagging between the boughs, unconcerned with the drama of the humans below. I wanted, desperately, to say more: to tell her about the way William made my heart jump, or how even the smallest kindness from him made me feel wild and exposed. But I couldn't. Not yet. I could only manage the one secret at a time.

When Sarah stood to leave, she put her hand on my head and ruffled it, like she might a nephew, "it gets easier," she said, "but only if you stop pretending. You're allowed to want what you want, without guilt or shame."

After she had gone, I sat on the bench until the damp found its way through my jeans. I watched the Hall, its windows yellow with the promise of a hundred smaller lives, and I wondered if any of them could see me here, hunched and shivering and hollowed out by the effort of speaking.

I thought of Mark, and the way his mouth tasted in the dark. I thought of William, and how I would never be brave enough to ask for what I wanted. I thought of the children, asleep and dreaming of conquests, and of the grass that would remember none of this in the morning.

Then, finally, I stood, stretched the stiffness from my back, and walked toward the lights, hoping that the world would be less frightening if I faced it head-on.

But for now, the night was quiet. For now, that was enough.

CHAPTER 7: A RAINY DAY DISCOVERY

The air tastes of copper before the rain begins—an acrid, metallic tang that stings the tongue and tightens the throat. I am on the cricket square, pacing out cones for fielding drills, when the first bruised clouds roll in from the northwest. Even the children sense what's coming: their voices grow shrill, arms windmilling with sudden, showy bravado, as if to impress the storm gods. A gust of wind flattens the outfield and sends my marker cones tumbling down the boundary line, orange and fluorescent against the frantic green. I watch as the nearest boy chases a fugitive cone, his hair lifted by the static, the whites of his eyes wide with the thrill of impending chaos.

"Sir," he calls, "is it safe to play?"

I weigh the question. Already the grounds pulse with kinetic possibility; the sky is a surgical grey, the grass shivering in expectation. I scan the horizon. A lance of distant lightning forks behind the copse of sycamores between the Hall and Home Farm, so bright it leaves an afterimage even when I close my eyes. The air buckles with the shock of it. I wait for the thunder—count out the seconds, then lose track in the mounting wind.

"Inside, everyone!" I shout, and my voice is more urgent than I intend. The children gather their gear in a tumult, feet thudding the sodden path toward the portico. I jog after, batting loose balls and rogue cones into the duffel as I go. The first, hesitant drops dimple the dust on my forearms. I relish the cool of it.

By the time I reach the Hall, rain strafes the windows with military precision, each drop amplified by the stone. The Great Hall is dense with bodies and humidity, every surface slick with sweat or condensation. The children have discovered the echo properties of the stairwell and are engaged in a massed experiment on the limits of sound.

Sue catches my arm as I pass, "weather's always dramatic here in the summer," she says, her clipboard damp with the day's exertion. "You can cancel the rest of your session, let them loose in the ballroom if you like. Just keep them away from the stage."

I nod, grateful, and dispatch my group to the designated rec room. Ash is already there, arranging chairs into a makeshift barricade and orchestrating a game of *capture the flag* with the theatrical supplies.

The other staff trickle in, rain-darkened, trailing the scents of ozone and wet polyester.

I claim the lull as my own. The corridor to the library is deserted. I find myself unaccountably cold, and press my hands to the wall as I walk, the stone sweating beneath my palms. At the threshold, I pause. The double French doors that open onto the terrace are blown wide, admitting not just the fitful light but a sheeting wind, which drags rain in long, slantwise bars across the floor. For a moment I consider leaving the doors, then think better of it, and move to close them.

The table in the centre is a slab of oak so massive it appears to grow from the flagstones themselves. On it is arrayed a scatter of papers, some official, most not: programs from vanished galas, a book of botanical sketches, a stack of postmarked letters in hand so spidery I have to tilt them against the light to read. I drop my duffel, shake the water from my hair, and let myself browse.

The rain continues to rattle the panes and draws the library's ambient silence even tighter. I am alone, for the first time in what seems like days. I let my fingers roam the spines, drawn to the peculiar gravity of the most abused volumes: a treatise on cricket tactics, *marginalia* so dense it resembles a palimpsest; a ledger from the 1880s, ink bled to sepia by the slow leak of time. I open a random page and find myself in a world of manorial rents, livestock tallies, and the names of men.

I am not sure what I am searching for. Maybe a pattern, maybe an excuse to believe that my own life, too, might be rendered legible by proper indexing. I thumb the stack of letters, their envelopes all addressed in the same looping

I return to the letter I had found previously, the intimacy is shocking for its time, and even now, the pulse of longing is preserved, like an insect in amber. I want to read more, to know how the story turns out, but the paper is trembling in my hands. Whether from cold or nerves I can't say.

The next envelope is heavier, double-folded, as if it contains some greater gravity. I am halfway through deciphering the return address when a shadow crosses the terrace, obscuring the light. I look up, startled. William stands in the doorway, hair plastered to his forehead, arms bare to the rain.

He says nothing at first, just walks in on silent feet and closes the doors behind him. The glass is instantly fogged by the contrast. He leans his back to the frame and looks at me, blinking water from his lashes.

"Had a feeling you'd be in here," he says, voice low and unhurried.

I try to speak, but my tongue is thick with the residue of rain and the echo of his name in my throat. "I… didn't expect… " I start, but the words are insufficient.

He shrugs, still hovering in the liminal zone between in and out, then advances. His hair is a riot of wet spikes, and there's a cut on his left forearm, beaded with water and the faintest trace of blood. He moves past me, fluid, and inspects the chaos I've left on the table. He picks up the cricket treatise, thumbs through the annotated pages, then glances at me sideways, eyes sharp under the slick fringe.

"Is this research, or just an excuse to stay dry?" he asks.

I try to compose myself. "Both," I say, "but mostly the former." I slide the open ledger in his direction, a token of truce.

He accepts it, turning the pages with surprising delicacy. The way his fingers move, careful but unselfconscious, reminds me of my mother's surgeon hands: precise, never hesitating.

He leans against the back of a chair, palms flat on the oak. "What's your interest in this old stuff, anyway?" He jerks his chin at the growing heap of documents.

I swallow, "history, mostly. The stories that get left behind." I hesitate, then add, "I found something. Not sure what it means yet." I gesture to the thin stack of letters, the one with the strange, insistent hand.

He studies my face a moment longer than seems necessary, then rounds the table and stands directly behind me, close enough that I can smell the after-rain on his skin. He peers over my shoulder at the letter I've just finished.

I tense, aware of the heat from his body despite the sodden clothes, "go on," he says, voice so low I feel it in my chest more than I hear it.

I read aloud the mysterious latter from *Kip* to *Jonny*.

I set it down, my fingers trembling, "it's… " I begin, but can't finish. I have no vocabulary for this.

William squeezes my shoulders, then slides into the seat beside me, "you think it's real?" he asks, voice back at its usual volume.

I nod, unable to look at him, "why keep it, otherwise?"

He shrugs again, "people hide what they care about." His knee presses lightly against mine beneath the table, and I wonder if it's intentional or just a byproduct of the narrow bench.

I risk a glance. The cut on his arm is bleeding a little more now, red tracking down to his wrist in a thin, elegant line. Without thinking, I reach for a tissue from my pocket, press it to his skin. He holds my gaze while I do it, a flicker of something unreadable passing over his face.

"Sorry," I say, withdrawing my hand too quickly.

He laughs, but the sound is not unkind, "it's only blood," he says. "You should see me after an afternoon in the wood yard." He takes the tissue, wraps it deftly around the cut, and returns his attention to the letters. I realise I am holding my breath. I let it out, quietly, and rest my hands on the table, palms flat.

The wind rattles the windows again, and though the rain remains constant the skies seem to be lighter. For a heartbeat, everything is sharp and unfiltered, the curve of William's mouth, the pulse in his throat, the fine stubble along his jaw. Then the moment is gone, and the ordinary shadows return.

"There's a *Thomas Cooper* mentioned somewhere too, a relation?," I ask, motioning at the stack.

"That will be my great-uncle Thomas, the one in the painting, he was in service here for most of his life," William offers.

"I saw that he was a valet in 1914."

"Oh yes, to Lord John Langley," another piece in the puzzle was laid down, "and then butler and estate manager to the last earl, Prince Christian," there is now almost a sense of pride in William's voice.

"Is that the *Jonny*' in the letter? How do I find out more?" I ask tentatively.

William smiles, slow and unhurried, "might be easier than you think. Old houses, someone's always keeping a ledger or journal."

"Like your great-uncle Thomas perhaps?" I ask hopefully, realising that he was slowly reeling me in.

William just winks, and flashes a smile that makes me want to pull him to me, "that, my friend, is a story for another time, as I had better get back to work now."

"I should too I suppose," I gesture toward the ballroom, where the children are surely plotting mutiny by now. I look outside where the first streaks of sun have reappeared, "is that the storm over then?"

"For now at least," he hesitates, then closes the folder for me, his hand lingering on mine for a beat too long, "you ever want to talk more or find out more," he says, "I'm usually around." I cannot quite work out who is being teased the most, the historian in me or just the man.

I say thank you, and I mean it.

He leaves the way he came, silent and unhurried, his passage marked only by the soft click of the door and the faint, metallic taste of rain left in his wake.

I stay a few minutes longer, reading and rereading the letters, trying to commit the feeling to memory. Then, with the storm dissipating outside and the world inside suddenly sharp with possibility, I gather my things and head back to the life that waits.

We try to keep the children entertained and active to use up their unspent energy from today. After tea we let them outside to just burn up whatever energy is left. Sue's cunning plan worked a treat, as all the dormitories settled into quiet slumber sooner than the norm, and I found myself in just my shorts on the bed an hour earlier than normal enjoying the peace.

I could feel the humidity rising and opening my window did little to ease it, so out of habit I pick up my copy of *Graves' 'I Claudius/Claudius the god'* hoping it would help me forget just how uncomfortable the atmosphere made me feel. I failed, and instead I replay every word, every gesture, every charged moment of contact with William until the memory is so bright it almost burns.

I do not sleep, I pace the edges of my own consciousness, replaying the encounter in the library, the weight of William's hands, the letters' raw ache, the tease of the story yet to unfold. I was just about to drift off, when I heard a gentle tapping at the door. Expecting it to be one of the boys, I leap up and open the door ready to berate the visitor about how late it was. To my surprise it was Will, standing there with his fingers pressed to his lips shushing me.

"What is it?" I mouth, heart drumming. William beams, eyes alight with mischief. He glances at my shoes and whispers, "Put some trainers on and come with me." Panic and curiosity war inside me. I shake my head, but his grin melts my resistance. "Trust me, you'll love it." Against my better judgment, I nod

I sit on the bed, tug on my trainers, and he hands me a tracksuit top hanging from the cupboard door, "you'll need this." My fingers tremble as I pull it on. Why all the secrecy? Part of me wants to bolt back to safety, another part aches for adventure

He beckons, and I follow him into the pitch-dark dormitory corridor. We tiptoe past closed doors, stifling giggles that feel half-thrill, half-fear. My pulse hammers: are we crazy? The silence around us seems to watch.

At the far landing, William presses on a wooden panel. It swings open to reveal a narrow staircase. "Old service stairs, too cramped for modern use," he whispers, flipping a switch. A single bulb flickers on. We slip inside, and he quietly shuts the panel. My chest tightens.

"My first secret passageway," I murmur, torn between awe and anxious guilt.

"There's more," he says, already climbing. Each creak underfoot echoes my racing heart. At the top, he pushes open a heavy door. A rush of humid air hits us. I glance down several stories. He offers his hand. My breath catches: heights, rule-breaking, the unknown. Yet I take it.

We emerge onto the leaded roof. William guides me to the stone balustrade overlooking the terrace. His grip is warm; I'm reluctant to pull away, even as doubt knits inside me.

"It's amazing up here," I whisper, voice wavering. He smiles, then points as clouds flicker. Lightning splits the sky, and thunder growls like a distant train. My stomach twists with exhilaration laced with dread.

"Is it coming this way?" I ask.

"When storms start northeast, they usually do," he says, "want to stay and watch?"

My heart vaults, and then sinks, "you couldn't drag me away now," I lie, though panic and exhilaration batter my ribs. Each lightning flash strips the world bare: patchwork fields, hedgerows, and the ragged edge of the sky. I'm electrified and petrified at once, torn between craving this rush and a gnawing dread that we shouldn't be perched up here at all.

After ten minutes, warm raindrops hiss against my skin, and the air cools sharply. I risk a glance at William and see awe shining in his eyes and I realise that he relishes nature's raw violence. The strobe-bright light puts every angle of his face on display: flawed, vulnerable, and achingly magnetic. Part of me aches to touch him; another part worries we're courting danger.

Then the downpour intensifies, wind shears through the treetops, and the temperature plunges further. A jagged bolt slams into a nearby oak with a deafening crack that rattles my chest. Instinctively I pivot closer to William, heart hammering, and he laughs, harsh and bright, before draping an arm around me. He pulls me into his warmth, and I cling to him, caught between relief and an absurd jealousy of this storm.

Rain sheets over us in torrents; we're drenched to the bone but rooted to the roof like sacrificial figures. My skin prickles as though the air itself is alive. Then, flash, another bolt sears the sky, far too close, and thunder booms so sharply I taste it. William's grip tightens around me; I catch his breath hitching as much as mine is.

"Time to go inside!" he shouts, face inches from mine, eyes wild with adrenaline. We stumble, laughing nervously, down to safety, hearts pounding in sync. I lead him into my room and fling us each a towel.

"I've never seen anything like that," I stammer, patting my hair-drenched scalp. "Thank you, for dragging me up there." He just smiles, as if he's been waiting for me to admit it.

"Nature's greatest show, if you know how to watch," he says softly. His words should comfort me, but I feel a tremor of unease.

I wrap the towel around my shoulders, "just one thing," I whisper. "We were alone up there, weren't we?"

He quirks an eyebrow, "of course. Why?"
I swallow, suddenly self-conscious. "I… I thought I heard children's laughter…footsteps splashing in the puddles." My voice falters. William's hand finds my thigh and squeezes.

"You heard kids, huh?" he murmurs, amused.

"I did, like two boys, then they ran off." My stomach twists.

He leans closer. "I'm sure you did… but they weren't ours."

A cold dread coils in my chest, "stop teasing me," I hiss, but my voice wavers.

"It's the ghosts," he says lightly. I snatch his hand away.

"The what?"

"Local legend says that during storms you can hear two boys playing on the roof." He watches me, half-smiling.

"Seriously?" The word feels heavy.

"Well, staff get in trouble every year for *'letting'* boys up there—though the door's locked. So this will have to be *'our secret'* because would have my guts for garters if he found out I took you up there."

My scalp prickles, and a shiver snakes down my spine. William's eyes search mine.

"Wow," he breathes. "You actually believe in that?"
I gape at him, caught between ridicule and fascination. "I don't know what to believe," I admit softly, "but some things…can't be explained."

"Fair enough," he replies kindly. He slaps my thigh. "I must go, but thanks for trusting me tonight." As he opens the door, he turns back to, winking, "our secret remember."

The dawn breaks with a show of innocence—sky clear, grass silvered, not a trace of last night's violence left in the air. I make tea and drink it black, the bitterness a necessary ballast. The children wake subdued, their usual tidal surge of noise replaced by a slow eddying around the corridors. I walk the length of the pitch and find it battered but intact; the wickets are upright, the boundary rope merely displaced, not destroyed. I right the cones, rake the mud into symmetry, and let the work absorb me.

By ten, the sun has burned off the last dew. I see William at the far end of the grounds, repairing a length of fence felled by the wind. He works without shirt, bare to the waist, his skin crosshatched with old scars and the new, raw pinkness of fresh abrasions. I watch, ashamed at my own hunger, then force myself back to the Hall, where the schedule is waiting and the day insists on its shape.

The routine persists, as it must: morning practice, lunch, supervised "quiet hour" in the dorms. I find a rhythm in it, but under the surface the restlessness never abates. At every interval, my mind returns to the library, the table, the spidery script of longing.

After breakfast, the children are dispatched to a scavenger hunt among the flowerbeds. I watch them go, arms flapping, hair streaming, voices raised in the tentative hope of victory and I feel, for once, both older and younger than my years. I make my way to the library on the pretext of organizing the next day's lesson, but really I want to be alone with the letters, and the memory of William's voice.

He finds me there, mid-morning, a faint line of sweat across his brow, carrying a clipboard and a faint air of apology.

"Bit of damage on the west side," he says. "Sue says there's a loose window in the nursery. Mind showing me where?"

I rise, all too eager to oblige. The nursery is two flights up and a world away from the library, dusty, sunstruck, its shelves lined with battered board games and the ghosts of long-expelled children. The window in question is only slightly out of true, the frame bowed by last night's violence.

William props it open, leans out, and inspects the stonework. "Just needs a wedge," he says, then glances at me, grinning, "old houses: nothing's ever really fixed."

I want to say something profound, but all I can muster is, "it's holding up better than I am."

He gives me a look, fond, maybe even indulgent and says, "you don't give yourself enough credit."

He tugs the sash shut, wipes his hands on his jeans, and then, without warning, says, "if you want to see more of the estate stuff, there's a box I've found. More family gossip, and the odd scandal." He hesitates, then adds, "some of it's personal. About my lot."

"I'd like that," I say, and I mean it more than I can say.

He nods, the gesture brisk but kind, then steps in closer, close enough that I can smell the earth on him. He rests a hand on my shoulder, warm and heavy, and lets it linger. "I'll let you know when I have got them all together for you."

Then, with a half-smile and a touch of shyness I have never seen on him before, he turns and is gone, taking the memory of his hand with him. I stand for a long time, willing myself not to read too much into the gesture, but failing, utterly.

I return to the library, to the table and the letters and study again the painting with the three boys playing cricket. I run my fingers over the raised texture of the paint, tracing the layers. The room is silent but for the hush of the trees outside, their leaves still trembling with aftershock.

I read the letters again, slower this time, savouring the ache and the hope, the possibility that two people could find each other, even for a moment, in a world so eager to keep them apart. I think of William, his voice low and careful, the way he says my name when no one else is listening. I think of the way our hands touched on the roof, and how neither of us let go.

By the time the children return from the garden, I have packed the letters back into their folder, replaced the journals in their box. The room feels charged, transformed, the old secrets awake and hungry for more.

As I close the door behind me, I know with a certainty that is both terrifying and exquisite that the story is not over. There are more letters to read, more truths to uncover, and maybe, if I am brave enough, more to want.

I walk the long corridor to the staff lounge, every step echoing with possibility.

For the first time since arriving, I am not afraid of what I might find.

CHAPTER 8: MOONLIT CONFESSION

The heat, even at midnight, is relentless—a wet, enveloping thing that refuses to break, as if the entire world is suspended between thunder and release. I stand on the terrace at the back of the Hall, forearms braced against the parapet, watching moths stutter and tumble in the halo of the lanterns. Every surface sweats. I sweep the back of my wrist across my brow and taste salt, the skin of my neck tacky beneath the collar. Insects whir at my ears, and from somewhere in the blackness down-slope, a chorus of frogs initiates a slow, measured crescendo.

The rest of the house is dead. Only the faintest blue squares of light in the farthest dorm windows indicate other insomniacs, or perhaps the glow of forbidden torches. I linger, restless, unable to return to the airless quarters that pass for my room, unable to stop replaying the last twenty-four hours on an endless tape loop.

Mark haunts me still. Even here, in a world designed to scrub away old attachments and force the body into new habits, his face drifts through every idle moment. I see him in the sharp corners of the moon, in the way the clouds bunch and collapse, in the bitter aftertaste of tea left too long to steep. He is an overlay, a watermark, present in everything I try to learn or unlearn. He would say I am being dramatic, that the world is full of beautiful things if only I would look, that I am a prisoner of my own nostalgia.

But William is the present tense. The unignorable, the animal. When I close my eyes, I see the fine dust of his arm hairs in the afternoon sun, the sullen line where his shirt pulls tight across his chest, the infinitesimal movements of mouth and jaw when he's listening, or deciding whether to laugh. The memory of his hand on my shoulder has already fossilized: I replay it with the obsessive repetition of a child picking at a scab.

I pace the length of the terrace, forty-seven steps end to end, flagstone to flagstone then back, then again, every lap an attempt to outrun my own pulse. The night is thick with humidity, the air shimmering over the lawns like the surface of a pond. I take deep breaths, tasting honeysuckle and stone dust and the sharp, almost electrical note of ozone.

A movement at the edge of the dark catches my eye. Someone is walking up from the rose gardens, a slow, deliberate stride that suggests purpose. For a moment, I hope it's no one, just a trick of the failing light, but as the figure draws closer I know without knowing that it is him.

William does not call out. He moves up the steps with a catlike grace, pausing just at the spill of the lantern, where the shadows make his eyes unreadable. For a few seconds, neither of us speaks. Then, as if we are returning to a conversation already begun, he says, "you can't sleep either, then."

I let my head fall back, the sweat on my nape cold in the brief breeze, "not for lack of trying," I admit. "Feels like the air's got teeth tonight."

He laughs, soft and low, "it'll break soon, probably with a storm. Don't tell the kids, or we'll have a riot on our hands."

We stand in parallel, not quite facing each other. I am hyperaware of the distance between us, the shape of him filling the periphery of my vision. His hair is damp, pressed flat at the temples and spiking up in uneven ridges. The moon is behind him, making a luminous corona of his shoulders.

He jerks his chin toward the far end of the lawn, "I was just checking the nets," he says. "Some of the little bastards have been nicking the pegs. If you fancy a walk…"

The invitation hovers, electric. I nod, mute, then follow him into the library and out through the great hall. Stepping through the portico, we encounter the darkness of night again. At the foot of the steps, the world is all shadow and faint, silvered outlines: the pitch a flat lake, the flowerbeds low black islands, the trees a confusion of depth and tangle.

For a while, we walk in silence. The gravel drive crunches under our feet, the sound magnified by the absence of other noise. I keep my hands in my pockets, not trusting them, and keep my gaze ahead, trying to will my heartbeat to something resembling normal. Eventually we step onto the playing fields and he points out the various scars and repairs on the grounds as we go, such as the places where last summer's drought split the turf. His voice is level, almost clinical, but there's a pleasure in the telling, a pride that slips through in the details. I nod, interject where required, but mostly I listen, absorbing the world as he sees it.

Near the nets, he crouches, inspects a length of guy rope, then stands again with a satisfied grunt, "they'll do," he says, and I hear in the words a kind of benediction.

We loop the long way back around the ballroom, skirting another rose garden. The flowers are closed, heads drooping in the dark, but the air is heavy with their perfume. I loosen my collar, feeling the sweat cooling on my skin, and risk a glance sideways. William is looking straight ahead, jaw set, but there's a softness in the way his hands move, he trails his fingers along the low hedge, breaking off a sprig of lavender and rolling it between thumb and forefinger.

"Do you ever miss it?" I ask, not sure what I mean until the question is already out.

He looks at me, a small smile playing at the edges, "miss what?"

"Being somewhere else. A city. University. I don't know."

He considers, then shrugs, "sometimes. There's a freedom to it I suppose. You can be whoever you want, or no one at all."

The words snag, "is that what you wanted?"

He picks and then tosses the lavender onto the path, watches it bounce, then says, "I thought it was. Turns out, I'm shit at being no one. I always end up making a nuisance of myself, even when I try not to."

We both laugh, and for a moment the tension eases.

At the far edge of the garden, we come to a bench beneath an old oak which screens Home Farm from the hall. He sits, not at the centre but to one side, leaving a gap that is both invitation and challenge. I join him, knees drawn up, elbows on thighs, head bowed.

The frogs are louder here, their chorus dense and insistent. A moth flutters in the halo of the path light, banging itself senseless against the glass. I watch it, feeling a sympathy so acute it is almost physical.

William breaks the silence, "you don't talk much about home," he says. "Is that by design, or are you just shy?"

I huff a laugh, feeling the old reflex of deflection rise and fall, "mostly by design," I admit. "Nothing worth reporting, really."

He nods, as if this is the most natural thing in the world. "That's the trouble with places like this," he says, "everyone wants to know your story. I used to invent new ones every summer, just to see how long it would take for people to catch on."

I turn to look at him, and he meets my gaze, unblinking. There's a candour in his face that is both exhilarating and terrifying—a sense that nothing I say would shock him, that I could lay out all the ugly, needy parts and he would just nod and make room for them.

"Did anyone ever figure you out?" I ask, my voice barely audible.

He grins, a crooked thing that makes my stomach flip. "Now and then. But mostly, people see what they want. You're the first person who's ever asked."

The confession hangs between us, ripe and dangerous. I want to touch him, his hand, his arm, the perfect arch of his cheekbone but I don't. Instead, I sit, vibrating with the effort of holding still.

He leans back, stretches his legs out, and lets his head fall against the bench, "you don't have to tell me anything," he says, eyes on the sky. "But if you want to, I'll listen."

I take a breath, let it out slow, "it's just…" I start, then stop. Try again. "It's hard to be one person in the day and someone else at night. Eventually you forget which one is real."

He nods, a flicker of understanding passing over his face. I risk a glance at him, and the moonlight catches in his hair, turning it silver at the edges. The lines of his face are softened by the dark, his eyes deep and reflective. I wonder, wildly, what it would be like to kiss him here, under the dumb, impassive gaze of the oak.

But I don't. Instead, I rest my palms on the bench, fingers splayed wide, and focus on the shared gravity of the wood beneath us. The air is alive, every molecule vibrating with the potential of what might happen next.

I glance at him, then away, then again, as if rehearsing an entrance. He notices, of course, "what's really on your mind, John?"

I exhale, once, hard, "I suppose I should just say it."
He waits, patient.
"There's…" I struggle for the right noun, the right level of safe ambiguity. "There's someone back home. Not that it's a

proper thing, or even a thing at all, but I've not really…" I fumble, mortified by the clumsiness of it. "I've never really talked about it to anyone, well…" correcting my lie, "to anyone like you."

He doesn't look away, "you don't have to, if you don't want."

But I do want, or at least, I need to. The pressure of it has built to the point where it's either this or burn alive.

I press the heel of my hand to my brow, as if I can force the words out, "it's always been secret. Not because it's exciting, but because it has to be. He…" The pronoun escapes before I can trap it. "He's got someone else. A real life. And I'm just… a side thing, I suppose. Only it never feels like enough to let go, even though I should."

I risk a look, expecting horror, or at least a nervous shuffle. But William is steady, his eyes bright with something I don't dare name.

"Does he know how you feel?" he asks.

I shake my head, "he must. Or maybe he doesn't care, so long as I play along." I draw a line along my thigh with a fingertip, watching the whiteness bloom then fade. "I always thought coming here would change it. That if I could just be someone else for a while, I'd be free of him."

William is silent, but in the silence there is no censure, only waiting.

"I'm sorry," I say. "I know it's path…."

He interrupts, not with words but with a motion: he turns, squares his shoulders to mine, and meets me eye to eye.

"It's not pathetic," he says, "everyone wants to be seen, even just for a minute."

The kindness of it knocks me sideways. I feel my chest hitch, as if the air has gone dense.

He continues, softly, "I've never had anything like that, not really. Apart from the odd shag at college, I've never been with someone I cared about."

I almost laugh, but the sound is ragged, "you make it look easy."

He shrugs, "only because I don't bother pretending. It's a village. If you've not shagged the farmer's son by eighteen, they ship you out to Norwich for training."

I snort, grateful for the pressure valve, and let myself smile.

He lets the joke settle, then says, "my dad never cared, so long as I could drive a tractor and keep the weeds down. The rest…" He shrugs. "No one expects much out here, so you get away with a lot. But it gets lonely, sometimes." The truth of this is so bald and unadorned it almost hurts to look at him.

He must sense it, because he adds, "I like talking to you, John. Feels like there's less to hide."

For a long time, neither of us moves. The heat builds, not from the sun but from the directness of his gaze, the way it settles on me as if testing every inch for weakness.

Without warning, he lifts his arm and lays it across my shoulders, not heavy, but definite. The warmth of it pours through my shirt, lighting every nerve. For a moment I think I might break in half.

I am very conscious of my own body, the dryness of my mouth, the sweat prickling at the base of my skull, the wild, ungoverned beat of my heart. I want to rest my head against his chest, or reach out and trace the line of his forearm, or any one of a dozen gestures I have never before had the courage to try.

Instead, I just sit, letting the contact settle me, the un-spoken permission of it a gift I cannot yet repay. We stay like that for a long time. No words. Only the warmth of his skin, and the certainty, for once, that I am exactly where I am meant to be. When at last he withdraws his arm, he gives my shoulder the briefest squeeze, like the punctuation on a story well told.

"If you ever want to talk about it," he says, "or anything else, you know where I am."

I nod, the hope in my chest so fierce it threatens to out-pace the ache.

"Walk with me?" he finally says, though it's less a question than a gentle imperative. "I have to check the barns," he says. "They'll fine me a fiver for every open door after midnight, and I can't afford to lose any more money to them."

At the service gate, he veers left, toward the old stable yard, a place as haunted by memory as the Hall itself I imagine. The gravel underfoot is loose and new, a recent fix for a chronic drainage problem. The smell of hay and old manure is faint, but persistent, a reminder that this world is older than any of us, and will be here long after we are reduced to stories.

When he reaches a small storage room, he opens the door and retrieves two torches. One he offers me, and I take it, surprised by the warmth left by his hand. We slip through the yard in sequence: first the tack room, then the feed store, then the long, low runs of the main stables themselves. Each door is a variation on the same routine: lift the latch, check inside for errant cats or foxes, slide the bolt, and give it a rattle for luck. The metal-on-metal rings through the yard, echoing off the old stone.

I let myself be useful. The rhythm of the work, predictable, finite, requiring only the smallest acts of trust manage to calm the wildness in my chest. Now and then our hands touch, not by accident, but by the simple necessity of the task. Every time, I feel the spark, the old voltage, but I do not look at him. I want him to be the one to break the spell.

Halfway down the row, we pause to breathe. The torch casts oblong shadows across the brick, and for a moment I am ten years old again, hiding in the school supply shed and hoping the world will never find me.

William leans against the frame of the next door, "you're good at this," he says, and the compliment is so unforced, so simple, that I want to cry.

"At what? Locking up?"

He shakes his head, "at being here. Most people, they act like they're allergic to the place. You fit. Even if you don't think you do."

I laugh, softly, "maybe I just haven't figured out how to leave."

He looks at me, not smiling now. The moment stretches, thin and dangerous.

"Maybe you don't have to," he says. Then he turns, unlocks the last door, and gestures for me to follow. The final barn is empty, the air inside cool and still. Dust motes catch the torch beam and swirl in lazy spirals. There is nothing to inspect, no animals to account for, just the two of us and the hollow sound of our breathing.

He sets down the torch, lets it roll until it settles against the wall. In the half-light, his face is all sharp angles and possibility.

He says, "I found some old photos and stuff of the staff and hall. You should come over tomorrow. If you're not busy."

The invitation is casual, but the undertow is not. I feel myself flush, from throat to ears.

"I'd like that," I say, "I can bring beer. Or biscuits. Or both."

"Beer, definitely." The smile is back, and this time it's wider, more reckless.

"Eight o'clock, then?" he says. I nod; certain I will not survive the hours between now and then.

We make our way back through the yard. The work is done, but I linger, reluctant to let the moment collapse into the ordinary. At the foot of the stairs that lead to his flat above the old carriage house, he pauses.

"Thanks for the help," he says.

"Anytime."

He looks at me for a beat longer than is strictly necessary, then says, "goodnight, John." He climbs the steps, his boots thudding the wood, and disappears into the darkness above.

I stay where I am, motionless, listening to the creak of the boards, the click of the latch, the silence that follows. The world has narrowed to a single, incandescent point: the promise of a meeting, the possibility of more, the strange and savage hope that perhaps I am not as alone as I once believed.

I tip my head back, gaze at the blunt edge of the moon, and let the fever of hope and fear work its way through me.

When at last I move, it is with the knowledge that tomorrow is not just another day, but the beginning of something else, something I do not yet have the words for, but will spend the rest of my life trying to name.

CHAPTER 9: THE STABLES RENDEZVOUS

Eight hours crawl by in the purgatory of a Tuesday, the day's heat building in slow, deliberate bands until it seems to set behind my teeth. By mid-afternoon, the cricket pitch is a mirage, a warped green membrane wavering above baked, root-splintered earth. I stand at square leg, whistle pinched between my lips, and pretend not to mind the sweat pooling behind my knees or the way the sun sharpens every edge until even the children seem made of glass.

It's not the first time I've sought escape in routine: drills, matches, the precise choreography of coaching. If I keep moving, I can almost convince myself I'm more coach than ghost, less a tangle of nerves and hope than the sum of my responsibilities. I run the children through shadow batting, then a relay sprint to keep them distracted from the heat. Their chatter is mercifully undirected; every question is a gift, every misfield a reprieve from my own thoughts.

But the pitch is only half the theatre. William arrives, as scheduled, but with the improvisational flair of someone who knows he is being watched. He's atop the Hall's old tractor, a machine that looks more at home in a black-and-white war documentary than a school field, and his silhouette—capped, sleeveless, impervious—draws every eye. My group stops in unison, as if by magnetic compulsion, and several of the older boys stare with the slack-jawed adulation usually reserved for pop stars or professional athletes.

I can't help myself: I look too. The tractor coughs and rattles, then dies. William hops down, the motion fluid and easy, and waves a mock salute at my direction. For a second, the sun catches him in full profile: arms tanned and dusted with gold, shirt clinging at the chest, grin wolfish and white. I feel the flush crawl up my neck, ridiculous as that is in the open air.

He walks the boundary, inspecting the line with studied detachment, then stops a few yards away. "Square's looking good," he says, just loud enough for the nearest kids to hear. "No rabbits today?"

"Not unless you count this lot," I reply, nodding toward my giddy, collapsing fielders.

He grins, all teeth and kindness, then kneels to adjust one of the marker cones. "Don't let them near the new wicket, if you can help it. She's fragile."

There's an implied you there, I know, but I ignore it. "We'll stay off. Promise."

He stands, brushes dirt from his knees, and lowers his voice. "You remember? Eight o'clock. Stable yard. Bottom door's always open."

I nod, trying to keep my face unreadable. "Wouldn't miss it."

"Good man," he says, and the words are less a compliment than a binding contract.

He moves on, arms folded behind his back, whistling something unplaceable. The boys' attention lingers a beat longer, then the world snaps back into focus. I blow my whistle, and the match resumes as if nothing at all has shifted, even though everything has.

The rest of the session passes in a fugue: fielding drills, a water break that degenerates into a soaking free-for-all, then a half-hearted attempt at a match that no one wants to win. I let them go a few minutes early, using the excuse of "heat exhaustion," but really I am desperate to be alone, to let the future unspool itself without witness.

In the changing rooms, the children peel off their kits with the urgency of moulting insects. The showers hiss and steam, drowning out most other sound, and I lean against the cool tile, willing myself not to count the seconds until evening. I catch my own reflection in the mirror—pale, jaw clenched, hair plastered to my forehead—and think: who is this person, this man so undone by a single invitation?

Back in the staffroom, the air is thicker, less forgiving. The fridge has been raided of anything caloric, but I find a case of 'communal' Carling on the floor. I do the social thing and cram as many as I can into the fridge assuming that demand will be high soon enough. I slip four of them into a discarded Sainsbury's bag and head back to my room.

Every fifteen minutes, I check the clock. At seven-thirty, I change shirts twice, finally settling on the one least likely to show sweat. I brush my teeth, then do it again. I pick up the plastic bag and spend two full minutes rehearsing what to say when I arrive: some combination of "thanks for inviting me" and "don't expect too much," but when I say it aloud, it sounds pathetic, so I try not saying anything at all.

At seven-fifty, I leave my room. The air is marginally cooler, the lawns humming with insects, the Hall's windows bright and expectant. I follow the path to the stable yard, every step slowing as if the world itself is trying to delay the inevitable. There is no one around, but the echo of my trainers on the gravel is so loud that I wince, twice.

The stable block is a long, two-story tangle of brick and timber, half converted to storage and half left in its original state. There is a light in the upper flat, gold and alive, and as I reach the bottom of the exterior staircase, I hesitate. The door is ajar, and the air from inside is heavy with soap and aftershave—mint and something sharper, almost resinous.

I stand at the foot of the stairs, and my stomach knots itself twice. I am suddenly, inexplicably terrified. Of what? That I'll make a fool of myself, or worse, that this is all a game and I've read it wrong? I replay the last conversation, searching for clues, but there is no comfort in autopsy.

Above, the window grinds open. William leans out, freshly showered, his hair damp and sticking up in chaotic whorls. He is shirtless, a white towel thrown careless around his neck, and the line of his chest is bisected by a pale scar I have not noticed before. His eyes catch mine, and he grins, the mischief obvious and unhidden.

"Straight up the stairs," he calls, then points down to a narrow side door. "Door's open."

I nod, unable to summon an actual reply. My hand grips the carrier bag until the plastic creaks. I step into the stairwell, which is dark and close, the wood worn to a satin sheen by decades of passage. Every stair is an act of will. I count them—ten, then twelve, then sixteen—until I stand at the landing, heart thudding so loud I worry he'll hear it through the door.

I pause at the threshold, wipe my hands on my jeans, then knock. Once, sharp and fast.

His voice, closer now: "Come in, it's open."

I open the door and step inside, eyes adjusting to the dim, the hush, the shock of being exactly where I had most wanted to be.

The door opens onto a room that is, at first glance, less a flat than an annexed memory: low-ceilinged, timber-braced, cluttered with the relics of three or four generations' inertia. The first thing I notice is a battered, small open trunk on the coffee table. The box, roughly one foot by two foot and one foot deep, is dense with papers— mostly envelopes and photographs. Someone has scrawled "FAMILY" in black marker across the side, the slant of the letters a minor rebellion.

The air is thick with a mingling of aftershave, clean laundry, and the unignorable signature of outdoors. Not unpleasant—just omnipresent, the same way the sound of the clock on the mantelpiece insists itself on every silence.

William is nowhere to be seen at first, and for a moment I am suspended, unsure whether to knock again or retreat. Then, from the bathroom, a voice: "Through to the main room. Just give me a second."

I step in, shoes clapping against old pine, and take in the rest. The space is—there's no other word for it—lived in. Two battered armchairs flank the Formica coffee table, its surface mapped with ancient rings. The fridge is covered in a mosaic of yellowing magnets, a photo of William as a child in wellies and a Liverpool kit, another of what must be his father, caught mid-laugh. There are books everywhere, the shelves sagging with the weight of biographies, gardening manuals, and more than a few mystery paperbacks. Tacked to the walls in no particular order are black-and-white photographs: men in uniforms, women in hats, children lined up outside a church. The effect is less nostalgia than a refusal to let the dead be lost.

Next to the trunk, arranged with what might be intention, is an empty teacup, three stubby pencils, and a sheaf of Polaroids. I hesitate, but curiosity gets the better of me. The top Polaroid is of a cricket team, eleven boys in white, squinting into the sun. The caption, written in a deliberate, almost ceremonial hand, reads: "Langley XI, 1973. Dad's last year."

I am so engrossed that I don't hear William return until he's at my elbow, damp hair tamed and tucked behind his ears, now in a faded black t-shirt and clean jeans. He moves close enough that his breath stirs the fringe above my brow.

"You found the box, then," he says, voice low but not un-friendly.

I snap the photo back into its stack. "Sorry. I didn't mean to pry."

He waves it away. "That's what it's for. I keep meaning to sort it all, but every time I open the box, I end up reading old letters instead." He notices the beers in my hand and grins, a lopsided thing that makes his eyes crinkle at the corners. "You came prepared."

I offer him the Sainsbury's bag. He removes two cans, sets them on the table, then gestures for me to sit in the armchair opposite. When I do, the springs sigh in relief, and I feel the tension in my body ease by degrees. William opens both cans, passes me one, and raises his in salute. "To surviving another day," he says.

We drink. The beer is only mildly cool, and the first mouthful settles something that's been trembling in me since I left the pitch.

For a while, we talk around the obvious. He asks about my home, my university, whether I ever played "proper cricket" or just coached. I answer as best I can, trying not to let my voice betray how much I am cataloguing every detail of him: the faint stubble on his cheek, the small half-moons of dirt under his nails, the way the lamp-light behind him turns the edge of his ear translucent.

He talks about the Hall—about the "big house" and the people who float through it each year. "They come and go," he says, "always thinking they're the first to see the place for what it is. But it's the staff who remember. We're the ones who hold the map."

I nod, not because I know, but because I want to.

After the second beer, the conversation thins out into the kind of quiet that only occurs when both parties are comfortable with the silence, or equally afraid of breaking it. I let my gaze wander again, this time to the wall above the trunk. There, in pride of place, is a photograph of a man.

William catches me looking. "That's him," he says, voice almost reverent. "He worked at the Hall for fifty years. Started as a hall boy, ended as butler and estate manager. Never married, never left."

I ask, "Did he keep diaries?" because I can't help myself.

William's smile deepens, something almost sly at its core. "He did. But most of his papers ended up in his cottage's attic when it was let out. He left the cottage to me and my sister when he died, but we were both at uni."

He leans in, lowering his voice as if the old man might overhear. "If you're really interested, we could maybe get up there sometime?. The attic's a mess, but I reckon you'd find what you're looking for."

The prospect fills me with a childlike, almost illicit glee. I say, "That would be—brilliant," and I mean it in every sense.

For a while, we sit in a shared, unspoken anticipation: me, of reading the secrets of the dead; him, of something I cannot yet name. He fetches a chilled bottle of white wine and fills two glasses, "Uncle Thomas would never have let anyone drink cheap plonk."

I took my first ever taste Chablis, "this is, wow, very good." I smiled because it was, every drink of wine I had ever had before was obviously the 'plonk' William had been referring to. "You are the first wine snob I have ever known."

"As uncle Thomas would often say 'standards matter dear boy'," William's eyes show that he is in fond remembrance.

"You and he were close then?"

"Yes, we were," William's eyes looked far away for a moment, "especially in his last few years, it's been four years now…" he hesitated, blinking heavily as his eyes became watery,"…four years and every time I am at the pub, I want to walk down the lane and pop in to see him." For the first time I recognise vulnerability in his face.

"I'm sorry, I didn't mean to upset you," I reach forward and pat his knee, and he wipes a single tear from his cheek.

"No it's fine honestly, I feel better for it, it's just you're the first person I've told this to," he looks at me once more with a smile.

"I'm glad then that you feel you can trust me," and then, "tell me some more if you want to?"

The talk drifts into stories—some his, some communal. He tells me about the war years, how his grandfather and great uncle were in the Home Guard and how they once captured a German airman.

He asks if I ever wish I had a family archive, a history with depth, and I tell him about the one photo I have of my own father: a faded 5x7 of a man holding a baby, neither of them looking at the camera. "We don't talk much," I admit. "I think I disappointed him, somehow."

He gives me a long, appraising look, then says, "My old man was the same, in his way. Wanted me to take the farm with my eldest brother, but I convinced him it might be more useful learning about how things grow. Got a talent for making things grow, just not the patience to sell them after." He shrugs, the motion casual, but I sense an old wound there.

The talk slows, the room settling into a companionable dusk. Outside, the day has cooled; the window is open an inch, and the night brings with it a crosshatch of nature's nocturnal hunters, I am aware, with every passing minute, of the rare and possibly unrepeatable perfection of this arrangement: two men, two glasses of wine, and the whole machinery of the past at their feet, ticking softly.

We don't discuss Mark, or the phantom of my wanting. But it hovers, a third presence, not unwelcome.

At some point, William stands and stretches, shirt pulling tight over his shoulder blades, then sits on the edge of the armrest nearest me. Our knees brush; neither of us moves to widen the gap.

"Do you want to see the attic sometime and see what truth there is in Jonny and Kip's story?" he says, and I realize he means it literally. "Could take you up sometime with planning, if you're game. Might find something worth the dust."

I say yes, more quickly than I mean to, and his answering laugh is the happiest sound I have heard in years.

He looks at me, eyes steady, then lowers his voice to a hush. "It may be a wait until this lot of tenants vacate."

We finish the last of the wine in silence, the night outside now deep and resonant. I want to stay—would stay, if invited—but the clock on the wall tells me I have dorm duty in an hour. I gather myself, stand, and thank him for the hospitality.

He walks me to the door, his hand brushing my back as I pass. The contact is brief, but electric.

I get three steps down the stairs before I hear him call my name again, soft but insistent. I pause, one foot suspended in air, and look back. William stands at the threshold, the yellow light making a small, private theatre of the doorway. His expression is unreadable: half apology, half dare.

"I almost forgot," he says, with an upward jerk of the chin. "Saturday's my day off. If you're around, I could show you the grounds properly. Some of the old WWII stuff, and the air raid shelters. There's a pub lunch in it, if you're interested."

I swallow, my throat dry. "Yeah," I say, the word thinner and more naked than I mean it to be. "I'd like that."

He nods, as if confirming something to himself. Then, in a movement that feels both inevitable and utterly without precedent, he steps forward and pulls me in for a hug.

It is a brief, uncertain embrace—arms around shoulders, hands clapping once at the back, a squeeze that is more honest than any conversation we have had so far. But he does not let go immediately, and neither do I. For a second, the world narrows to the smell of his shirt, the warmth of his neck, the pressure of his chest against mine. The contact is everything and nothing, a benediction, a handshake, a promise of more.

When we break apart, I can't meet his eyes.

"See you then," he says, voice back to its usual register, but the vowels catch at the edges, softer than I remember.

I manage a "night," then retreat down the stairs, skin tingling with the aftershock of contact.

Outside, the air is cooler, the night rinsed clean by a wind that stirs the first leaves of the coming autumn. I walk the length of the drive back to the Hall in a state of quiet disbelief, replaying every microsecond of the evening: the touch of his fingers at my back, the flash of teeth in lamplight. I catalogue it all, every gesture filed and cross-referenced, as if I might decode the true meaning by sheer force of attention.

The Hall is black at the windows, the moon painting the columns in blunt relief. I enter by the side door, take the stairs two at a time, check that the dorms are sleeping, and slip into my room, closing the door with a soft click. The world here is silent, the only sound the faint groan of pipes and the distant rush of the river.

I undress, peel the shirt from my back and stand barechested in the half-light. My skin is alive, every inch humming, as if the touch of William's body has rearranged the circuitry beneath. I splash water on my face, then dry off, the towel rough and grounding. In the mirror, I see myself: hair wild, eyes too bright, mouth slack in a way that borders on idiotic. I laugh at the sight, then stop, suddenly and inexplicably close to tears.

I lie down, the bedsprings complaining, and stare at the ceiling. The moon is a white thumbprint on the wall, and I let my mind drift. I imagine the attic, dust motes swirling in the torch beam, the secrets of a dead man waiting in the dark. I imagine the curve of William's neck, the way he poured the wine, the little pause before he offered the next question. I imagine more, much more, and then am ashamed by the wanting.

But as I try to summon sleep, my mind loops sideways. It drags me backwards, to childhood, to the years before I had language for what I was. To the uncle at home, the one who smelled of tobacco and sherry and who, when my parents left me alone with him, would pull me onto his lap and tell me stories about how he'd been "special" too, once. I recall the roughness of his hand, the way he pressed his face into my hair, the way I would count the seconds until the ordeal ended, then the hours until my parents returned.

The next hour is a forensic reconstruction of the night: every word, every laugh, every flicker of William's gaze. I interrogate my own motives, cross-examine his. Was the hug a mistake, a product of alcohol and loneliness? Was it an opening, or a kindness? Did I hold on too long? Did he?

My mind jumps from hope to fear and back again. I am terrified of misreading the signals, of forcing meaning onto gestures that were never intended as such. I am even more terrified of what might happen if I am right, if William genuinely wants me, if I have somehow stumbled into a happiness that the universe does not intend for people like me.

But despite the doubt, despite the old, calcified terror, I cannot quite suppress the quiet, subversive thrill of possibility. For the first time in years, I want something without qualification, without the caveats of guilt or shame. I want to see him again. I want the attic, and the stories, and the walks through the Hall in the small hours. I want the permission to want, even if only for a little while.

I turn on my back, exhale, and let the night have its way with me.

Outside, the wind rattles the glass, and the moon slides across the wall, painting my body in slow, silver increments. I watch the light move, and feel the shape of my hope growing, even as the old fears circle and nip at its edges.

I tell myself I will survive it, either way. I tell myself that Saturday is not so far.

I close my eyes, and let sleep, at last, come for me.

CHAPTER 10: MARK'S UNEXPECTED MESSAGE

The blue airmail envelope trembled in my hands as if it possessed its own private pulse, fragile as the skin on the back of a pensioner's wrist. I regarded it on my desk, then lifted it to the light. Inside, Mark's spidery handwriting undulated along the lines with an energy I remembered too well from that first, improbable term—a brand of enthusiasm more suited to football terraces than matters of the heart. I did not open the letter straight away. I let it rest on the faux-leather blotter—Langley Hall's gesture towards clerical permanence—while I looked out across the lawns, where the sun was already cruelly bright and unkind to anything or anyone seeking shade. Only the willows along the lower field managed to look cool, and that by a kind of dogged persistence, their silver leaves resistant to the furnace.

My room in the Hall, appointed with the minimum comforts for a summer caretaker and thus deliberately stripped of character, did not encourage reverie. There were two pieces of furniture I might have called my own: a narrow iron bed, unyielding and plain, and the writing desk, which still bore, in scratches and palimpsests, the record of generations of boys pressed into the service of homework or penance. The remainder—the cane chair, the small wardrobe with a single bent hanger, and the enamel basin by the window—suggested a transient existence, a life in parentheses. I sat for a long time with the envelope pinched between my fingers, its lightness both contemptuous and damning.

The postmark was Monte Carlo, and the return address was a hotel whose name alone conjured all that I resented in Mark's family, and my own. I slit the flap carefully, folding it back with the same neurotic delicacy I had once used on his shirt cuffs, and drew out the letter. The scent of it was not the oily tang of foreign correspondence I had expected—no ghosts of Gauloises, no perfume, nothing—just the dry scent of stationary, which felt like the most insipid betrayal of all.

He opened with a joke about the heat and the size of his father's bar tab, a line that should have made me smile but instead sent a tightness across my chest. By the second paragraph he was recounting, with what passed for Mark's humility, his "triumphs" at the local tennis club, victories measured as much in points as in the number of girls who "seemed keen for post-match drinks." He italicized "keen," as if to make clear the word's double-meaning. And yet, as I read further, I realized this was not double-meaning at all. It was what he wanted to say, and what he wished me to know.

He mentioned, with the breezy disregard of a man reciting the shipping forecast, that he had "finally managed to get somewhere with that blonde from Liverpool," the phrase underlined twice. Her name, apparently, was Simone. He described her hair, her legs, her "incredible sense of humour." Not once did he refer to her as a friend. The entire affair was delivered as though in confidence, as though the details would amuse me or perhaps stoke in me a competitive urge. It did neither. My face flushed. I felt a trickle of sweat trace my sternum under my open-necked cricket top.

I flipped to the second page, hoping for some gesture, some evidence of memory or missing me. He closed with a line that might have been meant as a compliment, but felt instead like a thumb pressed to the bruise: "Don't be a stranger, mate. September'll be a laugh if we're both still alive. Can't wait for the fun."

No mention of what had happened between us in the hush of the library stacks, or the raw, confessional silences that followed, or the night in March when he'd pressed his forehead to mine and said—his voice barely above a whisper—that I was "the only one he really gave a damn about." All that vanished, erased by the blankness of "mate," the pretence of ordinary friendship, the universal solvent of plausible deniability. I folded the letter in half, then in half again, and pressed the edge with my thumbnail so hard that the paper threatened to split. Then I crumpled it, an ugly gesture, and launched it toward the far wall, where it struck a corner of the wardrobe and dropped, unceremonious, to the bare floorboards.

My hand shook, but I would not let myself cry. Instead, I leaned forward, elbows on desk, head in my hands, and tried to regulate my breathing. There was an art to this, learned in years of attending an all-boys grammar school: the containment of panic, the redirection of grief. I tried to summon anger, to loathe him, to see in his words the cold-hearted opportunist I'd always known lurked in him. But I could not muster it. Instead, I felt only the sting of having trusted someone unworthy, and the more prosaic humiliation of having thought myself special when I was, at best, a regrettable experiment.

The room did not help. The walls, painted in the shade of white peculiar to institutions, seemed to repel warmth, and the single, under-sized radiator beneath the window gave off the odour of stale dust even in summer. On the window ledge, someone—perhaps my predecessor, perhaps a housekeeper—had left a jam jar of field daisies, now brittle and browning at the edges. They radiated a stubborn kind of cheer, mocking the atmosphere within. Beyond the glass, the afternoon vibrated with life: bees in the phlox, the shriek of swifts as they circled the eaves, the intermittent whirr of a strimmer somewhere near the kitchen garden. I could see, on the drive below, two of the grounds staff unloading crates of tomatoes from a battered Transit van. They laughed as they worked, one of them pulling off his cap and using it to swat at the other, a pantomime of violence that ended in both men doubled over, convulsed by some private hilarity.

I envied them, these men whose lives seemed untroubled by ambivalence or longing. Their world was defined by the rhythms of the estate, the demands of grass, growth, and weather. My own world—of books, and imagined futures, and secret hopes—felt impossible by comparison. My future, in that moment, felt both trivial and unattainable.

After a while, I could not resist. I stood, walked to the corner, and retrieved the crumpled letter. The paper was creased and bruised, but readable. I smoothed it on the desk and, as if compelled, read it again from the start. The words had not changed. If anything, the tone was now more abrasive, the subtext more taunting. I found myself searching for signs of regret, some latent phrase that might have softened the verdict. There was none. Even the closing "Yours, M," with its careful absence of affection or intimacy, felt calculated, as if he knew I would parse every word, and wanted to leave me nothing.

I tried to imagine the return to university and our future shared digs - the first awkward encounter on the stairs carrying boxes, the unspoken negotiations over shared space, conversation, the false laughter and the shared cigarettes after dark. I pictured myself performing the role of the unconcerned, perhaps even superior, ex-lover. The prospect sickened me. I thought, then, of the other possibility: not returning at all. I could, in theory, fail to show up, send word that family matters or illness had prevented my return. It would not be the first time a promising scholar vanished from the rolls. Yet the thought of surrendering to that fate seemed worse than any humiliation. My mother would not forgive it, and neither would I.

The sky darkened a little, a passing cloud, but the light in my room remained pitiless. I set the letter aside, resolved to destroy it later, and stood by the window. The breeze carried in the scent of cut grass, sharp and alive, and for a moment I remembered William, the one whose presence in my life now confounded everything I thought I knew about desire and its objects.

I could not dislodge him from my thoughts. His voice, his posture, the way he spoke to me as if I were already a long-time friend, as if my opinions mattered. In his presence, I felt a different kind of gravity—a sense that I might be capable of something more than endurance. I did not know what I wanted from him, or whether he could want anything from me. But I knew, with a sudden clarity, that I would rather fail in that direction than persist in the old lie.

Below, the tomatoes were stacked in neat red pyramids, and the two men had moved on to other tasks. The day, indifferent, unspooled itself in heat, scent, and sound. Inside my room, the silence settled again, more complete for having been briefly disturbed.

I gathered the letter, pressed it flat, and slid it into the drawer. Not as a keepsake, but as a reminder of what could no longer be endured. I looked once more at the daisies, their heads bowed but unyielding, and decided to leave them there, at least until their petals gave up and dropped.

Tomorrow, I would have to face the world again. But tonight, I would allow myself the luxury of doing nothing, of letting the evening pass without purpose. I sat back at the desk and closed my eyes. I listened to the bees, and the wind, and somewhere, faintly, the sound of laughter coming from the kitchen. In the company of these things, my wounds felt both smaller and more honest. I could survive this, I told myself. I could even, one day, forgive it.

Saturday morning arrived with an overabundance of sun, as if the estate itself had something to prove. I awoke earlier than was strictly necessary and spent a quarter of an hour in pointless rearrangements—straightening the thin blanket on my bed, aligning the pens on the desk, inspecting the seat of my trousers for imaginary lint. When, at last, I made my way down the scuffed corridor to the main entrance, William was already there, his back to me as he considered a cluster of dusty sepia photographs in the vestibule. He wore the same khaki shirt as yesterday, sleeves rolled, exposing forearms that suggested both manual labour and a longstanding intimacy with sunlight. He turned at the sound of my shoes, offered a nod that felt somehow formal, and gestured wordlessly toward the double doors that led into the Hall proper.

He held them open for me, and as I passed, I caught the faint scent of lemon—polish, perhaps, or aftershave, or even the lingering residue of the pastry he'd carried into the staff room the day before. We stood for a moment just inside the threshold, taking in the room's proportions. Even empty, the children were all on a day trip to Great Yarmouth, the Hall retained the presumption of an audience, its dimensions calculated to awe and to discipline. Marble floors, black and white in a chevron that pulled the eye forward; pale yellow walls with ornate plasterwork overhead; Corinthian columns, each fluted with almost comic excess, supporting nothing more than a shallow entablature but managing, all the same, to impress.

"Eighteenth century," William said, voice low, "though the Langleys would have you believe there's been a house here since Henry the Eighth. This one was built by the third viscount and first earl, after the last place burned. Probably an insurance job," he winked," but my lot were just tenant farmers back then, so who knows?"

He said it with a smile, but there was no irony in the delivery, only the plain recitation of family lore. We moved along the periphery, our footfalls amplified by the hard stone. Occasionally our shoulders would brush as we maneuvered to regard a painting or a particularly flamboyant sconce, and each time I felt a prickle of awareness—first as discomfort, then, increasingly, as anticipation. I was unused to the choreography of such proximity. With Mark, every contact had been either the calculated aggression of the sports field or the orchestrated privacy of locked doors. Here, in open air and under daylight, I found my senses betrayed me at every turn.

He stopped before an oil painting, some ancestor of the Langleys, a pale stout man with an expression of invincible entitlement. "The Fifth Earl of Grafton. The next to last one."

I nodded, uncertain whether this was meant to be a warning or an aspiration.

We proceeded through a sequence of state rooms—drawing room, music room, a dining room big enough to feed the entire village if so inclined. William provided a running commentary that was equal parts encyclopaedic and local gossip, peppered with odd asides about the construction ("look at the thickness of that door, must be six inches at least—probably stopped more than one family row from turning into homicide") and the private foibles of long-dead scions ("the third Viscount, they weren't earls yet, kept a pet monkey, and let it eat at the table. Apparently it bit a bishop once. My great-granddad swore to it, and he never lied about animals").

The library was, predictably, the room that most interested me and the one I was familiar with, though I kept this enthusiasm contained. The shelves were crammed with a glorious disorder of books: leatherbound law volumes, forgotten novels, guidebooks to foreign capitals. I ran a finger along the spines, feeling the nicks and ridges, the interrupted journeys of generations of hands.

"Ever read any of them?" I asked, meaning to be light, but it came out tinged with genuine curiosity.

William shrugged. "A few. Not really my thing, though. I'm more outdoors than in. Never could see the point of reading about places you can just walk to." He paused, then added: "Not that I'm against it, mind. My sister, she'll sit for hours with her nose in a book."

There was a brief silence, filled by the ticking of a heavy clock somewhere out of sight. I picked up a volume at random—an etiquette manual, so old that the advice inside might have been contemporary with the first Langleys—and leafed through it.

"I suppose there's a rule for every situation," I said, more to myself than to him.

"Oh, definitely," William replied. "And if there isn't, someone will make one up."

His tone was ambiguous enough to suggest both complaint and admiration.

We left the library and cut through the service corridor, a narrow passage lined with framed plans of the estate and, on closer inspection, the occasional photograph of prize livestock. The air here was cooler, and I realized with a start that the sweat which had collected at my temples was already drying, leaving behind the faint sting of salt.

William led us outside through a side door, holding it open as before, and we stepped into a square of blinding light. The lawns, which from above appeared manicured and serene, revealed on closer inspection a tangle of dandelion heads and tufts of clover, as if the grass itself were engaged in a slow, ongoing rebellion. He pointed out features as we walked—a sundial, a stand of ancient beeches, the distant shimmer of the Home Farm's slate roofs against the horizon.

"My dad owns Home Farm now," he said. "Granddad before him. They reckon the Coopers have been working this land since King George the third. You can't go anywhere in the village without tripping over some cousin or other." He grinned, as if to apologize for this provincial boast, then added: "Means you get to know everything. The secrets, the shortcuts. Who's sleeping with who, and who's planning to burn the place down."

We reached a low hedge that separated the formal garden from what William called "the wild bits." The air was thick with the metallic tang of cut grass and something else—honeysuckle, perhaps, or the exhalations of nettles bruised underfoot. We took a narrow, rutted path that traced the old boundary wall, and as we walked, I could feel the heat radiate upward, gathering in the hollow of my neck.

William stopped suddenly, pointed to a patch of brambles threaded through with the ruins of corrugated metal. "That's the first of them," he said, and ducked through a gap in the thicket.

I hesitated, then followed, the branches scraping at my bare forearms. The interior, once my eyes adjusted, revealed the remnant of a Nissen hut—World War II, if I guessed right—half swallowed by the advancing undergrowth. William knelt and brushed away a drift of leaves, exposing a faint circle of concrete, pitted and lichen-stained.

"They used to keep anti-aircraft guns out here," he said, his voice suddenly quieter. "My granddad said the noise would shake the whole Hall. Sometimes they'd fire for practice, just to let the Germans know we were ready. He reckoned the only things they ever hit were rooks and the odd unlucky sheep. Great uncle Thomas was estate manager here then and head of the local Home Guard."

I tried to picture the scene: the sky turned black with the threat of bombs, the estate alive with the terror and thrill of history in motion. It was impossible, in this sunlit moment, to imagine fear so dense it altered the colour of the world.

We moved on, following the edge of the field, and William told stories as we walked—of rationing, and black-market eggs, and the night a stray shrapnel set fire to the Home Farm's hayloft. He spoke with a fluency that suggested these memories were not his own but had been entrusted to him, a legacy to be preserved and, if possible, improved upon.

I listened, contributing little. My mind replayed the words from Mark's letter, the parade of girls and the casual promise of "fun." I compared this to the afternoon unfolding around me, to the company of someone who seemed both impossibly alive and, at the same time, not quite real. I wondered if this was how longing worked: an endless oscillation between absence and presence, want and fulfilment, the mind always searching for a place to rest.

Eventually, the path opened onto a low rise, from which the entire sweep of the estate could be seen. William squinted into the glare, then pointed to a squat brick structure half-hidden by a stand of sycamores.

"Bomb shelter," he said. "Supposed to be big enough for all the Yanks living in the Hall, plus servants."

We walked down the incline, the grass brittle beneath our feet, and approached the entrance. The door, a rusted relic, hung open on a single hinge. William ducked inside, and after a brief hesitation, I followed.

The air within was shockingly cool. After the heat outside, it felt like entering another season. The space was low-ceilinged and cramped, the walls lined with shelves of mildewed tin cans and, incongruously, a child's tricycle with one pedal missing. There was only enough room to stand side by side or else move in awkward sequence, one person leading, the other shuffling behind.

William clicked on a torch, its beam slicing a bright wedge through the murk. "Still smells of damp, forty years on," he said. "They say the staff would only come down if the sirens were really close. Otherwise, they'd just wait it out with a bottle of gin in the servants' hall."

I ran my hand along the cold wall, surprised by the roughness of the surface. It felt oddly comforting, this evidence of survival, the stubborn endurance of matter.

For a moment, we stood in silence, the only sound the faint drip of water somewhere beyond the range of the light. Then, without warning, William turned and handed me the torch. Our hands brushed, and I felt an electric jolt—familiar, yes, but newly complicated by the uncertainty of context. I held the light steady as he crouched, examining something at floor level. When he stood, we were closer than before, and I realized how little separated us.

He looked at me, his expression unreadable in the half-dark. "You're quieter today," he said. "Sorry if I've been talking too much."

I tried to formulate a reply, but the words felt slow and unwieldy in my mouth. "No, it's good. I like it. Just… didn't sleep well, I guess."

He nodded, but didn't press.

We lingered a while longer, exploring the other end of the shelter, then retraced our steps to the door. As we emerged into the sun, the light struck me full in the face, forcing me to squint until my eyes watered. I blinked rapidly, embarrassed, and wiped at my cheeks, pretending it was just the glare.

William remained silent as we trudged up the hill back to the Hall, his steps perfectly synchronized with mine. It was as if we were locked in a delicate balance, neither taking the lead nor trailing behind. At the top, we halted, gazing over the landscape. It was a moment suspended in time, caught between what had been and what might be, leaving us uncertain about our next move.

"Let's take the village road - at least it will be in the shade," he suggested at last, before leaping over a fence. We landed on a familiar road, the one that stretched from the village to Norwich. The towering trees on either side concealed Home Farm and the Hall, casting deep, dappled shadows that turned the path into a tunnel leading toward the village, about three-quarters of a mile ahead. It was yet another seemingly perfect moment, filled with bird songs and our meandering chat. My heart urged me to reach for William's hand, yet I held back, torn by the fear that I might shatter whatever fragile connection lay between us.

Langley Village was built for the romance of postcards: a single, sinuous road lined with cottages whose thatch resisted modernization with the stubbornness of the ancestral. Even the telegraph wires, strung low and whistling in the wind, seemed to know their place in the tableau, providing an accidental music as we strolled beneath them. William walked slightly ahead, hands in pockets, his stride easy and loose, pausing now and then to point out some forgotten boundary stone or the place where, he claimed, the entire under-sixteen football team had once hidden from a vengeful groundskeeper.

At first, I let the rhythm of his voice wash over me, not caring to follow every detail, content to be led. But as we entered the heart of the village, the atmosphere changed. The air, already heavy with the promise of late afternoon, carried the scents of wet stone and distant baking. Windows along the lane were thrown open to admit the day, and behind net curtains I glimpsed the slow movements of old women at their chores, toddlers left unashamedly bare in the sun, men in rolled shirt-sleeves smoking with the deliberate idleness of men whose work was not in crisis. Each door, William explained, concealed a minor dynasty: the bakers had intermarried with the boatmen, the retired schoolmaster ran a black-market repair business from his garden shed, the pub landlord was cousin to half the constabulary and thus above certain laws.

We stopped outside the church, a Norman building that looked as if it had grown directly from the earth, its walls mottled with a crust of lichen and the scars of past repairs. The graveyard, hemmed in by a low flint wall, was improbably full—headstones at every angle, their inscriptions growing less legible the closer one approached our own time. William guided us through the gate, the hinges protesting, and led me along the gravel path.

"My mum's people are here," he said, not needing to specify which side of the plot. "Most Coopers get the same stone. No-nonsense, like they are. That's grandad, there." He pointed, and I followed, feeling a strange trespass in the act.

The inscription read simply: William Cooper, 1890–1972. Below it, a line that caught me off guard: Loved and remembered, every single day. The headstone next to it was for Thomas Cooper, and the dates were 1892-1980 and also William Thorne, 1900-1981 with the epitaph 'Reunited'; someone had left a posy of wildflowers, already wilting in the heat.

I tried to imagine the story behind these names—if they had been close, if the family gathered here on anniversaries, or if the flowers were the work of a village child sent on an errand by a mother with more sentimental debts than time.

"They say Thomas was the clever one," William said. "Entered service at the Hall at fourteen, worked his way up to eventually be Lord John's valet, and then the last Earl's Estate Manager."

"And William Thorne?" I asked with genuine interest. William smiled widely for a moment.

"He was great uncle Thomas'," he paused to find the words, "'special friend'." He winked making the insinuation that they were more than friends obvious.

He squatted to pull a weed from the base of the stone, exposing a thin vein of white root. "I always thought it was sad, him staying when he could have gone anywhere. But then, my dad used to say, sometimes you belong to a place, whether you want to or not." He guided us over to a set of memorials by the west entrance to the church which were much grander than the rest. "The Langley family," he announced and pointed at the newest looking of the set which read 'Lord Christian Langley, sixth Earl of Grafton, 1895-1963'.

We walked on, and the rows of stones gave way to the more recent graves—shiny granite, plastic flowers, the occasional incongruous teddy bear or football scarf. I found myself wondering, not for the first time, what my own memorial would look like, and whether anyone would think to bring flowers, or if that custom would die with my mother.

At the far end of the yard, the view opened onto the river, its surface muddied by the recent rain and carrying, on its slow current, a flotilla of duckweed and the odd discarded can. William led us to the bridge, where two boys fished with the timeless hope of boys everywhere, the oldest of them barefoot and red-kneed from climbing the bank.

"Used to do that," William said. "Me and my elder brother. Never caught anything worth keeping, but we tried." He watched the boys for a while, a fondness in his eyes that made me think of the way my mother looked at small children in supermarkets, as if marvelling at a version of me she'd lost.

For a while we stood in silence, leaning on the sun-warmed stone of the bridge, watching the world go about its unhurried business. I wanted to say something meaningful, to mark the moment, but every line I rehearsed sounded forced. William seemed content not to talk.

After a while, he straightened. "You alright?" he said, and this time the question was less casual, more pointed.

I started to lie, then stopped. "Not really," I said, surprised by the honesty.

He nodded, as if he'd expected no other answer. "Is it something you want to talk about?"

I hesitated. "It's stupid. Just—someone I know wrote and well I think we shouldn't see each other anymore."

"Someone from home?"

"From uni, actually."

He regarded me with a careful neutrality, the way a vet approaches a frightened animal. "I'm sorry," he said. "That's rough if it is who I think it is."

I shrugged, already regretting having said anything. "It is. Wasn't much, really. Probably for the best. We weren't…" I groped for a word that would not betray either of us. "We weren't well-matched."

He studied the river a moment longer, then turned to me, full on. "Still hurts, though. Even if you know it's coming."

I nodded, unable to look at him.

He kicked at the dust of the path, then spoke in a lower voice. "If it helps, I think anyone who lets you go must be an idiot. They don't know what they're missing."

The words took me by surprise—not just the sentiment, but the unguarded way he delivered it, as if the fact were obvious and required no further explanation. I felt a hotness in my face, and looked away, pretending to study the church tower.

"Thanks," I said, the syllable barely audible.

He laughed, but gently, not at me but at the awkwardness of the moment. "Sorry," he said. "Didn't mean to embarrass you. Just—seems like a waste, is all."

We started back toward the main street, and for a while neither of us spoke. The air was thick with the scent of roses and the exhaust of a passing delivery van. We walk along the riverbank and pick up Wherryman's Lane that leads back to the village road. Halfway along, we stop outside a cottage. "This William announces is my cottage," he pauses and then corrects himself, "well mine and my sisters."

"Left to you by your great uncle Thomas," a confirmation that I had been listening to his stories the other night.

"Maybe one day I will buy my sister's half," a little doubt became evident in his voice, "well once I get a job that pays enough for me to get a mortgage?"

"That's a worthy ambition for sure, and something your uncle Thomas would approve of," I offer in encouragement.

"I think you may be right," with that he pointed to the end of the lane, "onward."

In the distance, the pub sign creaked on its bracket, advertising the Langley Arms as a place of "Good Cheer & Honest Ale." We crossed the road and ducked into its cool interior, where the ceilings were so low that even I had to stoop. The walls were crowded with horse brasses, old photos of cricket teams, and, for some reason, a sepia portrait of the King George the sixth that looked as if it had never been dusted.

William ordered two pints and carried them to a corner table, where the light was filtered through a panel of stained glass, colouring the dust motes in an amber haze. I drank gratefully, the bitterness of the beer cutting through the woollen taste of defeat that had lingered in my mouth all morning.

We talked of safer things—his plans for the grounds, the latest in agricultural equipment, the chances of England advancing past the group stage in the next World Cup. But the earlier exchange hovered between us, unsaid but not forgotten, and I found myself replaying it with a kind of incredulous pleasure.

After the second round, I felt the knot in my stomach begin to loosen, and the room took on a softer quality, as if the world had decided, for once, not to press so hard. We sat there a while longer, the minutes slipping by in the hush of old wood and the clink of glass.

When it was time to leave, the sun had shifted, and the day was already promising to grow cooler. We walked back to the Hall at a slower pace, the road now nearly deserted. At the entrance, William paused.

"Let me know if you want to talk," he said, voice low. "About anything."

"I will," I said, and this time I meant it.

He smiled, a crooked thing, then turned down the path toward the stables, again whistling a tune I did not recognize. I watched until he was out of sight, then stood for a long time at the edge of the drive, not quite ready to go in.

Above me, the sky had turned the colour of watered milk, and the air was heavy with the promise of rain. I breathed in, then out, and found, to my surprise, that the world no longer felt so narrow.

CHAPTER 11: THE END-OF-CAMP PERFORMANCE

There is a particular hush peculiar to certain old buildings, a silence that seems not the absence of sound, but the presence of memory—a vibration between the walls, a tension woven into the grain of the wood itself. The ballroom of Langley Hall had such a hush, even on evenings like this, when the very air throbbed with nervous energy and the expectation of applause. It was the final night of the camp; Sarah's vision made manifest in tinsel, crepe paper, and more determination than the assembled audience of parents, siblings, and staff could comprehend.

The space had not hosted a proper dance in decades, but tonight, at her insistence, the scattered trestle tables and plastic chairs were banished, and the battered grand piano rolled into service at stage right. Lanterns, pressed into duty from the storeroom, hung from the flaking plaster cornices, shedding islands of golden light upon the polished emptiness of the floor. Even the scent was period-appropriate: a compound of lemon oil, melting candle wax, and the faint suggestion of mildew from the ragged velvet curtains that had been kept drawn all summer. I stood with William at the very back, just inside the shadows, as the first number commenced—Sarah herself, bounding onto the makeshift dais in a flurry of chiffon and practiced modesty.

There is something inherently humiliating in amateur theatre, and I suppose I had always been acutely sensitive to it. In a previous life, my own mother had once required me to perform in a nativity play; the memory persisted, undiminished, as a hot stone at the base of my throat. I did not enjoy public spectacles, and as Sarah's troupe of children scuttled and pirouetted across the boards, I watched the audience more than the action, collecting fragments of reactions like pressed flowers. Students and teachers alike craned, cameras lifted. Sarah, despite her radiance, did not quite meet my gaze; but I felt her performance was intended for my eyes regardless, an offering I was never certain I deserved.

The only person whose reactions I genuinely cared about was, at that moment, shifting his weight on the dusty boards beside me. William—tall, sunburnt from his days spent gardening, hair still damp from his hasty post-shift shower—exuded a smell of Nivea and grass stains. I had invited him, though the word "invited" seemed inadequate: more accurately, I had confessed to him the time and place of the event, and he had responded with a noncommittal shrug that nevertheless guaranteed his attendance. That was William's way—minimal effort, maximal presence.

For the first ten minutes, we exchanged nothing but the odd whispered aside: him mocking the earnestness of the performers, me correcting his misremembered pop culture references. ("It's Grease, not Dirty Dancing, you troglodyte.") These exchanges were a bulwark against the attention of others; a private patois developed over dozens of shared cigarettes and long walks around the perimeter of the Hall's gardens. Occasionally, our laughter would attract a brief, disapproving glance from Sue or a jealous flash of white eye from one of the other staff. I did not mind; we had, by mutual agreement, decided that the opinions of the rest of the world ended at the edge of our own small conspiracies.

As the performance unfolded, Sarah made her presence felt in every detail, even when offstage—her programs, printed on pilfered A4 and stapled slightly askew; her command of the curtain calls; the faintest hint of her perfume on the programs she'd passed out by hand. I envied her capacity for effortless authority, the way she commandeered a room and bent it, lightly, to her will. When she darted out to supervise a quick change or reposition a prop, the air seemed to bend around her. I felt myself, by contrast, diffuse—a piece of scenery, a backdrop. It was easier to observe than to participate.

Between the third and fourth acts (the "interval" so styled), the lights dimmed further, and the ambient noise of the audience retreated to a low, rolling mutter. In the shadowed periphery of the room, William and I migrated a few steps closer to the side wall, ostensibly for a better view. In reality, we orbited one another, neither wishing to stand apart nor to stand so close as to be conspicuous. The line between our arms became impossibly, magnetically charged. I remember the feeling not as desire, precisely, but as an anticipation of a future in which desire was possible. Something in the air had shifted, a confluence of proximity and accumulated unspoken sentences. And yet also too afraid to actively encourage anything.

Children took the stage in pairs and trios, clumsy yet determined, faces shining under the fierce lamps Sarah had begged off the Drama department. Their shadows doubled and trebled against the pale expanse of the back wall, strange and larger-than-life. I traced those shadows, and in them, found myself reflected—awkward, overgrown, straining for recognition. William must have sensed this, for he leaned toward me, his mouth barely a hand's width from my ear. "Do you reckon they'll get away with that?" he murmured, as two of the older boys attempted a hip-hop routine whose choreography was far more suggestive than Sarah could possibly have intended.

"If anyone's going to object, no one will ever know," I replied, keeping my tone light. My hand, hanging at my side, twitched. William's knuckles grazed mine. The effect was instantaneous and dizzying. All the borrowed confidence of the evening evaporated, replaced by a bristling animal panic that I might, through some reflex or miscalculation, reveal myself in the presence of the wrong eyes.

William leaned into me in the darkness and whispered in my ear that we should step outside for some air as he fanned his face with his hand. The heat of his breath on my cheek was almost suffocating. I lifted a teacher's finger to my lips and nodded, indicating that we should leave quietly.

It was a law of Langley Hall that any journey, no matter how direct in intention, became labyrinthine in the execution; the place was a perpetual work of architectural spite, refusing to yield a straight line or an unimpeded passage. William led the way, and I followed, careful to keep my footfalls silent on the flagstones as we left the echo chamber of the ballroom and threaded through the half-lit passages of the main wing. Overhead, the old gas pipes—disused but not removed—cast corrugated shadows, and our progress was shadow-play, two silhouettes gliding in and out of the light. We passed the empty cloakroom, the row of high windows ghostly with condensation, and then emerged, finally, into the open air of the side garden.

I had not realized, until that moment, how heavily the evening's events had pressed upon my chest. It was as though every room in the Hall had been a vacuum, extracting the air from my lungs, and only now could I truly breathe. The night was cool and sweet, the grass exhaling a scent of wet loam, the rose bushes—ancient, feral—spilling fragrance over the cobbled courtyard like a benediction. There was a bench, half-swallowed by the shadow of a rampant climbing rose, and it was toward this that William steered us, his hand guiding the small of my back with the lightest of pressure.

The roses had outlived their original owner by many decades, perhaps more, their trunks gnarled and black, the flowers themselves absurdly fragile in contrast. In the moonlight, petals glimmered like the remnants of a wedding confetti, and the trellis above us groaned softly as if protesting the weight of such a brief, perfumed excess. The bench itself was smooth with use, but cold; I hesitated to sit, not wishing to mark my trousers with dew, but William was already settled, his elbows resting on his knees, his face turned upward to the pale corona of the sky.

I joined him, gingerly, and let my gaze drift out over the grass, where the Hall's windows reflected a latticework of distant light. For a long minute, neither of us spoke. My hands, idle, found occupation in plucking invisible threads from my sleeve. The silence between us was not the comfortable one from before, but something taut and bruised, straining against the inevitability of words. I could sense William regarding me from the corner of his eye, and I tried to imagine the arrangement of my own features: did they betray the panic I felt, or had I succeeded in reconstructing my face into something bland and inscrutable?

At length, he said, "You can still hear them, if you listen. The kids, I mean." His tone was casual, but I caught the signal for what it was—a gentle cue to ease the entry into the next conversation.

I closed my eyes and let the wind bring me the echoes of the performance: a girl's high laughter, the thump of an ill-timed jump, the tide of applause swelling and receding. It was the kind of noise that reminded you, with a stab, how many lives could coexist in a single building, each unaware of the others except when forced to intersect. "They did well," I said, offering the olive branch of a safe topic.

"They did," he agreed. "You're a good liar."

It might have been an accusation, but he said it with a smile, and I allowed myself to smile in return. "I've had a lot of practice." That was a confession.

We let that sit for a while. I could sense him fidgeting beside me, a vibration that seemed to travel through the slats of the bench and into my own body. I wondered what it would feel like to lean into him, to rest my head against his shoulder and let the world recede to a manageable size. Instead, I kept my hands folded in my lap, fingers interlaced so tightly that the knuckles whitened.

"There's something I need to know," he said at last, and this time his voice was different—stripped of the usual scaffolding of sarcasm and bravado, earnest in a way that was almost unrecognizable.

I nodded, once. I did not trust myself to speak.

He shifted to face me more directly, knees angled toward mine, his profile luminous in the moonlight. "You've never really told me about him," he said. "The one you keep mentioning back at uni." He paused. "Is it serious?"

"Seemingly not after that last letter," I said, though my voice was so soft I barely heard it myself.

William waited, silent, his hands palm-up on his knees, "but it was serious to you?"

"I thought so."

He reached over and took both my hands in his, his grip firm but not forceful. I flinched, out of habit more than intent, but he did not let go. His thumbs pressed into the soft skin between my knuckles, grounding me.

"For the cleverest person I have ever met," he said, "you really can be obtuse at times."

I stared at him, uncomprehending. "What do you mean?"

He smiled—real, unguarded, a grin that showed the uneven line of his teeth. "I mean, you daft bastard, that I hoped it wasn't serious. I mean, I hoped it could be me."

The sense of relief was so immense that I laughed, a sound that started in my belly and burst out, raw and inelegant. William laughed too, and the sound bounced off the courtyard walls, a kind of new echo, fresh and unpractised.

He leaned in, his forehead resting against mine, and the world narrowed to the circle of our breathing. I could smell the night on him, the cut grass and the medicinal tang of his aftershave. His hands still cradled mine, their warmth and pressure an anchor.

With Mark, everything had always been so simple, or so I had convinced myself. It was pure physical attraction and nothing more, or at least that's what we both pretended. We never spoke of emotions, never admitted to feeling anything beyond desire. Despite this, I had undeniably grown to care for him, maybe even love him, though I was painfully aware after nearly three years that my feelings were not reciprocated. To him, I was nothing more than a potential blemish on his reputation, a risk he wasn't willing to take. Yet, in the fleeting moments since my candid conversation with William, I sensed he was different, profoundly different from any man I had known. This realization both exhilarated and terrified me.

I was just beginning to grapple with this overwhelming mix of emotions and thoughts when William leaned towards me. He kissed me —not a question but a confirmation, a punctuation mark. His lips were dry and chapped from the wind, and the first contact was almost a collision, both of us uncoordinated with expectation. We laughed again, but this time did not pull apart. The second kiss was slower, softer, and I felt my own hands tighten on his, afraid that letting go would break the spell and return us to the prior arrangement of the universe.

We sat like that, the two of us, beneath the tangled arms of the rose, and the cold and the possibility of interruption no longer mattered. The applause from the ballroom had faded, replaced by the patient creak of the trellis and the pulse of blood in my own ears.

After a while, William leaned back, his face still inches from mine. "So what now?" he said.

I shrugged, feeling at once ancient and new. "We finish the summer, I suppose. See the kids go home tomorrow and then have our staff party. We figure the rest out as we go." A new confidence rose inside me.

He grinned. "I can live with that."

I squeezed his hand, and together we looked out over the grass, the Hall's windows now mostly dark. It occurred to me, then, that the world was full of performance and confession and the wild, fearful hope that somewhere, someone would applaud the truth of you.

The roses shifted above us, a shower of petals drifting down to settle on our joined hands. I brushed them away, but not too quickly.

Some nights, you don't need an audience. Some nights, it is enough to find yourself seen.

CHAPTER 12: THE FAREWELL PARTY

The final night at Langley had always been, in theory, a celebration—a pseudo-wake for the season, complete with apologies and unclaimed lost property and the release of a communal breath held too long. It was not so much an end as an unspooling; the sharp edges of routine, of discipline, blurred first with exhaustion, then with drink. The main hall, stripped of its usual grandeur, wore a half-hearted regalia of fairy lights and bunting pilfered from the kitchen stores. The makeshift bar comprised two trestle tables set end-to-end, a battlement of supermarket wine, tepid lagers, and, if you knew where to look, Sarah's private stash of cheap Prosecco.

By nine, the air was thick with the signatures of too many bodies in too small a space: sweat, anxiety, the fermentation of both yeast and feeling. Teachers gathered in nervous clusters, their laughter just a decibel too high, the topic of "next year" floated with the brittle optimism of those already bracing for disappointment. Kitchen staff, less bound by hierarchy, claimed the dance floor and powered through an ancient boombox's greatest hits, the bassline juddering up through the parquet. Even the caretaker—a perennial ghost, seldom glimpsed in daylight—could be seen holding court near the doors, dispensing stories and double-measures with the same rough affection.

I hovered at the periphery, glass in hand, making periodic forays into the current of movement and conversation. Sarah intercepted me early, her arms already thrown wide as if she might literally engulf me in celebration. "I was so proud of you last night," she said, pronouncing it as though it had been my name in the program, not hers.

I accepted the hug, but with the same wariness I reserved for all contact, as if I suspected the warmth might be a trick of the lighting. "It was all your doing. I just fetched chairs."

"You never give yourself any credit," she chided, drawing away and tucking a stray strand of hair behind my ear with clinical tenderness. "You're a terrible liar, you know."

I was not, in fact, a terrible liar; I was merely a careful one, and I had trained myself never to lie about things that didn't matter. "Is that a compliment?" I said, not quite smiling.

She grinned, revealing the slightly snaggled teeth that made her, somehow, seem more trustworthy. "Only if you want it to be. But tonight, you're required to have fun. That's an order." She pressed another glass into my hand and vanished toward the bar, leaving me in a drift of perfume and obligation.

The night unspooled in increments of ten or fifteen minutes—segments measured not by the hour but by the frequency of glances toward the door. William was late, as I had predicted to myself knowing how busy he had been, and though I did not scan for him, I was acutely aware of each arrival, each silhouette parsed and dismissed with the speed of a survival reflex. When he did appear, just past ten, it was with the half-sheepish, half-smug air of one who knows he will be forgiven his tardiness. His hair was still damp from the shower, curling at the nape in a way that seemed deliberately careless, his shirt untucked and sleeves rolled to the elbow. He moved through the room with a sort of magnetic disruption: people pivoted to greet him, conversations realigned. I watched all this with a mixture of pride and unease, the latter more familiar and therefore, perversely, more comforting.

He caught my eye from across the room, lifted his chin in a gesture that could be construed as both greeting and challenge, then promptly allowed himself to be subsumed by the rugby scrum of kitchen staff. I sipped my drink and retreated further into the shadow of a curtain, content to observe. To want something was to risk having it taken away, and so I had mastered the art of wanting obliquely, by proxy.

Eventually, the crowd's centre of gravity shifted and I found myself standing adjacent to William, who had managed to acquire both a pint of bitter and the beginnings of a black eye, courtesy of an overzealous headbutt from one of the sous-chefs. He wore it with a rakish pride.

I looked down, tracing the rim of my glass with a thumb. "Are you having fun?"

He considered. "I am, actually. More than I thought I would." He paused, studying my face as if trying to decipher a code written in invisible ink. "Are you?"

I hesitated, unsure whether to betray the relief I felt at his presence, or the mounting dread of the imminent future, when the summer would end and I would be—again—alone in the city, living out a rehearsed version of myself. "Not sure yet," I said. "Ask me again in an hour."

He nodded, as if this was the answer he had expected. "Let's get some air," he suggested. "It's getting a bit warm in here."

Outside, the humidity had the quality of unwashed linen, heavy and faintly sour. The terrace was deserted except for a pair of smokers, their faces illuminated intermittently by the glow of their cigarettes. We walked a short distance, past the statuary and the water-logged urns, and settled on the low wall overlooking the gardens. The moon was high but veiled, and the world below seemed vague, as if rendered in watercolours.

For a while we sat in silence, our shoulders not quite touching. I sensed William building toward something, a pressure in the way he tapped his foot against the gravel, the way he exhaled sharply as though steeling himself against the next line.

Finally, he said, "You've been somewhere else all night."

I shrugged. "You know me. I like to keep a foot in the door of escape."

He laughed, but quietly. "You ever think about not escaping?"

I didn't answer right away. I thought about all the times I had left places before they could leave me—schools, teams, friendships that had grown a size too big for comfort. "Sometimes it seems easier to keep moving," I said. "If you don't stop, you don't have to admit you've arrived."

He was silent, digesting this, then: "But do you want to leave here?"

"No, of course not, and for the first time perhaps," I paused, "but I have to complete university."

I looked at him then, really looked, and for the first time felt something akin to safety in the way he held my gaze. "I know," he said, though the words came out sounding more like hope than fear. "What would you say to trying the long-distance thing? I mean, we'll share very similar and long holidays, won't we? Makes sense."

It was a practical argument, and for that I was grateful. I did not trust declarations, nor did I wish to make any tonight, under the influence of borrowed time and Sarah's Prosecco. But I understood what he was offering: increments, not promises. The idea of a future not as a leap but as a series of steps, tentative but cumulative.

"I'd like that," I said, feeling the relief pool in my chest. "I'd like that a lot." My eyes began to sting with unshed tears, and we sat there, the two of us, and the air seemed a fraction lighter. The party raged on behind the walls, the music and laughter rolling out in intermittent waves, but it was as though we occupied an eddy outside of time. I found myself no longer afraid to lean, just slightly, into the possibility of happiness.

Eventually, William stood, brushing dust from his jeans. "If we don't get back inside, they'll send out a search party."

"They'll manage," I said, and we walked in together, two points of a new constellation.

The rest of the night passed in a succession of rooms, each one hazier and more affectionate than the last. Sarah found us and insisted on a round of toasts; the kitchen staff demanded a group photo, arms thrown around necks in a facsimile of family. At one point I caught sight of myself in a mirror—hair mussed, cheeks flushed—and did not immediately recognize the person looking back. It was not a bad feeling.

As the clock inched toward morning and the guests began to trickle away, I found myself once again at the edge of the dance floor, William at my side, his arm slung casual and confident around my shoulders. We swayed slightly, not to the music, but to the rhythm of something larger, the collective exhale of a summer spent in each other's orbit.

When the lights were finally raised, Sarah made the ceremonial pronouncement that the party was over, but there was a reluctance to disperse, as if leaving would mean admitting that what had happened here was not permanent, that the world outside the Hall would not recognize the particular alchemy of this night.

William leaned in, voice pitched just for me: "Come back to mine?"

There was no hesitation. "Yes," I said. "God, yes."

We slipped out through the service entrance, the sound of laughter and clinking glasses fading behind us. The walk to the old stable block was silent, but the space between our hands was full of promise.

The way over to William's flat was an assault on the senses: the odour of ancient hay mingled with the petroleum ghost of farm machinery, the passageway echoing with a mosaic of footfalls from decades of stable boys and staff, each one leaving a trace. The steps themselves were worn into hollows, the banister sticky with generations of varnish and the invisible imprint of hands. It was nothing like the sterile corridors of the Hall proper, and for that, I found it immediately comforting.

The landing was illuminated only by the spill of moonlight through a half-open skylight, and the air in the stairwell vibrated faintly with the hum of insects drawn to the warmth of summer masonry. William's door was a battered composite of paint and memory, splintered at the bottom where some long-dead terrier had scratched for entry. He fished for his keys, dropped them once, then laughed as he retrieved them, the sound a release valve for the pressure that had been building since we left the party.

"Sorry," he said, pushing the door open. "It's a bit untidy; it's been a busy day."

William closed the door and flicked on a lamp, flooding the room with a low, amber warmth. For a moment, we stood in the hush of arrival, each waiting for the other to claim the first move.

It was William who did, surprising me. He stepped forward, cupped my jaw in his broad, work-rough hand, and kissed me. Not tentative or chaste, but with a fullness that said: this is what I want, and if you don't, then stop me now. I did not want him to stop, and so I kissed back, harder than I had intended, the shock of teeth a reminder that neither of us was entirely sure what came next.

We stumbled together toward the bed, pulling at buttons and belt-loops, both of us clumsy and urgent. My shirt caught on my elbow and for a moment we laughed, then William's hands were under the hem, warm against my skin, and the laughter bled into something else entirely. The taste of him—residual hops from the beer, an undertone of summer sweat, the mineral tang of salt—was somehow more intoxicating than anything I'd drunk at the party. My own pulse hammered so violently that I was certain he could feel it in my neck, my wrists, the hollow of my back where his hand settled as he pressed me to the mattress.

We unspooled each other piece by piece, every layer discarded an act of trust. When at last we lay in only our underwear, William paused. His chest rose and fell in shallow, rhythmic waves, and I sensed the momentary backpedal of nerves, the old animal fear of being seen and found wanting.

He looked at me, eyes serious now, and said, "I've never done this before. Not with a bloke, I mean. Only a few girls at college."

My own surprise must have registered, because he added, "Is that a deal-breaker?"

"Not at all," I said, and smiled, reaching up to trace the outline of his angular nose with the pad of my thumb. "Just do to me what I do to you."

He considered this, then: "Is it that simple?"

I grinned. "It is tonight."

We fell together again, our bodies negotiating the boundaries as we went. William's hands were heavy but careful, learning the contours of my ribs, the curve of my spine, the soft inside of my thigh. His mouth mapped me in small, reverent increments, and I returned the favour, marking a trail from collarbone to navel with lips and tongue. The world shrank to the span of the mattress and the heat between us.

At some point, my head slid under the sheet and I worked my way down, kissing every exposed inch with a kind of greedy reverence. William gasped and fumbled for my hand, squeezing it until our knuckles ground together, but he didn't protest. Instead, he let out a laugh—surprised, delighted—and then quieted, his whole-body arching toward me in an offering.

When it was over we lay side by side, both of us panting, neither sure what to do with our hands. The aftershocks were less physical than psychic—a sense of having crossed a border, the land behind us already receding. I rolled onto my back, stared up at the plaster ceiling, and listened to the synchrony of our breathing. William's fingers crept over and hooked into mine, lacing them tight.

"That was…" he began, then trailed off, searching for a word.

"Unrepeatable?" I offered.

He grinned. "No. Definitely worth repeating."

We lay there for a while, not speaking, letting the warmth settle over us like a blanket. Eventually, I propped myself up on one elbow and looked at him—really looked, taking in the mess of his hair, the flush on his cheeks, the childlike way he grinned when he caught me staring.

"I don't want to go back," I said. "Not ever."

"Don't, then," he replied. "Stay. I mean, if you want."

I did want. More than I had admitted to myself in all the days and nights leading to this one.

We slid under the covers, pulling them up to our chins despite the summer heat. William reached behind him, fumbled for the switch, and plunged the room into darkness. There, in the pitch black, I found his hand again, and we fell asleep like that—tangled, uncertain, but content.

It was the first time I had ever woken beside someone and not felt the urge to flee. Dawn arrived slyly, bleaching the ceiling in William's flat from blue-black to the colon of wet newsprint. I surfaced into consciousness with the lazy confusion of the newly contented, aware at first only of heat and weight and the faint, sour trace of sweat and last night's wine. For a moment, I lay perfectly still, the world stripped to the gentle ache of my own limbs and the unaccustomed comfort of another body pressed so close to mine. William was still asleep, one arm curled possessively across my stomach, his breath warm and even against my collarbone. His hair fanned out across the pillow, a copper blur in the soft light, and I was struck by the sheer ordinariness of it—the way, in sleep, he surrendered every defence and became just another sleeping boy.

I glanced at the small clock next to the bed and noted that is was just before six am, so I watched him for a long while, my thoughts looping not with anxiety, but with something like awe. This, I realized, was the thing I had been searching for: not the collision of bodies in the dark, but the gentle rightness of waking beside someone and knowing they wanted you to stay.

Eventually, William stirred, mouth twitching into a half-smile even before his eyes opened. "Are you staring at me?" he mumbled, voice hoarse with sleep.

"Maybe," I said. "You snore like a bear."

He snorted, rolled onto his back, and stretched luxuriously, every muscle articulating its own miniature drama. The sheets slipped down, baring a geography of his skin and constellations of freckles. I wanted to map them with my tongue, but for the moment I was content just to look.

William turned his head, blinking in the new light. "You all right?"

I nodded, then surprised myself by leaning in and kissing him, slow and deliberate. When I pulled back, he looked at me with something close to astonishment.

"Thank you," I said.

He frowned, brow furrowing. "For what?"

I hesitated, suddenly aware of how vulnerable the confession might make me. "That was my first time," I said, letting the words fall with all their weight.

He stared at me, searching for the punchline. "No, it wasn't," he said, kindly. "I mean, you knew what you were doing."

I laughed, embarrassed. "I've done things before. But never this. Never all night. Never… waking up with someone. That was new."

Comprehension dawned, his face softening. "What about Mark?" he asked, the name floating between us like a discarded receipt.

I shrugged. "He was always careful. Afraid someone might find out. We'd finish and then he'd send me back to my own bed, or tell me to leave. Just in case. It was never…" I gestured at the bed, at the sunlight and our bodies tangled together. "It was never this."

He reached for my hand and laced his fingers through mine. "Is it better?"

"Fuck yes," I said, and in a fit of spontaneity rolled on top of him, pinning his arms above his head. He grinned, then bucked me off and twisted so that we landed side by side, laughing like idiots. We kissed until the stubble on his jaw chafed my face raw, until my thighs ached from squeezing his hips, until the taste of him filled my mouth like an antidote to every bad morning-after I had ever known.

Afterward, we lay in a heap, the sheets kicked to the foot of the bed, both of us sweating and panting and not at all inclined to move. But eventually, necessity prevailed. William was the first to rise, stretching, scratching, and padding naked across the cold floorboards to put the kettle on. He stood at the window, water boiling, watching the day bloom over the gardens, and I joined him, arms wrapped around his waist from behind.

The intimacy of it—coffee made together, the casualness of skin against skin, the smell of him in the muggy air—was more disarming than any act of sex. We sat at the tiny table, knees touching, and ate toast with the butter straight from the knife, talking about nothing and everything. I told him about my mother's impossible expectations, about the pressure to be exceptional and the terror of letting anyone down. He told me about his childhood on the estate, about the way he'd always felt more at home in the stables than the house, about the time he'd broken his arm trying to impress a boy two years older and smarter than himself.

We talked, and with each story, each confession, the space between us shrank a little more. By the time I got dressed to leave after our shared shower, my nerves had transformed—not into confidence, but into a readiness I'd never possessed before.

At the door, William pressed a kiss to my forehead, then my mouth. "Don't be a stranger," he said. "I'll see you before you leave?"

"Of course," I said, and meant it.

The walk back across the stable yard was different in daylight—no longer a journey into the unknown, but a pilgrimage from one kind of home to another. The sun glared off the limestone facade of the Hall, dazzling and indifferent, but I no longer felt invisible beneath it. I let myself in through the service entrance, slipped past the early-rising caretakers, and climbed the stairs to my attic room, my body humming with the memory of the night.

There were bags to pack, tasks to complete, goodbyes to say. But none of it seemed quite so daunting anymore.

Some mornings, it is enough to wake up beside someone and know that, for once, you are exactly where you are meant to be.

CHAPTER 13: THE MORNING AFTER

The attic room was the highest and therefore the coolest in Langley Hall, and at seven am —it seemed entirely plausible that I was the last person alive in the house. All was quiet in the dorms and I decide to take thirty minutes on my bed before tackling the rest of the day. I lay propped on one elbow, watching the ceiling gradually extrude itself from darkness. The events of the previous night played in my head with the clarity and lack of logic of a silent film: William's laugh, the pressure of his hand on my hip, the shock of sunlight on his skin as morning breached the dormer window. It would be an exaggeration to say I was happy, but for the first time in months—possibly ever—I did not greet the start of the day with the usual rush of dread. Instead, it was an odd, insubstantial hollowness that filled my chest: not relief, exactly, but an absence where anxiety might have lodged itself.

Eventually, there were practicalities to be observed, and I went about them with the automaton's precision of someone rehearsing for their own departure. I showered in the common washroom at the end of the hall, my feet numb against the cracked tiles, and returned to my room wrapped in a towel and a sense of unreality. My suitcase, bought second-hand at the start of the summer and already shedding its threadbare lining, lay open on the bed, half-packed. Shirts and my few companion books, waited to be interred for the journey home. I folded things as quietly as I could, though the house had begun to stir.

Packing was a task I had always found curiously comforting, its logic immutable: the more you folded, the less you owned, and the nearer you came to a kind of weightless freedom. Today, though, my hands betrayed me. The left trembled so that I had to grip objects with both, and even then, a persistent flutter ran up my forearms into the hollow above my sternum, where it lodged like an electric insect. I tried to ignore it, to think only of the day's requirements—getting to Norwich and picking up my train north.

Below me, the soundscape of the house intensified: the clang of plates in the servery, the shriek of a vacuum, the shouts of children already released from supervision. It was a world that had no further claim on me, and yet I could not summon the will to stand.

The telephone was at the end of the ground floor hall, bolted to the wall in a kind of alcove just outside the linen room, as if to minimize both its presence and the possibility of eavesdroppers. I hesitated only a second before picking up the receiver, the familiar coiled cord brushing against my wrist, then dialled the number by muscle memory. Each rotary click felt both prehistoric and irreversible.

Mark answered on the third ring, his voice instantly recognizable and so practiced in its affability that I felt a pang of almost-love for the man I was about to discard. "You're up early," he said, and I could hear the thin patina of accusation beneath the greeting. "I thought you'd call last night."

"There's something I need to say," I interrupted, voice steadier than I had anticipated.

A pause. "What's happened?"

I listened to my own breathing for a moment, heard the way it trembled through the receiver. "I can't do this anymore. Not the way we have."

Another pause, longer. I imagined Mark, sitting in his threadbare armchair, pinching the bridge of his nose, already recalibrating his story for the next person who mattered to him. "Is this a joke?"

"No," I said, and surprised myself by not apologizing.

"You're being ridiculous. You're not thinking straight. Just come back and we'll—"

"I won't be back," I said, and this time it was almost easy. "I'm sorry, Mark. That's all there is to it."

He laughed, a brittle sound with no actual humour in it. "You can't just quit. Not like this."

"I just did."

The silence on his end was so complete that I imagined the line had died, but then I heard the familiar, ugly click of him slamming the receiver down.

I replaced the handset in its cradle, then stood there, blinking at nothing, for what could have been ten seconds or ten minutes. My hands, still white with pressure, unclenched themselves one finger at a time. I expected relief, or guilt, or the overwhelming urge to take it all back. Instead I felt only a thin, glacial clarity: the air around me seemed charged, as if I had stepped outside after a thunderstorm. Even the corridor's habitual funk of boiled cabbage and beeswax polish was muted, repulsed by the magnitude of what I had just done.

I returned to my room on legs that no longer shook. The suitcase accepted its final, haphazard contents. I zipped it shut, put on my coat, and surveyed the scene for anything I might regret leaving behind.

The house was fully awake now, the hallways perfumed with burnt toast and the floral air freshener that the cleaning staff deployed in defence against the boarding students. I made for the nearest exit, suitcase trailing behind like a recalcitrant pet, and stepped out into the late-summer chill. The shock of the cool air was bracing, almost medicinal; the world had the bruised, overexposed quality of a watercolour still in progress. I inhaled until my lungs ached, then set off across the sward toward the stables.

The path, still slick from the dew, glistened and the iridescent wreckage of fallen leaves. My shoes squelched, soaking through in the first ten paces, but I did not slow. My feet knew where to go, had been rehearsing this flight for weeks. The closer I got, the faster I moved, as if the inertia of the past three years could only be cancelled out by sheer velocity. I drop off my case and coat in the staffroom before venturing out to find William.

By the time I reached the stable yard, my pulse was a drumbeat in my temples, and I had to brace myself against the old stone wall to keep from collapsing altogether. William was there already, in the half-light of one of the old barns, working with an efficiency that belied the hour. He was silhouetted against the open doors, his body haloed by the dust and chaff that caught the morning sun. For a moment I simply watched him, collecting myself, and then, with a force that felt both alien and necessary, I called his name.

He turned; surprise etched in the set of his shoulders. I stepped into the yard, breath coming hard and visible in the cold, and waited for the rest of my life to begin.

For a moment, neither of us moved. The entire world seemed to crystallize around the two figures in the yard: me, hunched and breathless at the threshold; William, standing just inside the stable, a pitchfork slung over his shoulder like a parody of a constable. The day was still new, the sun not yet strong enough to be felt and the air was weighted with the scent of old straw, horses, and the sharp, ammoniac tang that never entirely left the stones.

He wiped his hands on his overalls, squinting at me as if he doubted his own senses. "You're early," he said, voice low and still pitched for private conversation despite the emptiness of the space.

"I've finished my packing," I replied. The words sounded insufficient, but they were true. My chest still vibrated with the aftershocks of the phone call, the tremor of having said—at last—exactly what I meant.

He leaned the pitchfork against the wall, stepped out into the open, and for the first time since I'd known him, seemed at a loss. There was a smudge of dirt on his cheek, and his hair, still unbrushed, caught the early light in coppery spikes. I wanted to touch him, but instead folded my arms over my chest, as though bracing myself against the possibility of rejection.

"I called Mark," I said, and immediately regretted the abruptness. "I mean—I ended it. For good. There's nothing left to go back to."

William stared, his eyes wide with surprise and something else, something dangerously close to hope.

"I couldn't—" My voice caught. I tried again. "I couldn't do it anymore. Not when there's—" I gestured at him, at the Hall behind us, at the dawn, as if the evidence were self-evident. "I want to be here. With you. Even if it's just—" I ran out of air, the old panic threatening to resurface.

He crossed the space between us in three strides, the impact of his boots echoing off the flagstones. For a second I thought he might hit me, or worse, turn away. Instead, he pulled me into a rough, awkward hug, crushing the breath out of me and nearly snapping the suitcase handle between us.

"Don't say 'even if,'" he said, his voice muffled in my hair. "Just say what you want."

"I want you," I said, unable to believe how easily the words fell. "I want this. All of it."

He laughed, a sound so sudden and so bright that it startled the stable cat from its perch. "You're a bloody idiot," he said, but his arms only tightened. "I thought you'd leave and I'd never see you again. I thought—" He trailed off, then released me enough to look at my face, his own uncertain and incredulous.

I nod, understanding at once.

He kissed me then—not with the nervous hunger of the night before, but with a deliberate, anchoring gentleness, as if to remind both of us that this was real and would endure the daylight. When we parted, the world seemed brighter; even the old Hall, with its centuries of secrets and sorrow, looked newly tolerant of the improbable happiness unfolding in its shadow.

We stood like that for a long moment, two figures in the threshold of possibility, watched by the ghosts of all who had come before. The day stretched ahead, unclaimed and immense, and for once I did not shrink from its promise.

I reached for his hand, and he let me take it, our fingers tangling together in the chill. There would be difficulties—of course there would—but for now, the only thing that mattered was the fact of us, rooted in the hard ground of the yard, beginning again with the simplest act of holding on.

CHAPTER 14: THE LONG-DISTANCE THING

The flat was less a residence than an essay in compromise, a thesis statement on the economics of solitude. Its ceiling sloped like the inside of a ship's hull, the walls still tacky with magnolia emulsion that had failed, despite best efforts, to mask the substratum of mildew and student squalor. The corridor from the stairwell narrowed at the threshold, funnelling the hum of city traffic and the drone of radios into a noise signature not unlike the persistent tinnitus of my own anxiety. The letting agent had described it as *'cosy'*, and if by cosy he meant a two-roomed cell above a kebab shop, then the description was, for once, accurate. I found myself unaccountably grateful for its honesty.

The process of moving in had not so much been a transition as a dispersal, my possessions, boxed and labelled and then relabelled when the first taxonomy proved insufficient, now sat in uneasy congress along the skirting boards. Each object seemed a rebuke or a relic: the cricket bat, dented from a long-ago season and still faintly resinous, propped in the corner as if it might at any moment be called upon for service; the clutch of history books, their margins annotated with a neurosis bordering on mania, arranged alphabetically by author and then again by year of publication, as if by imposing order I might summon a fragment of the old self I was supposed to inhabit.

A single poster, Langley Hall in early summer, its facade caught in impossible sunlight, hung above the desk, creased at the edges from its migration north, the thumbtacks bleeding tiny brown constellations into the paper.

Unpacking was less an act of settling than of curating an exhibit. I performed the work methodically, laying each item in its designated place, as though the objects themselves possessed agency and might protest improper arrangement. The framed photo of Will and me, snapped by Sarah on the last night at Langley, took pride of place on the shelf nearest the window. In it, we stood side by side on the Hall's terrace, sleeves rolled to the elbow, expressions uncertain but, in retrospect, unmistakably linked. It was the kind of image that could easily be misread as platonic, and perhaps that was the point: plausible deniability in glass and matting.

I placed the photo and stood back, surveying the tableau with a curator's detachment. The room did not become home, but it did, gradually, become mine.

The air, heavy with the residue of emulsion and second-hand curries, was sharp enough to sting the nose. I opened the window to the city's eastward aspect, letting in a draft tinged with petrol, wet brick, and the faintest hint of bakery from the row of shops across the way. The city did not so much wake as shift restlessly under its own weight. Sirens receded and approached in patterns as complex as birdcalls; from a lower floor, a woman's laughter arced up the stairwell, reckless and unselfconscious, punctuated by the slam of a door.

I sat at the desk, the only surface in the flat unadorned by the clutter of necessity, and attempted to grade a set of history essays for Monday. The words swam before my eyes, the students' handwriting alternately spidery and blockish, as though each sought to camouflage the uncertainty of their arguments with the bravado of their script. I found myself rewriting the same sentence over and over: "Your essay is promising but lacks evidentiary support." It felt too near the bone.

I abandoned the essays and instead busied myself with arranging the kitchen, such as it was. The fridge's interior was arctic and unwelcoming, its shelves bare save for a single bottle of supermarket wine and the stub of an unlabelled cheese. I set the wine on the counter and retrieved the glasses, thin enough to betray a lack of confidence in their own existence, from the back of the cupboard. The flat's previous occupant had left behind a mug emblazoned with the phrase *'Keep Calm and Carry On'*. I considered smashing it for emphasis, but instead exiled it to the shelf behind the sink, where it could serve as a cautionary emblem.

I make myself a coffee and settle back to my desk. I had received a letter from Sarah the day before, and I decide to pen a reply, so I could finally tell her about the developments with William. I reckon that the written word was a safer means of communicating my emotions as I could cross out and start again if I got it wrong, or if I gave away too much. Foremost in my mind at this time, was the long-planned first visit of William during the Autumn half-term break.

The anticipation of Will's imminent arrival pressed at the edges of my awareness, manifesting in a series of compulsive, pointless rearrangements: the straightening of the doormat, the wiping of already clean surfaces, the alignment of cutlery in the drawer. I checked my watch at seven-minute intervals, each time startled by the lateness of the hour and the corresponding quickening of my pulse. I debated whether to change my shirt, then decided that any attempt at sartorial effort would be met with mockery, gentle or otherwise.

At ten minutes past eight, a knock at the door, two sharp raps, then a third, tentative, as if seeking confirmation of its own existence. I waited a full count of three before opening it, willing my hands to be steady.

Will stood in the corridor, damp from the evening's drizzle, his hair plastered to his forehead in a way that would have seemed tragic on anyone else. He wore a jumper with the logo of some defunct football club, the fabric pilled and stretched at the cuffs, and carried in one hand a plastic bag bulging with groceries. His smile, when he saw me, was both wary and familiar, a private joke revived after a long dormancy.

"You made it," I said, and immediately regretted the banality.

"Course I did," he replied, "you think I'd miss a chance at free food and questionable wine?"

He stepped inside, shaking off the weather with the practiced indifference of a farm animal, and surveyed the flat with an appraising eye. "Not bad," he said, "bigger than I thought. Less blood on the walls, too." He set the bag on the counter, began unloading its contents: bread, cheese, a clutch of tomatoes still dusted with soil, a pair of bananas so green they looked manufactured. Then he stepped forward and took me in his arms, pulling me close for a full kiss.

"You brought provisions," I stutter, in shock from the warmth and intensity of his greeting..

"Didn't fancy starving to death in the name of romance," he replied, then flashed the grin again, wider this time, "speaking of which, where's your wine?"

I poured the wine, "bloody hell John, you can't afford this!" William notices that had bought my first ever bottle of posh wine.

"Standards Will, standards," I reply. My hands are only slightly unsteady, and we stood in the narrow galley of the kitchen, glasses raised but not quite touching, as if wary of the symbolic weight of the toast. The wine was sharp and dry, as I remembered from the summer, but the first sip chased away the lingering taste of paint and set my nerves alight.

We sat on the floor, using a cardboard box as an impromptu table, and ate the bread and cheese with our fingers. The conversation, at first, was all indirection: stories from the school, gossip about mutual acquaintances, a dissection of the relative merits of Manchester's public transport. We spoke of Langley only obliquely, in fragments and asides, as though to name it outright would risk puncturing the fragile surface of the present.

At one point, Will picked up the photo from the shelf and held it at arm's length, squinting through the glass, "we look like idiots," he said, but his voice was soft, almost reverent. He set it back with a care that belied the words.

"I miss it," I said, surprising even myself with the confession. "Not the place, really. The time."

He nodded, not looking at me, "yeah. Me too."

The rest of the evening was a gradual loosening, the conversation unspooling in ever longer stretches, punctuated only by the chime of the city's clocks and the thrum of traffic below. At some point, Will moved closer, so that our shoulders touched, and the contact was so casual, so natural, that it felt like a memory rather than a novelty.

When the wine was gone and the light from the street had thinned to a pale suggestion, Will yawned theatrically and stretched out on the floor, arms folded behind his head. "I could get used to this," he said, though whether he meant the flat, the city, or the fact of us, I could not say.

I lay beside him, our bodies aligned in the narrow corridor between the desk and the kitchen counter, and let the quiet settle around us. The sense of possibility, so easily extinguished in daylight, flickered to life in the hush of shared exhaustion.

In the stillness, I heard the city breathe: the siren's wail, the laughter from a distant party, the relentless churn of engines and ambition. I reached for Will's hand and, after a moment's hesitation, found it waiting, fingers interlaced with mine.

It was not home, not yet. But it was enough.

Morning arrived in the form of a tremulous grey light; the city's pallor filtered through curtains the colour of old bone. The flat, in this refracted dawn, was unrecognisable: its cheapness dignified, its squalor softened to a kind of noble imperfection. I surfaced from sleep not to the siren or the alarm but to the steady, reassuring rhythm of Will's breathing from the mattress beside me. He slept like the dead, one arm resting on my chest, the other curled around the topmost pillow as if subduing it by force of will.

I watched him for a long while, uncertain if it was permissible to stare at another person with this degree of intent. In the new light, the angularity of his face was almost architectural, sharp planes and unexpected hollows, a geometry rendered gentle only in repose. I catalogued every detail with the same obsessive precision I once reserved for the study of classical ruins: the stray curl at the base of his neck, the faint, silvery scar along the jaw (a childhood incident involving a potato peeler, according to previous confidences), the sun-bleached hairs on his forearms that glowed even in the absence of actual sun.

He blinked awake, looked up and caught my gaze, and grinned without preamble, "been awake long?"

"About a hundred years," I said.

He propped himself up on one elbow, surveyed the room as though its configuration might have shifted in the night, then sniffed the air with theatrical suspicion, "is that coffee?"

I had set the percolator on a timer, a small act of optimism from the day before and the aroma, though faint, managed to assert itself over the ambient smells of plaster and street. Will extracted himself from the heap of bedding, padded naked into the kitchen, and returned with two mugs and a triumphant expression.

"Milk?" he asked.

I shook my head, and he handed over the mug, fingers grazing mine. The touch, still novel, sent a minute shiver up my arm, "you're not going to get sentimental on me, are you?" he said, voice half-mocking.

"Depends how strong the coffee is, and how long it takes you to get back into bed."

He settled back beside me, both of us half-swaddled in the reconstituted duvet, and for a while we drank in silence, watching the morning assemble itself from the disparate sounds of the city: the whine of a delivery truck, the rattle of bins, the distant, syncopated

clatter of the tram. There was, in the quiet, an ease I had never
anticipated. The silence was not emptiness but ballast; it an-
chored rather than exposed.

Breakfast was a production. Will, in shorts now at least,
whose culinary credentials extended only so far as having once
not burnt an omelette, insisted on doing the cooking, which en-
tailed a great deal of banging pans and muttered curses as he
navigated my ill-equipped kitchen. I stood at the counter, simi-
larly attired, peeling fruit and assembling toast with a diligence
that masked my pleasure in the routine. At one point, we
reached for the same pan, and his hand closed over mine; neither of us withdrew immediately, and the moment stretched,
elastic, before he released it with a huff of laughter.

"You're hopeless," I said, though my own voice was
unsteady.

"Yeah, but you like me anyway," he replied, triumphant,
and resumed his assault on the eggs.

We ate at the desk, which now doubled as a dining table, knees knocking together beneath the surface. The food
was, by any standard, abysmal, but neither of us mentioned it.
Instead, we constructed elaborate plans for the day: a visit to
the museum, a walk through the new *'Gay Village'*, a tour of the
city's more improbable landmarks.

Will listened to my itinerary with the forbearance of a
man accustomed to digressions, only occasionally inserting a
sardonic "uh-huh" or "if you say so." It struck me, not for the
first time, how easily we had lapsed into a pattern, not quite do-
mesticity, but the rehearsal of it, the test drive before commit-
ment. On a very superficial level, I enjoyed the comfort of
simply sitting, eating and talking with another man in our underwear, as if it was the most natural thing in the world.

Outside, the city was slick with the residue of last
night's rain, the pavements a patchwork of puddles and discarded fast food. We navigated the streets with the casual urgency of locals, neither hurrying nor dawdling, our conversation drifting from the trivial to the confessional and back again.
Will had an inexhaustible supply of stories: the time he and a
mate had been trapped in a lift with a crate of onions; the year
his mother had adopted a succession of rescue rabbits, each

more neurotic than the last; the day he'd biked the length of the *Chet* in one go, stopping only when he crashed into the river and ruined his best trainers. I listened, and in listening, felt a kind of healing take place, old wounds sutured by the steady application of narrative.

I told him a few stories about my struggles with my workload and finally about my letter to Sarah telling her about us.

"You don't mind do you?" I asked, realising that Mark would have seen telling such a thing to be the ultimate betrayal. He must have seen the momentary look of panic in my eyes.

"Of course not, she was a good friend to both of us," he smiles warmly. "Maybe one time she could come up and share a weekend with us?"

I nod enthusiastically, "yes, that would be nice."

At the museum, I led the way with all the zeal of a born pedant, stopping at every placard, reading aloud the more egregious errors and correcting them for Will's benefit. He affected boredom but, every so often, asked a question that revealed he'd been paying attention all along. In the reconstruction of a Victorian street, he found a battered school desk and insisted I pose for a photo, "for posterity," though I suspected he meant something closer to, *'for blackmail'*. When I balked, he sat in the desk himself, folded his hands atop the faux-ink blotter, and assumed the expression of a boy who knew he'd be first against the wall come the revolution.

The day passed in increments: a shared pastry in a cafe crowded with students; a detour through the market in the *Arndale* centre, where we sampled cheese with toothpicks and debated the ethics of gentrification; a slow loop around the university's gothic quadrangle, its stones blackened by decades of Manchester rain. Will bought a bunch of flowers from a vendor with hands so arthritic she could barely make change, and handed them to me without a word. I took them, awkwardly, and for a moment we stood in the middle of the quad, neither quite able to meet the other's eye.

"Don't get used to it," he said, eventually, "I'm not made of money."

"Noted," I replied, but kept the flowers anyway. No one had ever bought *me* flowers before.

By late afternoon, the city's tempo had increased to a low, persistent throb. We walked back to the flat, groceries in hand, the bag straining at the handles from the weight of bread and tomatoes and a

cake Will had insisted on buying, "for dessert, or emergencies."
The building's stairwell was redolent with damp and the warm,
yeasty breath of the kebab shop below. At the landing, Will
paused, then reached out and smoothed a stray petal from the
top of the bouquet.

"You look knackered," he said, though his own face
was flushed and bright.

"I am," I admitted, "but in a good way."

Inside, the flat was warmer, suffused with the residual
heat of the day. We set the groceries on the counter and, without planning it, began to assemble the makings of a meal. There
was no choreography, only the instinctive give-and-take of people who have grown used to sharing a small space. I rinsed the
tomatoes; Will sliced bread with the focus of a man engaged in
surgery; we moved around each other with the ease of magnets
in a defined field.

As the meal took shape, I felt a shift in the atmosphere:
a relaxation, a giving-over. The kitchen's clutter, the hum of the
fridge, the scent of cut herbs, all coalesced into a sense of belonging that was as physical as it was emotional. I caught Will
watching me, once, and the look in his eyes, fond, amused, unguarded, stopped me mid-motion.

"What?" I said, too quickly.

He shrugged, mouth twisting into a half-smile. "Nothing. Just, didn't think I'd ever do this, you know?"

"Cook?"

He snorted, "no. This." He gestured at the flat, at me,
at the absurd little tableau we'd created, "thought I'd just…
drift. Like my old man. Didn't think I'd ever be someone's…"
He trailed off, embarrassed.

I set the knife down, turned to face him, "you are, *someone's*, if you'll let me be that person," I said, and let the words
hang.

He looked at me, searching for sarcasm or evasion, and
when he found none, nodded, "yeah," he said. "I want you to
be that *someone*."

We finished preparing the meal in silence, but it was a
companionable silence, stitched with small glances and the
brush of shoulders. At the table, still the desk, still our knees

touching beneath, I raised my glass to him, "to not drifting," I said.

He raised his own, "to anchoring, and having *someone*," he replied.

We ate, and as the city darkened beyond the window, I realised that I could no longer remember what it felt like to be alone. Night in Manchester descended not as a curtain but as a slow, greasy accretion, layer upon layer of sodium vapour, exhaust haze, and the migraine pulse of a thousand traffic lights. The city was no less alive for its darkness; if anything, it seemed to lean into the neon and the thrumming bodies, to insist on a collective energy that daylight only ever managed to dilute. The newness of it, the sheer electric possibility, had not yet worn off for me, but tonight's plan, Will's plan, required a different species of courage than my usual fortitude.

"Promise me you won't do that thing where you overthink until you potentially ruin everything," Will said, sprawled on the mattress and digging through his rucksack for a clean shirt. He had the infuriating ability to look effortlessly composed even in a state of total disarray, while I, having spent the last hour toggling between options in the wardrobe, was beginning to resemble a child's drawing of a teacher, all pressed collar and anxious elbows.

"I make no such promises," I replied, which earned a soft, derisive snort.

He changed shirts without fanfare, eschewing the mirror entirely, and then studied me with a gaze so direct it was briefly destabilising, "you look good. Like you belong here."

I doubted it, but said nothing. The prospect of the gay bar—a phrase I still could not say aloud without imagining my mother's face—had induced a kind of low-grade panic since its casual introduction over breakfast. Even after two months in the city, I had not ventured into that territory, content instead to watch from a theoretical remove: the sociologist's perch, the historian's lens. It was one thing to have a boyfriend; it was quite another to occupy a space dedicated to the celebration (and, I feared, the exhibition) of that difference. I worried about being recognised, outed, judged, or, perhaps worse, simply ignored.

We set out at half past nine, when the city had begun to shimmer with Friday-night expectation. Will led the way, his pace deliberate, his stride angled for the quickest route rather than the most scenic. I trailed half a step behind, cataloguing the subtle shifts in the street as we moved away from the university's periphery and toward the canal district. There, the bars and clubs nested together like hostile siblings, their windows fogged with condensation and promise. The air was damp, sharpened with the tang of wet stone and spilled cider.

The place itself was almost wilfully unhidden. A neon sign, one of those double entendres that would have mortified me if I'd been alone, buzzed above the door, its letters uneven in their fluorescence. From the street, the bar looked unremarkable: a blank door, a doormat, a patch of wall painted an unconvincing shade of navy.

Inside, however, the scene was instantaneous, a full-frontal assault of strobe and sweat and saturated sound. The lighting was a palette of impossible colours: magentas, acid yellows, blues so dense they approached the *Platonic* ideal of blue. At the threshold, I hesitated, momentarily blinded by the transition, and Will reached back to steer me in with a hand on my shoulder.

The first impression was of bodies, hundreds of them, pressed and jostling and lit from within by the pulse of the DJ booth. Every surface gleamed, every molecule of air charged with the collective exhale of men who had, for one night at least, permission to be entirely themselves. The music was less a sound than a physics problem, a vibration that travelled up through the floorboards and reorganized the nervous system around its beat.

"Not so scary, is it?" Will said, his lips grazing my ear as he leaned in to shout over the noise.

"I'm reserving judgment," I replied, though my voice was lost to the din.

We fought our way to the bar; a fortress of polished steel and liquor bottles illuminated from below like rare specimens. The barman, a preternaturally beautiful man in a mesh tank top and eyeliner, served us with the distracted grace of someone paid to be ogled. Will ordered a pint and, after a moment's hesitation, I ordered the same, eschewing the cocktail menu with its intimidating taxonomy of names and modifiers.

We stood, drinks in hand, and observed. To my surprise, the crowd did not feel predatory or even particularly sexualized; it was, rather, the exact inversion of every school disco I'd ever survived, a place where the self-consciousness was not erased but inverted, performed as a form of collective armour. Here, no one looked twice at us. No one cared if our hands touched as we leaned in to hear each other. The absence of scrutiny was at first terrifying, then liberating.

Will sipped his pint, surveying the room with the unhurried appraisal of a man who had nothing to prove. "So," he said, "do you approve?"

I tried to calibrate my response, torn between the instinct to minimize and the urge to confess, "it's a lot," I said. "But… I think I get it."

He nodded, satisfied, "you can always leave. But you should see the dance floor first. Am sure it will be the best part."

The idea of dancing was preposterous, I had not danced in public since the compulsory sixth-form Christmas party, and even then only under duress, but I allowed myself to be led into the roiling mass of bodies. There, the sound became absolute, a force that compressed time and space to the dimensions of movement and breath. It was impossible to think, or to worry; there was only the heat, the friction, the synchronised chaos of bodies in motion.

Will, contrary to expectation, was a dreadful dancer, enthusiastic, but entirely unschooled. He bounced in place, hands raised, his face open and unconcerned with the possibility of ridicule. I matched him, at first self-consciously, then with a growing sense of abandon. In that moment, the shame and anxiety that had tracked me for years sloughed off, replaced by something lighter and more resilient.

We danced until we were out of breath, until the sweat ran in rivulets down my back and my shirt clung to my skin. When we retreated to the bar for water, I caught my reflection in the mirror behind the shelves: hair plastered to my forehead, cheeks flushed, eyes bright and unguarded. For the first time, I looked at myself and saw someone not haunted by what he lacked.

We watched the room together, drinking water and catching our breath. The crowd was a mosaic of types, young and old, polished and rumpled, alone and entwined. There were men in drag, men in tailored shirts, men in nothing but shorts and trainers. They moved through each other's orbits with the easy gravity of planets, each radiating his own particular brand of light.

I realised, with a shock of recognition, that I was not afraid. That I was, in fact, happy.

Will must have sensed the change, because he bumped my shoulder and said, "see? It's not so bad. We fit, here."

"We do," I said, and meant it.

As the night wore on, the room thickened with the smell of cologne and sweat and spilled beer, but I hardly noticed. The city outside ceased to exist; there was only this: the heat of Will's arm, the throb of the music, the knowledge that I was, for once, exactly where I wanted to be.

We left the bar just before one, the inside of my skull still thrumming with aftershocks of light and sound. Outside, the city had undergone its nightly inversion: the crowds thinned to pockets of stragglers, laughter unspooled in echoes from closed shopfronts. The air was close, faintly metallic, with an undertone of ozone from the brief but vigorous rain that had swept through while we were dancing. Will flagged a cab, and we rode in companionable silence, the windows beading with condensation as the driver navigated the city's recursive grid.

Back in the flat, the transition to quiet was so abrupt it felt theatrical, as if we'd stepped from the stage into the hush of an empty auditorium. The fridge's intermittent growl was suddenly audible, and the faint tick of the radiators seemed to punctuate the dark. I shed my jacket, dropped it onto the desk, and sat down on the edge of the futon, exhaling in a long, ragged stream.

Will joined me, stretching his legs until his heels nearly touched the opposite wall. For a while we didn't speak, letting the adrenaline decant from our systems in silence. My heart, which had been hammering at a frenetic BPM since we left the bar, began to settle into something like a normal rhythm.

Eventually, Will said, "you survived," with a crooked smile.

"I did," I said, and realised it was true.

He watched me for a moment, then shifted closer, knees angled toward mine. "You're not like them," he said, kindly, "not really."

I shrugged, unsure whether to be flattered or insulted. "I don't know who I'm like," I admitted.

He considered this, then said, "you're like yourself. Which is more than most people manage."

I laughed, the sound softer and less brittle than before, "what about you?"

He grinned, "I'm just happy to be the sidekick."

We talked, then, in the low register reserved for night and confession. We compared notes on the men in the bar, their bravado and vulnerability, the way some of them seemed to wear confidence like a suit that never quite fit. Will told me about his first time in such a place in Norwich, how he'd spent the whole evening pretending to look for someone else, convinced he'd made a mistake, that any minute now someone would call him out as a fraud. I told him how I'd never thought I'd end up in one at all, how I'd always believed that happiness was a thing you only glimpsed in other people's lives, never your own.

"Did you like it?" he asked, voice so low I could barely hear.

I thought about the bar, the lights, the music, the beautiful men and the ordinary ones, the laughter and the brief, improbable moments of connection. I thought about Will's hand on my shoulder, the way it had steadied me, the way it made everything seem possible.

"I liked it," I said. "I liked it a lot."

The words hovered between us, and for once, there was no need to clarify or minimize. Will leaned in, rested his forehead against mine, and closed his eyes. In the half-light from the streetlamp, his face was all shadow and contour, the blue under his eyes deeper than ever, but softer somehow.

We stayed like that, unmoving, for a long minute. Then, gently, I reached for his hand, and he took it, his thumb tracing slow, deliberate circles on the back of mine.

We kissed, there on the edge of the futon, the city's pulse muted and distant. It was not a hungry or desperate kiss, but a careful one, as if both of us were determined not to squander the moment or break whatever fragile thing we'd managed to assemble between us.

After, we sat with our shoulders touching, watching the city lights flicker on the far side of the glass. The world outside kept turning, but in the small, illuminated rectangle of my flat, it was enough just to be still.

The transition from the sanctuary of my flat to the bright, surveillant corridors of the school was always jarring, but never more so than in the weeks and months after Will's first visit. It was as if the city had two entirely separate nervous systems: one that hummed with the animal certainties of desire and belonging, and another, a colder, more spectral network, which registered only the threat of exposure, of being seen in the wrong light. At Langley I'd mastered the art of camouflage, but here, in the relentless fluorescents of the sixth form block, my invisibility felt precarious, provisional. I could feel myself becoming the object of a different kind of gaze.

It began, as these things always do I suppose, in the smallest increments: the overlong glance from an upper sixth student at the end of the corridor, *'had he been one of the faces on the dancefloor in Manchester?'* I asked myself; the laughter from a group of Year 12s, pitch-shifted just loud enough to imply an audience. I heard the girls whispering, *'has he got a girlfriend?'*, and the boys, *'course he hasn't, looks like a puff to me'*. To confront these insinuations would only serve to empower them I thought, so I refused to answer any and all personal questions, but this only seemed to allow them to grow.

The lesson plans, meticulous and densely annotated, provided little cover against the murmured jokes and the sidelong exchanges. Every time I turned from the blackboard to face the class, I was met with a bristling awareness, not overt defiance, but a quality of attention that bordered on predation. Even my own voice, once the instrument of control, began to betray me; it trembled at the margins, as though unsure whether it was permitted to exist in the space it occupied.

On the day it became undeniable, the chalk dust on my fingers was visible proof of my distraction. I had spent the entire morning diagramming causes and consequences of the Great War, writing and erasing and rewriting in an effort to anchor myself in the facts. Behind me, the whispering had achieved a steady, high-frequency whine, like the buzz of an insect just out of reach.

I tried to ignore it, but my hands betrayed me, white-knuckled around the chalk, sweat blooming in my palms. When I turned, the class was a tableau of innocence, every head bowed studiously over their notes except for one, who met my gaze with a look of frank appraisal. He was clever, this one, and beautiful in the way that popular boys are, broad-shouldered, mouth set in a permanent smirk. He did not look away.

The silence that followed was so complete it rang in my ears. I put down the chalk, wiped my hands on my trousers, and tried to recover the lesson, but the momentum was lost. The remainder of the hour unfolded in a haze of rote recitation and performative discipline. When the bell finally sounded, the class filed out with an efficiency that felt rehearsed. The last to leave—the beautiful boy—paused in the doorway just long enough to look back, his expression equal parts curiosity and warning.

In the staff room, the change in atmosphere was subtler but no less potent. Where once I had been tolerated as an eccentric, now I was a cipher, the locus of a dozen conversations conducted in the register of plausible deniability. Colleagues smiled, but with the faintly condescending air of those who have already decided not to intervene. The head of department, a woman with a voice like a staple gun, sat next to me at lunch and asked, too casually, whether everything was "all right at home."

I said yes, of course, but my hands kept folding and unfolding the napkin until it split along the crease. After lunch I retreated to the classroom, the only space in the building where I could close the door and manufacture a sense of privacy. I graded essays with the compulsive intensity of a drowning man, the red pen skating over arguments that seemed suddenly juvenile, arbitrary. Outside, the sky shifted from blue to gunmetal, the light flattening the city into a series of silhouettes. The clock on the wall marked time with a stubborn indifference.

At four, the corridors emptied, leaving only the caretakers and the faint, echoing clang of lockers. I stood at the window and looked out over the city, the buildings rising like teeth from the wet pavements. In the reflection, I saw myself twice over: the external, jacket-and-tie version, and the internal, hunched and spectral, made translucent by the failing light.

The world outside was indifferent, relentless, and infinite. But inside the glass, I was contained, no less real, but visible only to myself. In my mind I consider that I was drawn back to William like a moth to a flame – dancing with the real possibility that if I got too close I would burn and fall. I stood like that for a long time, unsure which version I preferred.

Night in the flat was a different country, one governed by the laws of inertia and the slow gravitational pull of what couldn't be said in daylight. The city outside, which by day felt menacing in its indifference, now seemed to conspire in our favour: the traffic reduced to a distant hush, the only intrusion the mechanical heartbeat of the wall clock and the odd, disembodied shout from the kebab shop's closing hour. The rooms themselves shrank with the darkness, corners folding in, turning the world into a single pool of lamplight around the futon.

Will's visits became my lifeline and the one thing that made the hell, that my job had become, tolerable. After each visit, I performed a mental reset, convincing myself that it was all worthwhile.

During a visit the following Easter, Will was sprawled on his side, propped up by a cushion, the light accentuating the tiredness around his eyes. I sat cross-legged at the foot of the bed, picking at the frayed edge of the blanket, rehearsing in my head the speech I'd been avoiding for months. When at last I spoke, my voice came out brittle and higher than intended.

"I think they know," I said.

He didn't pretend to misunderstand. He nodded, once, and waited for me to go on.

"It's getting worse. The kids, some of the staff. I thought maybe it would just blow over, but…" I trailed off, embarrassed by the incompleteness of my own sentences.

"You want to quit?" Will's tone was even, neutral.

"No. But I don't want to…" I made a vague, helpless gesture. "…be that. The one everyone talks about."

For a long time neither of us spoke. The clock counted out each second with a judicial certainty, the seconds accumulating like evidence.

Finally, Will said, "you could leave. It wouldn't be the end of the world."

The idea was at once both repellent and comforting. I'd spent years constructing an identity out of achievement, discipline, the incremental rewards of conformity. The notion of stepping away, abandoning that careful edifice, was unthinkable, or should have been.

"I've never quit anything," I said.

"That's not always a virtue," Will replied. He reached for my hand, squeezed it gently. "Sometimes staying is just another way of running."

I looked at him, searching his face for irony, but found only exhaustion and a kind of fierce loyalty. He believed in me with a simplicity that bordered on the reckless.

"What would I do?" I asked, not really expecting an answer.

He shrugged. "Teach somewhere else. Write a book. Run away to Spain and open a bar. I don't care, as long as you're not miserable."

I tried to picture myself anywhere but here, anywhere but this tiny, provisional life we'd constructed. The prospect was terrifying, but also, if I let myself admit it, wildly liberating.

"I don't want to go," I said. "But I can't stay if it's going to be like this."

Will nodded, understanding in the way that only people who have had to reinvent themselves can. "We'll figure it out. We always do."

He pulled me down beside him, my head fitting into the hollow of his shoulder as if it had always belonged there. We lay like that, in silence, for a long time. The city's lights flickered on the ceiling, tracing invisible circuits that mapped out possibilities I was only now beginning to imagine.

Eventually, Will fell asleep, his breathing evening out, his grip on my hand slackening but never letting go. I stayed awake, counting the seconds between the ticks of the clock, listening to the world rearrange itself around us.

The future was undecided. But for the first time, the uncertainty felt like something I might survive, at least if I had Will by my side. The very fact that I knew that Will would support me whatever I decided, gave me the strength to decide to wait until the New Year to make any decisions. Therefore, I reverted back to my standard tactic of distraction and diversion, and in a bold gesture I booked Will and I a two-week holiday on the Norfolk Broads. I gave myself something good to look forward to.

When I told Will, he was happy if I was happy, but couldn't help but add, "cancel your booking, my cousin runs the boatyard in Langley, we can get 'family rates'," and that one simple phrase, in that single moment, meant more to me than anything ever. *I was part of Will's family*.

Will had plenty of notice in order to allow him to book his time off in August, and as we set sail from Langley Boatyard we just resolve to make up each day as it came along. Those plans never extended much beyond the next village and pub mooring. We were living a life I had never thought possible for two men, a life I had never thought possible for me.

We laugh together until we cry, at our early attempts to moor the cruiser, or when either of us fall into the water. We swim naked at midnight under the light of the stars and make love on the cabin roof. We also feel raw fear as a thunderstorm catches us as we cross *Oulton Broad,* and pure joy as we sit on deck and watch shooting stars streak the night sky.

For those two weeks, all the worries of my working life back up north just slip away, and I allow myself to become lost in this new life. On our last night, we moor a couple of miles along the *Chet* from Langley Village. We lay on top of the cabin, quietly enjoying a last bottle of posh wine. I lean into Will and lay my head on his shoulder, "thanks, this has been perfect," I whisper. He kisses my forehead.

"For once, I have to one hundred percent agree with you," William replies playfully. I reach up and place my hand on his cheek and gently turn his head to face me.

"I love you William Cooper," I say before kissing his lips. William lets out a long breath and then pulls me close.

"Good to know, as I've loved you since that night in my flat," he replies.

"You never said anything," I say with no criticism implied, and the smile on William's face showed that he did not feel any.

"Well you had stuff going on, Mark and then your work," he leans back in and kisses me, "and I didn't want to complicate things." He let his words settle for a moment, a long moment, as he looked with intent into my eyes, striping me bare. A single tear welled in his eye, "I love you John Williams."

My response is a physical reaction to the emotions I feel – my chest swells and aches, my stomach churns, my breath catches, my hands tremble. I could find no words, even if I had been able to utter them, and ultimately none were needed so I just hold him close and tight in my arms. In those moments, we are just two young men in love, and the world be damned. It feels good and purpose.

I returned to my second year in my job with a sense of regeneration and determination to succeed. I promise Will that I will give it a try at least, and think again in the new year. A new intake of students to my sixth form classes meant that the old rumours , I hope, have been forgotten and this might represent a clean slate. Initially, this seems to be the case until the night that Will and I are back in the bar in the Gay Village during our half terms.

A young guy approaches me on the edge of the dancefloor, "you're Mr Williams from school aren't you?" I am stunned and look quizzically at him. "I'm Steve Turner, I left this summer, at Manchester Poly now," he further explains.

"Oh hi Steve," I am faking it, "good to see you, I hope you have a good night." I turn away, a total look of panic in my eyes as I face Will.

"Don't worry, it will be ok John," he whispers. I don't believe him.

So, it started again, the rumours and the gossip, the questions about what I did at weekends, and who I spent my time with, *'was that guy in the nightclub your boyfriend?'*, and so by Christmas I had given up. There was a particular nastiness to some of the comments as the government at the time was running its *AIDS* campaign which served to provoke much anti-gay behaviour. One day, I entered my classroom early, as was my habit, to discover on the blackboard:

'AIDS = Arse Injected Death Sentence'.

It was then I decided I could no longer stay where I was and that I should look to find another job and Will, typically, was fully supportive.

The envelope arrived with the day's post, sandwiched between a gas bill and a charity appeal. It was heavy, denser than a standard letter, the weight of it disproportionate to its size. My name, printed in tight, impersonal capitals, glared up from the glossy sticker, and beneath it, in smaller type, the name of the international school I'd applied to almost on a dare. I held it for a long moment, thumb pressed against the flap, as if opening it would set some irreversible sequence in motion.

The flat was silent, emptied of Will until the weekend, the only sound the intermittent tick of the clock and the distant, ragged engine of a bin lorry making its rounds. I sat at the kitchen table—the one piece of furniture I'd purchased new, the rest scavenged or bequeathed—and placed the envelope in the centre, aligning it with the table's grain. I stared at it, willing it to vanish, or to disclose its contents without requiring the final, traitorous act of opening.

Eventually, I broke the seal. The letter inside was thick, several sheets stapled together, the first page alone dense with formality and the cool, lubricated optimism of corporate language. I read it once, twice, then a third time, the words blurring at the edges as my mind stuttered around the reality of what it promised: escape, anonymity, the possibility of being reinvented in a country where no one would care about my private history.

I set the letter down and steepled my fingers, trying to imagine the shape of a life transposed to *Kuwait*. I saw, in fragments, the sand-coloured buildings and the relentless blue of the desert sky. I tried to picture myself in those settings, a teacher among strangers, the days unmoored from the scrutiny and suspicion that had begun to choke me here. The prospect was both intoxicating and terrifying.

The clock ticked on. Outside, the city was a saturated watercolour, all the colours bleeding into each other under the heavy sky. I looked around the flat, cataloguing each item, Will's jacket draped over the back of the chair, the empty coffee mugs stacked in the sink, the curl of notebook paper on the desk where I'd last left my lesson plans. I tried to reconcile the permanence of these objects with the sudden, gaping absence their abandonment would create.

My hands were shaking. I reached for the phone, dialled Will's number, and listened to the rings coil out into the silence. He answered on the third ring, his voice low and thick with sleep or the remnants of last night's shift.

"Hello?"

"It's me," I said, and immediately hated how small my voice sounded.

"Hey. Everything all right?"

There was no good way to say it, so I said it flat: "I got the offer."

A beat. "For *Kuwait?*"

"Yes. It's… I think I have to take it."

He was quiet for a long time. I could hear, behind his silence, the slow exhalation of a cigarette, the distant whirr of traffic through his window.

"When?" he asked.

"End of term. September start."

He made a noise, neither assent nor disappointment, but something heavier, more resigned. "It's what you want, yeah?"

"Maybe. I don't know." I pressed my fingers into the bridge of my nose, tried to steady the tremor in my voice, "I'm scared, Will. I don't know if I can do it. But I can't stay here. Not like this."

He exhaled, the line buzzing with the sound, "I get it. I really do."

"I want to see you before I go. Maybe we could," I hesitated, the word sticking in my throat, "take a holiday? Go somewhere new?"

He laughed, softly, "always running, aren't you?"

"Only if you come with me," I said, and was surprised to find that I meant it.

There was another long pause, then, "all right. Deal."

We talked for a little while longer, the conversation meandering between practicalities and nostalgia, both of us avoiding the centre of the thing. When the call ended, I sat with the phone in my lap, staring at the letter on the table, its neat paragraphs spelling out a future I could not quite imagine.

Outside, the sky was clearing. The city, for all its noise and violence, looked newly gentle in the morning sun. I watched the clouds scud past, felt the soft ache of possibility and loss twined together, and waited for the next chapter to begin.

CHAPTER 15: ET IN ARCADIA EGO

There is a moment, always, at the threshold of travel, when the self is both doubled and erased. In the case of Aegina, it occurred as the ferry crested the final headland, the island's ochre ridgeline dividing the *Aegean* from the dome of untrafficked blue, and I felt myself both arriving and vanishing in a single pulse. The port was nothing as I had expected: not the antiseptic terminal of brochures and travelogues, but a slow-bleeding spill of fishing boats, mopeds, sunburnt children, and the smells, olive oil, diesel, and the marine tang of fish being gutted at the quay. We disembarked together, but in the crowd we could have been anyone: strangers, brothers, honeymooners, even, though the word stuck in my throat.

William had insisted on carrying both rucksacks, and now wore them slung crosswise like the victim of an improbable robbery. He squinted up at the hotel sign, one of several promising sea views and continental breakfast in the frantic, over-punctuated grammar of holiday English. I watched him, waiting for the moment he would realise I was not, in fact, as self-sufficient as I'd always pretended, that I could not even navigate a taxi queue without his hand on my elbow to steady me. But if he had noticed, he made no comment. Instead, he handed me the map, creased, annotated, a palimpsest of our joint anticipation and said, "you're the brains. Which way?"

The hotel was three streets off the main promenade, down a lane thick with the humming of bees and the almost indecent bloom of bougainvillea. The woman at reception was plump, relentless in her cheer, and ran her finger down the guestbook as though reading an omen. "Mister John, Mister William," she said, beaming, "two beds, yes?" Her eyes, black and bottomless, waited at the hinge of the question.

William shot me a glance, the kind that communicated three years of private dialogue in an instant. I felt the old reflex, deny, deflect, recite the well-practiced script of *just friends*, but in the humid pulse of the lobby, I found I had no energy for subterfuge. "One is fine," I heard myself say, and to my astonishment, my voice did not tremble.

Our room was on the top floor, a cell with walls the colour of an overripe melon and a balcony just large enough for two. The sea

view, so ardently promised, was mostly occluded by power lines
and the writhing bougainvillea, but it mattered less than I'd
thought. I dropped my bag and collapsed onto the bed, inhaling
the antiseptic tang of freshly laundered sheets. William flopped
down beside me, his arm brushing mine, and for a while neither
of us moved.

"Happy?" he said, after a minute, his accent flattening
the vowels.

I closed my eyes, tried to catalogue the absence of familiar pressure in my chest. "I think so," I said, and was surprised to find it true.

We unpacked in companionable disorder, shirts and
guidebooks and flip-flops arrayed with the random logic of
children at play. William, who prided himself on his travel discipline, lined his toiletries along the shelf in precise military formation. I arranged mine at careless intervals, a scatter of tubes
and brushes and the battered razor I'd never learned to wield
without drawing blood. There was a brief contest over who
would claim the single usable power socket; William, ever the
pragmatist, produced a battered extension lead from his rucksack and solved the problem without comment. It was these
small, improvisational acts of kindness that undid me, not the
grand gestures or the declarations. I wondered if he knew.

The first hours passed in a haze of heat and fatigue. We
walked the length of the promenade, stopping for orange juice
at a shaded taverna where the plastic chairs left red welts on the
backs of our legs. The menu was in five languages, none of
which William trusted, so we pointed at the nearest table's order and received, after a time, a platter of grilled sardines and a
mound of chips thickly crusted with salt. I watched him eat,
hands working with the economy of a person who has never in
his life been self-conscious, and felt a rush of gratitude so sharp
it bordered on pain.

It was late afternoon by the time we reached the nearest
beach—if it could be called a beach, the sand more rubble than
powder, dotted with the detritus of past seasons and the slow-
calcifying remains of shells. The water, however, was as promised: clear to the bottom, so cold that when we entered, I had
to suppress a shout. William dove headlong, resurfacing with a

whoop, while I advanced in increments, each step an experiment in ac-climatisation. We swam out until the buoy line, then floated on our backs, letting the sun cauterize the line of the horizon into a single, gold-threaded seam.

It was here, adrift and anonymous, that I first let myself look, really look, at him without the camouflage of context. In the harsh northern light of home, he was all edges and unfinished sentences, but here the sun rounded his features, softened the angles of his jaw, painted him in a palette of honey and bronze. He caught me staring and grinned, spitting a jet of seawater in my direction.

"You're staring," he said, mild amusement in his tone.

"Just making sure you don't drown," I replied.

He laughed, and the sound carried across the water, a sonic proof of our presence. For the first time, I did not care who heard.

The days resolved themselves into a routine, improvised but immediately natural. We would wake with the sun, drink coffee on the balcony while the town was still hushed and the air smelled of jasmine. William insisted on a morning swim, and so we would traipse down to the water, towels slung over our shoulders, sharing the path with old men walking dogs and small, feral children already sticky with break-fast. Afterward, we would eat at the bakery, a slab of spanakopita or a sugared, doughy thing I could never remember the name of, before re-turning to the hotel to plan the day's assault on the island.

There were ruins to see, temples half-reclaimed by the scrub, the agoras and amphitheaters where William would insist on testing the acoustics with an off-key snatch of pop music. There were hikes through the olive groves, where the air shimmered with the metallic click of cicadas and the ground was veined with the silver of spent leaves.

In the afternoons, we would rent a scooter and ride out along the coast, the engine's whine barely outpacing the swarm of bees that seemed to follow us at every turn. We stopped wherever the view com-pelled us, or wherever there was shade, or whenever either of us simply wanted to stop. There was no need to negotiate. For the first time in my life, there was nothing to prove.

It was in the small intervals, waiting for a table at the taverna, or lingering on a sun-warmed step outside some ruin, or simply walking side by side along the stony lanes that I became aware of a change. At first, I was hypervigilant: every brush of his arm against mine, every shared glance, was catalogued and interrogated for its potential to expose us. The years of self-policing had carved deep channels in my reflexes, and though *Aegina* was not *Manchester*, I could not entirely shed the old patterns.

As the days passed, nobody looked. Or, if they did, it was with a kind of distracted curiosity, the way you might glance at a pair of stray cats sunning themselves on a windowsill. We were, for all intents and purposes, invisible. The realisation was at once liberating and slightly mournful: I had wasted so much time guarding against an enemy who, in the end, was mostly indifferent.

The nights were William's favourite. After dinner, usually a contest of how much grilled octopus he could consume before I surrendered in disgust, we would walk the back streets, the town's shops and restaurants blinking out one by one until only the bars remained. There was a particular one he liked: no sign, no music, just a row of battered tables on the edge of the quay and a proprietor who poured the retsina with the solemnity of a priest. We would sit and watch the fishing boats drift in, the men unloading crates of gleaming, prehistoric-looking creatures by the light of a naked bulb. Sometimes, we talked; more often, we simply existed, letting the silence fill the spaces between us.

Back at the hotel, we would shower the salt from our skin, then lie on the bed, limbs entwined and cooling in the fan's sluggish breeze. William always brought the guidebook to bed, marking pages and annotating the margins with a stub of pencil. I would watch him, his brow furrowed in concentration, and marvel at the way he could be at once so methodical and so entirely present. Sometimes, he would read aloud the more improbable facts, "did you know the temple of *Aphaea* is older than the *Parthenon*? Or that *Aegina* once tried to conquer *Athens* with a fleet of fishing boats?," and I would pretend to be interested, though what I was really listening for was the cadence of his voice, the unconscious lilt that surfaced when he was tired or happy or both.

It was in these moments that I realised I was, perhaps, capable of loving him. Not the reckless, devouring love of myth, but something slower, more mineral, accreted in layers over the sediment of shared days. I did not say it. Not yet. But I think he knew.

On the fifth night, as we stood on the balcony watching the lights of the mainland flicker in the heat, he said, without preamble, "do you ever think about just… not going back?"

The question startled me, less for its content than for the way he phrased it, as if the idea had been fermenting in him all along, waiting only for the right ambient temperature to rise to the surface.

"Sometimes," I admitted, though the thought had never fully crystallised until now.

He shrugged, as if to say, why not? "We could be anyone, here. No one knows us. No one cares."

He reached for my hand, and this time I let him, the contact electric in its ordinariness. We stood like that for a long time, the sound of the sea and the distant music from the town blurring into a single, continuous note.

Later, in bed, I listened to his breathing slow, felt the weight of his arm across my chest, and wondered if it was possible to build a life out of such moments. It seemed improbable. But so, I thought, had everything else until now.

Some nights, the self is neither doubled nor erased, but simply held. And in the dark, it is enough.

You learn the landscape first by its shadows. This was true in Aegina, and truer still as we set out to conquer the mainland. Each day-trip was a careful foray, less a touristic checklist than a slow, deliberate trespass into the past. I had mapped it all in advance, of course; my whole adolescence had been an exercise in imaginary expeditions.

The ruins of *Greece*, as pictured in the library's battered *World Book*, had been my first true escape, and I approached their reality now with the reverence of a pilgrim, the scepticism of a man who had spent his life disappointed by the ratio of promise to fulfilment.

On the morning of our *Acropolis* venture, we joined the earliest ferry, the deck still slick with dew, the air so sharp it seemed to flense the last vestiges of sleep from our skin. William stood at the bow, hands tucked into the pockets of his windbreaker, eyes fixed on the receding line of the island. I wanted to ask him what he was thinking, but the silence was too fine to risk shattering.

Athens, when it finally unspooled itself along the horizon, was a paradox of light and entropy: marble and diesel, pigeons and buses, the endless spiral of the modern city constricting the ancient core like a python devouring its own tail. We navigated the port to find the coach tour we had booked ourselves on, and passed through the streets, lined with the pedlars of souvenirs and counterfeit handbags. We arrived at the foot of the hill just as the first wave of tour groups began their ascent.

The climb was less arduous than anticipated, though the heat already pressed at our backs with a force that felt both atmospheric and personal. I babbled facts as we mounted the marble steps, how the *Parthenon* was once painted in violent colours, how the Persians had razed the city before the *Athenians* rebuilt it as an act of collective will, how Lord Elgin had looted the best bits and left the bones behind. William grunted in appreciation or scepticism; it was never quite clear which, but I had learned to cherish his interruptions.

At the summit, the *Parthenon* loomed, not so much a ruin as an assertion: even in collapse, it refused to be humbled. The columns stood in ordered disarray, scaffolding weaving between them like a prosthetic skeleton. I ran my fingers along the fluted drum of a fallen pillar, expecting coldness but finding only the residual heat of the sun, stored and released like a secret. William traced the same line, his hand dwarfing mine, and I felt an odd twinge, pride, perhaps, that I had brought him here, or that he had agreed to come at all.

We wandered the precinct, ducking behind the less-trafficked temples, reading the inscriptions with varying degrees of literacy. At the *Erechtheion*, with its famous caryatids, William leaned against the rope barrier and said, "so these are just… women, holding up a roof?"

"Not just women," I said, delighted by the opening, "they're meant to be priestesses, or maybe representations of civic virtue. Nobody's sure. But yes, they hold up the porch."

He regarded them, head tilted, then looked at me, "looks heavy."

I laughed, the sound bouncing off the stone, "that's the point."

We sat on a sun-blasted slab, sharing a bottle of tepid water and a handful of almonds. The crowds eddied and surged, but we were outside their orbit. For a long time we watched the city seethe below, the avenues and alleys radiating out from the *Acropolis* like the veins of a living organism. I felt, for once, entirely present, not as a simulacrum or a witness, but as myself, bone and sinew, part of the world's brief attempt at order.

Back on *Aegina*, after the heat and the crowds and the unrelenting marble, the evenings took on the quality of reprieve. We would eat at whichever taverna looked least occupied by our fellow day-trippers, order whatever the owner recommended, and drink retsina until our mouths were too numb for complaint. It was in these moments, the languid postscript to the day's exertions, that I felt the boundaries between us, so long maintained, begin to blur. William, who was usually allergic to sentiment, would grow expansive under the influence of food and fatigue, telling stories from his childhood with a candour I had never managed to coax from him at home. I listened, as rapt as any congregation, and found myself wanting, impossibly, to tell him everything.

The next trip was to *Epidaurus* we chose as a cheap alternative to a paid for tour, this was a theatre carved into the hillside and famed for its perfect acoustics. The journey there was a saga of buses and wrong turns, each transfer a negotiation conducted in a hybrid of English, gesture, and the handful of Greek words I had managed to memorize from the phrasebook. William was the better navigator, but he indulged my stubborn adherence to the plan, letting me lead us in ever-widening circles until we arrived, sweat-soaked and sun-punished, at the ticket booth.

The theatre was empty but for a handful of early risers. We climbed to the topmost row, the stone seats worn smooth by centuries of use, and surveyed the bowl below. The stage was a simple circle, nothing like the ornate sets of the West End or the slick productions of my university days. It was raw, elemental, a space where words alone could remake the world. I left William at the top and ventured down to the stage.

I stood at the centre, looked up at the high rim where William sat, and without thinking, recited the only line of Greek tragedy I could remember: "whoever exalts himself shall be humbled, and whoever humbles himself shall be exalted." The words, plucked from some forgotten syllabus, ricocheted off the seats, returning to me not as echo but as amplification.

William grinned, cupping his hands around his mouth, "speak up, can't hear you!"

I tried again, louder this time, and the phrase fractured into a flock of syllables, each one darting up the rows and perching, somehow, exactly at his ear. He clapped, exaggerated, and shouted down, "you're wasted as a teacher."

I bowed, a parody of humility, and rejoined him at the top. We sat, catching our breath, letting the silence of the place thicken around us. It occurred to me that we had spent most of our lives performing, first as the versions of ourselves that parents, schools, and the world demanded; then as the men we thought each other wanted. Here, at last, there was nothing to perform. Only the stones, the sky, and the inscrutable presence of the other.

We descended into the surrounding countryside, the fields patched with poppies and wild thyme, the air so dense with the scent of herbs and sun that it was like breathing in the world's most sophisticated liqueur. William picked a sprig of something, held it to his nose, and made a face, "smells like soap," he said.

"It's sage," I offered, though I was guessing.

He tucked it behind my ear, "looks better on you than on the plate."

We walked for hours, down dusty paths and along the skeletons of ancient walls. There was an ease to it, a physical companionship that required neither explanation nor apology. We stopped at a roadside stand, bought a hunk of bread and a wedge of goat's cheese, and ate them in the shade of a lone cypress. William, who had never understood the point of ancient ruins, seemed content to simply exist in the sun, while I catalogued every detail for the future retelling.

By the time we made it back to the hotel, we were too tired for anything but sleep. We lay side by side, the sheets sticking to our skin, the fan clicking in its death throes. I dozed in and out, waking every so often to find William's arm draped across my chest, heavy and anchoring.

The last of our mainland excursions was to *Mycenae*. The bus wound through the hills, olive groves and cypress groves alternating in patterns that seemed both random and inevitable. I read aloud from the guidebook, summarizing the myths: the house of *Atreus*, the curse of *Agamemnon*, the legacy of blood and betrayal that had, in some obscure way, shaped the western imagination. William listened, occasionally asking questions that undercut the grandeur, "did they really kill each other over a woman?"; "why didn't they just leave if it was so cursed?", but mostly he let the stories wash over him, as if acclimating himself to a new species of time.

The site itself was a delirium of stone. *Cyclopean* walls, the *Lion Gate*, the deep-drowned shaft graves where archaeologists had unearthed gold masks and bones and fragments of improbable narrative. We wandered the citadel, our footsteps muffled by the dust and the sense of accumulated history. I was nearly giddy with the proximity of it: these were the stones that Schliemann had touched, that Homer had mythologized, that I had dreamt about as a child in the north of England, the rain lashing the windows while I traced floorplans in the margins of my exercise books.

At the *Treasury of Atreus,* a beehive tomb sunk into the side of the hill, William ducked inside and whistled, the sound spiralling up the dome and returning in a softened, altered key.

"I feel like a hobbit," he said, echoing down the passage.

I joined him, the air inside cooler than outside, redolent with the smell of ancient earth and the faint ammonia of bat droppings. We stood in the centre, our voices attenuated to whispers, and let the darkness close around us. I reached for his hand, and he did not pull away.

When we emerged, blinking, into the sun, it was as if we had been translated: no longer tourists or escapees, but something more elemental. A pair of bodies, unremarkable, coextensive with the landscape.

On the coach back we sat at the very rear, sharing a bottle of water and the leftover cheese, our knees pressed together in the close quarters. William dozed with his head on my shoulder, and I watched the hills unspool behind the glass, the olive trees flickering past in a pattern that felt both infinite and intimate.

That night, back on *Aegina*, we ate in near silence, too exhausted for conversation. The waiter brought us ouzo and a plate of something gelatinous and untranslatable; we ate it anyway, the taste so sharp and foreign that it burned away the residue of the day. Afterward, we walked the beach, the sand cool underfoot, the air alive with the sounds of the night: the distant music of a wedding, the yowl of cats fighting for territory, the undertone of waves, always the waves.

We sat on a breakwater, the rocks still warm from the day's sun, and watched the ferries wink out across the bay. William leaned against me, his hair damp from the swim, his hands idle in his lap.

"I like it here," he said, voice barely above a whisper.

"Me too," I replied, and let the confession hang in the salt-tinged air.

For a while we said nothing, content to simply absorb the world as it was, imperfect, unfinished, but ours for the moment. It occurred to me that the future, so often imagined as a thing to be conquered or survived, might also be something one could simply arrive at, unheralded and undeserving.

We walked back to the hotel in the hush of the midnight hour, the streets empty but for our footsteps. At the door, William paused, turned to look at me, and smiled.

"Best holiday ever," he said.

I smiled back, knowing he was right, and that nothing would ever be quite the same again.

There are places so precisely arranged in the memory that to describe them is simply to recite: the taverna at the end of the island's main road, the tables arranged in ragged procession along the beach, a flotilla of white-painted chairs facing west to catch the last possible sliver of sun. The evening was already spooling out in peach and lavender, the horizon knifed by the far line of the *Peloponnese*, the water agitated by a breeze that promised storms but delivered only the perfume of ozone and salt. We had walked there in near silence, William and I, the comfortable silence of men whose conversation had outstripped the day's capacity.

The proprietor, an ancient man in a shirt the colour of saffron, his arms corded with a lifetime of labour, ushered us to a table notched into the sand, barely a meter from the gentle wash of tide. No menu, only a promise of *'catch of the day'* and *'the best tomatoes in Greece'*, which was perhaps the only truth ever spoken in the entire history of the tourist trade.

As we waited, William constructed elaborate towers of pebbles and shells along the table's edge, his hands moving with the slow, deliberate grace of a gardener at dusk. I watched, feeling a pang of the old, almost adolescent tenderness, how was it possible, I wondered, to be so unguardedly oneself in front of another person, and not be undone by the knowledge of it?

The fish arrived, charred and glistening, perched atop a heap of wild greens so bitter they made the teeth ache. There was salad, all sharp feta and oiled cucumbers, and a loaf of bread whose crust required the application of both hands and, at one point, William's elbow. We ate with the abandon of the newly shipwrecked, our hands and mouths slick with olive oil, and it seemed briefly that there was nothing of the world but this: the waning light, the shared labour of disassembly, the briny, molten sweetness of each morsel.

When the sun at last breached the edge of the horizon, the air shifted, colder, more electric and the other guests fell into a kind of reverential hush. I looked at William, and in the inverted light his features were a study in contradiction: the line of the jaw, so often set against the world, now softened by the rose-gold wash; the eyes, which in England had been blue as December, here rendered almost translucent.

"I wish we could stay here forever," I said, not expecting an answer.

He regarded me with a seriousness that, in other men, might have signalled disapproval. But in William it meant only calculation, the weighing of possibilities.

"Maybe we will, one day," he replied.

I laughed, or tried to, but it caught in my throat, "be serious."

He shrugged, tearing another hunk of bread, "why not? You do your stint in Kuwait, save a load of money instead of pay tax. We buy a bit of land. Not near the touristy shite, somewhere with olives or goats, up in the hills. You can write your books. I'll learn to farm, it's in my genes after all or fix up a guesthouse. We could live like this, easy."

The logic of it was so matter-of-fact that for a moment I was dizzy with longing. I tried to picture the years ahead, the slow accretion of days just like this one, the rhythm of seasons and the possibility of peace. It was more than I had ever allowed myself to imagine.

William watched me, his expression unchanging, but I could sense the faintest ripple of concern beneath the surface. He reached across the table, catching my hand in his, and squeezed until the bones threatened to fuse.

"What is it, John?" he said.

I struggled to find words. "I don't know. I just... where do you get it from? The strength to believe that it'll all work out?"

He grinned, the same lopsided smirk that had, for years, been both his armour and his flag, "all my strength comes from you," he said, and then, unable to maintain the solemnity, added, "God knows what'll happen when you're gone for a year. I'll probably get eaten by feral cats."

I made a noise that was meant to be a laugh, but the effort of containment twisted my face into what I'm sure was an unlovely rictus. William noticed, of course, because he noticed everything. Without another word, he rose, came around behind me, and wrapped both arms around my chest, pinning me so that my breath came in small, embarrassed puffs.

"Don't be a daft bugger," he said into my ear, and then, softer, "I'm just off to the loo, so order more beer if you want it." Normally, the breath of someone so close on my neck would have left me in a raw panic, but this time I resisted the urge to shudder.

He squeezed once more, then strode up the sand toward the restaurant's back-lit doorway, leaving me with the imponderable horizon and the last scraps of our meal. As I tried to compose myself, I became aware of a couple at the next table, a man and a woman, late-middle-aged, their faces blurred by the afterglow of sun and a bottle of retsina. They'd been at the theatre in *Epidaurus*, I realised, and at the bakery on Tuesday. In small places, the repetitions accumulate.

The woman, white-haired and sharp-eyed, leaned across the narrow gap between tables, "he's a keeper, love," she said in a stage whisper, "so look after each other."

I blinked, surprised into candour, "yes," I said, "I will."

She smiled, satisfied, and returned to her plate. We sat in companionable silence until William returned, at which point she raised her glass in our direction, "cheers, boys," she said. "Hope you get your forever."

We toasted back, William none the wiser, and for the remainder of the meal I tried to memorise every detail: the taste of the bread, the cadence of the waves, the shape of William's hands as he gestured in the gathering dark.

Later, when the restaurant had emptied and the owner was stacking chairs, we lingered on the beach, our feet burrowed in cooling sand. William leaned into me, head heavy on my shoulder, and together we watched the stars take their places in the new, unblemished sky.

I thought about what the woman had said, and for the first time in my life, I found myself unafraid to hope.

The following morning arrived not with the soft hand of dawn, but with the unceremonious clang of the hotel's ancient bell system. We dressed, still sticky from sleep and too much sun, and trudged to the lobby where a bus was meant to collect us for the group excursion to *Poros*. The corridor outside smelled of *Nescafé* and floor polish; the breakfast room's sole concession to fresh produce was an orange, sealed in cellophane and arranged atop a pyramid of croissants. William pocketed two, winking at the proprietor, who pretended not to notice.

The coach was idling at the curb, its air-conditioning set to glacial. We shuffled down the aisle, searching for seats that would not expose us to the conversational crossfire of fellow travellers. At the halfway mark, we encountered the couple from the taverna, Beryl and Bert, as we later learned, from *Huddersfield*. They waved with the enthusiasm of old friends, and we surrendered to their orbit, squeezing in behind them just as the doors hissed shut.

Introductions were conducted at a volume appropriate for the front row of the *Palladium*. Beryl, whose hair was an improbable confection of platinum and lacquer, asked if we had enjoyed the fish at the beach, and before I could summon an answer, Bert replied that he himself was "more of a steak man, but you only live once, don't you?" William grinned, said something about the chips being "spot on," and Beryl, delighted, launched into a monologue about her ongoing search for the perfect Greek potato.

It became apparent, over the next hour, that the two of them had been together since the tail end of the *sixties*, and had spent the intervening decades as hairdressers, parents, then, liberated by retirement, professional tourists. Their love for each other was explicit, performative, and entirely without guile. Beryl's left hand rested on Bert's knee for the entire journey; when she needed both hands to count the islands they had visited, she simply pressed her shoulder against his and continued.

The ferry to *Poros* was chaos, a migration of the aged and the sunburned, all shoving toward the railing for a glimpse of the famed clock tower or the promise of a discount at the duty-free. Bert and William staked out a corner of the upper deck, their conversation immediately technical, engines, weather, the art of reversing a car ferry into a space that looked, to me, the exact size of the ferry itself. Beryl took my arm and led me to the side, where we watched the islands unspool behind us, beads on a thread of blue.

"You two been together long?" she asked, her tone equal parts curiosity and benign mischief.

I hesitated, still unaccustomed to the absence of risk in such questions, "a few years, on and off," I said, trying to keep my voice casual.

She smiled, eyes bright with the pleasure of a secret confirmed. "We clocked you last night," she said, "but don't worry, nobody cares out here. It's not like home."

I looked at her, searching for a hint of malice, but found only a warmth so intense it bordered on the maternal. "Thanks," I said, and meant it.

On *Poros*, we disembarked into a promenade lined with eucalyptus and palm, the air humming with scooters and the fragrance of something sweet and unknown. The group fractured immediately: Americans to the shops, Germans to the nearest archaeological ruin, Australians to the bar. The four of us set off up the waterfront, dodging cats and the more insistent of the local restaurant touts.

William and Bert lagged behind, heads bent in concentration over a guidebook, while Beryl led me through the maze of lanes leading up to the clock tower, "it's the only decent view on the whole island," she declared.

The climb was steeper than advertised, the path switching back through terraced gardens and small, precarious houses whose paint had faded to the colour of memory. At the summit, the tower presided over the bay like a pale sentinel, its face stuck permanently at a time nobody could agree upon. Beryl took the requisite photos, one with the sea, one with the tower, one with both of us grinning like idiots and then, somewhat winded, collapsed onto a shaded bench.

I watched William and Bert arrive, the former animated and gesturing at the rooftops below. There was a lightness to his step, a boyishness I had rarely seen in England, as if the act of being elsewhere had granted him permission to inhabit an earlier, uninjured self. The realisation struck me with a force so acute that I felt my knees go soft.

We descended as a unit, Beryl and Bert in front, William and I behind, careful not to tumble on the uneven stones. At the base, we were steered into a small taverna, its tables arranged in a haphazard line along a narrow spit of harbour. Bert ordered a carafe of the local wine; Beryl produced a pack of cigarettes and offered them around. William accepted, lighting his with a match struck off the tabletop. I demurred, and Beryl laughed, "just as well, these will be the end of me."

The conversation was at first the typical volley of travel anecdotes, missed trains, terrible hotels, the time Bert fell off a donkey in Corfu but soon it veered into more personal territory. Beryl spoke of their children, all now grown and scattered across England, and her one regret: that she'd never travelled more when she was young. Bert, when pressed, said he was grateful for the late start, that it meant each place was more precious for being new. William, in a gesture that felt almost ceremonial, raised his glass and toasted "to the old and the bold," which Beryl pronounced the best thing she'd heard all year.

Lunch was a cavalcade of shared plates: stuffed vine leaves, charred lamb, a salad so luminous it seemed to have absorbed the sun. William and Bert competed to see who could eat the most peppers; Beryl and I picked out the black olives and dropped them, one by one, into our wine glasses, where they bobbed like punctuation marks.

It was during this meal that I realised I had stopped editing myself. I spoke of school, of my fear of returning to England, of the new job in Kuwait and the plan to write a book. William chimed in with stories I hadn't told, or had only hinted at, rounding out my silences with the facts I couldn't bring myself to admit. When Beryl asked how we'd met, he recounted the story of our first summer at Langley Hall, complete with his disastrous attempt to impress me with his cricketing prowess. Bert, who'd apparently endured a similar ordeal, laughed so hard he snorted wine through his nose.

The meal ended with strong coffee and a dessert so sweet I thought my teeth would ache for days. We settled the bill, Bert, ever the gentleman, refused to let us pay and then drifted back toward the ferry, sated in body and spirit.

On the return journey, the sun dipped low, painting the water in stripes of gold and indigo. Beryl and Bert sat together at the front; heads bowed in the kind of conversation that requires no words. William and I lingered at the stern, watching the wake fan out behind us, a thread tying the island to the world we'd left, however temporarily, behind.

He slipped his hand into mine, and for the first time, I did not check to see who might be watching. The gesture felt as natural as breathing, as though it had always been this way.

That evening, the four of us met again for dinner, this time at a place Beryl had discovered on the main drag, "not fancy, but the moussakas to die for." The talk was looser now, the boundaries erased by food and sun and the collective effort of a day well-spent. We traded gossip about the other tourists; Beryl critiqued the owner's highlights ("Too brassy, needs a toner"), and Bert regaled us with stories from the golden age of the Yorkshire salon.

As the night wore on, the conversation turned to the future. Beryl asked, outright, if we were planning to live together permanently, and William, without missing a beat, said, "one day, when we can do it somewhere sunny." I blushed, but did not protest.

Later, after dessert and more wine, the four of us walked back along the promenade, the air heavy with the scent of jasmine and the low drone of mopeds. We paused at the beach to watch the moon rise, the tide slick and black at our feet.

Beryl hugged me, hard, and whispered, "you're all right, love. Don't let the bastards get you down." Bert clapped William on the back, said something about keeping him out of trouble. When we parted, it was with genuine regret, and the promise of postcards and a future meeting somewhere less windy.

Back at the hotel, I lay awake, the memory of the day running in loops behind my eyes. I thought about the oddness of happiness, how it could catch you off guard, build itself in increments until one day you looked around and found yourself, for once, in the exact place you were meant to be. I reached for William's hand in the dark, found it waiting, and held on until sleep claimed us both.

The last night on *Aegina* brought with it the inverse of anticipation: a kind of backflow, as if the time already spent was seeping back into the present, colouring every detail with the knowledge that it would soon be lost. We packed in a desultory, almost comic fashion, wrestling with the geometry of our rucksacks as if brute logic could contain all that the week had gathered. The souvenirs, William's impulsively acquired amphora-shaped mug, my small, luridly painted canvas of the harbour, a bottle of olive oil so well-sealed it might have survived *Troy*, threatened to swamp the permitted weight. William declared his intent to wear all remaining clothing at once to cheat the scale; I, more cautious, suggested he leave behind the worst of his socks as a peace offering to the maid.

In the end, everything fit. Barely. The bags bulged at their seams, and we sat on them in turn to force the zips into submission, laughing at my memory of a similar battle in my student days, when the sum of my possessions would have fit in a single bag. I took a photograph of William, his arms wrapped around his lumpy pack, grinning like a child at Christmas. The shutter caught him in half-light, the blue of the Aegean framed by the window behind, and I knew instantly it would be the image I would revisit most - except perhaps for the secret pictures I took of him in his speedoes on the beach.

We dined for the last time at our usual taverna, the owner now greeting us with the familiarity of a cousin, pressing into our hands a paper bag of leftover pastries, "for breakfast tomorrow, or in case of hunger on the plane." The other guests, the seasonal regulars and a rotating cast of sunburned German pensioners, waved at us as we departed, as though we'd been part of their story all along.

In the morning, we lugged our bags to the ferry in a hush more solemn than the hour required. The boat was crowded, the air below decks damp and close, so we stood on the windy top, the salt spray needling our faces. The sea was glassy, and the sun rose behind us with the mild, apologetic warmth of late September. William laced his fingers through mine, saying nothing, but the squeeze was enough.

At the port in *Piraeus*, Beryl and Bert awaited us, perched on their own monumental luggage pile. They hailed us across the concourse, and we exchanged addresses in the chaotic, pre-boarding rush,

Beryl insisting we must visit *Yorkshire*, "if only for a proper cup of tea and the best chippy north of the Trent." Bert pressed into my palm a dog-eared business card for their salon, now operated by their daughter, with the words, "family discount, just mention us." John promised them postcards from Kuwait, and we all hugged, awkward and public but unembarrassed.

The flight home was a fugue of transitions: the metal corridor of the boarding bridge, the close quarters of economy, the strange intimacy of being above the world together, yet separate from it. William fell asleep within minutes of takeoff, his head lolling against my shoulder, his breath warm and slow. I did not sleep. Instead, I watched the clouds scroll past the window, the endless mutability of light and air, and I thought of the weeks behind us.

I thought of Beryl and Bert, the first people to know us as we really were, and to celebrate it without question or irony. I thought of the silent conversations in the ancient theatres, the ease of sharing bread and space, the absence of the old, defensive postures. I wondered if this was what adulthood was supposed to feel like, and if so, why it had taken me so long to arrive.

I promised myself, and the sleeping William, that we would do this again, twice a year, if I could manage it, during the breaks from Kuwait. We would meet in the middle somewhere, find new places to be ordinary together, add to our collection of stories and mugs and slightly ridiculous art. I imagined, for the first time, the possibility of years ahead, not as a series of hurdles but as a horizon, open and unbounded.

The plane banked, and William's head slid off my shoulder. I steadied him, adjusted the angle so he would not wake with a crick in his neck. He murmured something, a half-formed word, and I smiled, smoothing the hair from his forehead.

We landed, as all things do, in a drizzle and a queue, the world resuming its unlovely habits. But I carried with me a small, fierce core of peace, a knowledge that we had been, even briefly, exactly as we wished to be.

At the customs line, William blinked himself awake, looked at me with that upside-down smile, and said, "next time, let's go somewhere mad. Like *Istanbul.* Or *Norway.*"

"Deal," I said, and meant it.

We stepped into the terminal, the new air cool and bracing. The city, waiting just beyond, felt less like an enemy and more like a challenge. William took my hand, in public, and this time I did not even look to see who noticed.

Whatever came next, we would face it together. And, for the first time in my life, I could not wait.

CHAPTER 16: THE CURE

William and I spent one more night together. I stage my journey to Heathrow with an overnight stay in Langley. The plan originally was to then get a train from Norwich into London, but William insisted that he drive me to the airport.

We travel mostly in silence having said all the things we need to say the previous night. After parking, William helps me with my luggage to the check-in desk, and once I had collected my boarding pass we solemnly walk to the lifts up to the departure level.

"Ready then?" he asks me quietly. I nod.

"Am I doing the right thing?" I look into William's eyes and my doubts find expression.

"Yes, go earn lots of money," he steps into me and holds me in a close hug, then whispers, "I'll be waiting for you when you get back."

I rest my head briefly against his, and feel the slightest of kisses on my neck before he steps back. William extends his hand and shakes mine, "take care John and good luck."

"Thank you Will," as our hands separate I begin to say, "I…I…"

"I know," he mouths silently, "now off you go."

I close my eyes slowly, and compose myself before turning to the lift. The doors open and I step inside. I turn around, and watch William disappear behind the closing doors as he raises a hand to wave. I try my best to smile.

The first hour in Kuwait was defined less by place than by climate. The air in the arrivals hall was not air at all, but something else—heavier, denser, infused with the particulate intention of heat. It pressed against the skin with the curiosity of a doctor's hand, a deliberate and unsparing touch. The terminal was a series of glass corridors, the light outside so blanched it seemed to repudiate colour, rendering everything within in shades of bone and aluminium.

I drifted on a tide of fellow expatriates, their passports held like talismans, their faces already daubed with the speculative fatigue of jet lag. At passport control, a woman in a navy abaya reviewed my documents with an expression that suggested disappointment, though whether in me or in the paperwork I could not say. A red-vested attendant barked my name ("John Williams—Mister John! Come now!"), then shepherded me with the efficiency of a livestock auctioneer through a series of glass doors and out onto the curb.

If I thought the concourse inside was hot, the parking lot delivered its own lesson in thermal physics. It was not merely the air but the light itself, a thing with mass and motive, a presence that hammered rather than illuminated. The smell was a stratigraphy - petrol, dust, ozone, the faint undertone of detergent from the bus idling at the curb. I followed the attendant's pointed finger and boarded, sagging into a plastic seat that retained the memory of every previous passenger in a matrix of sticky indentations.

The shuttle was a converted minibus, its interior tricked out in beige vinyl and chrome accents, the kind of vehicle more suited to a prom night or a municipal kidnapping. The windows were tinted nearly black, but still the sunlight found ways in, scribing slow-motion pulses across the floor. There were only two other passengers: a young woman in a *University of Manchester* tee, her hair scraped into a ponytail so tight it looked painful, and a bearded man in a suit so immaculate it seemed engineered rather than tailored. We ignored each other, the way people do when proximity has not yet graduated into social obligation.

The ride to the school's accommodation block was thirty minutes of unreality, the city streaming past in a sequence of architectural contradictions. Minarets jostled against brutalist office towers; luxury malls rose out of empty lots; the roads pulsed with *Toyotas* and battered *Peugeots* and, occasionally, a *Mercedes* so ostentatious it might have been a mirage. I watched it all with the detached interest of a minor character in someone else's origin story.

The block itself was an eight-story tower with four apartments per floor, sand-coloured, its windows rimed with the ghost of a thousand sandstorms. It was surrounded by a raised marble courtyard approached up by about half a dozen wide steps. The driver killed the engine, then announced our arrival in a tone suggesting both pride and resignation.

Once in the lobby, the temperature dropped by at least ten degrees, evidence, I would soon learn, of the building's central obsession with refrigeration. The lobby was bare but for a pair of sagging sofas and a noticeboard crammed with printouts: school calendars, exchange rates, warnings about heatstroke and the consumption of local water. My name was on a list at the front desk; the man behind the counter handed me a keycard and an envelope, then gestured wordlessly at the lifts.

My flat was on the second floor, the corridor a pelagic blue and lit with the institutional hum of fluorescents. At the threshold, I hesitated, then swiped the card. The door opened onto a rectangle of laminate flooring, a separate kitchen and bathroom and two good-sized double rooms. The living area already occupied by a pair of running shoes and a heap of textbooks. The air inside was frigid enough to induce gooseflesh. My new flatmate looked up from the coffee table, where he was assembling a scale model of the *Globe Theatre* out of cardboard and glue.

He was my age, maybe a year older, with the kind of healthful good looks that implied a long history of morning jogs and proper breakfasts. He wore shorts and a faded t-shirt from a cricket club I'd never heard of. His hair was a shock of blond curls; his arms corded with a tan I suspected was not of recent vintage.

"John Williams?" he said, voice pitched to the lilt of London.

"Present," I replied, setting my rucksack down with a thud.

"Martin," he said, rising and offering a hand. His shake was firm but not competitive; he seemed genuinely glad to see another living human. "History as well?"

I nodded. "Apparently head of department."

"My new boss!" He laughed. "I arrived yesterday with my girlfriend who works in the infant's department. Apparently they start earlier than the senior school." I gestured at the project on the table with a quizzical look. "Figured I'd get a head start. The Globe is for next month's unit, but the local shops are rubbish for supplies so I had to improvise."

I regarded the lopsided stage, its galleries painstakingly coloured in with marker, "looks better than the real thing," I said.

He grinned, and I realized I was already relaxing, my body unwinding from the contortions of travel and anticipation.

"Bit of a culture shock," he said, lowering himself back to the carpet. "Not just the heat, though that's murder. The rules here, they don't tell you until you're actually here. Did you bring anyone? Partner?"

I shook my head, thinking briefly of William, now installed back above the stables at Langley Hall and counting the days until the first break.

"I did," Martin said, "my girlfriend, Julie. She's in the women's block, next to the school. They won't let us share, not unless we're married." He rolled his eyes, then bent to fit a cardboard buttress to the side of the stage. "Still, it's an adventure."

He showed me the vacant bedroom and I unpacked in companionable silence. The bed was a king-size double with a foam mattress on a divan base, the sheets supplied by the school and printed with an improbable constellation of cartoon camels. I stowed my clothes in the armoire, hung the Aegina painting above the desk, and lined up my books along the sill.

An hour later, Martin knocked and suggested we explore the locality. The hallways were identical, the only distinguishing feature the scent of the cleaning product deployed in increasingly desperate concentrations as one ascended the floors. We met a handful of other teachers, their faces a mix of old-timer stoicism and new-recruit awe.

At seven, the school hosted a welcome dinner in the city. A minibus delivered us to the *SAS* hotel which was halfway between the apartment block and school. It sat on the beach side of the *Gulf Road* that ran all the way south to the *Saudi* border. The lobby displayed an opulence I had never experienced before and was upholstered in marble and gold. The event was staged in a ballroom; the ceiling hung with chandeliers so dense they seemed to threaten collapse. Along the walls, tapestries alternated between scenes of European debauchery, naked cherubs, velvet-draped nymphs and abstract, Islamic-inflected geometrics that pulsed and receded as one's gaze drifted. The effect was at once decadent and faintly accusatory, as if the room itself resented the intrusion of its own ornamentation.

I collected a plate of suspiciously Westernised canapés, then drifted to the edge of the proceedings. Martin and Julie disappeared into a huddle of PE teachers; the girl from the airport, still in her university tee, was arguing with the bartender about the definition of "fresh juice". I found a spot at the far end of the room and watched the flow of bodies, the way alliances and rivalries already seemed to coalesce around the buffet and the coat-check.

It was in this moment of relative calm that I saw him. Mark O'Toole. Last I had heard about him was from a mutual friend from university, who told me he was teaching in *Huddersfield*.

At first I thought the heat had rewired my vision, because the last time I'd actually seen Mark was at a university function several years before, and then only at a great and deliberate distance. But there he was, unmistakable: the angled chin, the blond hair shorn close to the scalp, the eyes blue and shifty as a robin's egg. He wore a short-sleeved shirt, ironed within an inch of its life, and stood surrounded by a small court of English instructors, his laughter rising above the din in sharp, predatory intervals.

I tried to blend into the potted palm behind me, but the illusion did not hold. Mark caught my gaze across the room, and for a moment there was an old, familiar lag, recognition, then calculation, then the predatory closing of distance. He detached from his circle and approached with the confident stride of a man who has never, in his life, doubted his right to an audience.

"John!" he called, too loudly, as he reached me. "Well, fuck me, I didn't know you were coming out here!"

I faked a smile, "last-minute decision," I said, voice arid.

He clapped my shoulder, a gesture meant to be both fraternal and anchoring, "God, it's been what, two years? You look the same. Thinner, maybe." He studied my face, then let his gaze slip over my clothes, my shoes and my face again.

He sipped from a glass of lemon soda, then leaned in, voice dropping half a register, "we should catch up. Properly. Meet me later by the pool?." He let the implication hang in the air, then added, "there's a lot of time to kill in a place like this."

I mumbled something noncommittal, then angled my body away, as if I might be summoned by someone at any second. Mark laughed, not unkindly, and rejoined his circle, already in full control of the story he would tell about me.

The remainder of the evening was a blur, as I bumped into another university friend who had also just taken a job in Kuwait. It soon became apparent that many of the international schools had undertaken a massive recruitment campaign following the conclusion of the

Iran-Iraq War. Eventually, I found myself shadowing Martin and Julie, their rapport a buffer against the possibility of a further encounter with Mark. The food was passable, the speeches mercifully brief. By the time the shuttles returned us to the accommodation block, the moon was a red coin pasted to the sky, the wind full of grit and electricity.

Back in my room, I stripped to my shorts and lay on the bed, the painting of *Aegina* staring back at me from the opposite wall. I tried to summon the feeling of that island, the suspension of expectation, the possibility of escape, but it eluded me. Instead, my thoughts ricocheted around the perimeter of the room, seeking purchase and finding none.

I closed my eyes and imagined William's voice, soft and certain, anchoring me to the present. But it was Martin's laugh that I heard through the wall, and beyond that, the city's low, unceasing hum.

Some places, I decided, one simply survives. For now, that would be enough.

The staff room was a compromise between cultures. The walls bore the institutional optimism of laminated posters: *'every child can achieve!'*; *'respect is a two-way street!'*; an incongruous, airbrushed portrait of the Emir. The air was permanently scented with the unholy alloy of instant coffee and lemony floor polish, but the first time I entered at 7:15 on a Saturday, the effect was almost comforting. Thursdays and Fridays were the weekend here.

Amanda Bourke had already established herself at the table nearest the window, a chipped porcelain mug cupped in both hands, her legs crossed under a skirt that was, by local standards, practically daring. She was from *Cheshire* by birth, the accent still palpable despite years away, but her eyes, sharp, pale, iridescent as a northern sea, were what people remembered. She wore her hair short, a cap of brown, and her laugh, which I heard before I ever met her, was clear and unforced, like a bell rung in an empty church.

I claimed the chair opposite, shuffling my stack of lesson plans as if to justify my presence.

"John Williams, isn't it?" she said, in the upward tilt that doubled as greeting.

"Guilty," I replied, stirring the granules in my own mug with a biro. "You're…?"

"Amanda. Bourke. PE and some social studies." She grinned, and I found myself grinning back.

For a while we worked in parallel: her annotating a battered desk planner with yellow stickies, me parsing the contradictions of the *IB History* curriculum. Outside, the sun turned the window into a pale, blinding shield; inside, the fluorescent tubes stuttered, then rallied. The quiet was punctuated by the arrhythmic thud of lockers and the distant peal of the school bell, already a minute late.

"You get used to it, so I have been told," Amanda said, breaking the silence. "The heat, the noise, the surreal sense that you're in a country club for children of oil executives."

"I'm not sure I want to get used to it," I admitted, "feels like cheating, somehow."

She considered this, then shrugged. "Cheating who? The students? They'd all be in *Geneva* or *Singapore* if their fathers hadn't drawn a bad lot. You or me? We're just passing through." She eyed me over the rim of her mug. "Anyway, I like the view. Beats the hell out of a Crewe comp."

We settled into a routine; the morning coffee break a sanctuary against the slow-motion lunacy of the school day. In those first weeks, we developed a taxonomy of our colleagues: Mary from maths, who hoarded tonic water in the fridge and drank it neat; Peter, the geography teacher, who wore his wedding ring on a chain and rotated it nervously during staff meetings; Don, a math instructor from *Dorset*, who obsessed over the daily exchange rate and could be provoked into a diatribe by any mention of the Bank of England.

Amanda chronicled these characters with a mixture of affection and mild contempt, I listened, absorbing the unofficial rules, and found that her judgment, though caustic, was almost always correct.

It was Amanda who introduced me to the rituals that made the place bearable. The Thursday *'pub quiz'* at the *Marriott,* where alcohol was covert and the prizes overtly bad. The Friday morning trip to the souq, where the stalls were a chaos of spices, knockoff perfumes, and Soviet surplus electronics. The long, twilight walks along the beachfront at *Salmiya,* where the sea breeze rendered the city briefly habitable, and where, once, we watched an electrical storm strobe the skyline to the east.

In these interludes, I found myself telling her things I had never managed to tell anyone in England. Not the whole story, never the whole story, but enough for her to map the contours of my life, to sketch in the negative space left by William's absence. She never pressed, never asked about family or lovers or the reason I'd chosen a year in the desert over the comparative luxury of the English education system. Instead, she filled the silence with stories of her own: a childhood in *Crewe*, a failed marriage to another teacher and a varied teaching career.

We spoke of books, of course. Of cricket, and the state of the Labour party, and, once, of the shape of our ideal funerals. She had a talent for pulling the heart from a topic, leaving the rest to be dusted off and reassembled at some later date.

I came to anticipate our morning coffees, the way the heat from the mug warmed my hands even as the air con goose-pimpled my arms. I noted the way she tucked a stray hair behind her ear when concentrating, the way she pronounced *'schedule,* with a hard *'sh'* that always made me smile. I found myself waiting for her laugh, for the way she could puncture a pretence with a glance, or convert a small misery into a joke that lingered long after the lesson had started.

I regularly received letters from William and Sarah and both were happy to hear my news that I had made a new friend. I suppose that both of them knew me well enough to worry that I might have chosen to isolate myself instead of embracing the new experience.

By the end of September, it was unthinkable that we should not share this ritual. If she was late, I waited. If I was late, I knew she would be there, a second mug already steaming, her eyes fixed on the horizon or the page, but alert, always, to my arrival.

It was not love, or anything close to it, but it was something close to being necessary. In the confounding architecture of that place and time, Amanda's presence was both compass and anchor, a proof that life could be measured in increments of kindness, even on the far side of the world.

Dinner with Amanda was a negotiated ritual. In the city, restaurants seemed divided along binary lines, either the gilded excesses of the international hotels, where you could order steak frites and pretend for a moment you'd never left Europe, or the tiled, echoing canteens where men ate in haste, their eyes fixed on the TV , barely registering the food or one another. Amanda preferred a place on the edge of the old souq, a bistro of sorts, its signboard stencilled in French and Arabic, the interior a warren of blue-and-white tile and brushed steel tables. At dusk, paper lanterns were strung above the windows, softening the edges of the room and rendering every patron faintly conspiratorial.

We sat at the back, near the kitchen, the table so narrow our knees grazed beneath the surface. The menu was a hybrid: grilled halloumi, ratatouille, kebabs, the odd imported pasta. Amanda ordered a mezze platter and a carafe of something the waiter insisted was *very like wine*, though the taste was less grape than the memory of grape, dissolved in sugar and regret.

She picked at the food, arranging the vegetables by size, never eating more than a forkful before moving on. I pretended not to notice. We talked, at first, about the week, lesson plans, the implacable bureaucracy of the school, the farcical attempts by admin to enforce *modest attire* on a faculty of post-hippie Brits and American divorcees.

Then, as always, the conversation curled around to our colleagues.

"Mary's trying to outrun her own liver," I said, watching Amanda's fingers as she dismantled a slice of cucumber, "you'd have to be desperate to come to a country where you have to break the law to have a drink."

Amanda smiled, the corners of her mouth sharp in the lantern light, "Peter's hiding from his ex-wife. Did you see how he jumps every time a woman with sunglasses comes into the staff room?"

"And Don?" I said, "I get the sense he's hiding from more than just the *Inland Revenue*."

She nodded.

I watched her assemble a spear of grilled pepper, feta, and olive. She paused, as if seeing it for the first time, then set it down on the edge of the plate.

"It's a pattern," she said, not quite looking at me, "the world's best collection of people who'd rather not be anywhere at all."

I laughed, but it felt thin, "you think we're running from something?"

"Aren't we?" She tilted her head, appraising me as if she could find the answer in the geometry of my collarbones, "otherwise, why here?"

For a while we listened to the clatter of plates, the staccato of the kitchen staff as they traded insults in three languages. The table between us grew more crowded with uneaten food. I reached for the bread, then hesitated.

"So what about you?" I said. "What brings you to the world's most exclusive teacher gulag?"

Amanda traced the rim of her glass. For a moment I thought she would deflect, make a joke, or refer me to her résumé. Instead, she drew a breath and, in a voice barely above the sibilant murmur of the room, said, "I had a problem. For years. Eating. Or not eating." She smiled, but it was not the bright, puncturing smile I knew from the staff room; this was something more private, an artifact turned over in the hand for examination, "I was very good at not eating. So good I nearly stopped, permanently."

She let the statement settle, then continued, "Crewe was small. My world was smaller. Everyone knew, or pretended not to. Coming here was a kind of exile, but also…" She searched for the word, "a reset."

I nodded, unsure whether to reach across the table, or to let her keep her distance, "does it help?" I said.

She shrugged, "some days. Here, there's always a next thing. Next job, next contract, next country. You keep moving, and nobody asks what you left behind."

We let that stand. Then, in the same tone, she asked, "and you, John? What do you run from?"

The answer was on my tongue, but it was still unfamiliar in my own voice, "I suppose I thought I was running toward something, at first." I swirled the juice in my glass, watched the sediment settle, "but lately it feels like I'm just keeping up with my own story."

She leaned in, her face open and without pity. "What story is that?"

I tried, then, to explain. Not the specifics, never the specifics, but the way I had always felt out of phase with myself, the sense that my life was something I'd borrowed and would one day have to return, with interest. "There is a man," I said, and watched her reaction, "and there was a life that might have been possible, if I'd been braver, or less… myself. We spent the summer together. On an island. It was perfect, which made it impossible." I felt guilt immediately for my understatement of William's importance.

Amanda listened, hands still, her gaze steady, "why impossible?"

"Because it was real, and everything else was…" I shrugged, "everything else." I told her about how things had worked out in my first school and how William had stood with me at every point in my journey. Then I finally say, "and now I just wonder when I get back to him and England, that the same thing will happen all over again." I let the words disappear into the air, and realise that with them some of the optimism I feel about a future with William dissolve too.

We sat in silence, the restaurant's acoustics swelling to fill the pause. At another table, a group of engineers argued about satellite dishes; beyond that, a waiter refilled glasses with an exaggerated flourish. I break the silence once the significance of my own words impact me, "maybe I am just a coward?"

When Amanda spoke again, it was with the careful softness of someone who had been here before, "you don't seem like a coward, John."

"But I run every time," I said, too quickly. "I just…" I stopped. "I keep thinking, if I make the right choices, if I do everything right, one day I'll catch up to the person I'm supposed to be. But I never do. I just keep… running."

She smiled, the sadness in it now mutual, and she reaches across to tap her finger against my knuckle, "maybe that's the trick. You never catch up, but you don't have to stop running."

We finished the meal in companionable silence. When the bill came, Amanda insisted on paying. "You can get the next one," she said, standing and smoothing her skirt.

Outside, the air was warm but less aggressive. The lanterns flickered against the night, and the city's roar felt, for the first time, distant and unthreatening. We walked back to the accommodation block, not quite touching, but moving in parallel, our shadows twin on the pavement. At the entrance, we paused.

"See you in the morning?" I said.

"Of course," she replied, and for a moment I thought she might say more. But instead, she only smiled, the sadness gone, and slipped inside, leaving me to stand alone, wondering if running was enough after all.

Autumn in *Kuwait* was a suggestion, not a season. The air shifted from infernal to merely aggressive, and with it the rhythms of life at the school settled into their own complex equations. Morning coffee gave way to lunchtime debriefs, then to the after-school ritual of tea in Amanda's apartment, a two-room cell in the newer, brighter block reserved for female staff. The place was tidier than my own, hung with framed postcards from her travels. In each, she stood apart from the foreground, not quite belonging but never out of place.

The rules for foreigners in *Kuwait* were labyrinthine, but the one that mattered most was this: single men and women could not cohabit, or even visit one another's apartments un-chaperoned after certain hours. This did not prevent Amanda from inviting me over, but every visit was coded, a dance of plausible deniability. She'd leave the door on the latch, make tea in a chipped *Wedgwood* set, and always, always set an extra cup on the tray, as if at any moment we might be interrupted by a neighbour, a custodian, the social police.

It was on a Tuesday in October, in the dusky margin between the end of the teaching day and the start of evening classes, that Amanda first broached the subject of marriage.

We were on the balcony, drinking over-steeped tea and watching the sun lower itself into a haze of sand and exhaust. Amanda's hair was caught up in a kerchief, and she wore a faded T-shirt and loose trousers that marked her, for once, as a tourist rather than a teacher.

"I've been thinking," she said, tracing the rim of her mug with a thumbnail, "about what comes next."

I laughed, a little, "a job in *Abu Dhabi*, or maybe *Bahrain*, if I'm really unlucky. At least booze is legal there."

She smiled, then shook her head, "I meant us."

I waited, unsure of the category in which to file this conversation.

"It's a practical question," she said, "you know the rules here. They are so suffocating in many ways."

She paused, "you know, I'd like to live with someone again. But I'm tired of doing it by halves. I'm tired of pretending."

I tried to assemble a response, but Amanda forged ahead, her voice brisk and kind.

"I know you're not…" she gestured, vaguely, as if to encompass my entire previous life. "I know what you told me, John. About the summer. About him. But I also know you. And if you wanted, I think we could make it work. I think we could be good, together. Help each other. After all, Martin and Julie are getting married in a few weeks and you will need a new flatmate."

"But, how could I help you?" I wonder immediately but out loud.

"You already do John," she continues, and her expression becomes vulnerable.

I am genuinely puzzled, "how?"

"You never judged me about my food issues, you just accepted it as being part of me, and …" she pauses, "don't you think I haven't noticed how you watch me when I eat, how you always manage to persuade me to eat a little more without forcing me or making an issue of it…?" her voice trailed away as tears formed in her eyes. "Without you these past few months, I don't know where I would be now."

"And the same is true for me," I take her hand and squeeze it gently.

The air between us was dense with possibility, and with it, a kind of safety I had never felt before. Amanda was offering not passion but peace, the prospect of a life lived in the broad light of day, a future plotted in increments rather than accidents, and it seems she needs the same things as I do.

I said, "are you proposing some sort of marriage of convenience?"

She grinned, "I'm negotiating one perhaps."

I finished my tea and set the cup on the ledge. The city below was coming alive; car horns and muezzin calls and the far-off clamour of the souq. I looked at Amanda, saw in her face a familiarity that felt as old as my own, and in that moment, I wanted it. I wanted her. Not as a substitute or a disguise, but as a promise that life could, after all, be ordinary and good.

"I'd like to try," I said, "but let's not decide anything until Christmas," I offer.

"Of course, I understand you will want to discuss it with William," and with these words I finally think that I have found someone who *'gets'* me.

We did not kiss, not then. Instead, Amanda leaned her head against my shoulder, and we watched the sun bleed out behind the skyline, neither speaking until it was gone.

I write straight away to William and explain to him my thinking. By my reasoning, the arrangement would give me relief from the kind of pressures that had drowned me in my first job. I could assume the mantle of normalcy with someone I enjoyed the company of and who understood me. I could envisage no downside, and after his own contemplation on the matter, nor could William.

In the weeks that followed, we constructed a relationship with the same diligence we brought to the classroom. There were applications to file, a tangle of embassy forms to fill, interviews with the school's Human Resources officer who, when we broke the news, merely nodded and said, "happens all the time, you'll be assigned a new flat at the end of term." We did not mention it to many colleagues, Martin was the exception, and when I told him, he only grinned and said, "could do worse, mate. She's a legend."

When Martin moved in with Julie after their wedding, we set a date for January, part hope, part desperation and my apartment turned into our fragile refuge. Walking those endless corridors of paperwork at the *Kuwait Ministry of Justice*, I felt both determined and hollow: miles from one office to the next, begging for translated pages, stamps, signatures. At last we stood before a stern Kuwaiti official in a gold-braided dishdasha. He asked if I'd paid the dowry (a token sum, one dinar or two pounds sterling). I said *'yes'*. Then he asked Amanda, "do you offer yourself to be his wife?" and watched her nod with that quiet certainty I envied. Finally he turned to me: "do you accept her?" My "I do" felt hollow even as it left my lips. He stamped two certificates and handed them over, "are we married now?" I asked.

"Yes," he grumbled, an anticlimax. Only at the exit did we remember the rings and slip them onto each other's fingers, as if completing a promise we both feared.

Our wedding breakfast, a buffet at the *Holiday Inn* by the airport, was attended by pretty much the whole staff. A carved ice swan sat at the centre, beautiful and yet doomed to melt. We escaped to *Dubai* for a weekend, our brief, blissful illusion of escape, and by Saturday we were back at work, back to reality.

At home we cooked side by side: pasta with too much garlic, curries that nearly burned our tongues, the occasional attempt at a local lamb dish we found in a dusty recipe book. Amanda spun old vinyl on a battered stereo, *Paul Simon, the Beatles,* though sometimes *Sinead O'Connor* and *Whitney Houson* would drift in, and she'd murmur the lyrics in a quiet, off-key falsetto that made my heart both ache and rage with longing.

Evenings saw us cramped on the sofa, knees tangled, the TV barely on. Sometimes we talked easily; other times our silence roared with all the things unsaid.

We hosted other couples, served elaborate dinners, played '*Risk*' until dawn. Amanda, small but fierce, moved with an athlete's surety, her touch both gentle and commanding. At night she'd curl against me like a secret, her breath hot against my neck. Part of me thrilled in the closeness; another part recoiled at the vulnerability.

A week or two after the "ceremony," after one of those nights, we had sex for the first time. It was not planned, not even imagined by me at any previous point. We share the largest bed I had ever slept on, but the space between was always comfortably within the *'friend zone'*.

So, on this night, I feel her leaning towards me and she places a gentle kiss on my lips, momentarily I freeze, but then respond instinctively. The intimacy of the moment arouses me in a way I had never been before with a woman. Afterwards, she lay with her head on my chest, tracing idle circles. Her voice was soft but direct, "you know this won't fix you."

"I know," I whispered.

Yet I wanted, needed, hoped it all to be my cure. My cowardice was as clear as the ring on my finger, and every time I looked at her, I found myself both comforted and terrified that I'd failed before we'd even begun. To my greatest shame, I realise the next morning that I hadn't once thought about William.

CHAPTER 17: A NEW LIFE

The year unspooled in increments: term reports, exam proctoring, weekends at the mall, the occasional trip to the *Gulf* for shopping or sightseeing. Amanda became pregnant in late January, and the news startled us both, though for different reasons. She greeted it with a fierce, pragmatic joy, buying books and vitamins and assembling a spreadsheet of recommended clinics. I responded by panic-buying every guide to parenthood in the English section of the city's one decent bookshop, and the sad realisation that my betrayal of William was complete.

Up until that point, I had hoped that a quick confession to him when we reunited, would lead to his eventual forgiveness. Now there was no going back. I could not undo the choice I had made – betrayal and cowardice over my love for William.

Amanda's belly swelled, then her ankles, and with it my sense of the imminent and the irreversible. We decorated the spare room, painted it a colour the manufacturer called *'celadon'*, and assembled a cot from a flat-packed box from the new *IKEA* that lacked all instructions and half its screws. I read aloud from baby books, tips for sleeping, for feeding, for soothing night terrors, and found, in the repetition of these rituals, a strange contentment.

If I thought of William, it was only in the quietest moments, late at night, lying awake while Amanda snored softly beside me. I would remember the beach, the Greek sunlight on his face, the way his laughter had, for a time, rewritten the physics of my world. And finally the pain I was yet to cause him. But, these memories receded, replaced by the new math of diapers and the prospect of a future untroubled by secrets.

The baby arrived mid- November, two weeks early and with a full head of black hair. We named her *Rose*, at my insistence, and when I first held her, I felt a giddy, vertiginous sense that at last, I had caught up to the version of myself I was meant to be. The heat from her tiny body burnt into my heart and soul as I held her blood covered body next to me. For a few, brief seconds I felt *'normal'*, the same as any other new father. Then from nowhere, a wave of guilt and shame hit me, as I realised that one day Rose would have to know or discover the truth about me.

I told everyone, "she's perfect." And she was.

That winter was the happiest I can remember, as the joys of fatherhood eclipsed the many doubts I held, but had largely buried. I knew I still had to tell William, but for now that could wait.

Amanda's recently widowed mother flew out to meet her granddaughter, and for a month the apartment was full of voices and tea and the scent of home-cooked bread. Martin came by with a teddy bear the size of a sheepdog and held Rose like she was made of glass and quickly remarked to Julie, "don't be getting any ideas!"

We employed a Sri Lankan maid which allowed Amanda to return to work as soon as her mother returned to England. Amanda said I was a natural father; I told her I was just making it up as I went along. We both laughed at this, but it was the kind of laughter that carried a freight of real, complicated feeling.

Sometimes, when the city was quiet and the sea was dark and calm, I would close my eyes and think '*this is what it means to be normal*'. This is what it means to be cured.

I wanted to believe it, and for a while, I almost did.

Manchester in late March was a city in abeyance, caught between the threat of spring and the certainty of rain, the air heavy with the aftertaste of coal dust and the promise of something about to fail. I landed at *Ringway* on a Tuesday, the flight from *Kuwait* a sleepless sequence of time zones and congealed airline meals, and took the train into the city under the pretext of "clearing up a few loose ends." The truth was, I wanted, needed, to see William one last time before I surrendered to the reality of my new life. He deserved my honesty, and I think Amanda knew and respected this.

We agreed to meet at our usual bar, the scene of that first foray in the gay life of Manchester. I arrived early and claimed a booth near the back, beneath a sepia print of the canal when it still carried boats instead of rubbish. The carpet was sticky and the air smelled of old beer and *Brasso*, but it was warmer than outside and the barmaid, a woman with pink hair and a face like a collapsed soufflé, brought my pint without being asked.

I sat with my hands wrapped around the glass, watching the condensation bead and slide, rehearsing the conversation I knew would not go as planned.

William arrived a quarter hour late, hair longer than I remembered, the edges of his coat damp and his cheeks flushed with cold. He spotted me instantly and made a show of weaving through the tables, grinning in the old, familiar way.

"John," he said, voice pitched low for privacy, and slid into the booth opposite, "it's good to see you. Though I wasn't expecting you until the summer."

He laughed, and the sound was so precisely as I remembered that I had to look away.

"I had to," I said. "there are things I need to tell you in person."

The barmaid delivered his pint, and for a few moments we drank in silence, the noise of the pub a shield against anything that needed to be said.

"So?" William asked, eventually. He always seemed to know instinctively when to wait and when to encourage me.

I opened my mouth to explain how it all began in *Kuwait*, how it had started as nothing more than a convenient friendship which he already knew. Then watched the colour drain from his face as my words landed. I swallowed and added, "and there's a baby."

William's gaze locked on the rain-smeared window behind me, the glass blurred by erratic streaks. He tapped his fingernail against his pint, then glanced down, and I saw him spot the wedding ring on my finger. His smile was polite but empty.

"Does she know about me?" he asked, voice quiet.

I hesitated, my heart tightening, "she knows enough," I said, not daring to say more.

He exhaled as if to laugh, shook his head, "always the diplomat," he muttered.

My fingertips itched to reach across the sticky tabletop, to trace the line of his jaw, to erase the distance that yawned between us. Instead, I picked at the bar mat and watched the paper fibres gather under my nail.

"It's not what I thought," I confessed at last. "Marriage. Fatherhood. I imagined they'd, fix something in me. Make me… normal."

William studied me, his eyes searching, "does it?"

I closed my eyes, fighting the urge to lie. The truth sat heavy in my chest, "no," I whispered, "but it's what I chose."

He looked down at his hands, voice low: "you didn't have to. You could have chosen me."

His words hit me like icy rain. I lifted my eyes to meet his, "I know," I said, "but I was scared. I still am."

His thin smile cracked, brittle as ice, "you always were."

We finished in silence. He ordered another pint; I declined. Outside, the rain pounded the window, drumming out a chaotic rhythm.

"I'll be in *Kuwait* for a while," I said, my throat thick. "Amanda's contract runs through next year. After that… I don't know."

William nodded once, gaze distant. Then I spoke again, "she's asked me to break off contact with you." The words snapped free his last restraint. Anger flared in his eyes.

"You'd better leave me now, John."

I stood, heart pounding. I reached out to touch his shoulder, but he recoiled, "I'm sorry, William," I managed.

He didn't look up. He sat hunched in the booth, cradling his pint as if bracing for a blow.

Outside, the streets ran silver with rain and sodium light. I walked to the station, hands shoved deep in my pockets, the pub's stale air clinging to me. I told myself I was doing the right thing, that I had chosen the life I wanted, the life I needed to follow now if only for Rose's sake. But with every step I felt the choice twisting in my gut.

On the platform, the train's headlights cut through the darkness, and I pressed my forehead to the cold glass, letting tears fall as quietly as the rain outside. Some choices, I realised, never stop echoing. They linger in the spaces you leave behind, and in the ones you can't return to.

I watched the lights of Manchester blur into the night as I headed to Crewe and a wife, a child and the in-laws, feeling the ache of lost possibilities pulse through me, unresolved.

By the summer of 1990, we had completed two years in *Kuwait* and recently signed on for at least one more. We had both been offered substantial pay rises to stay on and the promise of a new apartment nearer to the school. Amanda and Rose had left for a holiday in *Crewe*, whilst I was left in charge of completing the move to our new home. The plan was to join them for the last two weeks in England.

Life had been good, as we were both now accustomed to the vagaries of life in *Kuwait* – we learnt that all of the restrictions were mitigated by the opportunities on offer. I tried not to think too much about William, but this was difficult as I simply missed him. Every time I felt badly about how I had treated him, I would take a drive into the desert and test myself off-road. Danger focused my mind.

I woke into a silence so absolute I thought, for a moment, that I had died and been consigned to a neutral afterlife: no harps, no flames, just the soft, unyielding hum of the air conditioning. The bed, king-sized and empty but for myself, was a continent; the sheets clung only to my side, the other half untouched, the outline of Amanda and the baby already erased by the night's shifting. I lay for a long time, unmoving, until the pale rectangle of desert sun crept up the wall to the ceiling fan and I remembered: they were gone. England for the summer. I was alone, left to sort out a move to a new apartment next-door to the school.

In the weeks before, the apartment had been a war zone of baby detritus, plastic bottles, teething rings, board books, wipes that multiplied in the corners like so many paper moths. Amanda, whose approach to life was to occupy every available surface with evidence of her existence, had transformed the place into a kind of kinetic sculpture, a constantly updated proof that she and the child were more real, more present, than anything else. Now, the counters were bare. The floor, mopped to a high gloss by the silent Sri Lankan cleaner, reflected the light from the balcony. Even the fridge seemed to have rearranged itself, its contents reduced to the bare minimum: yogurt, mineral water, a block of feta.

I padded to the kitchen and made coffee in the stovetop *Bialetti* Amanda had once mocked as a "midlife crisis in chrome." The coffee was bitter and perfect. I poured it into the largest mug in the rack and drank standing, my feet cool on the tile, staring out at the heat-shocked street below. Nothing moved. The sky was so violently blue it looked fake, a movie director's idea of heaven. A convoy of *Toyota Land*

Cruisers sat in the car park, dusted with a veneer of sand. In the distance, a pair of crows picked at something on the curb, unmoving, even in their labour.

I drank two more cups, each one a little slower, then showered and shaved with a deliberation that bordered on performance art. I dressed in shorts and a loose shirt, left the top buttons undone, and skipped the socks, reasoning that nobody in *Kuwait* could possibly be watching me, least of all Amanda. I lingered in the act of choosing: a belt, sunglasses, the battered copy of the *TLS* I'd saved for just such a morning. I was not hurrying. There was nothing to hurry for, and in this fact I felt, for the first time in months, the exquisite relief of not being necessary to anyone. There was no need to rush the packing and the move as I had as long as I needed to do it. Amanda's, or rather *'our'* sensible family saloon car was put in storage until September, and I kept our first joint purchase, a four-wheel drive convertible, for my own use.

Midday, I drove to the café in the *SAS* hotel foyer that served as a kind of embassy for the Western teachers—an air-conditioned box lined with orange vinyl booths, the walls adorned with posters of French actresses and faded photographs of 1970s *New York*. The manager, a Lebanese man with the improbable name of *'Elvis'*, greeted me with a gesture equal parts salute and blessing. I ordered a *club sandwich* and sat at my usual booth, back to the wall, with a clear view of the entrance.

The others trickled in, as they always did: Peter from geography, Mary from maths, a new American couple whose names I had not yet learned and probably never would. There was the perfunctory exchange of news, Amanda's safe arrival in Manchester, the baby's first transcontinental shit, the rumour of another expansion in the school. Conversation was a volley of complaint and commiseration, but it was all surface, all glide; nobody was invested in anything beyond the parameters of the current day.

"Summer's when the real bachelors come out," Peter said, raising his lemonade, "all the women and children vanish like clockwork. It's like, what's that program? *'Survivors'*."

"*Lord of the Flies*," I said.

"Yeah, but with less ambition," he replied. The table laughed, and I realised I was laughing, too, not the polite exhale I'd mastered for Amanda's benefit but the kind that rearranges your face without permission.

Mary leaned across the table, the tip of her cigarette trailing a constellation of ash on the marble, "you'll go native, John. You watch. One month and you'll be pissing standing up and eating kebab for breakfast."

"I already do," I said, and she howled, smoke streaming from her nose. I had grown very fond of Mary over the past two years and was happy when she accepted my invitation to be the baby's Godmother - "despite her *Fenian* leanings" I had noted.

The *club sandwich* arrived, constructed with the architectural precision of the region. I ate slowly, listening to the rise and fall of voices, the ping of cutlery on plate, the hiss of the espresso machine behind the counter. There was comfort in the repetition, the way each teacher slotted into their assigned role, all of us complicit in the fiction of normalcy. It struck me that I felt more myself here, in this anodyne bubble of Englishness at the edge of the *Arabian Gulf*, than I had in the two years since leaving William. I was married, had a kid and no one could question that I was just *'normal'*. *'Thank God'*, I would often remark to myself that no one would ever know that this seemingly perfect life was born of an act of convenience and an accidental pregnancy.

The heat was a fact of life, a presence you learned to ignore by degrees. Inside, the temperature hovered at an English spring; outside, it was a different planet. When I finally stepped out, the air hit me with the force of a hairdryer set to max. My shirt stuck to my back in seconds, before I could even seek the sanctuary of my car and its AC. I drove home slowly, savouring the emptiness of the street, the way the light bleached everything to the edge of abstraction. I passed a corner shop, its owner slouched in the shadow, a radio tuned to the *BBC World Service*. For a moment I stood, pretending to browse the rack of cold drinks, listening to the litany of headlines, military movements, oil prices, the threat of some new regional *'crisis'*.

But none of it touched me. Not today. Today I was unburdened, invulnerable, the briefest of bachelors. I walked on, the can of *Pepsi* in my hand, and let myself believe that I could be this person, a man in his element, wanted by no one, answerable only to himself, forever.

Upstairs, the apartment was immaculate. I set the can on the windowsill, kicked off my shoes, and lay on the cool, empty bed. The silence was not oppressive now, but luminous, the white noise of a world that had, at last, receded to a safe and manageable distance. I closed my eyes and let the memory of the morning replay itself, frame by frame, until I drifted into a sleep so deep that I did not even dream. Eventually I stirred and began the process of packing into boxes our possessions.

The next morning, the sun took the city before the hour of six, pummelling every surface until the glass of the windows, the steel of the fire escapes, the car already hot inside beyond tolerance. I waited in the shade of the foyer for the AC to do its job, before climbing in to take the fifteen-minute drive to the health club attached to the *Holiday Inn*. For a monthly fee (subsidised by the school), you got access to a cramped weight room, two clay tennis courts, five squash courts, a sauna and a coffee bar, and, most importantly, the pool, a blue, kidney-shaped oasis, forty meters long, with a view, from the shallow end, of the skyline's stunted modernity.

It was empty when I arrived, save for the Filipino lifeguard asleep in his chair and a trio of middle-aged expats power-walking the perimeter. The air was already syrupy with heat, the smell of chlorine and coconut sunscreen hung over the deck, but the water itself was cold enough to numb the toes. I undressed in the changing room (blessedly deserted), locked my bag in the metal cubby, and strode out in my faded union jack (cliched I know!) trunks, the towel slung cape-like over one shoulder.

Swimming had become my principal self-improvement project. In theory, each lap was a rebuke to entropy, a staving-off of the inevitable collapse. In practice, it was a contest between boredom and the need to feel my muscles work against resistance, some token pushback against the general drift of things.

It was during my swims that I could also consider the nature of the life that I was living and how intoxicating expat life had become. Most people's plans usually revolved around completing a couple of years to save enough money to then do something else - a simple means to an end. As our social circle in the expat community expanded, I even found an English cricket team to play for, I began to notice that many of the couples we knew were into their tenth or fifteenth year.

The possibility of good earnings, which were tax free, subsidised schooling for children, petrol 10p a gallon, non-existent utility bills through free housing from our employees. It all came down to a standard of living beyond the reach of teachers back in the UK. The price I paid for this at times seemed a high one given the guilt I felt over William, and the general sense that my life was still based on a deception. A deception that Amanda at least went along with, even though her insecurities caused by her eating disorder could at times feel suffocating.

I set off from the deep end, slicing through the cold, focusing on form: elbow high, fingers together, reach, pull. I had made it five, maybe six lengths when I surfaced for air and saw, standing at the pool's edge, a figure both familiar and wholly out of context.

Mark O'Toole. Arms folded, sunglasses perched on his forehead, smile as precise as ever.

He wore blue swim shorts and a white singlet that looked to have never seen a day of honest labour. He watched me with the detached interest of a zoologist at feeding time. I considered ducking back under and swimming another lap, but it would have been childish, and anyway, he had already seen me.

"Morning, John," he said, just loud enough to carry over the slap of water on tile.

I nodded, treading water in the deep end, "you're up early."

He shrugged, "needed a change of scene. Gym's useless after seven, all the city boys hogging the machines."

He took off the shirt, folded it with almost ceremonial care, then walked to the diving board and sat on its edge, feet dangling, "no wife today?" he asked, the emphasis sly and unignorable.

"England for the summer," I said, and regretted the admission at once.

He grinned, "freedom, then."

I sculled to the edge, resting my arms on the coping, "something like that."

He kicked at the water, making small, deliberate splashes, "you always were a creature of habit, weren't you?" The line was harmless, but his eyes held a different intent, as if he was probing for a crack in the surface.

I looked away, watching the pensioners round the corner of the deck, their sunhats bobbing in silent conspiracy.

"Anyway," he said, stretching, "let's see what you've got." He dove in, slicing the water with a practiced ease, and for the next ten minutes we swam in parallel lanes, neither quite racing nor ignoring the other. Every turn at the wall, I caught a glimpse of him: streamlined, relentless, always a half-body length ahead.

After a while I gave up, hung onto the lane divider, and let my pulse slow. Mark finished his set, climbed the ladder, and towelled off, watching me with a crooked half-smile.

"You're getting better," he said, "next time, you'll beat me."

I hauled myself out of the water, shivering despite the heat. "I doubt it," I said.

He leaned in, voice lowered, "you know, if you ever get bored of the solo routine, there's a men's sauna as you know here. Strictly invitation-only, but I'm sure I could get you in."

I met his gaze. It was, as always, unreadable, equal parts dare and invitation, with a trace of something darker beneath. "Not today," I said, keeping my tone flat, "nor ever again as I have been telling you for nearly two years," my tone remained neutral.

He laughed, a single, sharp syllable, "suit yourself." He slid his sunglasses on, gathered his bag, and strode off, leaving a trail of wet footprints.

I dressed quickly, ignoring the quiver in my hands, and left the club by the back exit, cutting through the hotel to the car park. The sun was high now, and the heat assaulted the skin in waves, each step a negotiation with the mirage of shade.

A group of Kuwaiti businessmen, immaculate in their white dishdashas, stood near the entrance, smoking and talking in low, urgent voices. I caught snippets of English, "border," "*Basra,*" "emergency measures", interspersed with Arabic too rapid for my basic Arabic to understand. One of them, older, with a crescent scar above his eyebrow, gestured expansively, his voice rising: "they will not stop at oil. Mark my words, it's coming here."

The others nodded, flicked their cigarettes into the gutter, and shuffled back to their *Land Cruiser*, the doors thudding shut in rapid succession.

I drove up the avenue toward the government buildings. In front of the police headquarters, two blacked-out *Humvees* idled at the curb, their drivers slouched behind the wheel, faces expressionless. Further on, at the *Ministry of Health*, a crowd had gathered, nothing like a protest, more the solemn density of an airport terminal. I felt, for a moment, the uneasy thrill of history happening at a distance just close enough to touch.

Back home, I stripped and lay on the tile floor, letting the sweat pool and evaporate. I flicked on the TV, but the English news channels from Dubai had nothing new: grainy footage of Saddam Hussein in military uniform, a studio analyst in London talking about "sabre-rattling" and "the fine balance of power." The language was clinical, even bored, as if the entire region's fate was nothing more than a scheduling concern.

I called Martin. He answered on the first ring.

"Mate," he said, "you heard anything?"

"Just rumours. Some of the locals are spooked. The news isn't saying much."

He exhaled, the sound half static, half weariness, "my tutor group at the language school, they're all talking about it. Two of them didn't show today, parents kept them home. I rang Julie, but she says the embassy's telling everyone to stay put."

"Think we should be worried?"

A long pause, then: "it's probably nothing. But just in case, I packed a bag. Passport, money, a change of clothes. Couldn't hurt."

I thanked him, promised to call if I heard anything, and hung up.

The apartment, pristine just hours before, now felt airless, every surface radiating the slow accumulation of tension. I showered, dressed, and tried to read, but the words blurred on the page so I finished packing as far as I could. By six, the sky was an inferno, the clouds purpled at the edges, and I drove out to the edge of the city, wanting only the illusion of movement.

On the highway, a convoy of military trucks passed, their cabs filled with helmeted young men who stared straight ahead, faces shuttered against the world. They moved in tight formation, headlights on, the dust of their passing lingering long after the engines had faded. I pulled over and watched until the road was empty again.

Night fell. I returned home, made pasta, ate it standing at the counter. On the *BBC World Service*, the tone had changed: more *'breaking news'*, more experts, more interviews with breathless correspondents who could not, or would not, say what everyone was thinking.

I sat on the bed, the sheet damp with sweat, and let the radio play into the dark. At some point I must have slept, but it was not a sleep I remembered. When I woke, it was to the same dusty morning, the same blank expectation.

I showered, dressed, made coffee, and waited. For what, I did not know. The phone rang alarmingly early. I groggily answered. It was Martin.

"I'm at the school. Julie and I have decided to leave, and they can get us on today's *BA* flight. Want a seat? I need to know now, the bursar's on the other line booking as we speak."

My heart thudded. Part of me screamed caution, but I didn't hesitate, "yes, Martin, book it for me."

"Good, good," he said. "*BA 149*. See you at the airport about 10 pm." He hung up before I could add anything.

I lay there a moment, phone still clutched in my hand, mind spinning with *'what-ifs'*. Then, swallowing my panic, I swung my legs over the edge of the bed and dressed on automatic pilot: underpants, shorts, shirt, shoes, the minimal armour against whatever was coming. In four minutes I packed a rucksack: passport, bank cards, a handful of clothes, the *Aegina* painting, my lesson-plan notebook. The rest could burn. The rest probably would.

In the corridor other doors slid open. Two sleepy-faced Americans from Science, eyes swollen with dread, pulled suitcases toward the lift. A woman from Administration, her hair wrapped in a towel, cradled a pet carrier and a sheaf of passports. The air reeked of fear, every gesture amplified by the urgent need to evacuate.

I jumped into my car and drove to the bank on *Salmiya High Street.* A short queue had formed, and as I waited, a voice inside me whispered that I was overreacting. But caution won over guilt. I withdrew every last dinar but one and stuffed the wad of notes into my pocket. My pulse raced as I drove to the money souk, where I exchanged the lot for nearly twenty thousand pounds sterling in fifty-pound notes. Another bulging roll went into my pocket. I could feel its weight against my thigh, and the gravity of what I was doing.

Back near my apartment, I stopped at *SAS.* The café was eerily empty, no familiar faces, yet I stayed, ordering my usual snack and drink. As the adrenaline ebbed, doubt surged. Had I panicked? Clutching the thick bundle of notes through the material of my shorts, I realized it was more cash than I'd ever held, enough to buy a house back home, exactly what our savings were for. But keeping it here now felt too dangerous, embassy warnings or not.

I let out a shaky laugh. Amanda would kill me for forfeiting that interest. My jaw clenched at the thought of her scolding, "it's done," I muttered, more to steel myself than to admit comfort. Part of me felt safe; the other feared I was already too late.

Back at the apartment, I half-heartedly shovelled the last of our things into boxes, telling myself this was a small mercy, which come September, when we returned, these would still stand waiting. But each taped seam felt like slamming a door on everything I was leaving behind. I collapsed onto the balcony's edge, lit a cigarette, an illicit, guilty luxury and inhaled against the ghost of Amanda's reproach. The smoke curled upward and so did my chest, taut with relief and regret in equal measure.

The taxi arrived with mechanical punctuality. I threw one last glance at the building's pale facade and my car parked below, my stomach twisting with a blend of longing and liberation. Clutching the wad of cash in my jeans pocket, I climbed in, driven by a nervous pulse that thrummed beneath my skin.

At the airport, the usual chaos had ratcheted up to nerve-shredding levels. Dozens of expats clustered outside the terminal, children clinging to toys as if they were lifelines. The stifling heat, salty with sweat and panic, made my throat dry. Inside, harsh fluorescents flickered overhead, and a single snaking line shuffled toward the check-in desk. At its head, a woman with three screaming kids berated a clerk who met her fury with hollow indifference.

I spotted Martin and Julie farther down the queue. Seeing them grounded in the frenzy brought comfort, and guilt, as I wrestled with the urge to turn back. After check-in and baggage drop, we found seats in the departure lounge, trading wild rumours: Iraqis already storming the city, embassies evacuated, the British consulate doling out water and blank forms like rites of exile. I drifted to the window, watching aircraft taxi past. Each take-off felt like a final curtain.

Our flight was called over a crackling intercom. The announcement sent a ripple of tension through the hall, and we funnelled toward the gate. The *DC-10's* door yawned in welcome, its crew as silent as mourners. I claimed my spot in the smoking section at the rear, wedged between a burly Norwegian oil engineer reading a magnified thriller and a pale American schoolteacher who reeked of vodka and desperation.

As Martin tucked his bag into the overhead bin, our eyes met, two friends suspended between fear and hope. He nodded, voice soft: "see you on the other side, yeah?" My throat tight.

"Yeah," I said, though my heart lurched at what *'the other side'* might bring.

The engines rumbled, doors closed, and we taxied into the night. Below, the city lay bathed in empty orange glow. Streetlights traced deserted avenues; a lonely stadium still blazed in futile welcome. Then we lifted off, carrying all our splintered emotions into the dark.

The flight passed in restless stabs of sleep, waking to sterile meal trays and the constant drone of turbines. The Norwegian murmured each line of his paperback. The American stared straight ahead, knuckles white on her knees. I found myself perched between their silent worlds, caught in a jittery, jittered lull.

Landing at *Heathrow* felt like wading into another storm of lights and voices. I hugged Martin and Julie wordlessly, then drifted toward the *Manchester* connection. At the gate I nursed a bitter coffee, the news ticker scrolling dire headlines: *'Tensions Escalate in Persian Gulf'*, *'Evacuations Underway'*, *'World Watches Next Move'*. My chest tightened, craving the gut-punch I both feared and needed, but it never came.

Finally, I boarded the plane to *Manchester*. The cabin was nearly empty and colder than any I'd known in months. As we climbed into the pale sky, I stared down at the shrinking earth, torn between running from everything I'd built and running toward something I couldn't yet name.

We landed in drizzle. The runway shimmered with it; the terminal itself smudged behind a curtain of rain. I followed the crowd to baggage claim, then to *Arrivals*, where a wall of televisions glowed above the corridor.

It was there, in that space between airlocks, that I saw it: grainy, slow-motion footage of tanks rolling through the outskirts of *Kuwait City*. The anchor's voice was distant, irrelevant. The picture said it all.

I stood there, bags in hand, while the other passengers flowed around me, like a river diverted by a stone. The world had changed. My job, my apartment, the little order I'd built for myself, all of it was likely gone. A month ago, I'd imagined myself an exile; now I was simply unmoored.

My reflection, doubled in the glass, looked back at me with something close to astonishment. I wanted to call someone, Amanda, Martin, even William, but instead I just stood, blinking, and let the rain and the news and the new reality sink in. After a while, I picked up my bag and walked toward the exit, before taking the train into Manchester and the house rented for the summer.

CHAPTER 18: BACK IN *'BLIGHTY'*

First order of the day though was survival. I looked for work anywhere in the UK. A few weeks later I found myself at an interview in a prefab office at the edge of a London comprehensive, a building so reluctant to exist that even the rain seemed embarrassed to touch it. The headteacher, a woman with glasses so thick they distorted the shape of her face, studied my *CV* as if it contained a series of encrypted confessions. She sat behind a desk that belonged to another decade, its surface pockmarked with the ghosts of a thousand coffee mugs. I perched on the visitor chair, hands folded in my lap, trying to look both eager and unfazed.

"You were in Kuwait?" she said, after a long silence.

"Yes," I replied, "teaching history and some English, mostly to expat kids."

She nodded, lips pursed, then glanced at the next line, "and before that, *Manchester.*"

I said yes again. She set the *CV* down and regarded me over the rims of her glasses, "why London?"

I took a breath, "I needed a job. My family's in Manchester, but the schools there had nothing to offer."

She smiled, or nearly did, "indeed."

There was a perfunctory tour, corridors lined with handmade posters about bullying and tolerance, the occasional flash of adolescent menace in the stairwells. I was introduced to the deputy head, the head of department, a trio of admin staff who greeted me with the kind of brittle civility reserved for visiting clergy. The students, in their odd melange of uniforms, watched me with the bored insolence of a jury that's already delivered its verdict.

When the interview ended, the headteacher offered me the position on the spot, "it's a maternity cover," she said, as if apologising. "But it's yours if you want it." I nodded, thanked her, and left the office with the sensation of having been both hired and gently dismissed.

The reality of my new existence assembled itself in fragments: a rented room in the flat of a teacher friend, another Kuwait exile, who had a cat named *Pasha* and a fondness for Turkish soap operas. The commute from Manchester was a weekly ordeal: three to five hours on the motorway, broken only by the monotony of service stations and the slow accumulation of regret. I drove down Sunday nights, returned Friday evenings, sleeping in my own bed only two nights out of seven.

Amanda managed the *Manchester* house with a proficiency that bordered on military. The baby, now nearly a year old, was in daycare three days a week and with Amanda's mother on the other days. The fridge was always stocked, the floors always clean, but there was a tension to it, a tightness in the air that made every movement deliberate, every conversation a negotiation.

We spoke mostly in logistics: who would pick up Rose, when the rent was due, how much money I'd managed to save that month. Sometimes, in the lull between chores, Amanda would look at me as if seeing a stranger, her eyes scanning for evidence of some betrayal she couldn't quite articulate.

One evening, after Rose had finally succumbed to sleep, Amanda sat across from me at the kitchen table, a mug of tea cradled in both hands.

"Who was that man who answered your work phone yesterday?" she said, not looking up from the steam.

I thought back, retraced the day, "probably one of the junior teachers," I said, "I was in a meeting."

She nodded, slow and noncommittal, "he sounded very, familiar. Like he knew you well."

I shrugged, "we share an office."

A long pause, during which the only sound was the click of the fridge cycling on, "you're not seeing anyone, are you?"

"No," I said, too quickly but honestly.

She looked at me then, really looked, and I felt the full weight of her suspicion, "you'd tell me, if you were?"

"Of course," I said, "but I never would." To me this was the reality of my situation, I had committed to this relationship, to being a parent and I accepted it.

After that, we cleared the table together, moving around each other with the choreography of old, mismatched magnets. The next morning, she was up and gone before I finished my coffee, a note on the counter listing the day's shopping and a reminder to "call your mum."

In London, I settled into a routine so narrow it felt more like convalescence than work. I arrived early, taught my classes, lingered in the staffroom just long enough to absorb the gossip, then retreated to my room, where I graded papers and wrote up lesson plans in the blue light of the desk lamp.

I called Amanda every night, even when there was nothing to say. We spoke of Rose, of the weather, of the impossibility of finding decent bread in *London*. Once, I tried to tell her I missed her, but the words came out flat, as if someone else had written them.

On weekends, back in *Manchester,* I tried to repair what I could: took Rose to the park, cooked dinner, watched bad television with Amanda until one or both of us fell asleep. But the distance was there, cumulative and irreversible, a buffer that no amount of effort could cross.

Some nights, after Amanda and the baby had gone to bed, I would walk the streets of our estate enjoying illicit cigarettes, circling the same blocks, watching the blue glow of television in the windows, listening to the rise and fall of distant trains. I wondered if anyone else could see how temporary it all felt, how close everything was to vanishing.

In the end, I suppose, we stayed together out of habit, or inertia, or the hope that time would smooth over the cracks. But as the months unspooled, it became clear that neither of us believed it.

The last night before the Easter break, I found Amanda standing in the dark of the living room, baby monitor in hand, her silhouette limned by the sodium glow from the streetlamp outside. She turned as I entered, her expression unreadable.

"Do you want to stay?" she asked, voice quiet.

I thought of all the places I could be, all the other lives I might have lived, and said, "yes. I do."

She nodded, and for a long moment we stood there, two points on a line, neither willing to move closer or further apart.

In the silence, the house seemed to settle around us, as if recognizing the truth of our impasse.

We went to bed, and I held her, but it was like holding a memory, solid, but already drifting away. I made the long journey south on Sunday as usual, using the time to replay in my mind Amanda's words and wondering what could have motivated them. Next morning, a long narrow, legal-sized envelope was waiting for me on the door mat. I opened it in the car, and my stomach turned as I read that Amanda was seeking a divorce. I realised that she must have known the letter was on its way when she had wished me "a safe journey" the night before.

The office was on the fourth floor of a 1960s block, the kind that always seemed to be waiting for demolition. The rain washed the windows in sheets, blurring the city to a watercolour mess. I sat on a plastic chair, legs crossed, hands folded, trying not to leave sweat stains on the vinyl. The solicitor, a woman named Pritchard, wore a brown suit with shoulder pads and spoke in the clipped, impersonal register of someone who'd long ago grown immune to other people's dramas.

She read from a sheet of paper, lips pressed together in a single, unbroken line.

"Your wife alleges infidelity, specifically, a homosexual liaison during your time in London. She wishes to cite this as grounds for divorce."

I stared at my shoes, then up at the rain outside the window behind her..

"There was no such liaison," I said, voice steady, "I want to make that clear."

She nodded, making a note, "nevertheless, should your wife wish to, she would instead cite unreasonable behaviour as you behaved in such a way as to make her believe you were having an affair. The remainder of the petition covers child access, joint assets, etc.." She set the document before me, sliding it across the surface like a poker chip.

"So, it doesn't really matter what I say or what has really happened?" For the first time a hint of anger appeared in my voice as I felt the inevitability of what Amanda wanted.

"Unfortunately Mr Williams, it matters very little in reality. You can refuse of course, but after two years it would happen anyway," I detected a hint of sympathy for the first time, "and cost you a lot more." In total resignation I finally responded.

"I will not accept adultery, but if she goes down another route, then so be it."

"Very well, sign to instruct me and I will contact her solicitors immediately."

My hands hovered above the page. I remembered the years of tiptoeing around the possibility, the whispered rumours at school, the endless dread that one day the secret would go from rumour to evidence. The irony, I suppose, was that the secret she had weaponised was a ghost, real, but not in the way she thought.

I signed the first page, then the second, each pen stroke easier than the last.

She gathered the forms, placed them in a manila folder, and stood, "I will keep you informed. Is there anything else?"

I shook my head.

When I left, the rain had slowed to a sullen mist. I walked the mile to the station, but when I got there, I kept walking, following the canals through the old city, past the sagging backsides of warehouses and the bins behind the curry houses. My shoes filled with water, but I didn't care.

At the edge of *Canal Street*, I stopped. But here it was, *the Village*: banners and flags and a scatter of tables under patio umbrellas, the air heavy with the promise of rain and the sour-sweet reek of spilled beer.

I walked the length of the street. No one looked twice at me. Men held hands, women in *Doc Martens* shouted at each other over the throb of music from inside the bars. I watched them all, feeling both invisible and impossibly conspicuous.

At the corner, a group of men clustered around a pub called *New York, New York*. The door opened and closed, each time releasing a throb of synth, a baritone shout, the sharp edge of laughter. The men, some in shirtsleeves, some in leather, moved through the entrance with the kind of ease I'd never managed in my life. I stood on the pavement, watching them, envying the simplicity of their joy.

For a long time I just stood there, the neon from the sign painting my face green and pink, the rain pooling at my feet. I imagined what it would be like to go inside, to be seen and to see, to exist not as a secret or a hypothesis but as something actual.

I did not go in. Not yet.

But when I turned away, I felt a loosening, a subtle rearrangement of the molecules. I walked back through the city, spine straight, eyes forward, my reflection caught and multiplied in every wet shop window.

On the train home, I watched the dark slide past, the sodium lights smearing the world to lines and dots. I thought of Amanda, of Rose, of the house and the garden and the rhythm of years we had tried so hard to master. I thought of William, of the *Aegean*, of the freedom I'd never quite managed to take for myself.

For the first time in a long while, I smiled. Not the brittle, defensive smile of survival, but the real, involuntary kind that creases the corners of your eyes and makes you believe, if only for a second, that anything is possible, even if the cost was a small amount of self-respect.

When I got off at *Euston*, the rain had stopped. The sky was clearing, and somewhere behind the clouds, I imagined the stars were still there, waiting.

CHAPTER 19: "FREEDOM"

The envelope is the colour of institutional neglect: a shade between bandage and resignation, creased at the corners, as if even its contents are unwilling to present themselves. It arrives in the morning post, delivered by a man with nicotine skin and the eternal impatience of those who know exactly what they're delivering. He rings my bell, shoves it through the slot, and is already at the next door by the time I retrieve the letter from the mat.

I hold it by the edge, the way one might handle a used tissue, and carry it to the table. The flat is cold, the radiators not yet warm, and the table itself is a war veteran: pocked laminate, each burn and gouge a story left behind by a previous tenant. I place the envelope on the only clear patch, then circle it, as if proximity alone might clarify its threat.

I don't open it right away. Instead, I make tea, rinse the cup twice, and pretend for a moment that it is any other morning. It isn't. The postmark is a dead giveaway: *Chorlton-cum-Hardy*, home to the world's least forgiving ex-wife and the daughter who has started to call her new partner Dad, sometimes for laughs, sometimes for emphasis.

I sit, pull the envelope closer, and run a finger under the flap. It yields without resistance. Inside: a letterhead that is all business and no mercy, a cover sheet with my full name in triplicate, and the final, notarised *decree absolute*. *'You are now free to remarry'*, it says, though the only remarrying I can imagine is a brief, doomed entanglement with the empty wine bottle in the sink.

The urge is to laugh. Instead, I sign the bottom of the page, the ink bleeding through to the table, and seal it back up in the return envelope. There is nothing to do, no one to call, and nowhere to be before noon. I consider, briefly, a dramatic gesture, burning the page, or tearing it up and releasing the shreds into the wind off the *Thames*. But the window is painted shut and my capacity for symbolism has been dulled by years of secondary school invigilations and a diet of nothing but late-night television and regret.

From my seat at the kitchen window, the city is a catalogue of other people's forward motion. Buses heave past, glassed-in dioramas of the determined and the already defeated. Children, uniforms perfect and oversized, drag their mothers across the street toward the promise of structure and arithmetic. Even the pigeons are purposeful, marching along the ledge in a parade of hunger and opportunism.

My own reflection in the glass is indistinct: a suggestion of a man, spectral and out of alignment. I touch the surface and watch the finger smudge obscure the face behind it.

The flat, rented on a short lease with the unspoken understanding that the letting agent was doing me a favour, is not so much sparsely furnished as actively resentful of being furnished at all. The sofa is low, its stuffing arranged in geological layers by years of shifting weight; the television, a *Sony* inherited from a retiring history teacher, sits on a crate. There is a bookcase, its top shelf buckling under the combined weight of three sets of *'Advanced Level History'* textbooks and a dozen, never-opened volumes of the *'Great Thinkers'* series, bought in a fit of optimism and never consulted since.

The only item of real value is a photograph, framed and facing away from the light: Rose, aged four, her hair is impossibly straight, her smile defiant, as if daring the future to take her seriously. I look at her and feel nothing, or everything; the distinction is moot.

I check my watch. It is nine fifteen. The world expects me to be somewhere, standing at the front of a classroom, explaining the *Treaty of Versailles* to a collection of indifferent sixteen-year-olds, or at least pretending to be a man who has not just lost the last tie to his former life.

Instead, I pour a second cup of tea, ignoring the chill in the air and the odd, hollow ache in my chest, and return to the window.

On the street below, a pair of young men in matching bomber jackets and rolled-up jeans are negotiating the mechanics of a cigarette handoff. One lights the other's with a flourish, cupping his hand around the flame and holding it there, deliberately, a gesture of intimacy or maybe just the easiest way to avoid the wind. They laugh, their voices carrying up through the open vent, and then drift down the street, arm in arm for two strides before remembering themselves and separating, the space between them widening like a wound.

This is London in 1993. The shortly after *Section 28*, the week before another scandal, the season of never quite arriving at the moment you wanted. On the radio, the *Pet Shop Boys* are all over the *Top 40*; on the street, the threat and promise of acid house is fading into something more commercial, less dangerous. The city is alive with rumour and longing, but also with a sense that, even here, everything is watched, noted, and quietly filed away for use at a later date.

I shower, dress, and contemplate the logistics of the day. There is a supply gig at a local comprehensive, one of those places where the staffroom is divided along lines so subtle and old that even the PE teachers cannot remember who is at war with whom. I will arrive, sign in, take a battered stack of lesson plans from a secretary with the sullen charisma of a prisoner-of-war, and stand in for a teacher who is almost certainly hungover, or possibly detained at *Her Majesty's* pleasure. The students, spotting the lack of engagement, will test boundaries with all the desperation of men on a sinking ship. I will indulge them, just a little, because I recognise the look in their eyes.

Before leaving, I place the signed papers back in the envelope and lay it flat on the table. It looks, for a moment, like a white flag.

The school is three stops on the *Hammersmith and City Line* and a bus ride away, a cluster of concrete blocks huddled behind high fencing, its playground a battlefield of discarded crisp packets and unexploded chewing gum. I show my badge at reception, endure the scrutiny of the security guard (former *Metropolitan*, or so he claims), and navigate the labyrinthine corridors to the staffroom.

It is, as always, a scene of subtle warfare: the math department in one corner, clutching their tea and muttering about "targets"; the English faculty, resplendent in corduroy and despair, arching their brows at anyone who dares sit at their table; the science teachers, absent, probably in the pub.

I find my station, retrieve the day's schedule, and scan for anything resembling a break. There are none. Four straight periods of *'General Studies'* - the pedagogical equivalent of solitary confinement.

The first class is a blur of names, faces, and thinly-disguised derision. The boys at the back, jackets off and sleeves rolled to the elbow, immediately clock the newness of the supply and set about probing for weaknesses.

"All right, sir?" says the ringleader, voice pitched just above normal, "heard you were ex-military."

I shake my head, "history. Nothing so glamorous."

He considers this, then turns to his mate, "so what's the plan, then? Bit of *World War Two*, or just the usual propaganda?"

I smile, because it is expected, and launch into the day's topic: *'The Evolution of British Democracy'*. Eyes glaze over within seconds, but a few students at the front gamely take notes, the rest retreating into private worlds of doodle and daydream.

At lunch, I amble outside, the air sharp and bracing, and find a bench on the edge of the car park. From here, the city is visible in cross-section: the high-rises of *Canary Wharf* in the distance, a tangle of council estates nearer at hand, and in between the slow, methodical demolition of anything old enough to remember the War.

I eat a sandwich, aware that the bread is stale and the ham possibly from a previous millennium. As I chew, I think about Amanda, about the brief, disastrous span of our marriage, and about the particular cruelty of a love that begins in hope and ends in litigation.

It lasted four years, including the separation and divorce. The first two were fine, in the way that fine can mean functional but not memorable. Once we were forced back to England and I had to work away, the pressure of that and my absence somehow ignited Amanda's insecurities. I had quickly learned that her eating disorder was rooted deep in her past and could flare up for no apparent reasons. I had learnt to live with it and be supportive – something which when I was in London I couldn't do.

The next year was a series of skirmishes over nothing: who should have phoned who, who forgot the birthday, who spent too long in the bath. I was blind, or some might say *'insensitive'*, to whatever had changed between us. In my world I was working hard, driving four hundred and fifty miles every weekend to provide for my family. The final six months were spent arguing over the details of the divorce and I fought for custody of Rose, but Amanda made it clear she would out me to my family, our friends and work if I challenged her. *Thatcher's Britain* of the mid-1990s was not a place to be a gay martyr. I gave in of course, and she told my family and out friends anyway.

So, I lost, of course. I always do. But the loss was surgical, precise: I am free, now, to invent an updated version of myself. I am free to be gay, or not gay, or whatever the world will tolerate.

After work, I return to the flat. The envelope is still on the table. I stare at it, consider moving it to the bin, but instead place it in the drawer under the cutlery, next to the expired takeaway menus and the unopened gas bill.

The night is slow to arrive, the dusk stretching itself across the sky like a last-ditch argument. I open a bottle of wine, bought on the cheap at a *Tesco Express*, and I remember thinking '*William would not approve of plonk*', and drink it in the blue light of the television. The news is all recession and war. The next show is a repeat of something from the seventies, the jokes so out of date they circle around to become relevant again.

At ten, I turn off the TV and sit at the window, watching the world recede into itself. The young men from earlier are back, this time in a group, their voices louder and more certain. One of them glances up, catches my eye, and holds the gaze for a beat longer than is strictly necessary. There is a flicker of something, recognition, maybe, or just the curiosity of the young for the '*old*' – as this how I feel at thirty.

They move on, the street emptying behind them, and I am left with the city and its possibilities. Tomorrow, I will wake, and teach, and do all the things required to sustain the illusion of adulthood. But tonight, for just a moment, I am untethered. Alone, yes, but free.

I close the curtains, and let the darkness take the rest.

There is a physics to the opening of a pub door: the vacuum-sealed tension, the sudden collapse of one reality into another, the sense of having crossed a threshold after which nothing will quite align with the world you left behind. *Compton's* of *Soho* is no exception, if anything, it exaggerates the phenomenon, catching newcomers in its vestibule like specimens in amber.

It's a Thursday night, early by the clock but already crowded, the air inside warmer and heavier than the late-winter damp outside. I step in and halt, momentarily blinded by the interior: everything wood-panelled and gleaming, mirrors multiplying the crowd into infinity, coloured lights washing over men in a spectrum of intent. The bar itself is a Victorian slab, dark and lacquered, its surface as slick as an accusation.

For a full minute I hover at the edge, clutching the strap of my satchel, scanning for a place to stand that will not invite either challenge or pity. My coat, a relic of the *Oxfam* autumn line, marks me at once as an outsider; my shoes, polished but outdated, complete the effect. The men at the bar are younger, more tactical in their fashion: *Doc Martens*, acid-wash jeans, t-shirts under open shirts, some in leather or mesh as if daring the March chill to do its worst. There is a choreography here, a way of occupying space, of leaning, of letting the eye roam that I have not yet mastered.

I find a patch of floor near the end of the bar, wedge myself between a column and a fruit machine, and try to look as though I am waiting for someone. No one notices, or everyone does and elects to pretend otherwise. I run a hand through my hair, aware that the humidity of the tube has already undone the morning's labour, and order a pint from the barman. He is balding, with arms like rope and a tattoo that peeks from beneath his sleeve, but he offers a smile that is neither predatory nor patronizing, just the dry acknowledgment of one man who knows a lost soul when he sees one.

"First time?" he asks, pitching his voice so it doesn't carry.

I nod, "in here, yes. Is it that obvious?"

He shrugs, pulls the pint, and slides it toward me, "everyone's first time once. If you need a rescue, shout."

There is comfort in the transaction, in the clarity of roles. I sip the beer, feeling the coldness anchor me to the present, and survey the room. Most of the crowd is already deep into the evening, bodies pressed together at the bar or crowded into the booths that line the opposite wall. The laughter is loud, the gestures extravagant, and every conversation seems to be conducted at a pitch designed to overpower the piped-in soundtrack, a blend of *Madonna*, *Erasure*, and something with a backbeat so relentless it registers as threat.

A group of men stands in a loose cluster near the window, their collective gaze oscillating between the street outside and the pool table at the back. They are beautiful, or at least symmetrical, with the easy self-assurance of those who have never known a day of being the odd one out. I watch as one—

tall, angular, hair the colour of fresh coffee, leans in to whisper to another, whose face lights up in either amusement or desire. For a second, I think they have spotted me; I look away, focus on the print above the bar, and pretend to read the beer selection with the seriousness of a judge.

A hand lands on my shoulder, gently but with intention.

"Mind if I share your patch?"

The voice is light, teasing. I turn to find a man, maybe mid-thirties, dressed in an argyle sweater that would have been the punchline to a joke anywhere else. His smile is crooked, his eyes the kind of blue that had once been my undoing.

"Not at all," I say, trying for nonchalance and failing.

He introduces himself, Peter, and within seconds has summarised the room for me: who is who, who is dangerous, who is worth the effort and who is best avoided until at least midnight. His tone is conspiratorial, inclusive, and for the first time all evening I feel less like a lab rat and more like a participant in the experiment.

"You from London?" he asks, angling himself so we are both facing the bar, an orientation that feels both safe and slightly intimate.

I explain the situation: recently moved, still sorting my life, temporary teaching, the usual. He listens with an intensity that suggests he is genuinely interested, though I suspect part of it is performance, a script honed over hundreds of similar exchanges.

"I'm an accountant," he says, then laughs, "which is to say, I'm very boring, but I know a lot about other people's secrets. This place is good for that, everyone's running from something, or toward it."

I laugh, a little too loud, and spill a drop of beer on my hand. Peter notices but says nothing, instead pointing out the barman, now deep in conversation with a man in motorcycle leathers.

"That's Kev. He's a sweetheart, but don't play darts with him, he's lethal. Over there, the pool table, that's where the real action is after eleven. And if you want to impress, you have to get past the twins by the cigarette machine."

I glance over; the twins are identical only in their mutual disdain for everyone around them. They are both blonde, both tall, and both smoking with the deliberate slowness of men who know they are being watched.

Peter leans in, his shoulder brushing mine, "you seem all right," he says, "nervous, but all right. You with anyone?"

The question is casual, but also a test. I take a second to reply.

"No," I say. "Not really. I mean, not at all."

He grins, "good. Would have been awkward if you were."

I look at him, really look, and realise that the nerves have receded. The conversation is easy, the air charged with the potential for something, anything, other than the relentless sameness of the last six months.

After another round, Peter proposes a tour.

"Let me show you the circuit," he says, "unless you have an early start?"

I don't. I am off tomorrow. I nod, and we finish our pints, Peter dropping a tenner on the bar with the casual generosity of someone who wants to set the tone.

We step out into the night. The air is sharp, alive with the residue of rain and the distant, relentless thump of music from a dozen other venues. *Soho* is in full throat; the pavements lined with people in various states of undress that challenge the calendar. We walk, side by side, dodging the puddles and the slow-moving clusters of tourists.

Our destination is *The Admiral Duncan*, another pub on *Old Compton Street*. Peter greets the doorman by name; we enter into a narrow space that is all red velvet and low ceilings, the crowd denser and younger, the music more aggressive as we move to the back room.

Inside, the rules change. Conversation is not the currency; here, the economy is bodies, proximity, and the exchange of glances that carry more information than any curriculum ever devised. We elbow through to the bar, order a round of spirits (vodka for me, gin for Peter), and lean against the back wall.

Peter narrates, as before, but with a different energy, a little looser, a little more daring.

"This is where you come if you want to forget what tomorrow looks like," he says, "if you want to remember, you go to *The Village*, but that's for Sunday brunch, not for tonight."

I nod, let the vodka spread warmth into my chest, and observe the crowd. Here, men are dancing, but not in pairs, more in clusters, or alone, but always with a sense of being seen. There is a stage at the far end, currently empty, but the promise of something more lurks in the lighting, the way the floor seems to angle toward it.

Peter points out a man at the far end, surrounded by admirers, "that's Dom, he does the door at *Heaven*, but he comes here to recruit. If he likes you, he'll give you a pass, get you in for free. Don't stare, though. He hates that."

Of course, I stare. Dom is beautiful in a way that is almost parodic: tall, black hair cut close, jawline you could use as a ruler. He wears a white shirt, unbuttoned to the third, and his hands move as he talks, drawing attention to the veins that lace his forearms. At one point, he glances in our direction, and I freeze, certain that I have committed a breach of etiquette.

Peter laughs, "don't worry. He only bites if you ask."

The hours compress, as they do in places like this. The music is constant, but not repetitive; the crowd shifts and cycles, fresh faces every ten minutes, old ones dissolving into the night. I lose track of time, and of my anxieties, and when Peter proposes that we try *Heaven*, I agree without hesitation.

We exit *The Admiral*, the sudden blast of frigid air a shock after the furnace of the club. The walk to *Oxford Circus* is short, but Peter takes the long way, cutting through the alleys and letting the city unfold in all its late-night weirdness. There are men kissing in doorways, women arguing over taxis, a man in a business suit singing *ABBA* to an audience of zero. The city is a living, breathing organism, and for the first time in years I feel not only part of it, but necessary to its function.

At *Heaven*, the queue is short, the doorman (Dom again) smiles at Peter, and we are in with no entrance charge. The club is vast, a cathedral of light and noise. The dance floor is already packed, bodies moving in unison or in open rebellion against the beat. Above, platforms support dancers in various states of undress, each one a minor deity in the church of self-invention.

Peter grabs my hand, not in a predatory way, but as a matter of logistics, and pulls me through the crowd. We find a spot near the back, under an archway, and from here the room is a shifting sea of colour and motion.

I let the music take over, let the bass erase the nervousness, let the moment become the only thing that matters. For the first time, I am not watching; I am being watched, included, part of the circuit. The feeling is intoxicating, not just the alcohol, but the possibility of being new again, of rewriting the rules that had, for so long, seemed immutable.

We dance, or something close to it, Peter more rhythm than motion, me trying to find a way to inhabit the beat without looking ridiculous. At one point, we are pressed together, and I am aware of the heat, the sweat, the weight of another man's arm around my shoulder.

There is no moment of epiphany, no sudden clarity; only the slow dawning that this is a life, and I am living it.

We leave the club at two, or maybe three, the night spent but the city still restless. Peter offers to walk me home; I decline, not wanting to impose, or maybe wanting to be alone with the aftermath. We shake hands, a gesture that is both formal and intimate, and he disappears into the lights.

I make my way back to the flat, my ears ringing, my body humming with exhaustion and something else, something closer to hope than I've felt in years.

I sit at the kitchen table, pour the last of the wine, and stare at the envelope in the drawer.

For the first time, I consider throwing it out.

I don't, not yet. But I know that soon, I will.

The world's smallest urban park, if it even qualifies, is a triangular slice of pavement, ringed by a half-hearted iron fence and populated by three trees that look as if they're ashamed to be there. I meet Daniel here, he's always early, always perfectly composed, like the starter's pistol to a night that can only ever end in either glory or injury.

Tonight, he wears a white t-shirt tucked into jeans the shade of blue found only in newly painted railings. Over this, a *Harrington* jacket: the armour of the urban professional intent on remaining perennially adjacent to the class he's left behind. His hair is cropped close, his jaw angular, his smile a studied mix of indifference and promise.

We shake hands, a formality that is also a test, and head up the street to *G-A-Y*. He walks slightly ahead, as if clearing a path or, more likely, as if daring me to keep up. We duck past the line of underage hopefuls at the door, and are let in by a bouncer who remembers Daniel by name.

Inside, the lighting is an argument with nature. Every surface is lit from below; the faces of the men cast in shadows and purples that flatten and reanimate them in turn. The floor is sticky, the walls postered with flyers for upcoming events, and the air hums with the possibility of something happening, though what that might be is never quite specified.

We find a table near the back, away from the speakers, and order drinks from a woman who looks like she's been sent by Central Casting to provide plausibility to the premise that this is an equal-opportunity establishment. Daniel orders vodka and Red Bull; I stick to lager, unwilling to commit to anything stronger without first consulting the runes.

"So," he says, after we've settled, "how's the teaching life?"

I give him the abridged version: supply gigs, bad coffee, worse kids, the perpetual dance of being both present and invisible in a system that punishes both. He laughs, warmly.

"At least you don't have to sell yourself every day," he says.

"I do, though. Just not as efficiently as you."

He works in advertising, which means he spends his days convincing people to want things they neither need nor, in all likelihood, even really like. His job is a running joke, but it pays well enough that he can afford a flat in *Clapham* and a rotation of shoes that never seem to scuff.

We talk about nothing for a while, the kind of nothing that is really everything: music, politics, how the city is changing, which restaurants are still safe, and which are now contaminated by celebrity. There is an ease to it, a rhythm, and I catch myself relaxing, letting go of the constant self-surveillance that has defined every date since the divorce.

The conversation stalls, as all things must. There's a lull, filled by the ambient roar of the room, and Daniel watches me over the rim of his glass. His eyes are sharp, pale grey, and always look just to the left of your own.

"You never talk about your past," he says. It's not an accusation, but it isn't not an accusation, either.

I hesitate, then decide to tell the truth, or at least the version of it I've prepared for occasions like this.

"I was married," I say, "we have a daughter. I came out… late."

His face doesn't move, but everything else does. The energy in his shoulders, the set of his mouth, the way his left hand starts tracing invisible patterns on the table.

"So you're bisexual?" he says, and the word hangs there, as if waiting for a chaperone.

"I don't know. I don't think so. I think I just… made it work, until I couldn't."

He nods, slow, as if giving me points for originality but not for effort.

"My ex," I continue, "she's remarried. Our daughter's almost six now. I see her sometimes, but it's complicated."

Daniel sips his drink, eyes narrowing, "complicated how?"

I shrug, "she lives up north. I'm here. She's not thrilled about my new life."

There's a pause. A real one. He looks away, then back at me.

"So, what's the deal? Are you… experimenting, or is this for real?"

The question is razor thin, but it slices anyway. I shake my head.

"It's real. I just…" I search for the word, find nothing, "I just started late, that's all."

He nods again, but the calculation is visible now. The shift from maybe to probably not, the subtle rearrangement of the future to exclude me from it.

He finishes his drink in a single pull, sets the glass down with a click, and leans back.

"I'm not judging," he says, "but you should know, most people aren't going to want a project. They want someone who knows what they're doing."

"I know," I say, "I get it."

He taps the table, glances at the dance floor. The music has shifted, something by *Ace of Base*, which seems both topical and cruel.

"I should get going," he says, standing before I can answer, "early meeting tomorrow. But…" and here he softens, just a little, "it was good to meet you. Really."

He doesn't touch me on the way out, doesn't linger. I watch him thread his way through the crowd, pausing to say hello to a pair of men in the corner, one of whom grabs his arm and whispers something into his ear. Daniel laughs, and for a second, I see the version of him that was possible, had I met him in some other context, some other universe.

I sit for a while, nursing the remains of my pint, and let the room recalibrate around my absence. From this angle, the place is different: the men at the bar are older, the ones on the dance floor younger, and between them a hundred subtle gradations, each with its own language and set of permissions. There are couples, but more groups, and within each cluster a leader, a follower, and an exile. Even here, even now, the hierarchies replicate themselves.

A table over, a trio of twentysomethings in matching vests and bracelets are performing a ritual of belonging, shouting over the music, comparing notes on the men in the room. At the bar, a pair of men in business suits are deep in conversation, their faces flushed, their bodies angled in a way that says this is either the beginning or the end of something. Near the door, a solitary figure stands, drink untouched, eyes scanning the crowd with the nervous intensity of a man about to be tested on its contents.

I watch, and I learn. I catalogue the tribes: the muscle boys, the bears, the preening club kids, the misfits who cling to the periphery like barnacles to a hull. I see myself reflected, not in any one group, but in all of them, a composite of desire and uncertainty, held together by the thinnest thread of hope.

Eventually, I leave. The street outside is alive with noise, with men and women spilling from the bars, with taxi horns and the low, sullen hum of a city that refuses to sleep. I walk the length of *Old Compton Street*, hands in pockets, head down, trying to parse the difference between loneliness and simply being alone.

At the corner, a man bumps into me, apologises, then grins in a way that makes clear the apology was optional. He is handsome, but in the way of men who have never needed to try very hard. I consider, for a moment, whether to follow, to let the night spin out in a new direction, but the thought exhausts me.

I turn onto *Dean Street*, then *Wardour*, letting the city absorb me. The neon is bright, the air still heavy with anticipation. Every bar is full, every pavement crowded with the living proof that desire is both infinite and ultimately, impossibly, exclusive.

I stop in front of a record shop, its window lined with CDs and cassettes, and catch my reflection in the glass. For a second, I don't recognise the face: older, perhaps, or just worn at the edges. I stand there, waiting for the streetlight to change, and remember what Daniel said: *'most people want someone who knows what they're doing'*.

I don't. Not really. But I know enough to keep trying.

At home, the flat is dark, cold. I drop my keys on the table, toe off my shoes, and sit at the window. The city is still there, still moving, still relentless.

I look at the envelope in the drawer, the symbol of everything that came before.

Tomorrow, I'll throw it out.

Tonight, I let myself hope, just a little, that someday I'll find a place where the longing is enough.

CHAPTER 20: THE BLACK DOG

I moved into the new flat in *Billericay* on a Monday in August 1994, that seemed to have misplaced its weather. The air outside was a mere suggestion, neither warm nor cold, and the sky, a noncommittal slab of pearl, seemed perfectly matched to the featureless council flats along *South Green*. The building manager handed me the keys with the diffidence of someone accustomed to more interesting clients.

"There's a bottle in the fridge, housewarming from the estate agents," she said, with a gesture that managed to be both hopeful and apologetic.

After a year of moving around London from one temporary job to another, I finally took a permanent head of department job in a large tertiary college. I had saved what I could and was able to take on a mortgage for a small purpose-built apartment that was only two years old.

Inside: a single bed, a lounge the size of a railway carriage, and a galley kitchen designed by someone with a grudge against cooking. I made a circuit of the place, inventorying its blankness, running my palm along the painted windowsills to check for grit. There was none. The prior owner, evidently, had aspired to some higher grade of order. It left the space antiseptic, nothing but echo and the faint trace of air freshener, labelled *'Summer Rain'*.

I set my boxes down on the patch of carpet by the window, the contents bulging in suggestion rather than volume. Everything else would follow, Amanda had promised, as soon as the settlement cleared. In the interim, I was to make do with my own skeleton crew: books, toiletries, the requisite three changes of clothes, and a clutch of photos and mementos, hastily packed under Rose's supervision, "for when you get sad," she had said, threading a hand-knit scarf through the handle of the box as a kind of ward against loneliness. I told her I would wear it every day, even if the sun never stopped.

I opened the box with the reverence usually reserved for relics. On top was the scarf, its colours an undulating nausea of pink and blue. Below that, a stack of dog-eared paperbacks: *Roth, Nabokov, E.E. Smith*, a tattered *Penguin* of *David Lodge* whose cover featured a leering cartoon professor that looked, I now realised, unsettlingly like my own father. I lined them up along the single bookshelf, arranging them by height rather than author, just to spite the notion of continuity.

Then came the smaller items: a mug from the *Aegina* trip, the paint flaking from the letters; a coaster inlaid with the skyline of *Manchester*, the blue enamel chipped at the edge; a tin box of dominoes, legacy of a Christmas at Amanda's mother's, the inside lid annotated with the scorched shadow of a forgotten match.

It was at the bottom of the box that I found the photograph. I'd thought, or maybe hoped, it had been lost in one of the moves, left behind in some *Liverpool Road* attic to be discovered by a future tenant with no context for the frozen moment within. Instead, it stared up at me now, the image as sharp and unsparing as a headline.

Me and William, posed in front of Langley Hall, the evening sun flattening our features into the kind of stoic, pre-war handsomeness that made us look distantly related. I remembered the day, of course, the end of summer, the orchard behind the stables alight with wasps.

I held the photo between thumb and forefinger, appraising it as if for auction. It was the only image I had of us together, Amanda, with her bureaucratic zeal, had purged the rest during the first weeks of the separation, unwilling to let ghosts colonise her new world order. I couldn't blame her. If it had been me, I would have burned the lot.

Still, I set it on the shelf, centre position, and stood back to judge the effect. The photo looked both at home and entirely alien in the flat's blank geometry, as if it were a window into another dimension, a richer, denser one, where colour and intention meant something. The feeling it produced was not nostalgia, exactly, but its more complicated cousin: a longing for a time when longing had an object.

I left the box and moved to the window. The view, if it could be called that, was of the car park, ringed by the back ends of other flats, the odd dustbin, and a single lime tree that had somehow survived the civic landscaping. There was a slow, residual traffic of people returning from work, their movements staccato, as if aware of surveillance. I wondered if any of them lived alone, and if so, whether they felt it as a verdict or an accident.

Back at the shelf, I ran a finger along the edges of the books, letting them tilt and realign themselves. The photograph caught the late light, a small artifact of defiance. I thought of William, where he might be now, what shape his life had taken, whether he still ate his toast with marmalade and the faintest sliver of butter. Whether, in the quiet of his own flat, he ever thought of me.

I turned on the radio, found a station playing late-period *Bowie*, and let the sound fill the corners of the room. It was enough, for now. I brewed a cup of tea, sat on the edge of the single bed, and watched the dusk infiltrate the space, softening the angles until everything, books, photos, even the persistent ache in my chest, seemed negotiable.

The sky outside deepened into violet. The flat, empty but for me and the patient accumulation of memory, waited. And for the first time in months, I did not mind the waiting.

After a week of staring down the inventory of my own past, I decided to take a more active role in the present. It was Friday, and the train from *Billericay* to *Liverpool Street* was running its usual schedule of delays and compensations. I read the advertisements along the carriage, hair transplants, personal injury lawyers, an ad for *Turkish Delight* featuring a woman wrapped in marabou and what I could only describe as theatrical lust, and considered, with some detachment, whether any of these were appropriate metaphors for my life.

I arrived in a now increasingly familiar *Soho* just after sunset. The streets, slicked with last night's rain and the early condensation of weekend excess, pulsed with bodies in various states of undress and intent. The air was a mix of fried food, hot tarmac, and, rising above it, the cold shimmer of *Calvin Klein's* latest mass-market pheromone. Neon signs throbbed with the urgency of old debts; bouncers shivered at the doorways, nodding the regulars through with the faintest of smiles.

I chose a bar at random, a former bookshop, now converted into a minimalist grid of glass and steel, where the only evidence of its prior life was a single shelf of damp, uncollected paperbacks in the gents'. Inside, the atmosphere was not so much welcoming as charged: all chrome and blue light, the shadows rendered surgical and cruel. I found a stool at the bar and ordered a gin and tonic, the only drink I had ever learned to trust.

The bartender, a man in a shirt so tight it threatened to declare a state of emergency, poured the gin with the precision of a pharmacist, then added two ice cubes and a curl of lemon. He set the glass before me with a practiced wink, "first of the night?" he said, voice a drawl of a thousand repetitions.

I nodded, though it was already the third.

I scanned the room the way one scans the index of a bad book, hoping for a name, or at least a context, which would make the next hour more legible. There were the usual types: the young, still in the first act of their desirability, orbiting the pool table and each other with a kind of feral energy; the old, clustered at the window tables, their laughter brittle but determined; a scattering of tourists, cowed into silence by the proximity of the unfamiliar. I caught the eye of a man near the jukebox, tall, head shaved, dressed in a way that tried hard not to be noticed. He looked away before I could decide whether this was encouragement or its opposite.

The music, a steady diet of remixed anthems and the occasional ironic pop classic, warred with the conversation but did not win. At intervals, the room would swell with the noise of a shared chorus, then collapse again into the undertow of singles, each on their private errand.

My first interaction was with a man whose T-shirt read *PERFECTLY NORMAL*. He introduced himself as Liam, though he admitted this was not his actual name, "you can't be too careful, not these days," he said, and I tried to determine whether he meant it or was merely reciting the line for effect. He worked in finance, he said, but his real passion was gardening, though he had no garden. "You have nice hands," he told me, "are you a pianist?"

I shook my head, said I was a teacher, and watched as the interest in his eyes flickered and died.

He left to join a group of friends who, I realised, had been watching us the entire time. I finished my drink and considered leaving. Instead, I ordered another.

The second approach was more direct. A man in a plaid shirt slid onto the stool next to mine and, without preamble, asked whether I was "into younger guys." He looked about twenty, face freckled and open, the earnestness of the question almost enough to disarm the underlying calculation.

"I'm not sure," I said, "I haven't run the experiments."

He laughed, a little too loudly, then leaned in, as if for a secret, "well, I'm not into old men, but you seem all right."

He bought me a shot of tequila, then told me, in the space of three minutes, the story of his last three boyfriends and what each had done to deserve their fate, "it's a jungle out there," he concluded, raising the glass in salute.

I drank the shot, felt the fire chase away the residue of awkwardness, and said, "what are you hoping to find in here, then?"

He considered this, "someone who's not a dickhead," he said, and I could think of no better answer.

We danced, if it could be called that, at the edge of the bar, the music now so loud that conversation was a matter of proximity and guesswork. He pressed his body against mine, arms around my waist, and for a moment I let myself be carried by the possibility of it: the surge of blood, the chemical haze, the simple pleasure of a touch that did not require translation.

But as the song changed, and the spell with it, I saw the flicker of impatience in his eyes, the calculation of time and return, the certainty that this was not, in fact, going anywhere. He disengaged, made a joke about having to pee, and I watched him wend through the crowd, already scanning for the next prospect.

At the bar, I ordered a third drink and tried to look unconcerned. In the mirror behind the bottles, my face was a study in negative emotion: the slight pull at the corner of the mouth, the furrow between the brows, the eyes permanently tuned to some frequency of loss. I turned away from the reflection and looked, instead, at the dancefloor.

There were couples there, real ones, by the look of it, dancing in the shameless, surrendered way that people do when they have already done all the suffering they intend to. I watched as one man, older, balding, wrapped his arms around the waist of another, the pair of them moving in a loop that made no sense to the rhythm but perfect sense to each other. Their laughter, even from a distance, was a private thing; it made the rest of us invisible. I wondered, briefly, what it would be like to have that, if I would even know how to hold on to it if I did.

My next encounter was with a man who, in the logic of the place, should have been the answer to every question. He was my age, maybe a little older, with the kind of looks that had aged into sharpness rather than decay. He wore a navy jumper with a rip at the sleeve, and his eyes, green under the lights, were the sort that could pass for kind in a different context.

He introduced himself as Nick, and within minutes we had charted the topography of our lives, his work as a freelance graphic designer, his ex in *Berlin*, his absolute refusal to ever own a pet. We talked about books, about the weirdness of living outside *London*, about whether gin was really better than vodka or simply better marketed. He made me laugh, a real laugh, the kind that bypasses all the usual checkpoints.

We talked for an hour, maybe two. At some point, he reached over and squeezed my hand, an uncalculated gesture. I felt the warmth of it run all the way up my arm, and for a moment I thought this could be it. Not love, not yet, but the first stutter of hope.

But then the conversation, so alive and sharp, began to circle back on itself. He told the same story twice, then a third time, and when I pointed this out, he laughed, too loudly, and ordered another round. His hand, once gentle, became heavy on my knee; the warmth of it now more obligation than comfort.

After a while, the conversation turned from books to bodies, from hopes to logistics, "your place or mine?" he said, and I realised, with a sudden clarity, that I did not want either.

I made my excuses, thanked him for the drinks, and left. On the street, the air was cold, slicing through the buzz of alcohol and expectation.

I walked. Past the kebab shops, past the clubs where people queued in shivering lines, past the neon and the floodlights and the windows where, behind the glass, other men sat together, holding hands or just being near enough to count. I walked all the way to *Liverpool Street*, ignoring the taxis and the invitations, feeling the sting of failure but also, somehow, relief.

On the train back, I replayed the night in slow motion, searching for the moment when possibility had turned to certainty, when the hope of connection had become the dread of repetition. I found it, as I always did, at the place where I saw myself in the other man, where my own neediness, my own deficit, was mirrored back at me with perfect, clinical accuracy.

At the flat, I undressed and lay on the bed, the silence so profound that I could hear the tick of the heating pipe, the faint hum of the streetlamp outside. I reached for my phone, considered texting Amanda, an update, a confession, anything, but thought better of it.

Instead, I stared at the ceiling, letting the night settle into my bones.

It was not failure, I decided. Not really. It was just the ongoing negotiation of being alive, of wanting something more than the sum of the bodies in a room. I told myself that next week, or the week after, it would be better, that there would be a man who said the right things, who did not leave, who might even, in time, give me cause to want to stay.

But for tonight, the empty bed was enough. I closed my eyes and let the city fade to black, the residue of hope still sweet on my tongue.

Days collapsed into weeks, and I let them. My freedom had the increasing feeling of being a burden. I developed a taste for temporal drift, waking at noon (or later at weekends), working only as much as needed to keep the paychecks coming, subsisting on a diet of whatever could be delivered or, failing that, boiled into submission. The flat settled into a pattern of disorder: half-eaten toast on the windowsill, coffee rings spiralling out from the edges of every surface, the bin filling with bottles whose glass caught the afternoon sun and cast it back in wan, greenish fragments.

I told myself it was fine, that this was a phase, that everyone in *Billericay* drank alone and watched the light crawl across their carpet and waited for the next thing, whatever that was, to begin. But the evidence, accumulating in dirty laundry and unopened mail, suggested otherwise.

I tried to stay grounded by continuing to exchange letters with Sarah and genuinely enjoyed her good news about her own growing family and developing career. She tried her best to encourage me after each failed weekend out to *'be yourself'*, *'go with the flow'* or, in a typically blunt comment, *'go out a get laid'*.

Sometimes I followed her advice, especially once my face was recognised in *The Admiral Duncan* which became my favourite *Soho* haunt. None of this could happen though without being fuelled by substantial amounts of alcohol. Physically satisfied, the lonely train journey home did little, in the sober light of day, to give me any sense of hope for something more.

One Sunday, I made the mistake of finally opening one of Amanda's letters that had arrived on Saturday. She had written it in her lawyer voice, all clean lines and indexed grievances. The first page covered money, who owed what, who was late, who had failed to account for Rose's *'escalating emotional needs'*. The second page, in a smaller and more frenetic hand, catalogued the things I had failed to do as a father, as a husband, as a human. It was less a letter than a litany, and by the end, my name felt like a sentence in itself.

I read it twice, just to be sure I had not missed the part where she said anything about missing me, or about wanting me back, or even about regret. There was none of that. Just the facts, raw and unsparing, *'I hope you find what you are looking for'*, she wrote, and underlined it twice, as if by doing so she could will me into some other shape.

I folded the letter into a tiny square and dropped it into the empty gin bottle by the sink, an impromptu message in a shipwreck. Then I sat on the sofa and let the afternoon pass in silence, the only movement the shifting of the light and the occasional tremor in my hands.

The phone rang. I ignored it. It rang again.

When I did answer, the voice on the line was my mother's. She spoke in that strange combination of concern and exhaustion that made it clear she had not, in fact, expected me to pick up.

"John," she said, "it's your birthday next week."

I said, "yes," though it was the first I'd heard of it.

She asked if I would come up to Manchester for a visit, "bring the little one," as if Rose were an accessory that could be summoned at will. I made a noncommittal noise, then let the silence stretch until she gave up.

"I'm fine," I told her, and she pretended to believe me.

After the call, I sat for a long time on the floor, my back against the radiator, feeling the heat seep into my spine. I thought about driving north, about the three hours on the M6, about the way the country blurred into sameness outside the window. I imagined arriving, my mother's face lit by the cold blue TV, the smell of old fabric softener in the hall. I tried to remember a time when her voice had sounded less tired.

But the more I thought, the less I wanted to move.

Later, I stood in front of the bathroom mirror and did the thing I had been avoiding for months: really looked at myself. The face staring back was unfamiliar—not aged so much as weathered, the bones sharper, the eyes deeper in their sockets. I ran a finger along the line of my jaw and watched the skin move, slack, a quarter second behind the gesture.

I thought about William, about the last time he had seen me, about whether he would even recognise this version. I tried to summon the image of the photograph on the shelf, but it seemed distant now, faded, an artifact from a world I could not re-enter.

For a moment, I imagined smashing the mirror, the fragments cascading to the floor, each one holding a different angle of myself. But I didn't. Instead, I leaned in, close enough to see the pores, the veins, the tiny errors in construction.

"You'll be all right," I said, though it sounded like someone else.

I left the bathroom light on, just to prove it.

That night, I dreamed I was underwater, looking up at the surface as bodies swam overhead, lit by a sun I could not reach. Their voices distorted, coming through the water as music or lament, I could not tell. I woke before dawn, the sheets twisted, my mouth dry, the city still dark outside.

I sat in the silence, letting it fill me.

It was not peace, but it was something close.

The suicide attempt, when it finally arrived, was less an event than an experiment in physics. I woke one morning to the sun bar-coding the ceiling, the taste of gin and aspirin already thick on my tongue, and decided, without drama or ceremony, that I was done. I wrote a note, not for Amanda or Rose or even William, but for the caretaker who would find me: "sorry for the mess. I did try to avoid the curtains." Then I lined up the pills, filled a glass from the tap, and lay down on the bed in my best shirt, as if preparing for an interview with God.

"Mr. Williams," she said, reading the name from the chart, "do you know where you are?"

I said, "*Billericay*, I hope," and she almost smiled.

She asked if I knew what day it was. I did not. She asked if I wanted water. I did. She asked, finally, if I wanted to die.

"No," I said, though the truth was more complicated, "not today." I felt sore, like I had received a good kicking, which was explained to me later as a consequence of the efforts to resuscitate me. I felt numb, disappointed, frightened.

I remained in the main hospital for three days or so until they were satisfied that physically I was stable. I was then visited by the *psychiatric team'* who gave me a stark choice: submit to a voluntary seventy-two hours of observation, the requisite period for determining whether a life was worth returning to the wild. The alternative was to be sectioned anyway.

I was transferred to my new home, voluntarily, and I spent the time cataloguing the furniture, reading old issues of *Reader's Digest*, and learning the names of the sedatives they used to keep us level: *lorazepam*, *quetiapine*, a daily parade of white and yellow tablets, each one engineered to tamp down a different kind of chaos.

The ward was called *Ann Boleyn*, a joke so obvious it barely warranted a smile. On the first evening, a work colleague visited. Her name was Janet, and she brought a banana loaf and a stack of marking, as if reminding me that the world outside had not collapsed in my absence.

"I told them you'd make a pun," she said, sitting at the end of my bed, "*Ann Boleyn*, get it? Lost her head."

"I'm only here for assessment," I said, though we both knew it would not be so quick.

She watched me peel the banana loaf, her eyes cataloguing the tremor in my hands, the pale seam of hospital tape around my wrist where cannulas had been.

"You'll be fine," she said, "they always let the teachers out first. We're not a flight risk."

I asked about the school, about the exam schedule, about whether anyone else had noticed I was missing. She said *'no'*, everyone just assumed I was working from home, "as you always do."

When she left, she squeezed my arm in the way you do with relatives at funerals, firm, but not lingering, "come back soon," she said. "The kids need you."

I nodded, though the prospect of returning to a classroom now seemed as remote as anything else.

The nights were the worst. Even with the medication, the dreams were thick with noise and repetition. I woke at odd intervals, the ward dark but never silent. Someone always cried, or shouted, or laughed in the dry, spitting way that meant the meds were working but not well enough. I made a ritual of watching the clock, the phosphorescent hands ticking away the hours, each minute a small, private rehearsal for the life I was supposed to want.

On the third morning, a doctor appeared at the foot of my bed. He was young, with an accent I could not place and a name badge that read *Dr. Arun*. He sat in the visitor chair and folded his hands, as if preparing for a chess match.

He asked the standard questions: *'Did I regret the attempt?', 'Did I have plans for the future?', 'Was I still drinking?', 'Did I have a support system?'.* He listened to my answers without judgment, only pausing now and then to write in his notebook, the scratch of pen on paper somehow the most comforting sound I'd heard in weeks.

At the end, he said, "you are highly intelligent, Mr. Williams. That is both a blessing and a problem."

I waited for the punchline.

"The thing about intelligent people," he continued, "is that you are exceptionally good at talking yourselves into, or out of, anything. Even dying." He smiled, as if to show this was not an accusation, but a simple fact of taxonomy.

He adjusted my meds, prescribed a course of therapy, and told me I could leave the ward on condition I reported twice a week to the *'wellness clinic'* in *Chelmsford*.

I signed the discharge papers with a pen that barely worked, then waited for the orderly to bring my clothes. When he arrived, he handed me the banana loaf, still in its wrap, and said, "you'll want this." I took it, and for the first time in weeks, the weight of it in my hand felt almost reassuring.

Back in the flat, everything was as I'd left it. The bottles, the books, the damp smell of defeat rising from the carpet. I aired the place out, made a cup of tea, and sat by the window, watching the world resume its indifferent pace.

The phone rang. It was the therapist, another Sarah. She sounded young, brisk, her voice engineered to project a confidence she probably did not feel.

"Mr. Williams, we have you scheduled for next Tuesday. Will you be able to attend?"

I hesitated. My hand shook, not with fear but with the residual inertia of the drugs.

"Yes," I said, "I'll be there."

"Good," she said, "we'll see you at ten."

The call ended, and I sat for a long time, the dial tone buzzing like a fly in the quiet. I thought about not going, about letting the world fill in the space where I'd been. But I knew, even as I thought it, that I would show up. That I had to.

On Tuesday, I took the train to *Chelmsford*. The wellness clinic was located in part of the university. The waiting room was lined with pale chairs and magazines so old the people in them looked like characters from a lost civilization.

I sat with my hands in my lap, watching the door, feeling the pulse of my heart in my wrists. When Sarah called my name, I stood and followed her down a corridor painted in a shade of yellow I'd last seen in a kindergarten.

She asked me how I was feeling. I told her I was fine.

She asked me why I was there.

I told her the truth, or as much of it as I could.

"I wanted to stop," I said, "everything. The noise, the chaos inside my head, the feeling that nothing will ever be as good as it was, or as I wanted it to be."

She nodded, made a note, "and do you still feel that way?"

I stared at the carpet, at the pattern of blue and grey squares, and said, "sometimes."

She asked about Amanda, about Rose, about my life before this. I told her about William, about the summer in *Aegina*, about the brief, perfect moment where I thought I might be happy, or at least not miserable.

She listened, and did not judge.

When the hour was up, she said, "I'm glad you came today, John. I think we can help."

I stood to leave, my legs unsteady, my mind still humming with the residue of memory and regret. As I left the building, the sun was out. The light hurt my eyes, but I forced myself to look up, just to prove I could.

On the train home, I watched my reflection in the window, the ghost of myself superimposed on the passing fields. It was an odd comfort, this double exposure, the man I was, the man I wanted to be, never quite overlapping but moving, at least, in the same direction.

When I got home, I called my mother. I told her I was all right. She believed me this time.

I sat in the flat, the silence less threatening now, and opened the window to let the air in.

It was not happiness, but it was a beginning.

CHAPTER 21: THE ROAD TO RECOVERY

The summer of 1976 arrived in England with a vengeance, a fever that cracked open the pavements and set the evenings trembling with the drone of insects and the reek of scorched tarmac. My parents, in a rare eruption of marital consensus, had planned a week's holiday in the family caravan in *Towyn*. The coach to North Wales left at 6:05 a.m. from the town's bus station, and it was agreed I would sleep at my step uncle's the night before, "just so you're not yawning your head off for the first two days," my step-mother explained, while giving me a look that made clear she intended this as an act of mercy, not exile.

He lived alone in a Victorian terraced house near to the bus station, the kind of structure that seemed forever in the act of not quite falling down. The front door opened onto the street and to the rear was a backyard and now unused outside loo. I arrived just before six, winded from the bike ride up the hill, and stood for a moment in the resinous fug of hot evening, listening to the slow, stately approach of the local ice cream van as it prowled the streets.

Uncle Frank, always *'Uncle'*, never *'Frank'*, answered the back door in what I recognised as his second-best shirt, open at the collar, the sleeves rolled to show the war tattoo on his right forearm. "Christ, Johnnie, you look like you've run a marathon," he said, and ushered me in, his palm hot and dry on the back of my neck.

The interior of the house was a time capsule, airless and scruffy. In the kitchen: a coat rack bearing a single anorak and a flat cap; the umbrella stand held nothing. The living room was panelled in knotty pine and dominated by a massive teak sideboard, its glass-fronted cabinets filled with the artifacts of Frank's other, more spectacular life: a ceremonial dagger, its handle twisted into the shape of a serpent; an RAF model plane in flight; half a dozen trophies, each one more obscure than the last, their engraved plaques rendered illegible by the polish he insisted on applying every Friday. Above the electric fireplace hung a black-and-white photograph of a woman in WW2 military uniform - apparently the love of his life that had got away.

"Put your things in the spare room, lad," said Uncle Frank, already heading toward the kitchen, "I'm frying up sausage and chips, that I know you like."

The spare room was boxy; the walls covered in a psychedelic wallpaper of interlocking orange and avocado. I dropped my rucksack on the bed, a single, tight against the wall, and stood for a minute, listening to the sizzle of fat through the open door. The house smelled of tobacco, *Brasso*, chip oil, and the ghost of some lavender cleaning fluid. I washed my hands, dried them on a towel so stiff it might have doubled as insulation, and went to eat.

We ate in the kitchen, the table set for two with a gravity that made the meal seem more important than it was. Uncle Frank poured brown sauce in a perfect circle around his plate, then used the tines of his fork to drag it inwards, methodical, mesmeric. He had been a rear gunner in the war, shot down over *Bremen* and left for dead in a Belgian field; a fact he shared with me not as a boast, but as a kind of lesson in the benefits of paying attention. He quizzed me on my school marks, the football, the science teacher he'd never liked. His hands were restless, always in motion, drumming on the *Formica,* twisting the stem of his glass, toying with the lighter he kept on a chain in his shirt pocket. His nicotine fingers were deeply stained from the *Navy Cut* he smoked incessantly.

After dinner, he produced a packet of cigarettes and, with a glance toward the window, lit up, "don't tell your stepmother," he said, winking, "she thinks I quit." He offered me one, and when I declined, said, "good lad. But you'll change your mind in a few years, I'll bet my pension." I watched the way his lips shaped the smoke, the satisfaction in the exhale, the ritual precision of it.

At nine, he insisted on tea and a slice of *Battenberg,* which we ate in the living room, the television tuned to the news but the volume low enough that the anchors' voices sounded like distant relatives quarrelling in the next room. He explained the route to the coach station, repeated it three times, I remember wondering why he had as he was coming with me on the bus. He then checked his watch and declared it "bedtime for soldiers." He sent me to the bath, "use all the hot, it's no good to me," and I complied, scrubbing off the sweat of the day with *Imperial Leather* and a loofah that left my skin tingling and raw.

When I emerged, hair damp and shivering in my pyjamas, Uncle Frank was waiting in the hall, unbuttoned down to his vest, his cigarette hand cupped to hide the ember, "we'll share," he said, gesturing toward the single bed, "no sense making up two for one night, eh?"

I said, "it's fine," and meant it. I'd shared with my brother, my cousins and even a schoolmate on a trip one time.

He tapped the ash into his palm, then into the bin, and we stood for a moment, the silence between us held taut by the sound of the clock in the lounge. "Good lad," he said again, and ruffled my hair in a way that was both affectionate and proprietary.

We lay down back-to-back, me pressed against the wall, Uncle Frank on the outer edge, the mattress bowing toward his side under his greater mass. For a while we were both very still. I listened to the night, the distant tick of the hot-water pipes, the rhythmic expansion and contraction of the house as it surrendered the day's heat. Uncle Frank's breathing was loud, but even; I matched my own to it, half-hypnotised, the way a sleeper will sometimes pace their breath to a companion's, unconsciously deferring to their rhythm.

Sometime later, it could have been minutes, it could have been hours, I felt him shift, the faint disturbance of the sheet as he rolled onto his side. The bed was so narrow that even the smallest movement brought us into contact. His arm, heavy and impossibly hot, draped over my waist, fingers splayed on the cotton of my pyjama top. I lay still, not alarmed, only mildly inconvenienced, the way one is by the slow colonisation of a quilt by an aggressive sleeper.

But then the hand moved, sliding up from my waist to rest flat on my chest, then tracing a slow, spiralling path down the line of buttons. His breath was closer now, the smell of tobacco and toothpaste and something older, metallic, catching in the hollow beneath my ear. "You're a good lad, Johnnie," he whispered, and the sound of my name in that voice, the gruff softness of it, sent a ripple of something through my stomach that was not, at first, entirely unpleasant.

His hand found the drawstring of my pyjama trousers and hovered there, as if awaiting further instruction. I felt the coarseness of his fingertips through the fabric, the involuntary tightening of my lower belly, the strange weightlessness that comes when a decision is made for you. He pressed his face against the back of my neck, the stubble abrasive and electric.

The hand slipped inside the waistband, slow and methodical. His palm rested a moment on the shallow of my abdomen, then drifted lower, fingers navigating by touch alone, as if I were an object to be studied and then catalogued. My body tensed, but I did not move; the sensation was so alien, so far outside the range of anything I'd ever imagined, that it might as well have been happening to another version of myself, one who had made different choices and so arrived at a different night.

His hand closed around my penis, deliberate, unhurried, the grip practiced and assured. He began to stroke, the movement slow at first, then gathering a kind of rhythm. The friction was gentle, almost measured, and in spite of everything I felt myself responding, the blood rushing, the skin oversensitive and raw. I wanted to recoil, to run, to disappear, but the bed was a raft in a rising sea and there was nowhere to go.

He whispered again, nothing intelligible, just a string of syllables half-swallowed by the darkness. His other hand pressed between my shoulder blades, flattening me against the mattress. There was a second, a long, hanging second, when I thought it might stop, when the hand paused, its motion suspended, as if he'd remembered something or come to a decision.

Then he pulled at my hips, wrenching me backwards, the abruptness of the movement knocking the air from my lungs. I felt the hardness of him, the hot, insistent press through his pyjamas, the way he aligned our bodies with a precision that was suddenly, terrifyingly efficient. He spat into his palm and pushed it between my legs, then, with a kind of grim inevitability, forced himself against me, the head of his penis finding the tight, clenched resistance and pushing, slowly, inexorably, inside.

The pain was incandescent. I bit down on the pillow, muffling a sound that was neither scream nor moan, just a ragged exhale of disbelief. His arm locked around my chest, pinning me in place, while his hips rocked back and forth, each thrust a little deeper, a little more certain. The friction was unbearable, a tearing, splitting agony that seemed to radiate outward until every nerve was raw and exposed.

But worse, far worse, was the betrayal of my own body: the way the pain co-mingled with a feverish, sick excitement, a shameful, traitorous pleasure that built in parallel to the dread. I stiffened and throbbed with each movement, and I hated myself for it, hated the inevitability of it, the way my body responded even as my mind recoiled in horror, confusion and shame.

He climaxed with a grunt, a low, guttural sound that reverberated in my ribcage. The sudden stillness was more shocking than the act itself. He held me tight, for a minute or an hour, then exhaled a shuddering breath and withdrew, rolling away to the edge of the bed. The sheets were slick with sweat, the room suffocating with heat and the acid stench of semen.

I lay motionless, eyes open, staring at the wall and the shifting geometry of shadow and light. My hands trembled, though I tried to will them still. In the silence, I could hear the blood in my ears, the dull, persistent thud of my own heart. I thought of my siblings, of the bus leaving at dawn, of the green, seething lawns of the caravan park and the way the sea sometimes looked almost black against the sky.

I did not sleep, not really as I constantly mulled over the events of the night. I came to the realisation that this had all been my fault by so easily allowing him to share my bed. At some point before dawn, Uncle Frank got up, went to the bathroom, returned and sat on the edge of the bed, his back to me. He smoked a cigarette, the ember a tiny, angry eye in the darkness. When he spoke, it was in the voice he used for war stories, a tone of confession disguised as casual conversation.

"Wake up lad, we need to be getting on if we are to catch that bus," it was as if nothing had happened, nothing at all. He crushed the cigarette in the ashtray and left, the door closing with a softness that was almost respectful.

I got up, dressed in silence, and packed my bag. The house looked exactly as it had the night before, every object in its ordained place, every surface scrubbed of evidence. At the door, Uncle Frank's small, battered suitcase waited for us. Within minutes we were on our way to the bus station, my body sore and leaking, my mind a blank wall. I did not think of it again, not for years.

Twenty-three years later I headed to my next therapy session. The smell of hospital air still made my skin crawl. It was not precisely the same, here, in the annex of the university's psychology building, a faint mixture of filtered dust, green soap, and the anxious residue of other people's confessions, but the association was strong enough that each visit left a thin, invisible film on the insides of my lungs.

I remember paying a little more attention my surroundings this time. The room was purpose-built: beige carpet, two identical armchairs facing each other at a calculatedly nonconfrontational angle, and a low table bearing a box of tissues and a stack of university pamphlets. The wall art was abstract, chosen for its ambiguity, something in blue and brown, all suggestion and no story. I had been coming here every Thursday for almost three months.

The therapist, never *'my therapist'*, always *'the therapist'*, as if the definite article might inoculate me against intimacy, with hair the colour of printer toner and the composure of someone who had already heard the very worst thing I was capable of saying. Sarah had a way of folding her hands in her lap and waiting, unblinking, until you filled the silence with whatever was next on the treatment plan.

She began, as she always did, by asking how the week had been. I gave my standard answer: "nothing to report." She nodded, making a note in her spiral-bound pad. I wondered, as I often did, whether there was a code for *'not lying, but not really telling the truth, either'*. I imagined it would be something like *'suboptimal candour'*, and tried not to smile. I was resistant, but I felt that resistance weakening.

Today, though, she deviated from the script, "we've talked a lot about the recent past," she said, eyes fixed on the notepad. "Your marriage, the separation, the difficulties at work. But you've said almost nothing about your childhood."

I shrugged, "not much to tell. It was pretty normal." Even though of course I knew from my teaching experience that there was no such thing.

She looked up, "what does *'normal'* mean to you?"

This was the trap. I could feel it, the way an animal feels the voltage in the wire before the shock comes. I shifted in my chair, feigned interest in the painting on the wall.

"School was school," I said, "stepmother worked in an office; Dad was a plumber. No drama. No real money, but we managed. Cricket on weekends in the summer, telly in the evenings. I got decent marks. Nothing spectacular."

She nodded, as if agreeing that yes, it all sounded very normal indeed. She lured me in.

"Did you feel loved?" she asked, the question so bald it made me recoil.

I thought about it, "they did their best," I said, "Dad wasn't big on words, but he turned up to every parents' night. It wasn't like people got told they were loved in those days. You just… knew."

She let the silence grow. I watched the minute hand of the clock edge toward the half-hour, tried to estimate how many other men had sat in this chair and delivered the same routine, "and your extended family?" she asked, very softly. "Grandparents, aunts, uncles?."

"Yeah," I said, "had my gran from my mum's side, and then…." The memory rose inside me after being so deeply buried for so long. I could begin to feel my neck and then face warming. Sarah just watched me and took it all in.

Finally, she pounced, "who else was there John?"

"A step uncle. He was… fun. More fun than my dad, anyway. Took me and my brother to the pictures. Kind of spoiled us."

"Did you spend a lot of time with him?"

"Most holidays," I said, my voice quiet and trembling.

She waited; her pen poised above the pad.

The memory arrived, as it always did, in fragments, the colour of the bedspread, the sticky heat of that summer, the taste of tobacco on the rim of the glass he'd made me finish before bed. I saw my hands, small and sunburned, clutching the chipped enamel mug as if it were an award for bravery.

I cleared my throat, "he was a war hero," I said, by way of explanation, "rear gunner. Lancaster bombers. He got a medal in the war. People treated him like he was famous."

She did not respond, just nodded, letting the momentum build in whatever direction I was prepared to let it.

"He was always physical," I said, "would play fight, punch me on the arm. Grab my neck in a headlock. It's just what men did, back then. You were supposed to like it."

Her pen hovered, waiting.

"It was the summer of 1976," I started. Then the flood gates opened and the memories flooded out. Articulated externally for the very first time.

Sarah only interrupted me once, "how did you feel?" she asked, not looking up.

"Nothing," I said, too quickly. "I didn't feel anything." It was the closest I had come, in months of these sessions, to telling the truth, "I just wanted it to be over. I didn't think it would ever stop, so I just… waited."

She was quiet for a long time, "have you ever told anyone else?"

I shook my head, "not even myself, really. I just… put it away." I pressed the heel of my hand to my right eye, where a tension headache had begun to flower.

"John," she said, and for the first time I noticed the faintest quaver in her voice, "do you think this has anything to do with the way you feel now? The guilt you've described?"

I wanted to laugh, "you think I'm gay because I got fucked by my uncle?"

She did not smile, "I think you feel guilt because you learned, very early, that pleasure and pain can coexist. That they're sometimes indistinguishable. And that somewhere along the line, you learned it was easier to take the blame for what happened than to admit you'd been hurt."

I picked at the seam of my jeans, refusing to meet her eyes, "I don't want to be a victim," I said. The word tasted like a mouthful of sand.

"No one does," she replied. "But you are not to blame for what happened. The shame isn't yours to carry. It belongs to him."

This was the theme that we explored together for the next couple of sessions as she explained the concept of post-traumatic stress disorder. It was a new lens through which I viewed my many personal failures. PTSD was never an excuse I realised, but simply a means of explanation.

At the end of one of these sessions Sarah asked the simplest question: "how do you feel?"

I heard it, and for a long time, did not respond. At last I said, "I'm not happy," and was startled to find my voice did not break. "But for the first time, I think I might be content. I can live with it."

She closed her notebook, folded her hands, "you're ready to go back to work," she said. "I'll sign the form, but I want to see you once more, in two weeks. Just to make sure."

I nodded, stood, and felt the ghost of a smile cross my lips. It was not victory, not even relief, but the air in the room seemed a shade lighter, as if someone had opened a door in a sealed house.

Outside, the corridor was empty. The autumn light was grey and flat, but I saw it differently now, an unremarkable, ordinary world, waiting for me to return.

I paused at the exit, took a long, deliberate breath, and walked on.

CHAPTER 22: A SUMMER SEARCH

The heat in my apartment was not the kind that demanded relief, but the kind that made you question the physics of insulation: muggy, residual, as if the city had been slow-roasted and then left to rest under clingfilm. I sat at the table by the window, my left arm sheathed from knuckle to wrist in a plasticised cast, the fingers mottled with frustration and the faint yellowing of a long-resolved bruise. My right hand hovered uncertainly over the keyboard, unused to its solo duties.

The prescription bottle on the table vibrated with the hum of the passing bus, its label, fluoxetine, 20mg, take one daily, mocked me with its banality. The cast was courtesy of a spiral fracture to the fourth metacarpal, sustained in the classic fashion: a mistimed drive through the covers, a cricket ball with no respect for its social superiors, and a split-second failure of hand-eye coordination that would have disappointed several generations of my cricket-mad forebears.

The orthopaedic registrar had admired the clean break ("textbook," he'd said, before resetting and pinning the bone with what I could only describe as professional glee), and dispatched me home with instructions to "rest and, if possible, avoid vigorous activity." I had not been sure whether he was referring to the cricket or something more personal. Since the minor surgery I had contracted a mild infection to add to my woes.

Outside, the street simmered in the parody of an English summer: children with melting ice creams, shirtless men arguing at the bus stop, the air above the tarmac shivering in perpetual anticipation of a thunderstorm that never arrived. I had not left the flat in three days, not since the school year had lurched to its anticlimactic end with an assembly so devoid of meaning that even the headmaster failed to produce a metaphor.

I poured myself a glass of water, one-handed, which is harder than you'd think, and took the pill with the kind of deliberate, ceremonial gesture that I imagined would impress my therapist, were she here to witness it. I cradled the glass in my casted hand, feeling the condensation bead and slip, and watched the surface of the water as if it might, through some act of observation, resolve into clarity.

I'd spent the first days in a haze of self-pity and half-hearted walks, but this morning I'd been seized by a different malaise: the urge to catalogue, to inventory, to drag the evidence of my life out of the cupboards and into the unrelenting fluorescent light of the kitchen. I lined up the boxes on the floor, each one a stratum of failed intentions: photos, yearbooks, student projects, a handful of love letters folded so many times the creases had become their own kind of *Braille*.

I started with the easiest box, university ephemera. The plastic sleeve at the top contained my degree, which I examined with the same mixture of pride and disbelief I'd reserved for the Queen's Christmas address. The name, my name, looked fraudulent, as if it had been borrowed from a more plausible version of myself. Below that, a sheaf of term papers, each one annotated in a different red ink. I scanned the margins, reading the old criticisms as if hoping to find an omen.

Then came the photographs. A stack of polaroids from the eighties, the colours faded to the washed-out palette of a war film, each image ringed with a nimbus of chemical uncertainty. I shuffled through them with my uninjured hand, pausing at each, the faces arranged in a taxonomy of loss. Most were instantly forgettable: the cricket teams, the Christmas party, a succession of students who, in the years since, had been recast in the tabloid imagination as either victims or minor celebrities. But there were others—rarer, more dangerous.

I found one, near the bottom. Me and William, summer 1984, posed in the shade of the giant oak behind Langley Hall. His arm draped over my shoulder, our shirts already translucent with sweat, and in our faces the squint of men who had not yet learned the lesson of sunscreen, or of consequences. I remembered the day: the smell of mown grass, the chorus of insects in the heat, the taste of lime cordial and cheap white wine. I remembered how he'd looked at me, as if daring me to find a better moment. I held the photo close, as if the heat might leach the image into my palm.

I put the photo on the table, next to the pill bottle, and kept going. There were letters from Amanda, each one a compressed spiral of hate and complaint. I read the first few lines of each, then set them aside. There was a postcard from Sarah, the therapist, written after my last scheduled appointment: *Remember, unresolved issues have a way of waiting for you at the next stop*. She'd drawn a cartoon train, its engine trailing a plume of question marks.

I laughed, and then, involuntarily, cried. It was a small, animal sound, and it passed as quickly as it came, leaving only the vestige of moisture at the edge of my eye. I wiped it away with the back of my cast, and imagined what William would say to such a display. He'd have grinned, then punched my arm, then made a joke about how "real men only cry when *the Ashes* are lost."

I stood, the sudden movement making my head swim, and walked to the window. The view was nothing: a brick wall, a fire escape, the hint of rural Essex and the M25 somewhere beyond. I pressed my forehead to the glass and let the pane cool my skin.

I thought of calling Amanda. I imagined the conversation, the careful modulation of voices, the ritual exchange of "how are yous," the slow circling around the subject of Rose. I pictured her, somewhere in her new house in Chorlton, surrounded by the evidence of a life that had already made room for my absence. I imagined her with her new family, and felt nothing but relief and the hope that one day she would rescind my visit ban.

The computer, a recent upgrade courtesy of my department's summer budget, sat on the desk, its screen reflecting the distorted geometry of the room. I logged on, navigating the familiar gauntlet of passwords and security updates, and opened the browser. The home page was still set to the school's staff portal, a grid of news items and mandatory training.

On a whim, I typed "Langley Hall School" into the search bar, and hit return. The results were instantaneous: a homepage, garish and over-designed, with a banner photo of the main building and, beneath it, a carousel of *Notable Alumni*. I scrolled through, pausing at the faces, trying to spot any evidence of the world I'd known. There were links to the school's calendar, to the *Friends of Langley* reunion committee, to a directory of staff.

I clicked the last, and scrolled down. The groundsman: William Cooper. Head Groundsman, actually, if the site was to be believed. The photo was recent: his hair now shorter, flecked with grey, the eyes narrowed against the sun. He wore the high-viz vest of his station, but otherwise he was unchanged. The smile was there, the tilt of the head that said, *I know exactly what you're thinking*. I stared at the image until

the screen saver cut in, and then restarted the machine just to
see it again.

My heart raced, the pulse jumping in my throat with a
violence I hadn't felt since the accident. I squeezed my left
hand, feeling the tension in the broken bones, the satisfying
ache of something desperate to heal. I tried to imagine what I
would say, if I saw him again. The words failed, dissipating in
the static of adrenaline and long held regret.

I turned from the desk, sat back down at the kitchen table, and stared at the photograph. Me and William, the shadow
of the cedar tree darkening the ground at our feet, the future
still entirely theoretical. I placed the polaroid next to the image
on the screen, aligning them by instinct, as if the juxtaposition
might spark some kind of magic.

I thought about what Sarah had said, about "unresolved
issues." I thought about the choices I had made, the betrayals,
the evasions, the long, slow retreat from anything that might resemble happiness. I thought about the years I'd spent running,
and about what it might mean to finally stop.

I clenched my fist, feeling the drag of the cast and the
sharp, electric jolt of pain as the bone protested. I breathed in,
deep and slow, and let the heat of the afternoon fill my lungs.

I knew, in that moment, that I would have to see him.
That I would have to drive to Langley, and stand in the shadow
of the old house, and try, however inadequately, to account for
the distance I had put between us. I knew, too, that it would
probably be a disaster.

But for the first time in years, I felt something like
hope.

I stood, walked to the window, and watched the last of
the light leave the street. The heat had broken, replaced by the
cool, mineral smell of an evening rainstorm moving in from the
south. I breathed it in, and let myself believe, for a moment,
that the world might allow for one more reprieve.

Next I searched for a bed and breakfast in Langley Village, and of course it had to be *the Langley Arms*. I called and
made a booking. Then I turned from the monitor, and began to
pack.

The journey north-east was not long, but I made it last, as if prolonging the liminal state between intention and consequence might dilute the latter. Each gear change with my lefthand reminded me of the reason I was able to make the journey in the first place. I took the A12 out of *London*, resisting the urge to cede the wheel to the M11 and its more efficient, more brutal extraction from the city's gravity. Instead, I let the old *Nissan* idle at every roundabout, linger in the slipstream of every lorry, milk the miles for their slow, narcotic effect. The car, a hatchback purchased used from a retiring science teacher, had a tape deck and a cassette of *'Now That's What I Call Music 11'* jammed inside, so the soundtrack was equal parts nostalgia and abjection: *Kylie Minogue* followed by *Dire Straits* followed by a novelty hit about *Joe le Taxi*.

The landscape was a strobe of past and present. Out of *Chelmsford*, the fields widened, the hedgerows thickened, and the air began to taste of more honest things: manure, diesel, the faint sweetness of rotting barley. In the villages, signs of the old world, phone boxes with glass still intact, post offices doubling as newsagents, the odd pub with its half-hearted hanging baskets. In between: new builds, out-of-town supermarkets, carveries with menus advertising both carvery and *'American ribs'*.

It was a Thursday in late July, the kind of day that threatened rain but never quite delivered, and the lanes shimmered with heat. During the journey, I ruminated on the several ways my encounter with William might play out. The best-case scenario was a brisk handshake, a pint, and the polite sharing of shared stories, the worst, a cold shoulder and a quick walk in the opposite direction. Somewhere between these extremes lurked the more likely outcome: an hour of studied awkwardness, followed by a soft fade into mutual embarrassment, after which we would both pretend it had never happened.

In the car, I rehearsed my opening lines: *'it's been a while'*, *'you haven't changed'*, *'did you ever finish that landscaping project behind the gym?'* Each seemed, in its turn, both trivial and catastrophic. I tried for something more direct: *'I think about you, sometimes'*, *'I'm sorry, for what I did—or failed to do'*. These, predictably, landed with the impact of a wet sock, so I went back to the first category, then, after several repetitions, decided it would be best to say nothing at all, at least at the outset.

As I approached the turnoff for Langley, the landscape narrowed, the fields hemmed in by wire fences, the houses transitioning from council brick to the soft gold of local stone. The signage grew sparse, the lanes more intricate, until, at last, the familiar perimeter of the estate loomed into view: the high, knuckled trees lining the avenue, the squat gateposts at the entry, the long, winding drive that led to the Hall itself. I slowed the car, more out of reverence than necessity, and took the turn, the crunch of gravel under the tires both aural and tactile.

The village lay just beyond, a clutch of houses arrayed on each side of the village road with the forced nonchalance of a royal courtier. I crossed over the ancient stone bridge into the oldest part of the village, passing the church and then a row of shops and cottages. *The Langley Arms* appeared next after a narrow lane and looked much as it had in the 80s: a thatched roof, whitewashed walls, a sign depicting the Langley coat of arms. The car park was half full, the cars more new than not, their paint jobs the muted palette of modern affluence.

I parked, switched off the engine, and sat for a moment, letting the stillness of the place invade the cabin. My hand hovered over the gear stick, the nerves in my fingers a tangle of anticipation and dread.

Inside, the pub was unchanged. The same varnished beams, the same sticky carpet, the same air thickened by decades of fried food and the slow, dogged fermentation of cask ale. Behind the bar, a woman of indeterminate age polished glasses with a vigour that suggested either deep satisfaction or equally deep rage. She glanced up as I entered, took in my city clothes and the bandage on my left hand, and, after a beat, nodded toward the guestbook.

"Checking in?" she said, her voice even.

"Yes," I replied, and fumbled for my wallet, "Williams. John."

She leafed through the register, marked my arrival with a sharp flourish, and slid a key across the bar, "up the stairs, second left. Breakfast is seven to nine, but don't expect miracles. The chef's on his holidays."

I thanked her, took the key, and climbed the stairs, the carpet sucking at my shoes with each step. The room was small but clean, the bed made up with military corners, the window giving onto a view of the car park and, just beyond, the ragged edge of the river *Chet*. I dropped my overnight bag on the bed, sat, and listened to the murmur of voices from the beer garden below.

I tried, for a while, to read the book I'd brought, *Sebald*, for irony's sake, but the words would not settle. My mind kept cycling back to the image of William: the photo on the website, the memory of his hands, the way his voice, memorised as it was, had rendered me adolescent again. I tried to remember what he'd sounded like when he was angry, but in truth, I could not; the only anger I remembered was my own, and even that had faded, become less rage than shame.

I slept fitfully, the dreams a sequence of unresolved arguments and impossible reconciliations, all conducted in the labyrinthine corridors of a Hall that was both Langley and not-Langley, its architecture reconfigured by the logic of regret.

In the morning, I showered, dressed, took a cooked breakfast and walked to the Hall, the air thick with the smell of cut grass and the drone of distant mowers. The drive was as I remembered, the avenue lined with lime trees, the gravel path bordered by the kind of precisely unkempt shrubbery that suggested a tradition of highly competent, slightly mad gardeners. The Hall itself was unchanged as it slowly revealed itself as the drive turned to the right, its facade the colour of old bones, the windows reflecting the uncertain light of the early day. If the intention of the architect had been to inspire awe then he knew what he was doing I thought to myself.

I circled the building, following the path to the right and behind the ballroom heading for the stable block, hands in pockets, scanning for any sign of William. The grounds were empty, save for a lone dog walker in the distance. I peered into the greenhouse, the potting shed, the brick-walled garden. Nothing. The only human presence was a teenager with a battered strimmer, ear protection on, slicing through nettles with a mixture of boredom and aggression.

I approached him, rehearsing an introduction.

"Excuse me…"

He glanced up, one eye narrowed against the sun, "yeah?"

"Is William, Mr. Cooper, around?"

He shrugged, in the universal language of teenage indifference, "he's off-site until later, I think. He's got a place up near the river. You could try there. Or leave a message."

I hesitated, then said, "Can you tell him an old friend is staying at *the Langley Arms*?"

The boy nodded, then returned to his strimmer, the conversation hopefully not forgotten.

I walked back to the village, mind awash with the realisation that I'd built the entire morning on the assumption of immediacy, of encounter. The failure of this plan left me exposed, and I spent the hours until lunch in a kind of anxious stasis, walking the perimeter of the churchyard and boatyard, then retreating to the shade of the beer garden to drink tea and watch the traffic.

At one, I moved inside, ordered a sandwich, and took a table by the window. The place was nearly empty, two men in hi-vis jackets, a family with a toddler, and a woman reading a paperback at the far end of the bar. I watched the door, expecting every new arrival to be William, then cursing myself for the transparency of my own anticipation.

It was nearly two when he walked in.

He was thinner than I remembered, the lines of his face more pronounced, the jaw squared by either years or a stubborn refusal to acknowledge time's advance. His hair, which had always been a point of pride, was cropped short, flecked with grey at the temples. He wore a work polo shirt with the Hall's crest above the pocket, forearms tanned and marked with the fine crosshatch of old scars and new labour.

He paused in the doorway, eyes adjusting to the dim, then scanned the room with the slow, methodical sweep of a man who knows exactly what he's looking for. His gaze landed on me, held for a beat longer than comfort allowed, then moved away, as if to check the exits.

He walked to the bar, exchanged a few words with the landlady, then turned, pint in hand, and made his way to my table. His approach was unhurried, almost deliberate, and as he drew near I felt my heart contract, then expand, as if making space for all the things I'd not allowed myself to feel.

He stood over the table, regarding me with an expression that was neither welcome nor rejection, but some third thing, appraisal, perhaps.

"John," he said, voice lower than I remembered but unmistakable, "been a long time."

I stood, awkwardly, and offered my right hand. He took it, the grip firm, then released.

I gestured to the chair opposite, "will you…"

He nodded, sat, took a long pull from his pint. For a while we did not speak, the silence populated only by the clink of glass and the murmur of voices from the other end of the room.

At last, he said, "didn't think I'd ever see you again. Not here, anyway."

I shrugged, unsure how to begin.

He set down his glass, folded his arms, and fixed me with a look that was equal parts curiosity and caution.

"Well?" he said, "you've come all this way. What's on your mind?"

The words, when they came, were nothing like what I'd rehearsed.

"I missed you," I said, and felt the heat rise in my face.

He watched me for a moment, eyes unreadable. Then he smiled, just a little, and said, "yeah. I missed you too."

We sat, not speaking, while the afternoon light shifted through the window and the world outside went on, oblivious. And for the first time in years, I felt, not home, but something like it.

The table between us, varnished to a high, glassy shine, reflected our hands as if offering a split-screen of intent and anxiety. William's fingers, blunt and dirt-caked at the cuticles, tapped a steady, arrhythmic pattern; my own, paler now from too much time indoors, lay still, the left nestled uselessly in the blue sling the NHS had dispensed with more enthusiasm than instruction.

We let the silence settle, a silt of old grievances and newer, sharper ones. I wanted, very badly, to clear my throat, but I let him have the floor, even as the need to speak pressed at my chest like a knot of rising gas.

He looked up at last, the blue of his eyes undiminished, if ringed now with the weathering of forty years, "you look like shit, John," he said, but there was something not unkind in it.

"Teaching does that to a man and a cricket ball does that to a hand," I replied.

He smiled, or something close, "you always did blame the kids."

"Not always," I said, "sometimes it was the parents."

He took a long pull on his pint, leaving a foamy rime on his upper lip, "so, you're back. What happened?"

I had not thought, really, about how to explain this, so I went with the truth as it had been suggested to me in therapy: minimal, factual, stripped of all the grandeur I might have assigned it in a different era.

"I had a rough time," I said, "the marriage… didn't last. Amanda moved on, took Rose with her. I got a job in *London*. Last year, I went through a bit of bother and nearly killed myself. Ended up in hospital for a while. Meds, therapy, all that."

He nodded, slowly, "you tried to top yourself?"

I met his gaze, "yes. Well. I tried to stop the noise."

He mulled this over, then shrugged, "glad you failed."

"Me too," I said, and felt the oddest urge to laugh.

He watched me, not in the appraising, predatory way of our youth, but in the cautious, half-suspicious way you watch an animal you're not sure will bite or bolt, "what about the kid?" he said, and for a moment I had to remind myself who he meant.

"She's in Manchester," I said, "I am banned from seeing her. She's better off without me, probably."

He finished the pint, set it down with care, "that's not for you to decide."

"I know," I said, but left it at that.

He signalled to the bar for another round. I tried to wave off the offer, still on antibiotics, as the doctor had warned, though I doubted now that it mattered, but he ordered two anyway, and when the drinks arrived, he tipped his toward me in a gesture both familiar and ironic.

I took a sip, the taste immediately evocative of other summers, other afternoons spent chasing oblivion at the margins of respectability.

I braced myself, then said, "I wanted to see you." I made myself hold the silence after.

He nodded, almost imperceptibly.

"I never stopped," I said, and now my face was burning, "thinking about it. About you."

He let that land, then said, "you were always the clever one. I figured you'd worked it out eventually."

This time I did laugh, a short, sharp exhale, "turns out I'm a slow learner."

He leaned back, folded his arms, "so what do you want, John?"

The question, so bald, so clinical, so William, took me apart for a moment. I searched for the right answer, then decided on honesty, because there was no other currency between us anymore.

"I want to be less lonely," I said, "or at least, to know I tried."

He nodded again, but his jaw was tight, the muscle working at the hinge, "you could have come back anytime," he said. "You could have called. Even once."

"I know," I said, "I should have. But I…"

He cut me off, not angry, just urgent, "don't say you couldn't. That's the one thing I never believed."

I sat back, felt the fatigue in my spine. "I was a coward," I said, and it came out so soft I almost missed it myself.

He shook his head, "no. Not a coward. Just…" He broke off, as if the word wouldn't come, "you thought you could fix it. Fix yourself, find the straight life, the normal."

He said the last word as if it were a breed of livestock he'd spent a lifetime despising.

I nodded, but he was not done.

"You were the only man I have ever wanted," he said, voice level, "and you threw it away for what you thought was normal."

I could not look at him. The room was warm, and the surface of the table had become a smear of lights and shadows, impossible to focus on.

He stood, abruptly, the legs of his chair scraping a protest against the tile.

"I need a walk," he said, "you staying here?"

I nodded, not trusting myself to speak.

"Right," he said, and was gone, the door swinging behind him with a finality that felt like a judgment.

I finished my drink, both of them, in fact, and then sat for a while, staring out the window at the slow drift of cars through the village. The clouds had thickened, and a line of rain swept across the road, beading on the glass. I felt light, insubstantial, as if the only thing holding me to the seat was the gravity of memory.

I paid, left a tip too large for the service, and walked out into the wet air. The village was unchanged, but I was not, and the

dissonance of that realisation unsettled me. I walked, not toward the Hall, but around its periphery, following the footpaths
that circled the grounds, past the gatehouse and the cricket
pitch and the pond that, in summer, was a net for dragonflies
and, in autumn, a mirror for the failing light.

Every hundred meters, the landscape triggered a
memory: the time William and I had toured the village; the
night we'd lain on our backs in the garden, tracing the constellations with drunken, outstretched fingers; the evening we'd argued about history and its value.

It was all there, as vivid and sharp as the cold on my
face.

At dusk, I returned to the pub. The evening crowd had
replaced the lunchers, and the noise was pitched to a higher,
more convivial register. I found a corner table and ordered a
tea, decaffeinated, as if that might stave off the rising headache.

I watched the clock, the hands moving with the languid
precision of a machine that knows it is being watched.

At seven-thirty, the landlady appeared at my table, a slip
of paper in her hand.

"Message for you," she said, "from the groundsman."

I unfolded the note, the paper soft and warm from her
palm.

"*Cooper's Cottage.* 8pm."

I stared at it, the handwriting unmistakable, a compact,
upright scrawl that spoke of patience and stubbornness in equal
measure.

For a long time, I did not move. I sat, tracing the loops
of the *C*, the curl of the *p*, the almost mathematical neatness of
the numbers.

It could be anything, I told myself. A dismissal. A reprieve. A reckoning.

The rain had stopped when I walked out, the road shining with the residue of the day, the air fresher than it had any
right to be.

I followed the lane that led past the beer garden, my
heart drumming a staccato that was equal parts dread and hope.
At the end of the lane, the lights of the cottage glowed through
the hedge, a beacon in the gathering dark.

I stood at the gate, rehearsing again what I might say.

Then I opened it, and walked in.

The gate squealed as I pushed it open, the hinges in need of oil or mercy. The garden was a narrow slip of lawn bordered by beds of wild geranium and mint, the air sharp with the fragrance of bruised leaves and the clean, ozone scent of recent rain. I walked the path to the cottage door, hesitated, then raised my hand to knock.

Before I made contact, the door swung open.

William stood in the threshold, illuminated from behind by a low, golden light. He wore a fresh shirt, open at the neck, sleeves rolled in the style I remembered. The lines at the corners of his eyes were deeper now, but the eyes themselves were steady.

"I saw you at the gate," he said, voice even.

"I was…" I started, then let the sentence dissolve, "didn't want to barge in."

He stepped back, holding the door with one hand, "you never did."

I entered. The hallway was close, hung with the scent of cut wood and onions caramelizing on the stove. The space was both unfamiliar and immediately legible: a rack of boots by the mat, a stack of garden catalogues on the radiator, a pair of reading glasses on the sideboard.

He led me to the kitchen. A small table was set for two, a candle already lit, the surface arrayed with plates of sliced tomato, olives, crumbled feta, a loaf of dense, floury bread. A bowl of tzatziki. The food was a shock, an unmistakable reference.

He saw my reaction and smiled, just a flicker at the mouth, "thought we might need a reminder, and something you could eat one-handed," he said.

Of what? I wanted to ask. Instead I sat, aware of the sudden heaviness in my arms, the ache that had nothing to do with broken bone.

He brought two glasses, a bottle of *Chablis* in a nod to standards I guess, sweating faintly in its sleeve, and poured without comment. We clinked, the sound small but satisfying. He gestured for me to sit.

He said, "eat," and I did, scooping feta onto a slice of bread, chasing it with a sliver of olive. It was perfect: briny, cool, the taste immediately evocative of *Aegina*, of afternoons spent sprawled under a parasol, the world reduced to sun, sea, and the slow drift of cloud across sky.

We ate for a while in silence, the only sound the click of knife on plate, the slight sound of wind against the kitchen window.

At last, he said, "you wanted to tell me something."

I nodded, "it's a long list."

"Plenty of time," he said, and I realised he meant it.

I started with the childhood. The uncle, that summer, the feeling of being a conduit for someone else's will. I told it quickly, as if reciting a series of events I'd learned to distance myself from, but he listened as if each detail was news, each pause an opening for something larger.

I moved on to the years that followed, the double life, the chronic unease, the way every decision felt predicated on avoiding the one thing I wanted. I told him about Amanda, about the effort to be good, the slow unravelling that neither of us could admit was happening until it was far too late. I described the hospital, the months afterward, the therapy, the tentative peace that followed.

He sat, motionless, through all of it. Occasionally he would refill my glass, or pass the bread, or nod in a way that was more than mere acknowledgment.

When I had run out of words, he looked at me, and for the first time in years I saw the man I remembered, not the stranger from the bar.

He said, "you don't owe me an apology."

"I think I do," I said, "you deserved better."

He shook his head, "we were children. We did what we could."

I let this settle.

He set down his glass, "I was so angry," he said, quietly. "For years, I thought you'd just erased it all. That the holiday, the Hall, none of it mattered. I kept thinking, if I'd been different, braver, maybe you'd have stayed."

I reached across the table, my hand shaking just enough for him to notice.

"I thought the same," I said.

He covered my hand with his, the grip warm, callused, and very real. We sat like that for a while. Not speaking, not needing to.

Outside, the rain started again, gentle at first, then heavier. The candle guttered in the draft, but did not go out.

He said, "I suppose the question is, what now?"

"I don't know," I said, "I'm tired of running."

He nodded, "then don't run."

I smiled, the first real one in months, "I won't I promise."

"Good," he said, and squeezed my fingers once before letting go.

We cleared the table together, moving in an unspoken rhythm that felt at once new and utterly familiar. He handed me a dish to dry; I dropped it, nearly, and he caught it, then laughed, the sound so full and rich that I laughed, too.

Later, we stood in the garden, sheltered beneath the eave, watching the rain bead on the roses. He smoked a cigarette, passing it to me halfway down, the gesture so casual, so intimate, I nearly cried.

When it was late, he showed me the guest room. The bed was made, the sheets turned back. On the pillow, a spare tee shirt and pair of pyjama bottoms, "or you can go back to the pub?" I stepped inside brushing past William with a smile, an obvious acceptance of his invitation.

I changed, lay down, listened to the pulse of rain against the window. I waited for sleep, but it did not come, so I rose, padded barefoot to the door of his room.

It was open.

He was sitting on the edge of the bed, elbows on knees, head bowed. He looked up when I entered. I did not ask for permission. I sat beside him, rested my hand on his back, and for a while we just breathed in tandem.

After a time, I said, "is this all right?"

He nodded, reached for my hand, laced our fingers together.

We slept, eventually. In the morning, the sky was clear, the world washed new.

Over breakfast, he said, "you'll have to go back. London, the job, the flat."

I shook my head, "I don't."

"You're sure?"

I was. For once, entirely.

We finished eating. We walked the grounds, side by side, speaking of nothing in particular.

When it was time to call the school, to let them know I'd not be coming back, I used his phone, the line crackling with the distance but also, somehow, with a new sense of possibility. I watched him as he deadheaded roses, the movement expert, almost thoughtless. He looked up, met my gaze, and smiled.

There was nothing left to say. Not right now.

But everything, somehow, had been said.

I stood there, the air bright and full, and let myself belong.

CHAPTER 23: TURKISH DELIGHTS

For the next month, I commuted between *Billericay* and Langley with the regularity of a blood cell in a closed circuit, never quite certain whether the pulse that drove me was compulsion, habit, or the slow, inverted pressure of William's pull. At first, it was a matter of logistics: one could not simply abandon a life, even an unloved one, without first disentangling the cords that bound it. My flat, though small, was a museum of attachments. Every box I taped up and set by the door seemed to echo with the guilt of things unfinished, or memories misplaced.

The drive was monotonous but necessary, a two-hour drive that left the mind ample room to wander. Each time, I loaded the hatchback with another round of essentials, books, mostly, and the kind of clothing that refused to crease. The flat's materiality shrank with every trip, until its echoing rooms felt less like a home and more like the waiting room of someone else's future.

William's cottage, by contrast, expanded to absorb my arrivals. It was as if the space anticipated each new incursion: a shelf cleared here, a drawer emptied there, the subtle rearrangement of priorities that comes not from edict but from the accumulation of daily compromise. William had never once said, "move in," nor had I announced my intention to stay; rather, we orbited the idea, each pass a degree closer, until the point of no return simply became another step on the path.

The weather that March was more obstinate than usual. In *Essex*, a late frost hung over the lawns, silvering the daffodil shoots and making the walk from car park to front door a study in caution. *Norfolk* was windier, colder by a degree or two, and the little lane from *The Langley Arms* to *Cooper's Cottage* often required navigation through a slush of fallen petals and last autumn's leaf mould.

In the garden, William made his peace with the season by working the beds with a ferocity that bordered on the punitive. I'd watch from the kitchen window as he moved through the rose borders, stooped and methodical, his hands encased in battered gloves and his hair a permanent chaos of rain and sweat. It was not only roses, of course, the hedge required trimming, the apple trees needed their winter cut, and the vegetable patch, still only promise and intention, demanded constant vigilance against the return of nettles and ground elder.

Inside, the cottage was a study in weathered charm. The low ceilings and exposed beams conspired to create an atmosphere both intimate and mildly oppressive, the air thick with the competing scents of woodsmoke, onion, and the wet wool of William's jumpers. The division of labour, never formalized, was quickly established: he cooked, I washed up; I made the beds, he kept the fire going. Once, I tried to intervene in the garden, but after a brief tutorial on the correct way to set a rose cane, I returned to my books, suitably chastened.

The *University of London* had, after only two brief phone calls and a flurry of e-mailed references, offered me a remote examiner position: part-time, flexible, with no expectation of presence beyond the odd meeting in *London* at the *British Museum* - which was no great hardship, and the punctual return of marked scripts. It paid less than teaching, but the freedom to read and annotate in my own time, and, more importantly, in my own clothes, made it irresistible.

I converted the cottage's spare bedroom into a study, stacking my reference volumes along the window ledge and arranging a makeshift desk from a pair of trestles and a cut-down barn door that William had salvaged from the estate. The sunlight that entered this room in the morning was so pale and watery that it barely registered as light at all, but it was enough to bring out the gold lettering on the spines of my history books, and to illuminate the drift of dust that, no matter how often I cleaned, seemed always to return.

The marking itself was both numbing and addictive. Each stack of essays was a tripwire of barely concealed panic and odd, feral brilliance, the kind of writing only students with nothing to lose can produce. I worked through the pages with a red pen, making notes in the margin, *'Awkward, but interesting'*, *'Cite your sources'*, *'Excellent, but watch your dates'*, and marvelled at the endless ingenuity with which young people managed to misunderstand the past. Occasionally, William would come in and perch on the edge of the desk, watching me read. He'd pick up the top essay and leaf through it, lips pursed, brow furrowed in mock-seriousness.

"You ever get bored of it?" he asked once, laying the paper flat and squinting at the handwriting.

"All the time," I replied, "but it's better than most things."

"Better than gardening?" He raised an eyebrow, the challenge half playful.

I considered it, "some days, yes. Most days, no."

He grinned, then pushed off from the desk, "let me know if you want a hand. Marking, or anything else."

There was never any suggestion of privacy, or the need for it. The cottage was small enough that even the faintest sneeze in the sitting room carried through to the kitchen, and from there to the bathroom. I came to appreciate the particular rhythm of William's days: up at six, coffee and toast by seven, in the garden when not at work until the rain or food drove him inside. The evening's main event, dinner, wine, and whatever series we could agree upon for an hour's communal watching before bed.

By April, I'd managed to transfer the last of my things. The *Billericay* flat had sold within three weeks, the estate agent barely bothering to show me the paperwork before shoving a pen into my hand. I left the key with the neighbour across the hall, a retired postman with the suspicious gaze of someone who has spent a career sorting other people's secrets.

The final move, when it came, was less catharsis than anticlimax. I packed the car with what was left, drove to Langley with an aching back and the beginnings of a cold, then unloaded everything in one go, stacking the boxes by the back door. William was out at work when I arrived. I let myself in, dropped the bags in the hallway, then wandered through the rooms, reacquainting myself with their contours. It was not the grandeur of Langley Hall, nor the threadbare impermanence of the university flats, nor even the bland, suburban calm of Billericay; it was, instead, something between, a compromise space, provisional but real.

I made tea, sat on the sofa, and waited for William to return. Outside, the rain pelted the windows in sheets, muting the garden to a blur of green and grey. I watched the clock, counted the seconds, and felt, for the first time, a twinge of anxiety that I had miscalculated, that the sum of all these gestures would not, in the end, amount to home.

At six, the door banged open, and William entered with the weather still clinging to his boots. He shook off his jacket, stomped in the hallway, and peered into the sitting room, grinning when he saw me.

"You're back," he said, voice loud and unmistakably pleased.

"I'm back and now homeless," I replied, and held up my mug in salute.

He crossed the room in three strides, leaned over, and kissed me, quick, perfunctory, but very real, "welcome home, then," he said.

We spent the evening assembling a desk for my new office, and then arguing amiably over the best arrangement of bookcases and the merits of storing shoes by the back door versus the front. William insisted on the former; I gave way, reasoning that it was easier to let him win than to risk the silent censure of muddy footprints on the kitchen tile.

For dinner, he roasted a lamb shank with rosemary and garlic, serving it alongside a tray of root vegetables that he claimed were from his own garden (I suspected otherwise, but said nothing). The kitchen, already warm from the oven, filled with the scent of caramelized onion and scorched thyme, and the combination of food, wine, and fatigue rendered us both content and nearly speechless.

After the plates were cleared and the fire crackled for the night, I retrieved the folder from my rucksack, those mortgage papers, the legal forms, remnants of my past life in *Essex*. I set them on the table, the plastic sleeve's sound echoing against the oak, a sharp reminder of what I was about to do.

William eyed the stack with a mix of curiosity and wariness, "what's this?"

I opened the folder and slid the top sheet toward him, "the flat sold faster than I expected. I had the funds wired this morning," I indicated the settlement figure from the sale proceeds. "I want to pay off your mortgage." I hesitated, letting the weight of my decision hang in the air, "put the cottage in both our names."

He stared at the paper, as if waiting for it to reveal something else. Then he picked it up, reading the lines with deliberate care. I watched him closely, searching for any hint of disappointment or doubt. Instead, I saw only careful consideration of what I had just offered.

When he finished, he set the papers down and closed his eyes, "thank you," he said softly, "it means a lot."

I reached across the table, placing my hand on his, "it can be our home now," I said, surprised by the intensity of my own conviction.

He squeezed my fingers and then stood, gathering the empty glasses and the last of the bread. Pausing in the kitchen doorway, he glanced back at me and said, "it's the right thing to do, John. For once."

We laughed, an old joke easing the tension. Yet, as we lay in bed later, with the wind battering the cottage and rain whispering on the glass, I felt a stir of uncertainty. This new rhythm, this new possibility, it wasn't perfect, not even permanent. But it was ours, for now at least.

And I wondered, could that really be enough?

The attic was a time capsule in the truest sense, not an archive, not a curated nostalgia, but a slant-roofed limbo where the unloved and unremembered went to wait out their exile. The first time I ventured up, it was under the pretence of practical necessity ("if we don't sort it, the floorboards will give way and we'll end up with a conservatory in the kitchen," William had observed, only half-joking). But really, I was drawn by the possibility that some residue of the Hall's history, or at least of William's own, might have seeped through the ceiling and gathered here, a slow sediment of the past waiting to be disturbed.

The attic's insulation had slumped in on itself over the years, exposing a fretwork of joists and the occasional rotted rafter. The air, heavy with the scent of cellulose and mouse shit, forced me to breathe shallowly. Cardboard boxes, some labelled in William's handwriting, others anonymous, lined the edges, interspersed with plastic crates and the odd mildewed trunk. I started at one end and worked methodically, hauling each box into the shaft of light that fell through the skylight and opening it with the wary precision of a bomb disposal technician.

The first few boxes were anticlimax: Christmas decorations, yellowed tennis racquets, a broken slide projector that looked as if it had last seen service in the 70s. A crate marked *'Garden'* yielded a tangle of rusted secateurs, a length of knotted baling twine, and a trove of cigarette tins, each filled with a different permutation of nails, screws, or seeds, the contents homogenized by decades of entropy.

It wasn't until I reached the third row, under the eaves, where the dust lay thickest and the air grew colder, that I found what I hadn't known I was looking for. The box was unmarked, its tape yellowed but intact. Inside: a series of leather-bound journals, their spines cracked and their pages mottled with age, accompanied by a sheaf of letters, tied in bundles with twine the colour of old teeth.

I hauled the box into the open and sat cross-legged, hands already tingling with the electric possibility of what it might contain. The journals were heavier than they looked; each one bore, on the inside cover, the name *'T. Cooper'*, in a looping, rightward-leaning hand. I flipped a few pages at random, marvelling at the elegance of the script, the careful underlining and the rare, extravagant flourish of a doodled rose in the margin.

The letters were more varied: some addressed to *'Thomas'*, others to *'My Dearest T.'*, a handful in German and what I assumed was Polish. The paper was fragile, near-translucent in places, but the ink had endured, black and vigorous, each word a rebuke to the amnesia of the present.

I lost track of time, as I always did when presented with the physicality of the past. I spread the contents over the attic floor, arranging them by date and by colour, then by the idiosyncratic taxonomy that only a historian with nothing else to do on a wet Wednesday could devise. I read snatches of entries, letting the story assemble itself in fragments: an account of the Hall under RAF occupation ("the Officers are in every way as disagreeable as the Hun, only better dressed"), a breathless description of a clandestine night in a *Norwich* cinema, a poignant, trembling letter of apology to a *'W. Beswick'*, the lines so heavily revised they looked more like an ECG than a script.

I was in the middle of deciphering a page from 1943, something about a clandestine trip to *Portugal*, the urgency of the tone belying the dryness of the detail, when I heard the sound of boots on the attic ladder. William's head emerged, haloed by the weaker light of the landing.

"You're missing tea," he said, then caught sight of the archive I'd made of the attic floor. He stepped up and leaned against the stair-well, arms crossed, mouth curled into the faintest of smirks, "planning to move up here, are you?"

"Could do worse," I said, holding up the journal for emphasis, "are these your uncle Thomas' journals that you told me about that first summer?"

He made a noise that was neither assent nor denial, then knelt beside me and picked up the nearest bundle of letters, examining it as if it might be booby-trapped, "I forgot they were up here. My great uncle stashed them before he died. My dad wouldn't let me bin them, said it was family, not trash, and I put it up here when we rented out the cottage."

"I remember you telling me. Your great-uncle's writing is beautiful," I said, tracing a finger along the slope of a capital *T*.

William shrugged, "didn't pass down the line."

He watched as I rifled through the pages, and I felt, rather than saw, the faint pleasure he took in my fascination, "you really want to read all that?" he asked, incredulous but kindly.

"Absolutely," I said, "this is the story. I'll finally write it, like I promised all those years ago."

He shook his head, but there was amusement in his eyes, "you do that," he said, and stood, dusting off his hands. "Just don't get lost up here. We're having dinner at Mum's later. You'll want to look presentable."

I looked up at him, the outline of his body framed by the open hatch and the stark line of the banister, "how formal is it?"

"Shirt at least. No holes," he said, grinning, "and don't start an argument about politics with my sister, she's a *Tory* now. She's not as gentle as me."

I promised to behave, then watched as he retreated down the ladder, the echo of his steps fading into the hush of the house. I gathered the journals, bundled them carefully, and brought them to the study, arranging them on the windowsill where the light could find them in the morning.

We made the trek to William's mother's house, a low-slung brick semi across the bridge at the edge of the village, its garden a riot of snowdrops and crocus even in the indifferent chill of March. The interior was a shrine to the 1970s: orange kitchen cabinets, anaglypta wallpaper, the lingering afterlife of decades of Sunday roasts. The table was set for seven, William's two siblings, their spouses, a cluster of nieces and nephews already jostling for territory around the perimeter.

The meal itself was a minor spectacle: roast beef, Yorkshire pudding, three kinds of potatoes (mashed, roasted, and chipped, in a bow to democracy), and enough gravy to float a corgi. Conversation was a volley of sibling in-jokes and topical disputes, but the presence of a "guest" shifted the dynamic, everyone a little more self-conscious, a little more inclined to overexplain.

The children, for their part, were fascinated by me. One niece, who couldn't have been more than six, looked and giggled. Another, older and more attuned to the subtleties of social hierarchy, whispered that I "looked clever" and Uncle William had told her I was a teacher, she asked if I would help her with her geography homework later.

Between courses, William's widowed mother quizzed us gently about our lives: *'How was the work-from-home going?', 'Did we have plans for a summer holiday?', 'Was the garden "settling in" for the spring?'*. She managed, in a single conversation, to convey both her scepticism and her support, a balancing act that only the most practiced of matriarchs can pull off. I suspected she missed living at Home Farm and ruling the family from there.

After dinner, the adults retired to the living room while the children descended on me, bringing books and puzzles and, eventually, a football which they insisted I kick around the garden with them. William watched from the window, arms folded, his expression unreadable. I scored an accidental goal, and the older nephew, emboldened, perhaps, by my sudden athletic credibility, asked if I'd ever been married, and if not, why not.

I fumbled for an answer, but the moment was interrupted by the call for pudding and, later, by the inexorable pull of the evening and the walk home.

Once back home, I sat in the armchair closest to the hearth, the nearest of the journals on my knee. William was in the kitchen, working through the remnants of today's crossword, pausing now and then to mutter obscenities at the compilers or to ask, with faux innocence, for a synonym for *'hapless'*. I answered when I could, but most of my attention was on the pages in front of me, the gradual revelation of a life lived at the margins, its passions both hidden and, when the occasion demanded, defiantly exposed.

The entries were a map of longing, each one marked by the latitude and longitude of forbidden desire. There were coded references, of course, no one of Thomas Cooper's generation would have committed the truth to paper without the insurance of plausible deniability, but there were also moments of luminous honesty, sentences that seemed to pulse with the voltage of unspeakable things.

One letter, sent by a "Pete," from the *United States* in the 1950s was a litany of gratitude and regret, its paragraphs veering from effusive praise of the recipient's *'steadfastness in the face of ignominy'* to the pained confession of *'an affection so durable it embarrasses me to confess it, even to myself'*. The penmanship quavered on the final lines, as if the hand had grown uncertain at the threshold of its own exposure.

I read until my eyes blurred and the page began to tilt and swim. At some point, William entered the room, a mug of tea in one hand and a crumpled crossword in the other.

"You're still at it," he said, not a question.

"Couldn't stop if I tried."

He handed me the mug, then perched on the arm of the chair, the weight of him a comfortable counterbalance to my tendency toward abstraction. We sat that way for a while, sharing the silence, the crackle of the fire the only soundtrack.

"Which bits do you want to write about?" he asked, not looking at me.

"The history?" I said. "Or the story?"

He shrugged, a motion that seemed to take in the whole of the room. "Either. Both."

I considered it, "might be a way to make sense of it," I said, "all the years, all the versions of us."

He nodded, then rested his hand on my shoulder, "start with Uncle Thomas," he said, "he's family, after all."

And so I did. Every morning, after breakfast and before the day's marking, I took an hour to transcribe the most compelling entries, translating the florid, elliptical prose of the past into something that could withstand the scrutiny of the present. I kept a running list of questions, places, dates, names of people whose significance was lost to time, and set about cross-referencing them with the local archives, the Hall's own partial records, and, when desperation called, the long-forgotten alumni newsletters of the school.

There was an embarrassment of documents on the Cooper line and on Thomas himself, I'd combed through family scrapbooks, wills, even taken dusty notes at the county archive to understand Langley Hall and the Langleys who'd lived there. Yet every promising lead on Lord John Langley slipped away into nothingness. I felt the nagging suspicion that he was the missing axis around which the twentieth century at the Hall had turned. Still, week after week, the story remained stubbornly blank. I came within an inch of admitting defeat, of settling for a dry, conventional history of grand rooms, footmen and footnotes. My hope was fading, until the moment I knocked over a box of old audio tapes and spotted something braver, more dangerous. A single manilla legal envelope peeked out from beneath them, incongruous as a blackbird in a snowdrift.

I froze, breath caught, "what have you been hiding from me, Thomas Cooper?" I whispered to myself. I lifted the envelope: embossed at the top, a coat of arms crowned by the scales of justice; in bold red type below, *Messrs. Harrington & Whitby, Solicitors, Lincoln's Inn Fields, London'*. It was addressed to *Mr. T. Cooper, ESQ'*, postmarked June 1963. My pulse hammered as I eased out the double-folded foolscap. Every fibre of me trembled, this was the breakthrough I'd scorned, the complication I both craved and dreaded.

Footsteps creaked on the stairs. William was on his way down for tea. Panic rose in my throat. With shame-flushed cheeks, I clutched the letter as if it might vanish, and almost ran to meet him, "William… look!" I thrust the papers under his nose.

He took them hesitantly, brow knitting. I could see alarm sparking behind his calm hazel eyes. He read in silence, then raised a hand as though to ward off a blow, "what does, *'we concur that, given the sensitive nature of the documents, they remain sealed until at least May 2013,'* actually mean?"

I swallowed, lip trembling. A laugh burst out, nervous, unsteady, "it means," I said, too loudly, "that I've stumbled on the real story." I placed my hands on his shoulders, feeling the tension in his muscles. He frowned, not yet convinced. I pressed on, my voice dropping to a whisper: "The *'sensitive nature'*, it can only be what your great-uncle hinted at before. A relationship between Lord John and the sixth earl..."

"But 2013?" William asked.

"Well yes, it's a wait, but at least I know the direction that I am heading in now," I said this to console myself as much as anything else.

William's eyes darkened. I felt a flicker of guilt, had I dragged him into something we shouldn't unearth? But even as his expression hardened, I sensed the spark of fascination too. My heart thudded with excitement and dread, an uneasy mixture that chased away any tranquillity I'd claimed to find in this project.

Outside, the wind rattled the windows, but inside, the world was still. And in a vault in London, the stories waited, patient and for now undisturbed.

By the end of the spring in 2006, we had settled into a good routine and began to think again about expanding our travels together. Timing would be key and needed to fit into a slot between William's summer break beginning but before my summer exams arrived for marking.

In the city of domes and echoes, we found ourselves once again rehearsing the art of starting over. *Istanbul*, at the height of July, was a fever dream: the air above the tarmac shivered with heat, the *Bosphorus* pulsed with ferries and shadows, and the skyline, so often reduced to the stock images of guidebooks, emerged, in person, as something at once mythic and indecently alive.

We had chosen *Istanbul* almost at random, on the premise that a holiday meant escaping the gravitational field of Englishness, and because neither of us had ever been. The arrival was unscripted: a red-eye from *Stansted,* the lurching, airless shuffle through passport control, the taxi ride in darkness along the old city walls, where the minarets appeared and vanished like the teeth of an elaborate machine. At the hotel, a five-storey tangle of carpets and lamps five minutes downhill from *Taksim Square*, we collapsed into the twin beds and let the jetlag rearrange us.

The first morning was all wrong, in the best way. The call to prayer broke in through the window at dawn, peeling us from sleep with its layered, insistent beauty. William, who claimed to be indifferent to religion, was the first to pull on shorts and a faded cricket T-shirt and drag me into the street, already dense with the churn of mopeds and the oily sweetness of simit vendors. The air was a shock, not only for its heat but for its insistence: every breath thick with diesel, roasting nuts, the sweet-and-rot of open drains, and above it all, the low metallic reek of the sea.

We walked without plan, letting the city organise itself around us. The main square was already mobbed by nine: tourist groups massed at the threshold of the *Blue Mosque*, children in matching hats eating ice cream for breakfast, the intermittent, half-hearted protester with a cardboard sign scrawled in English and a handful of local TV crews ignoring him in favour of more promising spectacle.

We queued for the *Blue Mosque* behind a family of Russians whose children tormented each other with plastic swords. William rolled his eyes and muttered, "diplomacy's wasted on children," then winked at the youngest, who returned the gesture with a tongue stuck defiantly out. The interior was somehow both vast and close, a trick of geometry or a function of the velvet ropes corralling us into a slow, shuffling circuit. The carpet was thick, the air surprisingly cool, and above us, the domes tessellated with the blues and whites of *Iznik* tiles, so fine they seemed painted by the pulse of the city itself.

We stood for a long time under the central dome, our heads thrown back in the classic posture of the tourist, "they built this in less than a decade," William whispered, awe leaking through the studied irony, "the Victorians couldn't even finish a railway station in ten years."

"Divine inspiration," I said.

He grinned, "and a workforce paid in actual bread."

The call to prayer began while we were still inside. The imam's voice, amplified into submission, ricocheted around the stone like the memory of thunder. Conversation stopped, even among the tour groups, and I felt, in that hush, the same humility I'd experienced once in a lecture hall when confronted by the original *Magna Carta*, a recognition that the present, for all its distractions, is a footnote to the things that survive us.

Afterwards we wandered, unmoored by time zones and the absence of agenda. We walked the perimeter of the old *Hippodrome*, where William insisted on reading every plaque, then detoured into the *Basilica Cistern*, descending into the echoing cold as if entering the city's secret twin. The Medusa heads, half submerged, seemed less menacing than resigned, remnants of a time when meaning was a matter of stacking old gods atop new. We pressed coins into the water and watched as they joined the slow drift of other wishes, neither of us admitting to what we'd hoped for.

At *Hagia Sophia*, the line wound around the plaza, but the movement was brisk, almost purposeful. Inside, the scale was impossible: the nave a canyon of light, the apse draped in scaffolding, the air thick with the quiet astonishment of several hundred people trying not to lose their footing on the worn marble floors. We navigated the outer galleries, leaning over the balustrades to peer down at the ants-in-motion below. "They say if you rub this," William pointed to a pillar with a thumb-sized dimple worn into it, "you get a wish." I did as instructed, the gesture absurd and moving at once, then made him do it too. He rolled his eyes, but I saw the way he lingered, his fingers pressing the stone as if to unlock a password.

We escaped into the afternoon heat, blinking at the crush of sun and humanity, "lunch?" I said, but William was already leading us down a side street, following his nose toward a bakery window stacked with baklava and syrup-drenched tulumba. We ordered by gesture and shared the loot on a bench in *Gülhane Park*, letting the sugar crash soften the sharpness of the day.

The *Grand Bazaar* was next, less by intent than by the city's own gravitational pull. The entrances were guarded by men in blue shirts and plastic name badges, but inside, the order dissolved. We wandered the labyrinth, each turn a new permutation of colour, noise, and the logic of commerce. Every third stall sold spices in pyramids so precise they could have been arranged by laser. Saffron, sumac, dried rose petals, a dozen kinds of pepper I'd never tasted. William bargained with the first stallholder for a packet of saffron, accepted the tea he offered in return, and then, to my surprise, launched into a conversation about the merits of Turkish versus English breakfast. "Ours is just builder's dust in a bag," he confessed, and the man laughed, slapping William on the back and offering a second round of tea. I bought a small azure glass evil eye for Rose, though I didn't yet know when, or if, I'd see her next. It would join an ever-growing collection of undelivered birthday and Christmas gifts.

The rest of the afternoon blurred: street cats weaving between our legs, a meander through a bookshop where every volume was in Turkish, the spiral up to the *Galata Tower* and the vertigo-inducing view across the *Golden Horn*. By evening we were exhausted, but unwilling to retreat to the hotel. We found a restaurant with plastic chairs set out on the street, the menu scrawled on a whiteboard, and ate lamb kofta and bread so hot it singed the fingers. William drained two *Efes* beers and started on a third, his face flushed from the sun.

"Happy?" I asked.

He considered, "better than I've been in years." He picked at the plate with his fork, then said, quietly, "I'm glad we did this, John."

It was the first time either of us had named the holiday as a thing we'd done together, rather than as the accident of two men moving in the same direction.

That night, the streets were louder, the shadows deeper. From our window, the city sparkled with a thousand shifting lights. We lay on the twin beds and tried to watch Turkish TV, neither of us bothering to guess the plots, then drifted into a sleep troubled only by the sudden, beautiful din of the early call to prayer.

The next morning, we boarded a ferry at *Eminönü*, following the procession of commuters and schoolchildren down the gangway. The boat was broad and white, its benches scrubbed to the colour of bone, and the upper deck offered a view of the strait that, in its scale, made the *Thames* seem a garden canal. We found seats at the stern and watched as the city unfurled behind us: the domes and minarets receding, then multiplying as the ferry traced its zigzag across the water.

William took out his phone and tried, with only partial success, to photograph the seagulls that trailed the wake, their wings lit gold by the sun, "you'll never catch them," I said.

He grinned, not looking away from the birds, "some things are worth the trying."

The ferry hugged the *Asian* shore for a while, stopping at small piers where the crowds thinned, then returned to the *European* side near the ruins of an *Ottoman* fortress. We disembarked and climbed a hill to a café that promised "the best view in *Istanbul*," a claim so universal it bordered on the metaphysical. From the terrace, the city spread in every direction, stitched together by bridges and the infinite, slanting light of a day that seemed unwilling to end.

We ordered coffee, thick, black, and sweet enough to etch enamel, and sat in silence for a while, watching the world move around us. The other tables were filled with couples, families, the occasional solitary reader. I felt, for a moment, the weight of all the stories unfolding in parallel, the impossibility of knowing which ones would matter in a week, or a year, or a lifetime.

After a time, William said, "what do you think happens to people like us?"

"Which people?"

He considered, "the ones who leave everything behind. The ones who try to begin again."

I sipped the coffee, letting the grit settle at the bottom, "I think they keep moving," I said. "Or they freeze in place, and hope the world catches up."

He nodded, as if this were answer enough.

We walked back down the hill, took the ferry in reverse, and by evening were too tired to do more than sit at the hotel bar and drink *Efes* out of tiny, sweating bottles. The bartender played eighties synthpop, and William, three drinks in, confessed that he'd always wanted to dance, but "never quite had the nerve." I told him he was in luck, as I had even less. He called my bluff, but neither of us moved.

The next day, we took the train to *İzmir*, then a bus to the coast. *Kuşadası*, in August, was a resort town in the throes of overachievement: beaches crowded with Dutch and German tourists, the air thick with sunscreen and the promise of a tan that would last until September. Our hotel, booked at the last minute, was an unapologetic slab of whitewashed concrete, but the view from the balcony was a liquid expanse of blue, interrupted only by the ferries and cruise ships that traced the horizon between the mainland and *Samos*.

The first evening, we ate at a harborside restaurant, the air vibrating with cicadas and the smell of salt. The owner, a man with a moustache so elaborate it deserved its own post code, delivered plates of grilled sea bass and olives, then lingered at the table to ask, with genuine curiosity, if we were brothers or friends or "the other." William blushed, but answered, "the other," and the man, delighted, insisted on pouring us both a glass of raki, "on the house, for love."

Afterwards we walked the marina, stopping at the edge of the breakwater to watch the moonrise. The air was softer here, the heat less urgent, and I felt, for the first time in ages, the possibility of future tense.

At dawn, we took a taxi to *Ephesus*, reasoning that only the very early or the very foolish would brave the site in high summer. Even so, the car park was nearly full, and the entrance thrummed with the low, combative energy of groups competing for the narrow ribbon of shade that followed the path down to the ruins.

William led the way, dodging the tour groups, his stride purposeful. The main avenue of *Ephesus* was a corridor of marble and pollen; the stones still cool from the night but already shimmering with the promise of noon. We passed the *Library of Celsus*, its façade a jigsaw of restoration and loss, then detoured to the amphitheatre, where the guides let their voices boom out, testing the famous acoustics for an audience of pigeons.

At one of the smaller temples, I lingered, reading the inscription, and looked up to see William standing at the far end of the colonnade, hands on hips, surveying the lay of the city as if he owned it. He turned and caught my gaze, smiled, then beckoned. I joined him, and for a while we sat on a fallen capital, watching the sun inch up the sky.

"Imagine living here," he said, sweeping an arm at the vista.

"Imagine dying here," I replied, less morbid than I'd intended.

He snorted, "I suppose it comes to the same thing, in the end."

We walked the rest of the site in a companionable hush, stopping now and then to read the plaques or, more often, to invent alternate histories for the statues and fragments that littered the ground.

By midmorning, the crowds had thickened, and we retreated to the car, dusted off, and drove inland to a village where a weekly market spilled across the main street. We bought apricots and soft cheese and ate them on the bonnet, juice running down our wrists. William found a crate of local wine at a roadside shop and, with the solemnity of a man doing his duty, strapped it into the backseat.

Back in *Kusadasi*, the day folded into the pattern of all perfect holidays: naps in the stuttering air conditioning, swims in the glassy, unchlorinated pool, and, later, the slow walk to the harbour for dinner. Each evening, we tried a new restaurant, though in truth the menus were identical and the real pleasure was in the people-watching. We became regulars at a gelato stand, where the young man behind the counter flirted with William and sneaked him extra scoops, no matter how vehemently he protested, "you're a dangerous man, John," he told me, licking pistachio from his thumb, "I've never eaten so much in my life."

The end of the holiday came too soon, as such things always do. On the last night, we returned to the same harborside restaurant, and the owner greeted us with a grin and an admonition to "remember each other, even when the sea is far away." We ordered the grilled fish again, and this time, when the raki came, I toasted him: "to the next time, and the time after."

William clinked his glass to mine and said, "to the best holiday, with the best man," and for a moment, the world stilled, a freeze-frame, sunlight and salt and the certainty that, even if nothing lasted, this would.

Later, as we walked the breakwater under the city lights, he said, "if you write the book, you'll have to add a chapter for this."

I squeezed his hand, feeling the pulse of him, the line of his knuckle under my thumb, "I will," I promised, "but I'll need your help with the ending."

He smiled, kissed my forehead, and said, "we'll write it together, then."

The moon traced our shadows on the stones, and the air, thick with jasmine and the memory of the day, carried us forward.

Even after we left, even as the flight home bucked through the turbulence above the *Alps*, the scent of the city, its dust, its spices, its particular, untranslatable brightness, clung to us. And when we arrived back in *England*, stepping into the soft, mossy dusk of *Norfolk*, I felt no

sense of loss, only the knowledge that the world was vast
enough for return, and that home was wherever we chose to
name it.

We unpacked, we slept, we fell back into the slow
rhythm of marking and gardening and the thousand gestures
that make up a life. But at night, when the wind carried in the
sound of the river, I'd close my eyes and remember the *Blue
Mosque,* the call to prayer, and the hand in mine, steady as the
stones at *Ephesus.*

And I knew, with the certainty of the truly lucky, that
the story was not over.

Over the next few years life, for the first time, was comfortable; I was exactly where I wanted to be and with the person I wanted to be with. I even dared to think that I was happy
- even though there was a lingering disappointment that I
would have to wait to view the *Langley Archive.* In the mean-
while, I devoted myself to William and our travels - building a
memory bank of happy times which could warm even coldest
and dampest of winter days.

CHAPTER 24: AN ACT OF FORGIVENESS

After the Turkish holiday, and its shuddering air and syruped heat and the untranslatable brightness, we fell back to earth, to the cottage, to the sort of life that, at arm's length, looked indistinguishable from happiness. The days at *Cooper's Cottage* lengthen into each other, and though I pretend it is the light that does this, I know better: the boundaries are eroding not because of any seasonal drift, but because the routines we have assembled are so precise they run on rails, welded together by habit and the careful, unspoken calculation of forgiveness.

This morning, as with every morning, William is up before six. He pads through the house in bare feet, collecting the necessary implements, thermos, pruning knife, wool hat still damp from the day before, and returns to our bed only briefly, to nudge me into the world. I pretend to resist, but the truth is I am always half-awake, listening for the kettle, the first cautious opening of the back door, the cough as he clears his throat against the cold. It is a choreography, or perhaps a waltz: he leads, I follow, we circle the same steps until we can no longer hear the music.

The first order of business is always the garden. In spring, this means kneeling in the mud and gouging out the rot from last year's optimism; in summer, it means a siege against the weeds that, given a single night's inattention, will reclaim every border and bed. I am not a natural gardener, but I have learned the necessary moves: how to distinguish a weed from a flower (always harder than it looks), how to deadhead a rose without severing the next year's promise, how to accept the loss of a plant with stoic detachment. William, on the other hand, treats every living thing as if it were both fragile and infinitely renewable. He speaks to the tomatoes as he tends them, tells the runner beans to "pull their socks up" as if they are underperforming trainees in a boot camp.

The first time he caught me watching him, he grinned and said, "you're waiting for me to lose my temper, aren't you?"

I shrugged, denying it with more force than was necessary, "I'm just trying to learn the ropes."

He squinted at me, the lines at the corners of his eyes deepening, and then said, "it's not a test, John."

But it was, and we both knew it.

Inside, the cottage is a controlled entropy. William's systems are everywhere: the hooks for coats, the rack for muddy boots, the cubby for outgoing post, the weekly rota for shopping and bins. My own contributions are less visible, more a matter of curation: books lined up by colour and author, the optimal arrangement of breakfast cereals for ease of access, the subtle shifting of furniture to maximise conversation angles. The war is never overt, but it is ongoing; every rearranged cushion is an act of mild insurrection.

We breakfast together, always at the window facing the garden. The food is secondary, a quick porridge, a poached egg on toast, yogurt with the last of the summer berries, but the ritual is inviolable. The first time I tried to check my email at the table, William snatched the phone and dropped it in the sink, grinning as it skittered across the enamel.

"Breakfast is for eating, not for work," he said, and though I protested, I have never tried it again.

Evenings are my domain. I build the fire, even in the shoulder months, and select the wine in the hope of William's approval, which sometimes even he pretends to find pretentious, but drinks with undisguised delight. We read, mostly, or watch documentaries about places we will never visit, or argue over the finer points of test cricket and the relative merits of the various *James Bonds*. Once a week, William invites friends or family for dinner, and I play the gracious host, amazed each time at my capacity for sociability. Much of my adult life, apart from the period in Kuwait, had usually been a solitary one.

But even as I settle into the role, there is a counter-melody of doubt. I watch William, in these unguarded moments, for signs of resentment or deferred judgment. I inventory the angles of his mouth, the set of his jaw, the way his hands move when he is tired or annoyed. I look for clues: a sigh too sharp, a silence too long, a joke that lands with a hollow ring. There is nothing, not really, but I keep looking.

The truth is, I am waiting for the reckoning. Old habits it seems are hard to break.

The Turkish holiday was supposed to be a reset, a blank page, but the ink of the past seeps through no matter how many times you turn it over. I remember the night in *Kusadasi*, after too much wine and an ill-advised bout of karaoke, when William caught my hand under the table and said, "I forgive you, you know." I wanted to believe him, wanted it so badly that I said nothing, letting the phrase hang between us like an ornament or a noose.

Now, back in the English winter, I find myself replaying the words, searching for a clue in the intonation, a cipher that might reveal the real meaning underneath. I think about Amanda, about the years in *Kuwait*, about the damage I did by trying to be something I wasn't. I think about William's mother, who, after our second dinner at her house, took me aside and said, "he's been waiting for you to come home since 1988, you know. Don't make a fool of him again." I laughed it off, but the gravity of her stare has haunted me ever since.

Tonight, we eat by candlelight, an indulgence needing no justification. William has cooked lamb shanks, slow-braised and falling apart under the weight of their own anticipation, and the potatoes are so perfect I suspect a conspiracy. We eat in near silence, the fire's pop and hiss providing all the soundtrack we need.

Halfway through the second course, I break.

"I still wonder if you might resent me," I say, staring at the candle flame as if it might blink out a *Morse* code reply, "for what I did. For *Kuwait*. For Amanda."

William does not answer right away. He sets his fork down with care, wipes his mouth with a napkin, and studies me across the table. In the flicker of the candlelight, his face is both younger and impossibly older.

"Why would I?" he says at last, the words slow and deliberate.

I hesitate, then, because the answer is both obvious and embarrassing, "because I left. Because I picked the safe option, the normal one. Because I let you think…" I stop, uncertain how much truth I want to spill.

William shakes his head, the faintest smile on his lips, "I never thought you'd stay, John. Not really. I hoped, but I knew you. You always needed to prove to yourself you weren't going to live a gay life."

I want to protest, to deny it, but I cannot. Instead, I say, "do you ever regret it? The way it turned out?"

He leans back in his chair, folds his arms, "every day, at first. Now, not so much. I've got what and who, I always wanted." He gestures at the table, at the house, at me, "this is enough."

I look down at my plate, the food suddenly unappetising, "it doesn't feel like enough," I say, the words so small they nearly vanish in the space between us.

William watches me for a long time, then reaches across the table and lays his hand on mine, "you're a clever man, John, but you're an idiot about some things. You keep waiting for a disaster that's already happened."

I squeeze his fingers, unsure whether to laugh or cry.

We finish the meal in silence. Afterward, we sit by the fire, each in our chair, the wine a slow bleed against the ache of memory. Outside, the wind drums against the window, and I imagine, for a moment, that we are the only people left in the world.

Before bed, as we brush our teeth in unison, William catches my eye in the mirror, "I need to think about something," he says, voice muffled by the foam.

"What's that?"

But he shakes his head, spits, and says, "nothing. Go to sleep."

I do, but it is not a restful night.

Instead, I dream of the ferry in *Istanbul*, of the city dissolving in the wake behind us, of the endless blue and the feeling of falling, falling, always just about to hit the water.

When I wake, William is already gone, his side of the bed still warm. I listen for the sound of him in the garden, and when I hear it, I breathe, once, and let the air settle inside me.

It is not forgiveness, not really.

But it is something like peace.

A week passes. In that span, the world turns exactly seven times, the bins go out once, and I read, by my own count, two hundred and six essays on *'the impact of colonial administration in modern Egypt'*. None of them are memorable, except perhaps the one that proposes *Nasser* as a tragic figure in the Greek sense and then spends two pages likening him to *James Bond*. The days cycle through with the same frictionless inertia as before, the only notable event being William's muttered complaints about the gooseberry sawfly "waging biological war" in the fruit cage.

On Thursday, at precisely 10:14 a.m., William appears in the kitchen, tracking muddy footprints across the tiles. I am hunched over the table, red pen in hand, fuming at a particularly egregious comma. He drops an envelope in front of me, fat with paper, and announces: "it's done."

I am not prepared for the shift in tone, "what's done?"

He stares at me as if I have missed an obvious cue, "our civil partnership. May 24th. *Norwich Town Hall.*" He says this with the same effect as if announcing a delivery slot from *Sainsbury's.*

I drop the pen, "you're joking." I realise he has picked my birthday.

He sits opposite, lips pressed thin in a line that is either amusement or challenge, "do I look like I'm joking?"

For a second, I think I might faint, which is absurd because I am neither Victorian nor in poor health. But the room tilts and the essays swim, and I am forced to steady myself against the edge of the table.

"You just... booked it?"

He shrugs, "it's not like it's *St Paul's Cathedral.* Or even a football stadium. You just fill out the form. Pay the deposit."

I pick up the envelope. Inside: a sheaf of appointment letters, confirmation slips, instructions for *'making your day special',* a luridly illustrated pamphlet on the legal status of civil unions. I sift through it, numbly, until I find the formal notification. There is my name, and his, and the date, written in bureaucratic blue.

"You did this without asking?" I say, and instantly regret it. The words come out petulant, the voice of a child whose birthday party is not to their taste.

William levels his gaze at me, "if I asked, you'd say *'no'.* Or you'd say *'yes',* then spend the next six months tying yourself in knots about it. This way it's settled."

I flounder, but immediately recognise the truth in his words, "but, what about guests? What about..." I grasp for the next logical step, "what about Sarah? Or your mother? Or my mother?"

He reaches behind and produces another stack: invitations, already addressed, "all sorted. Sarah is your witness. Mum and both my sisters are coming. The nephews are banned, for everyone's sake. As for your side..." He pauses, the first hint of uncertainty in his eyes, "I sent your family invitations. Whether they'll show is another matter."

I laugh, or try to, but it comes out as something else, a shudder, a cough, a noise that could be mistaken for panic. "You are a monster," I say, and he grins, wicked.

"That's why you love me."

For the rest of the day, I do not touch the essays. I walk the perimeter of the garden four times, getting lost twice in the apple copse because my head is spinning with the idea of it. Not the event itself, but the fact that it is real, that it is happening, that I am now required to step forward into the present and accept, publicly, legally, that I belong to someone. To this man, this idiot, this miracle.

At dinner, William insists on *'champagne'* (*Cava*, technically, but the label is angled away from me) and makes a risotto that is just a little too salty. We eat in silence, the candlelight throwing our shadows long and theatrical on the wall. I want to thank him, or at least to acknowledge the risk he's taken, but the words feel like a foreign language. Instead, I say, "you could have at least let me pick the date."

He lifts his glass, "I picked your birthday, then neither of us ever has an excuse to forget an anniversary, and besides, you can pick the honeymoon."

Later, in bed, I lie awake and try to parse the motivation. Is this forgiveness? A rebuke? A final, strategic act of possession? William snores softly, oblivious to my interior monologue. I stare at the ceiling, listening to the sound of the wind working the old house. Eventually, I sleep.

The next week is a fugue of logistics and the kind of mild dread usually reserved for dental appointments and parents' evenings. William's family takes the news with a kind of professional glee. His mother rings me to ask whether I'd prefer roast beef or salmon at the post-ceremony lunch, then proceeds to tell me, in granular detail, what William was like as a child and exactly which vegetables I must avoid on his behalf. His older sister, the *'Tory'*, volunteers to bring the wine and, with the air of a seasoned party planner, asks for a guest list and any colour-coordination preferences I might have. "He always liked you in blue," she says, voice sly, and I blush into the phone, unsure whether to laugh or hang up.

My own family is a different matter. My mother, on receiving the invitation, leaves a voicemail that is at once apologetic and loaded: "it's not that we don't support you, love, it's just… well, your father is still not quite himself, and your brother has his feelings, and you know how Gran is about these things."

My sister, bless her, calls me directly and asks what she should wear, "I'm thinking something non-rainbow, just to avoid the cliches," she says, and I love her more in that moment than I have since we were children.

Sarah is ecstatic. She calls three times in the first twenty-four hours, offers to book hair and makeup for both of us ("it's your big day, darlings, not mine, but you know I live vicariously"), and says, more than once, "I told you this would happen." When I ask what she means, she only laughs and says, "you two were doomed from the start. In the best possible way."

William, true to form, is unflappable. He books the venue, the registry, the lunch. He even arranges for a photographer, a friend from the Hall who, he assures me, "owes him several favours and will make us look younger than we are." For the ceremony, he insists we wear matching suits, dark blue, with white shirts and, for some reason, yellow ties. "Sunflowers," he says, when I object. "it's the only way to make you smile on camera."

The week before, we drive to *Norwich* for a fitting. The tailor, an ancient man with hands like bird claws, measures us with a tape that seems to double as an interrogation device, "you two together, then?" he asks, not looking up from the numbers.

William replies, "you could say that, and permanently so in week."

I remember my inner doubts had always been present with Amanda especially the day we married or the day Rose was born. Then it hits me, this is different – I have no doubts. This is what I want and this is the man I want.

"Till death do we part," I add which provokes a look from William which simply says, *'you bet it is'.*

We leave with the suits in garment bags and a sense that the future, while still terrifying, may at least fit properly.

The day before the ceremony, Sarah arrives at the cottage, bearing a basket of pastries and a bottle of *prosecco*. She breezes through the house, commenting on the decor ("charming in a rustic way"), the garden ("a bit funereal, but I like it"), and William, who she hugs twice in rapid succession, before turning her attention to me. She takes me aside in the study, closing the door with the solemnity of a confessor.

"Are you all right?" she says, eyes sharp.

I nod, too quickly, "it's just… happening very fast."

She smiles, tucks a stray hair behind my ear, "you deserve this. Don't let your brain talk you out of happiness. You're allowed, you know."

I want to believe her. I really do.

That night, William's family arrives for dinner. The house is suddenly alive with voices, laughter, the crash and tumble of half a dozen people moving in and out of the kitchen. The meal is loud, the wine flows, and I find myself, against all odds, enjoying the chaos. William's sister flirts outrageously with Sarah, who flirts right back, and by the end of the evening they have exchanged numbers and made plans to "escape the men and see the real *Norwich*."

After everyone leaves, the house returns to silence. William sits on the sofa, polishing off the last glass of wine, and gestures for me to join him. He doesn't say anything, just wraps his arm around my shoulders and pulls me in. We sit that way for a long time, the only sound the crackle of the fire and the distant ticking of the hall clock.

"You nervous?" he asks, eventually.

"Yes."

He squeezes my arm, "me too."

And that is the sum of it.

Tomorrow, we will stand in front of the registrar, say the words, sign the register. Tomorrow, I will belong to him, and he to me, in a way that cannot be revoked by distance or denial or the habits of the past. But tonight, we are just two men, side by side, waiting for the future to arrive.

And for the first time in my life, I am almost ready.

The morning of the ceremony is absurdly bright, the kind of light that makes everything, pavement, brick, skin, all looking washed and new. I wake before the alarm, William's arm a deadweight across my chest, and stare at the ceiling until my pulse slows enough to count as human. The house is silent, the world outside still damp from last night's rain, the birds, optimistic, relentless are already at war in the trees.

We dress in tandem, the way we always do. The suits are a perfect match, save for the ties (mine a muted yellow, his a shade closer to gold) and the buttonholes (his with rosemary, mine with a small, pale rose). In the mirror, we look like twins or like an after image, one version slightly brighter, the other fading toward blue.

Sarah arrives at 8:15 from her room at *The Langley Arms*, five minutes early and beaming. She wears a blue shift dress and heels so high I expect her to topple. She hugs us both, adjusting our lapels with the fierce, proprietary affection of a stage mother at opening night.

"You both look gorgeous," she declares, spinning me around for inspection, "is this what you're wearing to the registry?"

"Yes," I say, then, "should we have something else?"

She waves the thought away, "it's perfect. Let's not overthink it, darling, or you'll be changing clothes until next year."

We drive into *Norwich* together, William at the wheel, Sarah pretending to navigate, forgetting that we both live in Norfolk. The city is awake but subdued, the traffic sparse, the air sharp with the promise of summer. We park opposite the *Town Hall* and walk up the steps, three abreast, as if daring the world to comment.

Inside, the waiting room is both grand and faintly ludicrous, velvet benches, portraits of past mayors, a carpet patterned like a migraine. The other couples waiting for their slots are a study in contrast: a pair of pensioners in matching twinsets; two women in white, laughing and holding hands; a nervous-looking man with a slicked-back ponytail and a girlfriend who, judging by the tension in her jaw, has not fully consented to the day.

The registrar, a woman of perhaps fifty in a skirt suit of indeterminate colour, welcomes us with the poise of a headmistress at the end of term. She ushers us through the procedure: read the vows, sign the register, accept the applause, with a brisk efficiency that is almost comforting. There is no time for panic. We follow her down the corridor, past a mural of the city in medieval times, and into a sunlit room where the guests are already waiting.

William's mother sits in the front row, dabbing her eyes with a tissue. His sisters, perfectly arrayed, smile at us in a way that is both sincere and mischievous. My sister sits at the end of the row, having arrived the night before and stayed in a city hotel, hands folded in her lap, a look on her face that I cannot quite decipher. Sarah, ever the pro, stands ready with the camera, the lens already trained on the stage.

The ceremony itself is over in minutes, though I suspect I will remember every second for the rest of my life. The vows are simple, the legal language rendered oddly beautiful by the quaver in the registrar's voice. William's hand is warm and dry as he slides the ring onto my finger, his eyes fixed on mine with a steadiness that undoes me entirely. When it is my turn, I have to clear my throat twice before the words will come. My voice cracks, once, and the entire room seems to exhale at once.

We sign the register, our names looping together on the page. Sarah leans in and whispers, "I told you both back in '84 that you were perfect for each other." I want to answer, to thank her, to confess how much it means, but the words won't come.

The reception is at *the Langley Arms*, a marquee in the garden hung with paper lanterns and strings of wildflowers. The village has turned out in force: neighbours, friends, the grounds crew from the Hall, a surprising number of people from William's cricket team (including one man I'd long suspected of being a closet homophobe, now pink-faced and carrying a bottle of fizz like a peace offering). The food is simple, sandwiches, pork pies, trifle in plastic cups, but the mood is effusive, even wild. Children run riot on the lawn, someone brings a guitar and starts an impromptu singalong, and for a brief, dazzling hour the world forgets its boundaries.

William makes a speech, short and brutal in its wit. "Thanks for coming. We're not made of money, so please don't stay too long or eat too much. John says I have to be nice to everyone today, but if you're still here after midnight, I'm turning the hose on you."

People laugh, genuinely, and I see for the first time how much they love him. I make my own speech, which is more apology than address, but it lands. William squeezes my knee under the table, and the warmth of it radiates upward until I think I might actually glow.

After the cake (fruit, of course, because William is nothing if not traditional), the music starts, a playlist of 1980s disco hits, curated by Sarah and designed, I'm sure, to mortify us. The first song is *'Don't You Want Me'*, and it is impossible not to dance. We do, awkward at first, then looser, then wild, as if thirty years have vanished and we are once again at the threshold of our own story, the world unresolved but somehow within reach.

As the sun dips, the party spills into the pub proper. I find my sister on the terrace, smoking a cigarette. She turns, offering me one, "you happy?" she asks, voice low.

I nod, "I think so."

She looks at me, searching, "you deserve it, John. Whatever anyone says."

I lean against the rail, the taste of smoke in my mouth, the air cooling around us.

Inside, William is holding court at the bar, his laughter the loudest in the room. Sarah sits on a high stool, watching it all with the satisfied air of a matchmaker at her own wedding. For a second, I let myself see it through her eyes: two men, grey at the temples and still slightly ill-fitting in their new roles, but radiant in the way that only the truly lucky ever are.

We stay until closing, then walk home under a sky furred with stars. The silence between us is companionable, as if every conversation has already been had, and only the walking remains.

The next morning, there are no hangovers, only an ache in my feet and a strange reluctance to let the day begin. William makes tea, then climbs back into bed, dragging me with him. We lie together, the duvet cocooning us against the pale morning.

"So," I say, "the honeymoon."

He laughs, "you really want to fly somewhere after all this?"

"Not really."

He kisses my shoulder, his stubble rough but familiar, "let's just stay here. Best place on earth."

But we do go, in the end. To *Paris*, for a weekend. The city is as advertised: beautiful, indifferent, hung with the smell of bread and rain and cigarette smoke. We walk the bridges, eat in small bistros, drink wine on the hotel balcony and watch the lights of the city flicker on and off, as if the whole place runs on the same ancient, unreliable fuse as our own house. We don't talk much, but we don't need to.

On the last night, near our hotel in *St Michel,* we sit by the *Seine,* legs dangling over the embankment. William throws a pebble into the river, watches the ripples fade.

"Did you ever think," he says, "that we'd make it here?"

I shake my head, "I didn't think we'd make it any-where."

He smiles, then, and I am undone, as always.

We return to England changed, but only slightly. The cottage is the same, the garden more overrun than before, the stacks of essays on my desk multiplying at a rate that seems al-most supernatural. But there is something new, or maybe something old and recovered: a sense that this is not the begin-ning of the end, but the end of the beginning. That, after every-thing, we have given ourselves permission to be happy.

On the first warm evening of June, we sit outside with a bottle of wine, watching the sun set through the leaves of the old apple tree. The air is thick with midges and the scent of cut grass. William rests his head on my shoulder and closes his eyes.

I think of *Istanbul,* of the ferry wake dissolving behind us, of the city we left and the one we returned to. I think of the two decades spent in orbit around each other, the collisions and near misses, the years lost and the ones yet to come.

I think, finally, of the promise we made in that sunlit room, and how strange and beautiful it will be to keep it.

And for the first time, ever, I am certain: this is home, or rather *'home'* is wherever I am with William.

CHAPTER 23: AN AMBITION RESOLVED

Finally, 2013 arrived and I eventually negotiated with the solicitors to have appointments to begin to review the *Langley Archive*. However, they had taken their responsibilities seriously, and requested that I submit my *curriculum vitae*, a copy of my degree and an outline of why I wanted to view the documents in order to establish my credentials. I said nothing about my suspicion about the nature of the relationship between Jonny and Kip, but instead spoke about wishing to investigate a wider history of the earls of Grafton, and how the dynasty adjusted to social change in the twentieth century.

I remember vividly the first time I saw the large oak box, the Langley crest inlaid in tarnished silver on its lid, and being presented with the key. Before I could open it, two more large cardboard document boxes arrived labelled *'Fifth Earl of Grafton: Political Memoirs'*. It was almost too much to bear. With a pounding heart and tremble in my hands, I broke the paper seal and unlocked the box. The first thing I saw, atop the box's contents, was a letter written in a hand I recognised immediately:

To Messrs. Harrington & Whitby, Solicitors
Lincoln's Inn Fields, London
18th May 1963
Gentlemen,
Enclosed please find personal materials belonging to the late Lord Christian Langley, Earl of Grafton, to be held in your secure storage facilities alongside the existing Langley family papers.

These documents and artifacts are to remain sealed for a period of fifty years from the date of Lord Christian's death (14th May 1963), to be opened on or after 14 May 2013.

Upon that date, these materials shall be made available to qualified historical researchers with appropriate credentials and legitimate scholarly interest in Anglo-German relations, aristocratic life in the twentieth century, or related fields of inquiry.

Should Langley Hall remain in family possession at that time, the current titleholder shall be notified before any materials are accessed. However, family objections may not prevent access after the specified date has passed.

I immediately realised that this was Thomas' attempt in
some way to protect these two people, but also his feeling that
there was a story that needed to be told and not forgotten. Underneath this letter was a navy-blue leather-bound foolscap
journal. Was this going to be the story told in a way that was
honest and not sanitised for the times? I opened it, and the first
page, in Thomas' hand again, allayed any fears I might have
had:

Thomas Cooper, dead for thirty years, spoke to me directly with these final words before his catalogue of artifacts
and document:

final day. These items reveal aspects of their bond unknown to all except myself and a wartime friend of us all.'

'The careful preservation of these materials suggests Christian's desire that their true relationship not be entirely lost to history, even as he protected it from contemporary scrutiny.'

'As the sole remaining witness to their private life together, I consider it my final duty to ensure these items—and the truth they represent—survive to reach a more understanding age.'

It must have a taken eighteen months of twice monthly visits to review all the contents of the archive, by the end of which each of the main characters lived inside my head in a way I had never experienced before. It seemed every time I closed my eyes I heard the conversations of these long dead people. I must have written half a dozen outlines and drafts before I finally settled on the three books I would write. William was supportive throughout and nursed me through some early disappointments. Writing soon became as much a part of our routine as my marking and William's work and gardening.

By the spring of 2018, the lines of the world had shifted again, less by force than by the slow, tectonic grind of time and the patient erosion of excuses. We had lived at *Cooper's Cottage* for twelve years, long enough to see some of the trees in the lane double in size, to track the rising and falling fortunes of half a dozen local pubs, to attend, in person or in spirit, the weddings, funerals, and inconclusive retirements of everyone who had once mattered to us. William's hair was almost entirely white now, though his beard retained a stubborn streak of the old ginger, and the only way I could tell the difference between myself and the men I'd once mocked for their generational inertia was by the relative lack of cardigans in my wardrobe.

It was during one of those late-March mornings, mist over the meadows, the threat of frost in the air but the sun already hinting at better things, that I broached the idea of leaving it all behind.

We were at the kitchen table, sharing the newspaper and an unspoken agreement to ignore the latest round of international catastrophe. William had just set down his mug and was surveying the window box for evidence of new growth, his expression that of a man determined to will the tulips into early bloom.

"What if," I began, affecting the tone of the purely hypothetical, "we just… stopped?"

He didn't turn, but I saw the corner of his mouth tick up, "stopped what, exactly?"

"Everything. The garden, the house, the marking, the endless bloody cycle of winter and minor celebrity in the village. Just… retired, properly. Went somewhere warm and did nothing but eat, drink, and watch the sea."

He let this hang for a moment, then said, "you wouldn't last a week."

"Try me."

He looked at me then, the sceptical lift of his brow a genetic inheritance passed through a thousand years of *East Anglian* pragmatism, "you want to move to *Spain* and drink sangria with the rest of the refugees?"

"*Crete*," I said, not missing a beat, "there's a place for sale on a bluff outside *Chania*. Olive trees, a view of the sea, and an outbuilding you could turn into a studio. I've done the research."

He snorted, but I saw the calculation begin behind his eyes, the silent, meticulous sorting of risk and reward, the inventory of all the things that could go wrong and the handful of things that might, for once, go right.

"You've already decided, haven't you?" he said.

I shrugged, "I've decided we need a change. That's not the same as knowing what comes next, but I've finished my books more or less. So maybe we both need a new challenge?"

He grinned, then reached for my hand, the gesture casual and, after all these years, still electric, "let's think about it," he said, "see what the estate agents say, eh?"

But I knew, even then, that we were already halfway out the door.

The sale was quicker than expected, as William's sister gladly took the opportunity to purchase it back as part of her *'property portfolio'* for her retirement. *Cooper's Cottage* survived in the family, something which I knew was important to William.

The last weeks in Langley were a montage of reverse nostalgia: the slow packing of books and kitchenware, the ceremonial culling of clothes, the final visits to the pub where the landlady pressed a bottle of single malt into our hands and said, "for when the food gets boring." William threw himself into the planning, contacting shipping companies, negotiating with his sister over the fate of the garden shed, Great Uncle Thomas' archive, and finally arranging an all-hands-on-deck roast for the extended clan.

The day of departure, we signed the papers at the solicitors, then walked the boundary of the property one last time, the air soft with the promise of summer. William paused by the rose bed, fingers tracing the canes as if committing them to memory.

"Will you miss it?" I asked.

He considered, "some of it. Not all."

I nodded, understanding, "me too."

CHAPTER 26: SANCTUARY IN THE OLIVE GROVES

The car is heavier than when I had originally left *Billericay*, even though most of what we owned had been auctioned, donated, or consigned to that great English boneyard of storage units: *'the attic'*. William had packed the boot with a *Tetris* logic that bordered on the neurotic: every towel, every stray mug, every battered plant pot ranked and nested, the whole operation bound in the scratchy blue of moving blankets and optimism. My contribution was less material and more directional: the route, the weather report, the checklists annotated and re-annotated in my own restless hand.

We left *Norfolk* before the light, William's two eldest nephews followed us so that the youngest one could drive back in our car, which we had given to him. The horizon an electrified margin above the dark winter fields. William drove, knuckles white, a silence between us as steady as the hum of the A11. It was not the silence of anger or of secrets, those had been used up years ago, but the hush of two men balanced, for once, on the edge of something unspoiled by memory or expectation. He fiddled with the radio but found only news, then music so synthetic it sounded as if made by computers for the benefit of other, lesser computers. We rode most of the way south in the company of windscreen wipers and our own private rehearsals of what might come next.

At *Stansted*, we passed our keys to the car's new owner and gestured to the shuttle. We checked in our luggage, two massive suitcases, one taped shut in a way that suggested both competence and incipient collapse, and drifted through *Security*, and then to the departure lounge was a strip-lit aquarium, its glassy surfaces slick with the residue of a thousand anxious departures. We found a table by the window, ignoring the overpriced coffee and the insistent, nasal shouts of the budget airline's announcements.

William peered out at the tarmac, tracking the slow choreography of men in hi-vis jackets. I thumbed through a battered paperback, *Sebald* again, though I could not for the life of me recall ever having finished one, and watched, in my periphery, the way the dawn light stuttered along the wing of our waiting plane.

"Are you nervous?" I asked, in the voice I reserved for small children and the recently concussed.

William shrugged, "does it matter?" He rolled a euro coin across his knuckles, over and over, as if hypnotising a snake, "we'll land, one way or the other."

At the gate, the crowd surged forward in a parody of urgency, everyone keen to claim a patch of plastic seat or overhead locker before the next person did. Our row was at the back, next to the lavatory, and reeked of whatever spray the airline had used to neutralise the more persistent aromas of past occupants. I stowed our bags, sat, and felt the years slide off in a slow, slightly sickening spiral as the engines began their low, volcanic purr.

William slept almost before we left the runway, one of his abilities I lacked and *was* jealous of. His head drooped against my shoulder, a weight I hadn't realised I missed. I read, or pretended to, letting the words blur as I monitored the evenness of his breath, the twitch of his eyelid at some half-remembered dream. When the drink cart came, I ordered two teas, declined the plastic-wrapped pastries, and looked out the window at the ice-scabbed continent unspooling below us. It was beautiful, and meaningless, and utterly beyond the reach of regret.

We landed in *Chania* under a sky so blue it seemed absurd, a tone reserved for cartoons and pharmaceuticals. The air, even in the jet bridge, was different, less a medium than an imperative. The customs official, a woman with the tragic eyebrows of Greek statuary, scanned our passports and waved us through with a bored flick of her wrist. Outside, a man in a polo shirt met us with a cardboard sign that read *'COOPER'*, then pointed at the old *Peugeot* he'd parked haphazardly on the curb. The car was smaller than I'd imagined, but William whistled with approval, "that will do for now," he said, palming the roof as if greeting a horse.

We drove west in silence, past rows of olive trees and the occasional shrine to a traffic fatality: a blue-and-white box, a lamp burning even at midday, a sepia photo of a dead youth grinning against the void. I navigated, holding the printout of directions the estate agent had emailed the week before. William's hands were steady on the wheel, his attention tuned to the narrowness of the roads and the bright, angry persistence of the local drivers.

Our new house, about six miles from the airport, *'villa'* the agent had called it, though the word seemed an overreach, sat at the end of a gravel track, flanked on all sides by the kind of dry, rustling undergrowth that is one cigarette away from becoming next year's news. The building was two storeys of sun-bleached stone, the windows shuttered, the roof tiled in red clay that was already succumbing to moss and lichen. A fence, or the memory of one, separated the front yard from the dirt lane; the gate was a contraption of wire and hope, sagging but still functional.

William turned off the engine and let the silence settle, as if waiting for the house to acknowledge our arrival. I felt, more than heard, the change in the air: a sudden density, the pressure of expectation or of some other, less nameable thing. We hauled our bags up the path, pausing every few steps to let the sweat evaporate from our faces. The key, a battered brass thing on a string, fit the lock with an obstinacy that boded ill for the rest of the house.

Inside, it was cool and dark. The air smelled of stone and something older, a residue of disuse or perhaps of the family who had last called this place home. I blinked, letting my eyes adjust, and took in the details: a stone fireplace, empty but for a scatter of charred olive wood; a staircase of uneven treads winding up into darkness; a kitchen with cabinets the colour of old bones, their doors hanging open like mouths at rest.

William flicked the light switch. Nothing happened.

He tried a second time, then shrugged. "fuse?"

"Could be," I said, though I doubted it.

We explored by the available light as we pushed open the shutters from the inside, each room a study in absence. The upstairs was two bedrooms and a bathroom, the latter dominated by a claw-footed tub that had seen better, more sanitary decades. There was a bed, bare mattress, no linens, a curl of dust at each corner, and a dresser whose drawers were lined with faded, floral paper and nothing else. In the second room, more of the same: a desk, a bookshelf warped by the heat, a window looking out at the olive groves and, beyond, the sliver of the sea.

Back downstairs, William investigated the kitchen, "it's all here," he called, his voice echoing in the stone, "plates, pots, even a corkscrew."

I found the fridge unplugged, its interior haunted by the ghost of a single, blue ice cube tray. The tap ran, after a fashion, and the water came out cold but tinged with a mineral taste that suggested the pipes were on the wrong side of the twentieth century.

"Gas?" William asked, gesturing at the hob.

I looked and kicked the cylinder under the sink - it was empty, "not today," I said.

He leaned on the counter, face illuminated from below by his phone, and grinned, "it's like camping," he said, "only the tent is made of rocks, and there's a better chance of being murdered in our sleep."

I smiled, though I was not entirely convinced he was joking. We carried the suitcases upstairs and flopped onto the mattress, a cloud of dust rising around us in protest. For a long time, we lay still, listening to the house acclimate to its new inhabitants: the crack of settling beams, the gradual return of the outside world as the air began to circulate through the opened windows.

I dozed, or thought I did, but was awakened by the sound of William rummaging around the kitchen. I found him bent double behind the door; one hand braced against the wall for support.

"What are you doing?" I asked.

He held up a slip of folded paper, thick as a bandage and stained with what I hoped was only coffee, "it was taped here," he said, passing it over.

The handwriting was the estate agent's, large, round, a script trained in the business of making the unsettling seem like reassurance.

Welcome', it read. *The utilities are not always reliable in the off season, but the neighbours (Dionysios at the taverna, his daughter Maria) will know what to do. Electrician: Spiros (number below). Bottled gas: ask at the shop in the square. Please do not feed the local cats, as they will not leave you alone. Good luck*'.

Below was a list of phone numbers, as well as a map, hand-drawn, but precise, of the village's essential services.

William read it over my shoulder, then chuckled, "we're officially locals, then."

"Only until the first time we try to buy a lightbulb," I said.

He straightened, stretching his back with a series of pops that suggested he was made of older, less durable parts than he let on, "we'll manage," he said, the finality of the phrase a comfort and a challenge all at once.

The light was fading outside, the sky veined with the last pink and gold of the day. I took a bottle of water from a bag, set it on the sill, and watched as the first stars burned through the haze.

In the other room, William unpacked, his movements efficient, nearly silent. I sat on the edge of the bed and let my thoughts drift, the smallness of our possessions making the space seem at once infinite and provisional. There would be days, I knew, when the house would seem too much, too old, too far, too filled with the ghosts of other lives. But there would be other days, too: mornings when the sea caught the light just right, or when the air was so thick with rosemary and heat that the old England in me would dissolve, and I would be, for a moment, exactly where I meant to be.

I drank the water. It tasted, at last, of nothing but itself.

Morning arrived as a contradiction, brighter than any I'd known, but hesitant, a reluctant casting-off of the blue-shadowed dark that filled every stone cavity in the house. I woke to the noise of William pacing in the kitchen, the clatter of crockery followed by a muttered curse as he remembered the stove was still a useless relic. The house was cool, the flagstones feeling damp underfoot, but the air tasted of green things, a tang of wild oregano that must have come in through the broken window latch above the sink.

We dressed in the clothes we'd travelled in, which were still creased and haunted by the recycled air of the plane. Outside, the landscape had rearranged itself: the sun striking the low hills to the east, the olive trees glittering with dew, the track to the road churned to a paste by yesterday's rain. William produced a loaf of bread from our emergency rations, along with a packet of sweating cheese and a pot of instant coffee. He set it all on the kitchen table, silent, except for the slow, meditative tapping of his fingers against the mug.

"We need to go into the village," he said at last, "find the gas, the…" he waved the estate agent's note, "the rest of it."

He had written out a list on the back of a supermarket receipt, the items annotated with their probable Greek equivalents, most of which were spelled phonetically. I added to it, for my own comfort, a list of questions: *'Who is responsible for the water meter?', 'Where can we buy eggs that do not come in plastic?', 'Is there a place to print and post letters?'*

We drove, creeping down the lane with the caution of the newly arrived. At the main road, a herd of goats blocked our way, their bells clanging in a fugue of insistent disinterest. William braked, rolled down the window, and waited as the animals parted around us, their eyes unreadable, yellow and flat.

The village was, at first, indistinct. A handful of buildings crouched at a curve in the road: the bakery, the taverna, a *'supermarket'* no larger than a double garage, a municipal building with paint peeling off the portico in long, deliberate strips. In the square, a single tree leafed out in a bright, indecent green, birds squabbling over a scrap of bread on the flagstones.

We parked in front of the shop, unsure whether this was permitted, and stepped inside. The air was warmer, perfumed with the sweet rot of fruit and the sharpness of cleaning fluid. A man sat behind the counter reading a newspaper, his moustache a preposterous, architectural thing. He glanced up, clocked our faces, and returned to his paper.

William approached, estate agent's note in hand. "*Kalimera*," he said, pronouncing it as *'cull-a-mare-a'* and smiling with the intensity of a man performing CPR.

The shopkeeper looked up again, eyes narrowing in a calculation that took in both our height and our lack of tan. William tried again, holding up the note, tapping at the word *'GAS'* written in capitals and underlined twice.

The man's face brightened with sudden understanding. He barked a phrase, entirely incomprehensible, but clearly imperative, and pointed at the alley beside the shop. We followed, trailing our own confusion.

Out back, a battered metal rack held three blue canisters. The shopkeeper, now following, gestured with his whole arm, his enthusiasm not entirely matched by the efficiency of the operation. He lifted a cylinder, tested its weight with a grunt, and motioned for William to bring the car closer. William backed up to the alley, bumping over the curb and nearly decapitating a parked scooter. The shopkeeper and I manhandled the canister into the boot, where it nestled beside the box of books and a stray trowel.

Money was exchanged, too much, probably, but neither of us had the energy to argue. The shopkeeper wrote a phone number on the receipt, then drew a careful, childlike map of the village square, marking the location of the taverna, the bakery, and the municipal office with three dots.

"Super," William said, and the shopkeeper, sensing the transaction was over, returned to his paper.

The taverna was already open, its terrace shaded by a faded umbrella advertising *Amstel*. We sat at a table near the door, not sure whether to wait for service or to proceed inside. After a few minutes, a girl appeared, hair pulled back with a green ribbon, her English almost perfect.

"Good morning. You are new here?" she said, without malice.

William nodded, then explained the issue with the electricity, the gas, and the mysterious third thing, some paperwork the agent had hinted at but not explained.

The girl, her name was Maria, as luck would have it, smiled with a mixture of sympathy and amusement, "you will need to see my uncle at the municipal. After you eat. He is only there after eleven." She handed us menus, but seeing our confusion, said, "I will bring you the breakfast. It is easy."

She disappeared, returning moments later with a tray: thick yogurt, a jar of honey, fresh bread, and two coffees in little glass cups. William tasted the yogurt and smiled, his first real one of the day.

Over breakfast, I watched the street. Two women argued by the bakery, their hands moving faster than their words. A battered *Fiat* trundled by, its paint faded to the colour of regret, the boot tied down with a length of string. Birds fought over a crust of bread, one of them victorious, the rest sulking in the gutter.

Maria returned, carrying a stack of forms and a pen, "for the electricity," she explained, "you fill in here, here, and here. Your passport, yes?"

We produced the documents, and she wrote our names with careful, almost calligraphic letters. She took William's mobile, dialled the number written on the map, and spoke rapid Greek for a minute or so, glancing at us occasionally as if to gauge whether we were absorbing any of it.

"He will come this afternoon," she announced, setting down the phone, "maybe three, maybe four. He is very busy." She smiled again, this time in solidarity, "in *Crete*, time is different. You will learn."

We paid, left a tip, and wandered the square for an hour, buying a dozen eggs and a bottle of water from the *'supermarket'*, then sitting on a low stone wall to watch the village get on with its business. I was struck by how little noise there was, how much of the day was carried forward on the energy of sun and inertia. Even the children, in their blue uniforms, walked slowly, as if the bell for school was more of a suggestion than a demand.

Back at the house, William installed the gas cylinder with the focus of a heart surgeon. The stove, when lit, responded with a gentle whoosh and the faintest hint of sulphur. He made coffee, then boiled water for a test batch of pasta, just to see if it could be done.

I wandered the rooms, letting the house reacquaint itself with the idea of being lived in. The air grew warmer as the afternoon passed, and the shadows in the stairwell sharpened to the clarity of ink.

At three-thirty, a battered pickup arrived, scattering dust and the odd goat from its path. The electrician, a man of indeterminate age and infinite patience, came in, listened to William's explanation, and fixed the problem in less than five minutes. He nodded at his own work, pocketed the tip William pressed into his hand, and left with the dignity of a departing cardinal.

That night, we celebrated by eating pasta with jarred sauce, washed down with local white wine from a plastic jug. The table was a door propped on two crates; our plates, unmatched, had come from the previous tenants, who'd left behind a legacy of chipped ceramic and a single, violently orange mug.

We slept on the mattress, now topped with a borrowed sheet, our suitcases pressed into service as bedside tables. The house creaked and groaned in the wind, the unfamiliarity of it rendering sleep a series of shallow, easily disturbed episodes. I woke at midnight to the sound of an owl, its cry fluting down the chimney and into the room like a question.

I listened, feeling the slow reconfiguration of my body against the newness of the place. I imagined the house as a patient, waking after a long anaesthesia, each sound and shudder a sign of systems coming back online.

William turned over, muttered something, and reached for my hand. His grip was loose, but insistent, as if he meant to keep me from drifting too far from shore.

In the dark, I felt the pressure of his fingers and thought, not for the first time, that we might actually make a home here. The owl called again, further off this time, and I drifted back to sleep, content to let the future arrange itself in the hours ahead.

On the third morning, the sound of engines woke me before the sun had cleared the ridge. William was already up, barefoot on the chilly tiles, a mug of coffee balanced in one hand and a clipboard in the other. He peered out the window, then smiled, a smile not at me, but at the evidence of things finally beginning to happen.

The truck was bigger than the lane allowed, and it took the driver four attempts to back the container past the gate without shearing off a chunk of the stone wall. When he finally managed it, two young men in matching shirts leapt from the cab and began unloading our life, box by box, with the bored precision of people who have done this for too many summers.

William supervised with the benign tyranny of a man who knows exactly where every bag of compost, every garden fork, every crate of books is meant to go. I tried to help, but it quickly became apparent that the division of labour would be more efficient if I simply stood to one side and signed the necessary forms.

The house filled rapidly. The boxes stacked in the hall, the sitting room, even the alcove beneath the stairs, each labelled in my hand: *'KITCHEN'*, *'BOOKS 1-4'*, *'MISCELLANEOUS'*, *'BEDDING'*. There was a certain pleasure in seeing the familiar words in this new, sun-blasted light, as if the years we had spent waiting to escape the English climate had finally condensed into a sequence of manageable tasks.

The last thing off the truck was the battered chest of drawers that had belonged to William's grandmother. The movers set it down in the bedroom, then departed with a wave and the promise to collect the empty boxes "next month, maybe two." William stood over the chest for a long time, hands folded, as if waiting for the ghost of its former owner to either scold him for abandoning *Norfolk* or approve his choice of view.

We spent the afternoon unpacking. By mutual, unspoken agreement, the books were first. I lined the walls of the study with them, arranging the spines in the same sequence they had occupied in the old house. William made a desultory effort to sort the kitchen, but after breaking the handle off a saucepan and discovering the *'antique'* corkscrew was more antique than corkscrew, he gave up and set about assembling the table for our evening meal.

It was not so much a table as a board balanced across two battered saw-horses, but it served. We ate bread and cheese and olives from the village shop, drank the wine we had bought on a whim, and watched as the dusk folded the olive groves into shadow.

William, always most himself with a project at hand, spread a sheet of paper across the table and began to draw, his pen tracing the shape of the house, the yard, the sloping path that led down to the grove, "we'll need to fix the bathroom first and get a gas water heater," he said, not looking up, "then the walls, see here, and here, and after that, the garden."

He sketched rows of tomatoes, a trellis for beans, a patch for herbs, "the climate's right," he said, "if we can keep the goats out."

I nodded, though my mind was elsewhere: on the half-assembled computer upstairs, the pile of marked scripts waiting for me to upload them, the schedule for my next call with the publishers, "we should sort the internet," I said. "I'll need it working as soon as we can."

William frowned, as if the suggestion of a router threatened the integrity of his garden plans, "you'll have it," he said, but his voice was absent, already retreating into the world of rootstock and mulch.

For an hour we worked side by side, him with his sketches, me with my phone, sending emails to the estate agent and searching for the Greek equivalents of *'broadband'* and , *'Wi-Fi'*. It was a minor miracle, then, when a neighbour appeared at dusk with a loaf of bread and the news that the village had *Wi-Fi* at the taverna

That night, we sat at our makeshift table, the paper plans now covered in stains and crumbs. William poured the last of the wine, raised his glass, and said, "to the future," in a tone that made the phrase both a joke and a promise.

"To the future," I echoed, and meant it.

The breeze through the open window smelled of thyme and something else, an undercurrent of earth and old stone that reminded me of nothing I had ever called home, but everything I'd ever wanted one to be.

In bed, I listened to the house shifting around us, the wind pushing at the shutters, the settling of boxes and intentions. I reached for William's hand, found it already there, warm and certain in the dark.

"Tomorrow?" I said.

"Tomorrow," he agreed.

And we lay like that, two men in the middle of a new story, waiting to see what shape it would take.

In almost every sense the timing of our relocation was fortuitous, as we had avoided the consequences of *BREXIT* and then the impact of *Covid* in the UK, and Spring arrived on the island in slow increments, a day of sun, two of rain, then a sudden riot of flowers clinging to every rock and verge. By the end of March, the news from England had gone from anxious speculation to outright panic, but here in the high olive groves, the world shrank to a handful of square kilometres and the range of our recently purchased blue *Fiat*.

The *Fiat* was twenty years old, paint faded to a colour best described as post-traumatic sky, its seats mended with tape and the dash lined with the sticky ghosts of stickers long since evaporated. We bought it from a neighbour, who declared it a "family heirloom" and then, with a wink, confessed he'd always expected it to die on the main road to *Chania*. Instead, it ran. Each trip to the village was an act of faith, the engine coughing to life with a shudder, the steering only loosely connected to the wheels, but the car never once failed to bring us back home.

With the world in lockdown, our days developed a monastic regularity. We woke at first light, made coffee, and sat on the east-facing steps to watch the valley. William worked in the garden, digging out old roots, planting beans and squash in the patch behind the house. I converted the second bedroom into an office, *'the scriptorium'*, William called it, mocking but affectionate, and spent the mornings marking essays, reviewing publisher proofs, and trying to find a way to describe our new life that wasn't a cliche about escape or renewal.

Lunch was usually bread and cheese, sometimes fruit if the market had anything fresh. Afternoons were for errands or small repairs, the painting of a wall, the caulking of a window, the laborious process of ridding the house of its population of sugar ants. The pace was slow, and we felt ourselves adapting to it, our movements unhurried, our conversations looping and revisiting the same subjects until they wore down to a mutual, companionable silence.

On weekends, when the road was clear, we'd take the *Fiat* down to the coast. The sea was always different, sometimes glass, sometimes steel, sometimes a mottled, agitated blue that threatened to leap the retaining wall and drag the whole road into its undertow. We'd park on the promontory, eat sandwiches, and watch the waves smash themselves to pieces against the rocks. Once, we found a tortoise crossing the road. William picked it up, examined its shell, and set it on the other side with a pat' "good luck," he said, and for the rest of the day we referred to each other by the honorific, *'Mr. Tortoise'*.

The book proofs arrived in late May, dropped off at the bottom of our drive by a courier who wouldn't get out of his van. I took the package upstairs, opened it on the desk, and stared at the cover: my name, my title, printed in a font I'd never seen before but already decided I disliked. The text block was slightly off-centre. I flipped through the pages, reading at random, embarrassed by the mistakes I found on every other line.

William noticed my mood at dinner, "what's wrong with it?" he asked, nodding at the copy propped against the breadbasket.

"Everything," I said, "the typeface, the spacing, the typos." I shut the book, sliding it away.

He poured wine into two mismatched glasses and set one in front of me, "they'll fix it. Isn't it meant to be surreal, seeing your own words in print?"

"I suppose."

He opened the book and read a passage at random, his lips moving, then looked up and grinned. "I remember this story," he said, "but I like it better the way you told it to me."

"Because you're in it."

He shrugged, "a good story needs a villain."

I laughed, and the mood broke, the evening unfolding as all our best ones did: wine, and a meal that was mostly improvisation, and a walk out under the stars, where the air smelled of woodsmoke and the low, resinous heat of sage.

That night, I read the proofs again, this time with William beside me. He listened, interrupting now and then to point out a memory or a mistake, and when I reached the end, he said, "you did it, John. You really did it."

I lay awake for a long time after, listening to the wind in the chimney and thinking how improbable it all was: this house, this man, this book, this life. For the first time in years, the sense of dread that usually crept in around midnight failed to arrive. In its place, there was only the gentle persistence of the night, and the certainty that, for as long as it lasted, this would be enough.

I reached for William's hand, felt him squeeze back, and slept without dreams until morning.

By December, the cold had moved in for good. The house, built for the *Mediterranean* sun, was not persuaded by a single portable heater or the logic of our English layering. Each night the temperature dropped, and by dawn it was a contest to see who could make it to the kettle first, the flagstones cold enough to rouse a corpse.

William's solution was to light the fireplace, a massive old beast that dominated the sitting room. We cleared a nest of books and papers from the hearth, crumpled newspaper, and laid in split olive wood, the smell sharp and resinous. At the first strike of the match, smoke filled the room. Not a gradual seepage, but an instant inversion, black, chemical, merciless. We staggered back, coughing, eyes streaming. The alarms, long starved for attention, began a demented duet in the stairwell.

"It's blocked," William said, stating the obvious in the measured tone of a man preparing for war.

He spent the next morning climbing the roof, negotiating the slick tiles with a confidence that bordered on suicidal. I passed him the tools, the brushes, a length of wire he insisted would do the trick. The sky was a flat sheet of iron, and the wind from the sea brought with it a mist so fine it soaked the skin in minutes.

Three hours later, the blockage, birds' nests, twigs, the mummified remains of something, relented, and William returned, face smudged, hands trembling, but triumphant.

"Try it now," he said.

The fire caught, drew, and for the first time the room was warmer than the air outside. We sat in front of it, clothes still damp from the cool air outside, and drank toddies made from the last of the whiskey and a stolen wedge of lemon. The smoke faded, replaced by the honest smell of wood and heat. The exhaustion was a pleasure, our limbs heavy, our conversation reduced to grunts and the occasional, "not bad, this."

The cold, however, was not so easily defeated. That night, I woke with a throat of glass and a fever that sloshed behind my eyes. William muttered in his sleep, then woke fully, diagnosed me with flu, and went to fetch paracetamol and a tepid mug of honeyed water.

The illness lasted weeks. I marked the time by the changing angle of sunlight in the office, by the progression from cough to malaise to that slow, dragging fatigue that makes every motion a negotiation. William cooked, cleaned, and fetched soup from the taverna; when I was up to it, he insisted we walk the garden, to "get the stink of sick out of your clothes." He'd point out the first shoots of spinach, the evidence that the compost heap was working, the improvement in the drainage along the west wall.

In January, the rains found the weak spots in the roof. We woke to a puddle at the foot of the bed, the mattress wicking moisture up into the blankets. William patched the worst of it with a tarpaulin and silicone caulk, but admitted, "it'll need a proper job in the spring."

The windows rattled in the wind, and when the tap ran dry, we discovered the well pump was both ancient and insulted by the recent cold. I spent my days researching replacement parts, comparing models, and navigating the labyrinthine process of online ordering from the nearest city. Each victory was temporary, provisional, a new leak, a fresh set of drafts, the problem of the water never quite resolved.

But with every challenge, the house seemed to adapt, to accept us a little more. The kitchen, once dark and cold, became the locus of the day, the smell of bread or soup or whatever we'd managed to assemble anchoring the place in a way no architectural feature ever could.

In the evenings, after the news on the *'BBC's World Service'* and the second round of tea, we'd sit by the fire, reading or, when the mood struck, watching reruns on William's battered old laptop. Sometimes, in the midst of a particularly bleak update from the outside world, I'd look over at him, hair grown wild, face chapped from the cold and the wind, and feel a certainty that, despite the litany of small disasters, this was exactly where I was supposed to be.

One night, as a storm lashed the windows and the power flickered, I caught William looking at the ceiling, a line of worry creasing his forehead.

"What?" I asked.

He shook his head, "just thinking how long this will last. If we can keep it together."

I thought of the leaks, the broken pipes, the months of locked-down silence, and smiled, "we'll fix it," I said, "we always do."

He laughed, the sound bouncing off the stone walls, and leaned over to rest his head on my shoulder.

"For now," he said, "I'm just glad we're here."

And I was, too. Even with the mess, the damp, the unfinished edges of our new life, there was something beautiful in the way the place, imperfect as it was, held us together against the winter.

We slept with the window cracked, the night air cold but bracing, and woke to a room full of light and the certainty that, with the house still standing, the rest would follow.

It was early summer when the first visitors arrived. Travel restrictions, like the tides, receded just enough to make the journey plausible if not entirely safe, and William's mother and sister booked flights before we had time to even contemplate the implications.

We prepared the house in a frenzy: scrubbing the bathroom, washing the windows, making up the spare room with linens purchased at the last minute from a supermarket on the outskirts of *Chania*. Our own things migrated to the downstairs storage room, and I drove to the village to buy an inflatable mattress, the kind guaranteed to deflate under the weight of expectation.

William's mother, Judith, had not been abroad in a decade. She arrived with a single suitcase and an air of mild confusion, as if suspecting the whole thing might be a particularly elaborate joke. His sister, Miranda, was more sanguine, adapting instantly to the heat and the lack of reliable *WiFi*, snapping photos of the garden and the front of the house from every possible angle.

The first evening, we ate *al fresco*. The air was soft, the table crowded with plates of mezze and bread, the bottle of wine replaced twice before the conversation even touched on the pandemic. Judith sat quietly, hands folded in her lap, watching us with the sceptical eye of a woman who has spent a lifetime watching men try to impress her.

After dinner, as the sky shifted from blue to black, she helped me clear the table. In the kitchen, she asked about the routines, who cooked, who cleaned, who remembered to water the plants. I answered honestly, surprised at the interest, and by the end of the night she had confided her recipe for *'real'* English scones, which she promised to make if we could find decent flour.

During the week, we took Judith and Miranda to the coast, to ruins, to the market. Judith found a stall selling hand-embroidered linens and spent an hour negotiating with the owner, emerging with a tablecloth and the first real smile I'd seen on her face since she landed.

At night, William and I made up the inflatable mattress, listening to it hiss with the inevitability of disappointment. We lay there, too close for real sleep, whispering about the future, next year's garden, the slow improvement of the house, the possibility of a grandchild ("From Miranda," William clarified, "unless you've been hiding something.")

By the end of their visit, the dynamic had shifted. Judith insisted on helping in the kitchen, correcting my posture with the rolling pin, teaching me how to fold dough for a proper *Cornish* pasty. She told stories about William as a child, some of which he tried to deny, most of which I relished as evidence of his long, improbable journey to this place.

When it was time to say goodbye, Judith hugged us both, then held William for a long moment.

"I'm glad you found somewhere," she said. "I'm glad you found each other."

On the drive back from the airport, the car felt larger, the air heavier with what had been said and what had only been implied. At home, the house seemed both emptier and more fully ours. We ate leftovers at the kitchen table, the new tablecloth soft under our wrists, and talked about the visit, about family, about the strange luck that had brought us here.

Later, in the quiet, William ran a hand along the edge of the table and said, "she'll come back, you know. And next time, she'll bring her own flour."

I laughed, the sound echoing in the open space, and for the first time in a long time, I felt the truth of it settle in my bones: this was home.

We went to bed, the house creaking around us, the night scented with lavender from the garden. In the darkness, William whispered, "still glad you came?"

I pulled him closer, and said, "yes. Always."

And I meant it.

By autumn, we knew enough to know we would never quite be locals. The language came slowly, every new verb learned pushing two old ones out of the brain. We could order lunch, ask for directions, apologise for our driving, but the finer points of conversation remained, like the coastline, elusive and always just beyond reach.

The turning point came in the produce section of the supermarket. A man, older but immaculate, greeted us in crisp English and asked if we were "the couple in the stone house up the road." He introduced himself as Henry; his partner, Marco, was "the other half of the vegetable garden experiment." Within minutes, we were invited to a weekly gathering at the taverna in the village square, a "salon," as Henry called it, "for those of us who once assumed we'd never leave England."

That Thursday, we walked in to find a table of expats and semi-expats: the retired diplomat with a voice like port, the artist husband (tall, silent, prone to sketches on napkins), a widow who'd left *Kent* after her husband's death and bought a rescue dog "to avoid drinking alone," and a young couple who ran an online business and claimed they could never live in the *UK* again. There was a rhythm to the talk, complaints about bureaucracy, jokes about English weather, long debates about the best route to the airport.

The owner of the taverna, having served us before, brought drinks without being asked. William got a beer, I a glass of the sharp local white, and a plate of olives appeared as if by magic. There was a moment of collective, appraising silence, as if the group needed to decide whether we belonged. Then the artist said, "you're the ones fixing up the old place," and after that, it was easy.

We learned more in a single evening than in months of solitary effort: which plumber to trust, which builder to avoid, how to bribe the post office into actually delivering packages, the number for the only reliable vet in a 30-kilometer radius, *'should either of us need putting down'* I whisper to William. He swapped gardening tips with Marco, while Henry and I compared notes on the byzantine process of getting a bank account. The young couple invited us to their place for Sunday lunch, and the widow offered us cuttings from her lemon trees.

Driving home in the blue dark, the road winding through olive groves and empty fields, I felt something I hadn't in years, an anticipation for the days ahead, the sense that the project of our lives here was no longer just about survival, but about participation, maybe even contribution.

At the house, we stood on the terrace and looked up at the sky, the stars wild and uncountable. William reached for my hand, a gesture as unconscious as breathing, and said, "we'll need to fix up the porch if we're going to have people round. And the paint in the hallway is still a disaster."

"Not tonight," I said, but already I was listing the tasks in my head, each one a marker of progress, of time passing, of a future taking root in the Cretan stone.

Inside, we found an envelope on the kitchen table, a note from Marco with instructions for composting, a list of recommended seed varieties, and a bottle of home-pressed olive oil.

We poured two glasses, toasted the new friends, and sat together in the half-finished kitchen, the air sweet with the memory of the meal and the promise of more to come.

The work, we knew, would never be finished. The house would always want something: a new roof tile, a coat of paint, a better way to keep out the goats. But for the first time, the list felt less like a burden and more like an invitation, to stay, to invest, to become part of the landscape.

And so, as the nights grew longer and the harvest began, we settled in, certain only that whatever happened next, we would face it together.

In the morning, there would be more work. But tonight, there was light, and laughter, and the feeling, strange, but welcome, that we were finally home.

EPILOGUE: FULL CIRCLE

The ferry from *Piraeus* arrives late in *Souda*, Sarah had decided they wanted a sea adventure more than the convenience of landing six miles away, as they always do, as if the entire transport infrastructure of the Greek islands is held together by a sequence of amiable shrugs. I wait for them at the end of the causeway, hands in my pockets, the limestone light painting the port authority sign to a blindness. The usual crowd is here: a few old men with cigarettes and nowhere to go, the fisherman's wife in a *Housemartins* t-shirt, two taxi drivers arguing without urgency over who has the next fare. I lean against my car's bonnet and squint down the line of the quay until the family emerges, their silhouettes a series of hesitant exclamation marks against the hammerhead of the boat.

The children appear first, a girl and a boy, the precise ages evaporating as soon as I try to assign them, only their energy and limb-to-body ratio giving any hint. Sarah's new husband comes next, the drag of the suitcase a steady, self-effacing presence; his arms are tanned, his face unguarded, a man who wears his Englishness as apology rather than assertion. And then Sarah herself, hair a sharp, impossible black in the sunlight, sunglasses perched on her head, the only one of the party who does not look for me immediately. She takes three steps ahead of her family and only then scans the arrivals with a mathematician's method, as if plotting the most efficient vector to the next drinkable coffee.

When she sees me, her mouth compresses into a smile and she raises a hand, the gesture both casual and unambiguous, as if to say, *'here we are again, improbably, beautifully, again'*. The family vectors toward me, luggage rolling like artillery. I step forward, forced to remember how to greet her. In the end we settle for a continental double-kiss, her cheek cool and dry in the shade.

"You haven't changed," she says, and I almost believe her.

"You have," I say, and she laughs, brushing the fringe from her eyes, "you look like someone who belongs here."

"I belong nowhere," she says, "which is precisely why I'm perfect for the islands."

She introduces her husband, Ollie, and the children, whose names I immediately forget and then recover, as if I have to earn them by a series of small observations. The girl, perhaps twelve, is already the avatar of a future Sarah: hair loose, gaze unfixed, suspicion sheathed but always ready. The boy is younger, rounder, the ears large and untrained, his arms splayed as if waiting for some emergency to befall him.

We load the bags into the boot, an operation watched in silence by the taxi drivers, and begin the slow, switchback climb out of *Souda*. The car is immediately full of sun and the foreignness of new company; I adjust the air conditioning and glance at Sarah in the rearview, where she is already cataloguing the topography.

"It's greener than I expected," she says, "I thought *Crete* was all rocks and goats."

I gesture to the ridgeline, the scrub and the dark olive trees, "give it three months. Then it's just rocks and ghosts."

Ollie laughs at this, a sound surprisingly high, and I decide I like him. The boy asks why the sea is "so blue it hurts," and I offer some lie about the way light refracts off limestone, which seems to satisfy him.

The cottage is twenty minutes west, perched at the lip of a ravine where the wind works overtime, shuttling weather up from *Africa* and regret down from the mountains. William has spent the better part of two years converting it from its former life as a humble farmhouse, into something both more honest and more impossible. The main house faces out to sea, each window a frame for the kind of view that used to appear on desktop wallpapers. The new extension, which William designed and built from timber dragged down from the *White Mountains*, juts out at a right angle, its broad glass panes trapping the light and radiating it inward.

As we pull up on the gravel drive, William is waiting on the step, a linen shirt open at the neck, one hand in a wave, the other behind his back as if concealing either a weapon or a welcome. He comes forward as the car halts, and for a moment there is a standoff between British reticence and island candour before the children decide on the latter, racing past him to the door.

"Good journey?" he says to Ollie, then, to Sarah, "you look happy." He means it. He always does.

Sarah hugs him, the kind of hug that draws strength from the other person's spine, then steps back to take in the house, her hands on her hips, "you finished it," she says, half to herself, "I wasn't sure you would."

"Neither was I," he says, "but once I started, it felt like the only job in the world. So much for a restful retirement"

He looks at me, the old conspirator, and I realise he wants me to do the grand tour, "show them the sea first," he says, as if the rest of the cottage is just a delivery system for the view.

We leave the bags in a heap by the steps and follow the children around the side, where the path winds through a tangle of rosemary and lavender and spills out onto the terrace. The drop is abrupt; below, the hillside crumbles into a sequence of terraces, each one planted with olives. Beyond them, the sea, a band of blue so electric it seems at war with the air.

The girl stops at the edge, her hands on the rough stone of the parapet, "you can see forever," she says, and though the phrase is trite, the way she says it makes it new.

The boy leans over, searching for a route down the hill, "are those your trees?"

"Some," William says, "mostly the village owns them. I just do the picking and the drinking."

Sarah drapes herself over a deckchair, sunglasses on now, hair already wild in the wind, "it's exactly as I pictured," she says, "but also not. It's more... lived in. Like you've always been here."

I pour wine, there is always wine, the local white so dry it stings, the bottle sweating in the sun. The children are already exploring, taking stock of the herb beds and the stone troughs William has set out as makeshift fountains. Sarah's husband joins her on the deck, the two of them an incongruous but not unhappy pair.

I walk Sarah through the inside of the house, the floors tiled in the old hexagons, the ceiling beams sanded to a driftwood smoothness. The main room is simple: a long table for eating, the fireplace for the few nights a year it gets cold, and bookcases lining the walls, already half-surrendered to William's growing collection of local field guides and weather-beaten paperbacks.

"Did you do all this?" Sarah asks, trailing her fingers along the mortared stones of the old hearth.

"Mostly him," I say, nodding toward the back garden where William is digging a hole for a new pomegranate, "I'm more the curator."

She smiles, inspecting the joinery at the window frame, "he's better at it than you ever were."

"He's better at most things," I say, and she laughs, but it's not a competition. Not anymore.

The tour ends at the new extension, a long, airy space with broad plank floors and a view up the gorge, "this is the guest wing," I say, though it serves as a catchall for books, paperwork, and anything else waiting for a permanent home.

Sarah stands at the glass, arms folded, "it's like living in a painting."

"It's a cliché, but I'll take it."

She leans in, her voice lower, "you seem different, John. Settled. I didn't know if you had that in you."

I want to answer her; to explain the way the days settle into each other here, the way the heat erases boundaries and ambition. But instead I say, "I'm still a mess, just on a better background."

She snorts, and for a moment, we are back at Langley Hall, two younger versions of ourselves measuring the size of the world through each other's ambition.

The children have found the hammock, and are currently attempting to weaponise it. Ollie is lighting the grill; William is setting the table on the stone terrace, dropping the cutlery with an efficiency that bespeaks long habit.

I help with the bread, slicing the thick, salt-encrusted slabs and laying them out with small bowls of oil and olives. When I return, William is showing Ollie the firepit, a squat, brick-built affair with a half-moon of local stone for seating.

"Built it myself," he says, voice full of pride, "the stones came from the next ravine over, the brick from a demolition in the village."

Ollie nods, running a hand over the mortar, "solid work," he says, and I can see the way William puffs up, the compliment warming him from the inside out.

The first hour blurs with the business of catching up. Sarah wants to know about the book, "is it any good?" I get up and fetch the newly published first and second book.

"Here, decide for yourself," I say handing two paperbacks to her. Sarah opens the cover of one of them then sees my inscription inside: *To Sarah, the best of friends*. "And the message is from both of us," I add.

"Thank you John, that means a lot," she stood up and grabbed me into the tightest and warmest of hugs. I simply smile.

Ollie wants to know about the garden, the weather, the politics of the village. The children reappear at regular intervals to demand food, or to show off some new find, a lizard, a seashell, the half-decayed remains of a tortoise. William answers every question, and never once betrays the impatience I know he sometimes feels.

As dusk approaches, the wind dies, leaving the garden in a bubble of stillness. Sarah sips her wine, eyes on the horizon, and says, "I never thought I'd see the day you two were so happy. I mean properly, quietly happy."

I don't answer at first. There's too much to say, and none of it new. The world, in its infinite perversity, has delivered me to this place, sunburnt, softened, and content. Not cured, not remade, but content.

"You make it sound like a defeat," I say, finally.

She shakes her head, "no. It's an achievement. Most people never get there."

William comes over, wiping his hands on a towel, "get where?"

"Here," Sarah says, gesturing at the air, "this. You, him, the house, the world. It suits you."

He glances at me, a flicker of the old shyness passing through his eyes, "it's not so bad," he says, "gets better every year."

I can't help it, I reach for his hand, just for a moment, and the shock of touch is as new as the first time.

The children are yelling, the lamb is ready, the table is set. Sarah's hair is already wild from the wind, and she is laughing at something William has said about the futility of grass in this climate. The light is going gold; the air is honey-thick with the promise of another day.

For a moment, it is enough. More than enough.

And I let myself have it.

By seven, the sun is an afterthought, the horizon a velvet strip that frames the sea and the low, lambent smudge of the first offshore lights. The air is perfect for eating *al fresco*, just enough residual heat to warm the stone underfoot, just enough cool to make the idea of grilled meat and bread seem necessary, almost medicinal. William is already in his element, tongs in one hand, the other wrapped around a glass of the new red he found at the market. He stands at the fire with the composure of a man who is both host and subject, his only audience the children and whatever mythic ancestor first invented charred protein.

The cicadas are audible, but not omnipresent; the children chase their rasping, impossible bodies through the garden, the older girl strategising, the younger boy simply launching himself at random into the rosemary beds. Sarah sits on the terrace steps, knees drawn up, a glass balanced on her shin. She watches Ollie set the table, the ritual gestures of plates and cutlery and napkins somehow both foreign and foundational, as if she is seeing her own childhood in negative.

I'm in charge of the wine. This is not a trivial task as William has opinions and his *'standards'*, and the proper sequencing of whites and reds is apparently crucial to the success of any meal. I open the first bottle and test the cork, then pour a small measure for myself. It tastes of stone and something unresolved, which is as much as I can ever say about wine. I bring Sarah a refill and sit beside her, our legs just touching.

"You all right?" I ask.

She nods, tracing the rim of her glass with a finger, "I am. You?"

I shrug, unsure how much honesty the moment requires, "it's easier than I thought it would be."

She smiles, the teeth visible, and says, "isn't that always the way with the good things?"

Before I can answer, William calls out from the grill: "if you want yours less cremated, now's the time to claim it."

The children arrive in a blitz of grass stains and dirt, the boy's cheeks flushed, the girl affecting boredom but eyeing the food with interest. We gather around the table, the spread a riot of colour and texture, grilled lamb, eggplant, peppers blistered to sweet collapse, olives, salad, bread cut thick as doorstep. Ollie sits at the head, the children on either side, William at the foot. Sarah and I take the flanks, each with a view of the whole operation.

We eat.

At first, the conversation is all surface: how was the journey, is the house cold in winter, do the goats ever come up this far? The children provide a running commentary on everything, how the tomatoes here are so much better, why does the sea have so many jellyfish, can we swim tomorrow if the weather holds? William answers each question, sometimes inventing answers, sometimes telling the truth, and I watch as the children lean toward him, drawn by the gravity of his confidence.

Sarah is quiet for a while, but then, over the second helping, she asks about the book, "is it out yet?" she says, and though her tone is light, I sense the freight behind the question.

"Next month," I say, "I finally approved the proofs last month."

Ollie perks up, "you've written a book?"

Sarah snorts, "not just any book. It's a trilogy, an epic, family history, forbidden love, trauma, the works. He's underselling it, as usual."

William grins, chewing, "he never talks much about it, always moaning about this font or that format, but he finally got there."

"It's easier to write than to explain," I say, which is both true and not.

Sarah sets her glass down, leans across the table, "what I wanted to say," she says, "is that you've turned your pain into hopefully something beautiful." The words are blunt, unsentimental, and land with a weight I can feel in the tips of my fingers.

I look at William; he looks back, the faintest nod passing between us. I reach for his hand, and, I don't care who sees. Our wedding bands are nearly identical, plain, gold, engraved inside with the same two words: still here. The fire throws light across the metal, catching in the groove, making it glow.

Ollie raises his glass, "to beautiful things," he says, and for a moment, the whole world seems in on the secret.

We drink.

The conversation drifts, Sarah talks about her new life, the teaching job in Brighton, the way the school system is both better and worse than anywhere else. She talks about the difficulties of blending families, how the children have learned to trust her, but never entirely, and how she's learned to accept that. Ollie listens, nods, adds the occasional joke about the futility of step-parenting. The children, bored by grownup talk, sneak away from the table and return minutes later with a board game, which they lay out on the warm stones beside us.

William keeps the fire going, feeding it driftwood and olive branches, the flames a constant, low conversation. I watch the scene unfold, the way the children play, the way Sarah watches Ollie, the way William leans into my shoulder when he laughs. I realise, with a lurch of gratitude, that I am present in this moment. Not observing, not critiquing, but here.

Every so often, my hand strays to the pocket where the letter waits. I have not told anyone about it, not even William, though I suspect he knows.

He catches my glance once, his eyes bright in the firelight, and gives the smallest, most decisive nod. Later, he will ask me if I want to talk about it; for now, he lets it rest.

The food is gone, the bones picked clean and the bread reduced to crumbs. The children have moved on to some complicated, endless game involving dice and imaginary currency. Sarah and Ollie clear the table, working together with an ease that only comes from having done it a hundred times before. William pours a final glass of wine and sits beside me, both of us facing the darkening sea.

"Are you happy?" he asks, not quite a whisper.

I think about it. The old answers are still there, the reflexive, self-deprecating denials. But I let them pass.

"Yes," I say, and mean it.

We sit in silence, the night growing around us, the warmth from the fire lingering in our arms and faces.

The children tire, drifting toward the deck chairs, their heads heavy with sun and food. Ollie follows them, tucking a blanket around their knees, then returns to Sarah's side. She leans her head on his shoulder, her hair uncoiling in the breeze.

For a while, no one speaks. The only sounds are the hiss of embers and, somewhere up the slope, the mutter of a nightjar.

It is a perfect, fragile silence.

And in that silence, I know what I will do with the letter.

After the plates are cleared, the wine and coffee persist. There's a cake, Sarah's, made in the morning and ferried here with the gravity of an heirloom; there are bowls of cherries and small glasses of some aniseed liqueur William found in a duty-free. The children have migrated to the edge of the terrace, their board game halfway to collapse, the girl now reading from her phone, the boy spinning the dice and testing how many times it will land on six before anyone notices.

The adults sprawl in their chairs, the small aches of a long day's sun sinking into the soft tissue. The light is almost gone from the world, the sky a single, deepening gradient, the sea now a flat slate with only the faintest echo of day.

Sarah leans forward, refilling her glass. "Do you remember our summer in *Norfolk*?" she asks. "That world-shattering thunderstorm??"

William groans, "don't remind me. I lost half my tomatoes that night."

Ollie laughs, "sounds like my children."

Sarah turns to me, "you wrote about it, didn't you? In the book?"

I nod, "with better words, I hope," I grin in challenge.

There is laughter, the low, satisfied kind that only happens when everyone has been fed and is safely among their own. The night is so still I can hear the game pieces clicking, the children's occasional bickering, the distant thump of a fishing boat's engine.

And then I think of the letter, and the conversation recedes to the background, every sense telescoping inward to the shape of paper and what it contains. I stand, brush crumbs from my lap. William glances up, questioning; I shake my head, then gesture for him to follow me down to the stone wall. He does, and we stand together, shoulder to shoulder, looking out over the blue-black stretch of sea.

"Do you want me here?" he asks, quietly.

"Yes," I say, "I think I need it."

He places a hand at the small of my back, steady, anchoring and I pull the letter from my pocket. The envelope is ordinary, the postmark faded, the handwriting half-familiar from birthday and Christmas cards. My name is written in her hand, formal, careful, as if the act of writing it cost her something.

I open it, unfold the sheet, and for a moment I can't bring myself to read. My eyes skim the lines, but the meaning won't coalesce. William waits, patient, and when I finally find the words, I read them aloud, so they're not just mine:

'Dear Dad,

I know it's been a long time, and I know I haven't answered your last few letters. But I've been thinking about it a lot, and I wanted you to know that I'm okay. I hope you're okay too.

I'm going to finish uni next year, and after that I want to travel. Mum says you're living somewhere in Greece now. That sounds amazing. I've always wanted to see Greece.

Maybe, if you still want to, we could meet again? I don't know what to say, really. I'm not angry anymore, and I hope you aren't either.

After all, who can resist a free holiday?

Love,

Rose'.

I let the silence settle over the lines, the old, unhealed thing inside my chest both heavier and lighter at once. William slides his hand up my spine, cups the back of my neck, and for a moment I lean into him, letting my forehead rest against his.

"Do you think I'll fuck it up again?" I ask, voice barely there.

He turns my face so I'm looking at him, "probably. But then you'll try harder. You always do."

We stand like that until the ache recedes, until the sky is properly dark and the stars are out in force, and then we walk back up to the house. At the table, Sarah has already guessed, she is the first to ask, her hand landing softly on my arm as I sit, "good news?" she says.

I nod, unable to say more.

William, who has always been better at this, says, "his daughter wants to see him again. She might come here."

Ollie claps me on the back, so hard it rattles my teeth, "that's bloody brilliant."

Sarah, who never learned to wait for a right moment, raises her glass, "to new beginnings, then," she says, "and to not being angry anymore."

The toast goes around the table, and I drink, and it tastes of everything I have ever missed and everything I have managed to keep. We sit for a while longer, the conversation winding down, the night settling around us like a loose blanket. Eventually the children drift off to bed, and Ollie helps Sarah clear the last of the plates.

William and I step outside, down to the end of the garden, where the land falls away and the world opens. The moon is up now, bright enough to paint our shadows on the pale stone. We stand together, his arm around my shoulders, my hand in his, our bodies balanced against the dark.

I think of everything that brought us here, every hurt and grace, every false ending and return. I think of the next day, and the day after, and the letter still folded in my hand, the possibility it contains.

"I love you," I say, quietly, as if it might spook the night.

William squeezes my hand, "still here," he says.

And for the first time in forever, I believe him.

THE END

ABOUT THE AUTHOR:

John Williams is a retired teacher of history from the north-west of England in the United Kingdom. He is a published local historian, and author of the "A Forbidden Love" series of historical fiction books.

Check out his other work at:
https://linktr.ee/john.williams3599